THEORIZING THE ANGURA SPACE

BRILL'S
JAPANESE STUDIES
LIBRARY

EDITED BY

H. BOLITHO AND K.W. RADTKE

VOLUME 23

THEORIZING THE ANGURA SPACE

Avant-garde Performance and Politics in Japan,
1960–2000

BY

PETER ECKERSALL

BRILL
LEIDEN · BOSTON
2006

This book is printed on acid-free paper.

Library of Congress Cataloging-in-Publication Data

Eckersall, Peter.
 Theorizing the angura space : avant-garde performance and politics in Japan,
1960-2000 / by Peter Eckersall.
   p. cm. — (Brill's Japanese studies library, ISSN 0925-6512 ; v. 23)
 Includes bibliographical references and index.
 ISBN-13: 978-90-04-15199-4
 ISBN-10: 90-04-15199-0 (hardback : alk. paper)
 1. Experimental theater—Japan. 2. Theater—Japan—History—20th century.
3. Theater—Political aspects—Japan. I. Title. II. Series.

PN2193.E86E35 2006
792.095209045—dc22

                                                                        2006044004

ISSN   0925-6512
ISBN-13: 978-90-04-15199-4
ISBN-10: 90-04-15199-0

For my parents Ken and Laurel

CONTENTS

ACKNOWLEDGMENTS

There are a great many people who have contributed time, energy and inspiration to this project.

Although substantially expanded, some of the material here began as research for my PhD at Monash University (1999). I owe thanks to the many people who generously gave their friendship and support, especially Barbara Hatley, Alison Tokita and Ross Mouer. I also thank Denise Varney, Angela O'Brien and Paul Monaghan, my colleagues in theatre studies at the School of Creative Arts, University of Melbourne.

The research for this book necessitated long stays in Japan and there are many people who have made my visits to Japan enjoyable and productive. I would like to give special thanks to Uchino Tadashi of the University of Tokyo. His expert advice and assistance I wish to acknowledge with deep gratitude. Many scholars have been important to this project. In particular, I would like to thank Alan Cummings, Toshiko Ellis, Rachel Fensham, Fujii Hidetata, David Goodman, William Marotti, Moriyama Naoto, Edward Scheer, Stanca Scholz-Cionca and Totani Yoko, all of whom gave insightful feedback and generous friendship and support at various phases of my research.

Without the energy, vision and commitment, of Japan's theatre artists, this book would not have been undertaken. Many artists discussed have given freely of their time and allowed me entry into their worlds. They have shown great generosity of spirit and openness. Their artistic achievements are the inspiration for this work.

I would like to thank my parents, Ken and Laurel, for their continuing support and friends who have been with me, helped and sustained me for parts of this journey. I would like to specially acknowledge Aoki Michiko, Lauren Bain, Robert Fuchs, Greg Gardiner, Simon Hill, Rosemary Hinde, Sara Jansen, Kawamura Takeshi, Don Kenny, Oikawa Hironobu, Paddy O'Reilly, Otori Hidenaga, David Pledger, John Romeril, Shimizu Shinjin and Shiozaki Toshiko. There are many others.

I would like to thank Patricia Radder and the people at Brill for their excellent support in publishing this book. I also thank Diane Brown for her careful and professional editing.

Material from Chapters 7 and 9—substantially revised here—was previously published as: 'Japan as Dystopia: An Overview of Kawamura Takeshi's Daisan Erotica', *The Drama Review* (TDR T-165) 97–106, 2000; and 'The Performing Body and Cultural Representation in the Theatre of Gekidan Kaitaisha', *Japanese Theatre and the International Stage*, edited by Stanca Scholz-Cionca & Samuel Leiter, Leiden: Brill, 313–28, 2001. I thank Kawamura Takeshi for allowing me to publish my translation of his wonderful play *Hamletclone*.

The Faculty of Arts, University of Melbourne has supported research for this book through their small grants scheme. I undertook research and wrote much of the manuscript while supported by a Japan Foundation research fellowship in 2003. I thank the excellent staff at The Japan Foundation. Publication of this work was assisted by a publication grant from the University of Melbourne.

Japanese names are written family name first as is the convention. Long vowel sounds are indicated by diacritical marks, unless in common usage in Romanized form (e.g. Tokyo not Tōkyo).

Peter Eckersall
January 2006

INTRODUCTION

> For art to be 'unpolitical' means only to ally itself
> with the 'ruling' group.
>
> (Brecht 1974: 196)

> One does not create art in the theatre out of a
> desire for self satisfaction . . . it is in order to engage
> in a fight.
>
> (Suzuki 1996)

Theorising the Angura Space investigates the interrelationship of aesthetics
and politics in the Japanese theatrical "underground" (*angura*), an
avant-garde "small theatre" (*shōgekijō*) movement that arose in the
1960s. The notion of the avant-garde as a political sensibility in the
Japanese context is central to this inquiry. To this end, specific qualities of Japanese avant-garde performance are discussed in detail and
in relation to broader dimensions of Japan's recent cultural history.

Japanese theatre since the 1960s has been of immense and lasting significance. Beginning with a contest over modern and experimental genres of theatrical expression in its dialectic struggles with
shingeki (new theatre/modern theatre), the *angura* movement looked
to Japan's theatrical past for inspiration. It explored premodern cultures of Japan—especially those aspects of cultural history shunned
by modern society. Meanwhile, even while *angura* was steeped in a
vision of the past, it also looked to the wider world of contemporary theatre. Theatre internationally experienced a revolution that
was in equal parts an artistic and political transformation. Japanese
theatre in the 1960s was deeply influenced by these cosmopolitan
trends as well. In fact, the exceptional capacities of *angura* to distil
and refine transhistorical cultural practices meant that it became an
influential marker of the wider 1960s avant-garde movement in its
own right.

Many theatre artists relate to theatre as a unique and persuasive
form of political expression and/or experience (see prefatory cita-
tions above). To make theatre, according to Bertolt Brecht, is to
engage in politics without exception. For Suzuki Tadashi, one of
Japan's most important *angura* era directors, good theatre aims to
transform society. Theatre is investigated as deeply invested in political

practice and in the task of representing and critically transforming Japan's cultural experience. *Angura* is therefore both responding to Japanese cultural experience and determining some its constituent features. Thus, while *angura* is one mechanism for mapping the cultural history of Japan, it is also ineluctably an active player in shaping social, political and cultural processes. Theatre, like all arts, grows in significance and is more satisfying in artistic terms when it seeks to broach such broad aesthetic, intellectual and political interactions and contexts. Accordingly, to reflect on the Japanese avant-garde theatre brings forth a continuing sense of dialogue with Japan's social world.

Making and watching theatre are messy, overflowing acts of cultural invention. Theatre is widely appreciated as a unique site of artistic expression. Performance explores social and cultural issues alongside and through the experience of physical, dynamic and spatial sensibilities. As a moment in time, a live performance is simultaneously immersed in an extended experience of time; it is ephemeral and one of the oldest forms of expression known to humankind. The occasion of watching theatre is sometimes expressed as an act of becoming; narrative, language, bodies and senses mingle with the recognition of history, identity, and the world outside. Furthermore, while we can say that all theatre in all genres exhibits these tendencies, the theatrical avant-garde has sought to highlight them and to create dramaturgical platforms from these elements of theatrical production. In his famous essay on avant-garde theatre where he compares the intensity of theatre to that of the plagues that scarred medieval Europe, Antonin Artaud proposes such a revolutionary outlook: "The theatre, like the plague . . . releases conflicts, disengages powers and liberates possibilities, and if these possibilities and these powers are dark, it is the fault not of plague nor of theatre, but of life. . . . The theatre like the plague is a crisis which is resolved by death or cure" (Artaud 1970: 31).

As will be seen, *angura* is a vital and extraordinary expression of Artaud's proposal and is an avant-garde that sought to explore these extended capacities for theatre to affect the social organism. Work through the body, the senses, the dimensions of space and time and not forgetting darkness (the underground), are constituent features of the *angura* movement. In the following chapters, a new understanding of subjectivity (*shutaisei*) as a politics of experience and action and as a cure for social malaise is proposed in the link between the avant-garde and the social world. This in turn extends into other cultural dimensions and is a corollary to Japan's transformation after the 1960s.

To this end, the world beyond theatre has increasingly taken an important place in performance creation and analysis. As the performance studies theorist Marvin Carlson writes: "With performance as a kind of critical wedge, the metaphor of theatricality has moved out of the arts and into almost every aspect of modern attempts to understand our condition" (Carlson 1996: 6). We will see such thinking applied in chapter 2 where student demonstrations from the 1960s are discussed as a performance of radical politics. Further evidence of this trend will be seen in a wide-ranging discussion of politics and theatre in the emergent postmodern context of Japan after the 1960s. For groups such as Gekidan Kaitaisha and dumb type, questions about politics and artistic representation, including the overriding sense that the world has become increasingly performative, have been central themes in their work.

Theatre and culture are always interconnected. In this sense, the book explores two compelling, interacting and shifting histories predominant in contemporary life in Japan. In one sense, I aim to analyse the rise and fall of counterculture politics and the ongoing problems and possibilities for alternatives to manifest and contest dominating forms of power and social control in Japan. A second point that also relates to this asks questions about contemporary art and the avant-garde. How can theatre remain vital and manifest a continuing sense of cultural inquiry and spirit of innovation? As will be seen, Japanese contemporary and experimental theatre—the cutting edge of the avant-garde—have offered some powerful insights but also explored the sense of crisis for the avant-garde. This is a history of the rise and fall of *angura* in the same critical moment.

Theorizing the Angura Space: angura and avant-garde theatre

I propose expanded uses of the terms *angura* and avant-garde than is more typically the case in Japanese theatre scholarship. Both have specific and generalised meanings in contemporary cultural history. *Angura* describes the 1960s alternative theatre and performance scene; as will be revealed in the third and fourth chapters, the term has specific meaning and relates to alternative theatre in the 1960s political context.[1] At the same time, *angura* established new hallmarks for Japanese theatre as well, and the term can be used to describe the continuing development of the Japanese avant-garde. Indeed, it is intentionally provocative to continue to explore the dimensions of the terminology of *angura* in relation to the recent history of Japanese performance for it is this critical frame that continues to insist on reading the politics of new forms.

The same case applies to the term avant-garde (and *angura* and the 1960s avant-garde theatre in Japan are interchangeable terms). The avant-garde emerged in the late nineteenth and early twentieth centuries as a "leading edge" or "shockwave" in the arts. For some theorists, such as Peter Bürger, the term only truly applies to arts from the early modernist period (Bürger 1984). Principal to theorising the avant-garde is the idea that art should transcend convention, be marginal, inspirational and prophetic (Kostelanetz 1990: 109). Conceived of as a revolution in aesthetics and in culture, the avant-garde is an attack on the status of art as autonomous in the bourgeois society. For Bürger, it demands a reordering of the sensorium and the discovery of a life praxis drawn from a basis in art. Thus, art, not social power, is the organising system; the avant-garde proposes art as a model for living one's life.

In this sense, avant-garde art—although sometimes criticised for its sense of abstraction and disorder—is actually based in observations and forms from the material world. As evident in the work discussed, avant-garde theatre displays the following general characteristics:

- An interest in everydayness and making the world into art.
- Corporeality and a concern with the body and flesh.
- The use of materials and forms essential to artistic practice; it reveals or displays those forms as art.

---

[1] The term *shōgekijō* or "little theatre" is a more generalised term also used to refer to Japan's contemporary theatre. The term derives from the small, converted shopfront spaces that were used by little theatre groups, who also had few resources and, in some instances, created a "poor theatre" style of production (after Grotowski 1968) *Shōgekijō* also calls to mind the Tsukiji Little Theatre (*Tsukiji Shōgekijō*), the first modern theatre in prewar Japan (discussed in Chapter 1). Unlike *angura*, no sense of turbulence or transgressive reality is *ipso facto* assumed in using the term. Although small theatre may also be *angura*, the latter is always dark. Goodman's use of the term post-*shingeki* to theorize *angura*—which connotes avant-garde sensibilities—is discussed in Chapter 4.

- A privileging of experience and communal acts of participation.
- It is systematic and manifesto-like, but also spontaneous.

What is more, the avant-garde simultaneously ruptures with the past and is an arbiter of the future. Its reflex is to explore hitherto unknown forms of expression and representation. Paradoxically though, there can be no innovation without context, for the avant-garde is dependent on an object of resistance for its act of rebellion. That is to say, something can only be avant-garde in relation to something that it has moved forward from. The subversive transgressive potential of the avant-garde is tempered by this notion of continuum. The avant-garde reacts against but sits within; it is contra to, although requires continuum. Seen in this light, the avant-garde only exists in relation to the context of events and issues in society at large, and in dialogue with other modes of expression and cultural experience. It is ineluctably drawn into such a framework of historical consciousness.

The 1960s is often seen as a second wave or new phase of the avant-garde in which theatre was most active and original. Moreover, the idea that theatre should be socially and culturally interactive and speak to the themes, issues and experiences of a generation, is a new aspect of avant-gardism arising from the 1960s movement. So too are the connections that form between art and radical expressions of selfhood, agency and collective national forms of cultural experience. The avant-garde of this period is characterised by its attempts to speak to and for a radical vision of Japan's cultural memory, and to interrogate and renegotiate its complex history and formation of identity politics.

Focus on diverse performance practices

There are many important artists and groups to be discussed. Unavoidably, other notable figures have been regretfully overlooked here. My choice of material is determined by a number of considerations. Principally, I am guided by the composite tendencies of *angura*. As Terayama Shūji stated in his Tenjō Sajiki company manifesto: "Our concern is not to collect new evidence that drama is literature" (Terayama 1975: 86). Play texts are therefore considered as one source of material relevant to the project alongside interviews, observations of work in rehearsal and performance, archival work, and an immersion in the Japanese contemporary theatre world. Works that suggest composite innovations in staging, narrative and form are favoured, while playwrights and plays are less under consideration. My aim is to consider diverse and contrasting expressions of *angura* so as to better understand the complexity of the movement as a whole.

A consequence of this approach, however, is the relative displacement of textual analysis and critique of narrative. In fact, my approach redresses an imbalance in scholarship that has predominantly focused on the history of drama as the history of playwrights. Nonetheless, I acknowledge that significant figures are overlooked. Notable in this regard are playwrights including Betsuyaku Minoru, Shimizu Kunio and Tsuka Kōhei—active since the 1960s and 1970s—and such notable dramatists and directors from the 1980s and 1990s, including Kisaragi Koharu, Watanabe Eriko, Hirata Oriza, and Sakate Yōji. While chiefly considered as playwrights, many of these artists are also innovators of theatrical form. For example, the body as a percussive instrument of expression was a vital stylistic dimension to the success of Kisaragi's company, Noise. Hirata's "contemporary colloquial theatre" (*gendai kogo engeki*)—or as newspaper critics coined the phrase, "quiet theatre" (*shizukana engeki*)—as performed by his Seinendan theatre group, demonstrates subtle and nuanced transformations of theatrical space. Nor should their absence in this discussion be seen as negating the political motivations of many of these artists. Bestuyaku, Watanabe and Hirata, to name but three, who are important critics of the present day political system, have been outspoken in their criticisms of right wing trends in Japan's society. Sakate, whose plays have often focused on community issues and questions of social conflict, must be considered one of the most successful political artists of the last twenty years. However, while each of these artists is significant to the contemporary theatre movement as a whole, their work does not closely fit the investigation of radical dramaturgical forms and polysemic aims of analysis here. Fortunately, other scholarly work on many of their activities has been underway for sometime.[2] What is more urgent in the consideration

---

[2] Many of these artists have been discussed elsewhere, see for example: (Hirata 2002; Rolf and Gillespie 1992; Senda 1997). The Japan Playwright's Association have published English translations of plays by prominent contemporary playwrights in the *Half a Century of Japanese Theatre* series, published by Kinokuniya. New studies are also underway.

of Japanese theatre is precisely the study of the liminal and hybrid performance culture of the avant-garde, where considerable gaps in the research remain.

Avant-garde performance and politics in Japan 1960–2000

Nineteen sixties Japan was a period of immense artistic invention. The first part of this book on the theme of the 1960s space: performance and protest, explores this extraordinary era across four chapters.

The first chapter investigates the pre-1960s history of avant-garde performance in Japan. It casts an overview of modern Japanese theatre in the early part of the twentieth century and introduces relevant pre- and postwar modern and experimental theatre movements. Key cultural and political developments, the role of subjectivity, and the rise of student organizations are introduced as pivotal factors in prefiguring the radical space of the 1960s.

The second chapter focuses on cultural and political developments in the 1960s and theorizes the performative dimensions of an emergent radical subjectivity (*shutaisei*). Developments in mainstream political institutions and the riots protesting the US–Japan security treaty are explored in relation to the rise of the new left student movement (*zengakuren*) and counterculture. It is argued that the idea of being radical in the 1960s came to be theatrical and performative.

The theme of *angura* and protest is explored in the third chapter and considers the emergent split between *shingeki* artists and the nascent avant-garde. It continues with an extended discussion of the influence of the 1960s demonstrations on the evolution of *angura*. Narratives sourced directly from demonstrations are discussed in relation to specific artworks.

In the fourth and final chapter of this section, the evolving philosophical and symbolic dimensions of the relationship between *angura* and the new left are examined. A theory of *angura* is formulated as being centrally concerned with the exploration of subjectivity. The chapter concludes, however, with a pessimistic assessment of the 1960s space, as is evident in a seminal *angura* work, *The Dance of Angels Who Burn Their Own Wings* (*Tsubasa O Moyasu Tenshi-Tachi no Butō*, Satoh, Yamamoto et al. 1988).

The discussion then continues with an investigation of *angura* after the 1960s. Part Two considers the rise of postmodern culture and its relationship to the avant-garde. Thus, chapter 5 is set against the backdrop of the speculative economic boom period of the 1980s in Japan, known as the "bubble economy." This chapter explores the commodification and appropriation of *angura* by a society under the influence of postmodern forms of capitalism. It also considers the "*shōgekijō* boom," wherein aesthetics and strategies developed in the radical new wave were reapplied by a number of immensely popular theatre groups. As a result of this trend, the avant-garde was divested of radical or subversive functions and transformed into an aspect of the status quo.

Part Three aims to address this sense of crisis in proactive terms and explores the possible rethinking of radical spaces in avant-garde theatre. Four diverse and contrasting performance groups and their key works are analysed in terms that explore conditions for the renewal of alternative cultural politics in the post-1960s *angura* space.

The first of these, in chapter 6, reads Kishida Rio's important play *Woven Hell* (*Ito Jigoku*). I situate the play in a discussion about a feminist politics and dramaturgy developing from the *angura* method. The feminist rereading of Japan's imperial–military history, as evidenced in this play and the distinctive *angura* style production by Kishida Jimusho+Rakutendan, forms the basis of the discussion.

In chapter 7, the focus shifts to works that explore contemporary Japan in a study of Kawamura Takeshi and Daisan Erotica, and their critical representations of the 1990s dystopian space. This influential company has been working since 1980 and pioneered an unusual mix of theatre and *manga*-science fiction narratives, as well as eclectic performance styles. Key works that mark the increasing sense of social crisis in Japan are discussed at length. A discussion of *Hamletclone* (*Hamuretto Kurōn*), Kawamura's evocative play reflecting on the post-1960s space at the turn of the century concludes this chapter. It is also a preface for my translation of the play in chapter 10.

Chapters 8 and 9 address recent trends in performance art in Japan as new politically operative sites of avant-garde expression. The 1990s work of dumb type is discussed in respect of new forms of cultural politics that explore border terrains and personal transformations through multimedia performance and dance. Dumb type are one of the most notable media-performance art groups in the world today, and the discussion analysing key works *pH* and *S/N* begins to impinge on theories of globalisation, cultural politics and the appearance of a postmodern avant-garde.

Likewise, the work of Gekidan Kaitaisha has become well-known around the world. Working under the influence of *ankoku butō*, Kaitaisha also explores a radical, post-structural view of the body in relation to society. This chapter analyzes their keynote work from the 1990s, *Tokyo Ghetto: Hard Core*, in connection with philosophical writings by Michel Foucault and Elizabeth Grosz on processes that describe bodily inscriptions of power. Kaitaisha's work in the 1990s is shown to be concerned with questions of how bodies are socially and culturally inscribed.

Finally, chapter 10 takes the form of an annotated play translation of *Hamletclone* by Kawamura Takeshi. Written in 2000, this intertextual and multidimensional work offers a bitter critique of Japan's modern history with a particular emphasis on questioning the progress of radical politics and the hopes of *angura*. Sometimes viciously humorous, *Hamletclone* also marks the end of an era. In its awry, concentrated focus on the collapse of alternatives, the play neatly bookends the formation of the *angura* space.

Thus, in closing, we note that although many of the artists discussed are becoming increasing successful in national and global arenas, the cultural space of Japan has been radically transformed. It is no longer an *angura space*, but rather a *space of flows* associated with globalisation (Eckersall, Uchino et al. 2004b). Consequently, we have probably reached the end of the time of *angura*.

PART ONE

THE 1960s SPACE: PERFORMANCE AND PROTEST

CHAPTER ONE

PREFIGURING THE 1960s SPACE

> You must bear in mind that when modern Japanese
> theatre began, all we had to work with was a group
> of actors who could only deliver lines in chanting,
> Kabuki fashion—even when they performed Natur-
> alistic plays.
>
> (Senda 1970: 55)

This chapter discusses the circumstances that gave rise to the transformational space of 1960s Japan, a moment characterized by alternative politics and debates about Japanese history, culture and identity.
As will be seen, these developments prefigure and centrally inform
the rise of alternative Japanese theatre as well as the emergent
counter-culture. This will not be an exhaustive survey; rather my
aim is to map the critical space preceding and subsequently framing the 1960s era. In light of this fact, I will briefly discuss the conditions for modern theatre (*shingeki*) in prewar Japanese society, and
then consider in more detail the critical space in Japan during the
occupation and subsequent remaking of Japan in the 1950s. Alongside
theatre, pivotal events such as the formation of the national student
body (*zengakuren*), the fortunes of communist and socialist groups, and
debates about subjectivity (*shutaisei*) will be discussed as moments that
prefigure 1960s society and culture.

Historians have long debated the interplay of forces that led to
the historic split among left-wing political groups in Japan during the
late 1950s and early 1960s, and the subsequent appearance of the
new left or counter-culture movement. In retrospect, it has become
clear that the left never experienced such levels of transformational
potential in Japan than in the 1960s. As will be seen though, there
is no singular explanation for this rising influence; changes in ideology, or innovative new policies alone cannot account for its creativity and success, for the new left was always a fragmentary and
contradictory formation. Only a combination of factors and their
formal and informal networks of interaction, as seen through the
dramatic and often terrible events of Japan's modern history, can
account for the rise of the 1960s space.

Early shingeki

Some of these factors can be traced to developments in prewar Japan and the daily struggles by small groups of intellectuals and artists to understand and put into practice the modern theatre in ways meaningful to their situation. From as far back as the 1880s, Tsubouchi Shōyō called for changes in art and literature that might educate people and reflect their concerns and experiences of their rapidly changing world (Tsubouchi 1999). Tsubouchi's calls for a modern theatre were formulated in essays on aesthetics, and through the translation and study of canonical western texts, especially Shakespeare. He later formed a performance study group with *kabuki* actors at Waseda University where he was a professor. In fact, the parallel evolution of the idea of the public-national space in Meiji era Japan (1868–1911), and the growing awareness of modern theatre as a national theatre project, has been widely discussed by cultural historians. Suga Hidemi, for example, notes that legislative practices associated with the formation of the Meiji state expected that the arts would serve important modernising functions and act as tools of statecraft and nation building (Suga 2003: 145–6). Kano Ayoko neatly describes processes by which modern theatre represents a "straightening" of cultural expression in Japan in a self-conscious rejection of the liminal, ambiguous spaces of traditional theatre worlds. "Straightening theatre," she writes, "was a process of dissociating theatre from the world of *kabuki* and pleasure quarters and associating it with the world of business and the military" (Kano 2001: 75).

The development of *shingeki* in Japan gained momentum during the 1920s and included experiments with theatrical genres such as naturalism, realism, social realism, and the avant-garde. The Tsukiji Little Theatre (*Tsukiji Shōgekijō*) founded by Osanai Kaoru and Hijikata Yoshi in 1924 was the first regular repertory theatre in Japan, and offered a range of almost exclusively European plays to its cosmopolitan and mainly left-leaning audiences. As will become apparent, the fact that local plays were actively discouraged and rarely performed at Tsukiji came to be a problem for *shingeki* in its later forms. In December 1925, the Japan League for Proletarian Arts and Literature (*Nihon Puroretaria Bungei Renmei* or *Puroren*) was established and included a drama division and mobile agit-prop theatre called Trunk Theatre (*Torunku Gekijō*). Torunku Gekijō was a mobile theatre, easily transportable to communities and workplaces. The sets, props and costumes for the show came from the trunk, making a kind of *Lehrstücke*, or "learning-play," that could spontaneously address events and political causes.

However, the emergent liberalism and rising Marxist tone of prewar theatre was short-lived. As nationalist-military forces became stronger they sought to control all forms of artistic and cultural expression. Between 1925, when Peace Preservation Laws (*Chian Iji Hō*) limiting free expression were first introduced, until Japan's surrender in 1945, artists worked in an environment of ever increasing censorship and extreme nationalism. Murayama Tomoyoshi, a well-known socialist theatre artist in prewar Japan, described how the law was so intentionally vague as to allow any form of censorship to be imposed at the whim of authorities (Murayama 1991: 22). This had serious consequences for artists who faced imprisonment for perceived transgressions against the vaguely defined code of national polity (*kokutai*). Overall, the development of modern theatre in Japan was severely curtailed.

Murayama's 1927 play *Nero in a Skirt* (*Sukato o Haita Nero*; Murayama 1977)[1] has been read as an anti-war text that challenged the censorship laws. Written as a puppet play and evidently referencing Alfred Jarry's *Ubu* plays,[2] *Nero* was set in Russia in 1788. The main character of Catherine the Second is depicted as an Ubu-like queen who holds power through a mix of corruption, personal aggrandizement, and terror. Likewise, her court—the officials who surround her—are authoritarian and decadent. The soldiers brazenly sent to war by the blood thirsty regime and the hapless character of Lanskoi, Catherine's doomed and unenthusiastic lover, are images from the play that prefigure Japan's military adventurism and suggest a strong criticism of ruling powers and their disregard for the lives of normal people. As I have argued elsewhere, in the context of the rising of militarism, Murayama's theatre marks a broad trend in the prewar avant-garde. Beginning in the relative liberalism of the Taishō era with explorations of the performing body as a site of experience and personal expression, Murayama's theatre gradually transformed

---

[1] *Sukato o Haita Nero* was first published in Engeki Shincho (New Wave Theatre), May 1927. It was performed by Shin za (New Troupe) in 1928.

[2] The *Ubu* plays of which *Ubu Roi* is perhaps best-known are grotesque satirical works loosely based on *Macbeth* and written for the puppet theatre by Alfred Jarry in Paris in the 1890s.

into a quasi-socialist form: this transformation marked an emergent critique of the *kokutai*, the emperor centred "national polity" ideals of the military powers in Japan. Moreover, the situation for artists became extremely difficult in the 1930s. On August 1, 1940, hundreds of left-wing artists were arrested and the main *shingeki* groups dispersed. At the outbreak of the Pacific War, all theatre was mobilized for "national goals" (Powell 2002: 113–114) and the modern theatre was all but silenced.[3]

It is not my aim to discuss in detail theatre and culture in wartime Japan,[4] however, the immense problem of dealing with Japanese cultural developments during the war needs to be noted. In the imperial era, the Japanese State mobilized theatre as an instrument of propaganda. Historical *kabuki* plays (*jidai mono*) were the preferred model and were exploited for their espousal of so-called unique Japanese warrior values; the code of *bushido*, sacrifice, fidelity, loyalty, and the sacred, civilising mission of Japanese culture. Theatre troupes were sent to entertain soldiers in the field, *shingeki* artists, alongside *shinpa* and *kabuki* performers who needed work participated in these tours of propaganda plays. As in Britain and Germany, many actors performed in wartime propaganda films. Among the most controversial figures were artists who publicly recanted their opposition to Japanese imperialism (*tenkō*) and agreed to work in ways that would not undermine wartime society. One's degree of collaboration or resistance, however, could not be measured easily and the whole issue of wartime collaboration was a vexed question for the generation that followed.

Debates about Kishida Kunio, a leading figure in the postwar Japanese theatre, show how complex questions of wartime complicity and resistance were for the generation of theatre makers that re-established modern theatre following the war. Characterized by J. Thomas Rimer as Japan's pre-eminent humanist playwright of the *shingeki* tradition, Kishida's humanist perspective can be recognized as essentially an anti-war one (Rimer 1974: 234–6). What rankled many 1960s artists though was Kishida's wartime silence.[5] Moreover,

---

[3] For extended discussions of the prewar theatre in the context of State power, see (Kano 2001; Powell 2002).

[4] For an extended discussion of Japanese culture in wartime, see (Shillony 1981).

[5] Powell notes that Kishida Kunio and Bungaku za were perceived, by some at least, to be collaborators in progressing the wartime ethos (Powell 2002: 128–9).

the self-consciously 'art-for-art sake' Literary Theatre (*Bungaku za*) that Kishida helped to establish—one of Japan's best known *shingeki* companies—came to represent, for the 1960s generation, an apolitical and bourgeois theatre movement that was all the more suspicious because of its lack of anti-war perspectives. Unlike openly leftist authors such as Senda Koreya, who aimed to collapse the differences between art and politics (and were imprisoned during the war for their efforts), Kishida maintained that art was separate to real world events. For Kishida, as for Bungaku za, theatre's purpose was to reflect on the personal-literary dimensions of the human condition. From the perspective of the 1960s generation, however, the potential for theatrical realism to develop further seemed to be at an end. In the 1960s space, such performance was more likely to be simply replicating and hence naturalising a real world state of affairs. Such theatre was criticized for being uninterested in the notion of political intervention and for being complicit with ruling values of the day. What the younger artists were wanting was something far more spontaneous and chaotic; actions that spoke louder than words.

More immediate events informing *angura's* development arise from the way that the postwar cultural space came about. In one sense, modern theatre and alternative politics flourished in the generally liberalized society of postwar Japan. The Japanese Communist and Socialist Parties, of necessity underground groups during the war, enjoyed strong support; for a time they prospered as an effective opposition to conservative political forces that were also reforming. The socialists won the 1947 election and briefly formed government. Trade unions and citizens groups banned during the wartime regime were encouraged to organize and evolved into symbolic, as well as concrete examples of democracy, anti-feudalism, and collective action. In the first years after Japan's surrender, cultural practices including everything from *Shinto* worship to martial arts and festival celebrations were viewed with critical scepticism and an eye to their ideological and state-military functions. Occupation-force censors, for example, tightly controlled *kabuki*; in the wider sphere, aspects of education, landownership, and business were given radical and lasting reform.

Brian Powell notes how *shingeki's* fears of the wholesale imposition of an American view of theatre during the occupation were not realized, despite some clumsy attempts to persuade Japanese artists to perform American plays. Although suspicious of *shingeki's* collective company structures—something akin to a military hierarchy, but, in fact, a commonplace organizational structure in Japan—*shingeki* was given wide-ranging freedoms in the aftermath of 1945 by occupation authorities. Incredibly, in what must have been a remarkable feat of improvisation in the ruins of war torn Tokyo, the first theatre performances to take place following surrender on August 15 were only two weeks later on September 1 when a *kabuki* program was performed. In December, the first postwar *shingeki* production of Anton Chekhov's *The Cherry Orchid* played to full houses (Powell 2002: 136–8).[6] The 1950s were in many ways *shingeki's* most successful decade. Three companies in particular came to dominate the postwar theatre scene: Haiyū za (Actors' Theatre), Mingei (Peoples' Theatre) and the aforementioned Bungaku za. Each grew impressive networks among artists, audiences and the wider community. They built theatres, developed training programs, and, for the first time, began to seriously develop Japanese play writing. *Shingeki* groups also became influential in film and television industries and trained many of the generation of artists who would later rebel against them.

Undoubtedly, the director and theatre theorist Senda Koreya (1904–95) was one the most important people in 1950s theatre and his work marks the progress of *shingeki's* many achievements. Senda's real name was Ito Kuneo; he took the name Senda Koreya as a gesture of protest, marking his arrest by police who mistook him for a Korean in the Tokyo suburb of Sendagaya in the aftermath of the devastating 1923 earthquake. Japanese survivors killed many Koreans and the name symbolized a form of political protest and alliance with the underdog that came to be characteristic of Senda's life, work and politics. Although Senda was born into a wealthy family situation with *kabuki* connections, he entered the Tsukiji Shōgekijō in its first year and remained working in the modern theatre for the rest of his life. Like many of his generation, Senda was influenced by German theatre during the Weimar Republic (1919–29), an extraordinary period of European theatrical innovation. He studied in Berlin with Erwin Piscator and developed an enduring interest in the work of the Russian artist Vsevolod Meyerhold. Piscator and

---

[6] Although Senda Koreya (who I gather from Nishidō's account was the director), with false modesty perhaps, says it was not a very accomplished work (Nishidō 2002: 13).

Meyerhold pioneered new forms of theatre that mixed socialist politics with radical stage presentations. Senda was imprisoned numerous times for his political views and was said to use the time in captivity to write about theatre. In 1944, he helped found Haiyū za where he applied a holistic philosophy of theatre that stressed not only the literary and aesthetic values of a work, but also the need for skilled actors who could use their bodies and voices effectively and achieve a convincing depth of character.

In 1953, Senda directed the first play by Bertolt Brecht presented in Japan; a production of *Fear and Misery in the Third Reich* that marked a shift in Senda's creative process away from the genres of naturalism and psychological realism and towards the politically nuanced representational dramaturgy of Brecht. First staged in 1938, *Fear and Misery in the Third Reich* comprizes twenty-four scenes about everyday life under Nazi rule, and this play is a study of how fear and misery come to be the normal conditions of life under totalitarian rule. Reinforcing this message, the play is also called *The Private Life of the Master Race*. Senda made a lifelong study of Brecht's plays and dramatic theory stating that:

> The postwar presence of Brecht was large. No one else had done such extensive thinking about theatre as well as being involved in practice. The greater the confusion in the world became, the more Brecht's ideological method became useful. (Nishidō 2002: 15)

Senda also called for the establishment of a national theatre. For him, modern theatre rightly functions as a site of national debate and historical reflection. Nishidō Kōjin makes the point that for Senda *shingeki* was an attempt to restore the ground lost by theatre because of conscious decisions by governments, from as far back as the Edo era, to abandon its vital force (Nishidô 2002: 18). This suggests that for Senda, postwar *shingeki* was not simply a theatre of modern techniques, contemporary plays or political debates, but something that could become intrinsic to Japan's sense of history and identity. But this sensibility was never completely discovered in *shingeki*. Japan's modern theatre had not localized, consequentially a steady measuring of Japan's theatre against the values of global modern theatre culture is evident. This hypersensitive world of otherness imported onto the bodies of local actors—what the playwright Hirata Oriza calls "the incomplete project of modern theatre" (Hirata 2003)— struck at the minds of all those grappling with imported theatre models in local situations. It remains a powerful statement of cultural struggle in Japan. Senda is the representative figure of these dimensions and inherent contradictions in *shingeki*. And even as the next generation rejected the *shingeki* system, they could not ignore Senda.

Selective reform

Meanwhile, postwar reforms of Japanese culture were curtailed by shifting political forces. From the perspective of many leftists, reform was selective. Marked by the occupation and memories of war, they hoped that Japan might have come to reflect on recent history and develop a sense of collective responsibility for the catastrophe of the war. However, such thoughts were successfully elided in the public sphere and written over by the energising rhetorics of reconstruction, democracy, and capitalism. The Imperial House was not brought to task for their role in prosecuting the war and only a handful of wartime figures were eventually tried in war crimes trials. Nor did Japan examine its cult of imperial–military extremism. Moreover, Japan's US-authored postwar constitution has saddled Japanese political processes with at times a contradictory and unworkable framework that defined Japanese democracy always in relation to its American progeny; no indigenous democratic formula was able to emerge. To this day, casting a shadow over democracy in Japan is American power. As Igarashi Yoshikuni suggests, democracy "never existed as an abstract construct, but always as a historically specific condition under the hegemony of US military power in East Asia" (Igarashi 2000: 137). In 1951 the first US-Japan security treaty was signed. A decade later, massive demonstrations against the re-signing of this treaty marked the beginning of the era of protest. As will be seen, the sense of identity crisis and ineffectual resistance to this outsider hegemony that is evident from these events came to consume the modern theatre of Japan. Political and cultural institutions were transformed for similar reasons.

The onset of the cold war gave momentum to the "Reverse Course" of 1947–48 at which time many of the so called 'new deal' political and social reform programs of the occupation were curtailed, especially in the areas of business reform and political freedom. The revival of the fortunes of individuals and institutions associated with the wartime society must have appeared to some as *déjà vu*. From the critical perspectives of Marxist historians for example, who were influential figures in the universities but not in society-at-large, an ideology of corporate-nationalism was emerging as a key factor in the construction of the postwar space. It is further suggested that resurgent right wing corporate interests in Japan (*zaibatsu/keiretsu*), regardless of their wartime complicity, began to work in concert with those in the US to comprehensively undermine the liberal politics of the early occupation (Roberts 1979). During the "Red Purge" in the latter half of 1950, open violence directed against the left was tolerated, if not encouraged: workers in unions, Marxist intellectuals, and artists were among those targeted and removed from positions of influence. Throughout the 1950s, organized crime groups (*yakuza*), with links to ruling politicians and the police, and right wing students on university campuses, were paid to break strikes and fight battles with anti-establishment forces.

A parallel sense of crisis for the left is seen in the theatre. Powell characterizes the 1950s as the era that saw the final stages of leftist theatre groups and the subsequent domination of theatrical realism across the board (Powell 2002: 151). In this oppressive political climate, consciously left-leaning theatres such as Tokyo Geijitsu Gekijō (Tokyo Arts Theatre) and Murayama's democracy-vanguard theatre Shinkyō Gekijō disbanded. Thus, despite *shingeki's* many achievements in the 1950s, recently revived symbols of the democratic process, such as theatre, were seriously strained by the evolving logic of the cold war.

Nevertheless, the reconstruction of Japan was well underway and creative centres of resistance to cold war hegemony were continually active in the period. Two interrelating factors are of particular importance in prefiguring the 1960s space. These are the founding of the *Zengakuren* National Students Federation in 1948 and an underlying philosophical examination of the relationship between subjectivity and identity formation.

Zengakuren

Campus-based student organizations (*Gakuyūkai, Jichikai*) existed long before 1945, however, the founding of the All-Japan Federation of Student Self Governing Associations (*Zen Nihon Gakusei Jichikai Sōrengō* or *Zengakuren*) on September 18, 1948 was the first time that student

politics gained a national forum. In seeking wider political participation extending beyond campus issues and developing policies on
national and international themes, *Zengakuren* became an important
site for the formation of the new left. Hereafter, the new left, although
a broad-based coalition of people from a variety of political and cultural fields, was strongly associated with university students. In turn,
the overriding sense of disorder and anarchy that often shaped new
left thinking was compounded by *Zengakuren's* internal and continual
sense of fragmentation and reinvention. As Stuart Dowsey notes:
"About the only thing that all *Zengakuren* students will agree on is
that Japan needs a revolution" (Dowsey 1970: 6).

Given the prominence of student politics in the collective history
of radical Japan, it is perhaps ironic that until the 1960s student
politics involved a relatively small clique. Although all university students were technically *Zengakuren* members, a small group of highly
motivated students tussled over *Zengakuren* policy. Throughout the
postwar period until the end of the 1960s, *Zengakuren* volatility increased
as it moved between control by students who supported an alliance
with the Japan Communist Party (JCP), and those who formed anti-
JCP (*bund*) breakaway factions (Smith 1972: 283). Thus, while the
radical core membership of *Zengakuren* displayed a strong sense of
social activism across the board, the development of new left politics lay in an historic split with the communists. Radical students
often voiced criticisms of the JCP charging that it was contaminated
by "authoritarianism and absolutism" (Tsurumi 1975: 200). Students
were divided over the Party's disregard of the Soviet politburo's critique of Josef Stalin in 1956, when the former leader of the USSR
was officially denounced, and the genocide associated with his regime
made public. Moreover, a softening of the communist's revolutionary zeal was apparent in the JCP's participation in and implicit support for the mainstream political model: the US-authored constitution,
and the semblance of a multi-party system and parliamentary government. This trend was confirmed for the students when the JCP
rejected the goal of class revolution all together, and adopted in its
place a policy of "peaceful gradualism" at its sixth party congress in
1957. Further disenchantment was evident when students who stormed
the Japanese parliament building (*Diet*) on November 11, 1958, were
met with condemnation by JCP and Socialist *Diet* members.[7] On

---

[7] One can hardly expect the members of Parliament to support incursions on its

June 1, 1958, the *Zengakuren* passed a motion of no confidence in the JCP's central committee, citing grounds that the JCP had been ineffective in criticising Stalin and was doctrinaire and interfering in student affairs. In response, the Party expelled *Zengakuren* members who supported the motion. In all, over 2000 JCP student members left the Party, or were expelled. The resulting splinter group *Kyōsanshugisha* (Communist League/*Bund*) that formed in December 1958 soon wrest control of the leadership of the *Zengakuren* from pro-JCP members. Within *Zengakuren* there were now the mainstream or *bund* faction (*kyakukyōdo*)—an anti-mainstream and pro-JCP faction—and the *Shakaishugi Gakusei Dōmeikai* (Socialist Student League).

A widely discussed event from 1967 demonstrates how large the gap between old and new left forces would become. On October 8, as part of a rolling series of increasingly violent actions, militant students protesting against Prime Minister Satō's planned trip to Korea—the latest in an on-going series of issues that the students opposed—demonstrated in Tokyo. They burned vehicles and fought with police resulting in several hundred protestors being arrested and one killed. Meanwhile, on the same day in another part of Tokyo, 80,000 members of *Minsei* (The Socialist Party) were enjoying a picnic sponsored by the Communist Party newspaper *Akihata*. Thomas Havens suggests that this event signalled a new level of violence among anti-JCP factions (Havens 1987: 134). From the perspective of the activists who were bloodied in battle on that day, the image of their supposed comrades enjoying food and drinks in Tama Park while they fought against the paramilitary force of the State must have appeared bitterly ironic, yet truly revealing of the sorry state of the old guard. Thus, the stage was set, not only for confrontations between the left and right, but among the left itself. As is often the case, some of the most energetic and hard-fought campaigns on the left were not waged against the common enemy but between the factions.[8]

---

sanctity. Somewhat ironically, however, in May 1960, socialist members of the house were themselves prevented from entering the *Diet*. In a complete collapse of parliamentary process, Prime Minister Kishi used police to keep opposition members at bay, while controversial US-Japan Security Bills were passed (see chapter 2).

[8] For a wide-ranging discussion of *Zengakuren* infighting and the ideological clashes with the JCP, see (Matsunami 1970); (Nakanishi 1970); (Suga 2003).

A comparable sense of growing discontent with *shingeki* is evident among young artists. As we have seen, many *shingeki* artists in the 1950s were former opponents of Japanese militarism and had been rehabilitated because of the quasi-democratic impetus of the occupation. Well documented also, are the financial and political ties that *shingeki* developed with sections of the union movement. While it is not clear that the theatre had a large support base among working people, nevertheless, the large theatre companies received funds in the form of tickets bought by unions and espoused a belief in democratic worker participation and control. The *Rōen* (*Kinrōsha Engeki Kyōkai*) or Workers Council for Theatre and the Arts was the main trade union arts organization that recruited audiences for *shingeki*. A. Horie-Weber's account of *shingeki*, however, shows that the theatre was inflexible and resistant to change in ways that are similar to the leftist political parties (Horie-Weber 1975). In each case, the layering of democratic participation was at best superficial and made unworkable by a more classically Japanese bureaucratic structure that is typically less than transparent. Young company members were usually unable to gain power and influence in these organizations; consequently younger artists were generally unable to find creative outlets for their work. The growing sense of unease and frustration with *shingeki* fostered in an environment where *shingeki* was becoming, for the younger generation at least, a bourgeois institution with a propensity towards naturalism (with a more or less complacent outlook as a result) led the young critic Tsuno Kaitarō to conclude that: "beneath *shingeki's* prosperous exterior there is decadence" (Tsuno 1978: 11). In other words, despite the originality and topicality of a new generation of writers such as Abe Kōbō and Mishima Yukio working in *shingeki*, the modern theatre was regarded as too comfortable (for the artists and the audiences), too western, not involved with Japanese aesthetic or political sensibilities, too removed from the people (in their smooth new buildings), too intellectual, and subsequently lacking visceral engagement with the everyday world.

As will be seen though, political structures for theatre groups remained a problematic issue among *angura* groups and contradictions arose in their tentative moves towards new left counter-culture democratic structures. At the same time as *angura* attested to the political critique of *shingeki*, their own groups tended to ascribe features of traditional Japanese theatre models. Some groups continue the practice of *deshi* (young trainees), for example, who submit to a regime of obedience as part of their apprenticeship. Artistic leaders in the community, as with the student-politicians within the protest movement, sometimes cultivated "guru-like" status among their followers. Even while they might have espoused notions of democratic reform, the structures for achieving this were often parochial and unyielding to change. The fact that *angura* companies sometimes evolved models of organization more akin to traditional theatres, and new left groups were under the influence of charismatic leaders meant that institutionally they were both torn between ideals of freedom and worker participation on the one hand, and the maintenance of hierarchical power structures on the other. The former ideal defined their aims while the latter organizational structures determined their modes of operation. Hence, attempts to banish "*shingeki* as a system" were often unable to disentangle from older, problematically feudal, modes of power.[9]

Experiencing selfhood

Gaining a solid understanding of the idea of subjectivity and self-hood awareness (*shutaisei*) is a difficult, but nevertheless, essential task for this study as a whole. In many ways, theatre exists as a marker of subjectivity, through telling stories and embodying the medium of social interactions, for example. *Shingeki's* delineation of individual complex characters and explorations of the subconscious through the genre of psychological realism shows how it too was immersed in ideas of subjectivity. Selfhood was also a central focus in *angura*, wherein, it will be argued, the sense of selfhood that emerged—a form of embodied expression with radical political sensibilities—underlay the avant-garde nature of the work as a whole.

---

[9] Perhaps what is most problematic in this regard was the treatment of women in many *angura* companies of the 1960s. Women generally waited on senior males at post show drinking parties, did cleaning, and public relations work. These roles, of course, reinforce sexist stereotypes. Women *butō* dancers were often sent to work in strip clubs, while the men would fantasize about being gangsters and pimps; a part of the outsider Jean Genet-devil-may-care likeness that they cultivated. It is problematic that *angura* pioneered strong and pivotal theatrical representations of women and saw a generation of singularly important women performers emerge, and yet remained so uncritical of sexual exploitation.

While subjectivity has been debated as a philosophical principal of modernity in the west for a number of centuries, its impact on Japanese cultural history has been most striking in the postwar era. Selfhood's problematizing of individual experience and self-identity was a powerful and radical theorization of political change in postwar Japan; a society long-conditioned to accept hierarchy and interdependence as a method of social organization, not only for survival, but also for control. Here, it will be argued that *shutaisei* was an essential aspect of new left politics and culture; moreover, it is the key to understanding the interpretive dimensions of *angura* in political terms.

J. Victor Koschmann shows that various formations of *shutaisei* have been crucial to our understanding of the critical space of the left in Japan before 1960, and remains an important reference point for ongoing discussions of subjectivity and identity:

> For existentialists (*shutaisei*) implied a leap of faith associated with the philosopher Sören Kierkegaard; for Marxists the materialist subjectivity posited by Karl Marx in the first of the "Theses on Feuerbach"— or for Communists, partisanship (*tōhasei*); for students of the sociologist Max Weber it was an individualistic ethos modelled on the Protestant ethic; for behavioural scientists the capacity to make decisions based on either utility or value consistency. (Koschmann 1996: 1)

Koschmann's work shows that there was never one prevailing model of selfhood. Moreover, his work prefigures the rejection of leftist orthodoxy in the 1960s and shows that dissenting cliques inside the left were already formulating selfhood positions in opposition to the main ideological thrust of these organizations.[10] The wide ranging responses to *shutaisei* that Koschmann points to undermine the ordered sense of progress and control espoused by mainstream political institutions, including those on the left. *Shutaisei*, in its very plurality then, seems to invite a kind of critical reflection and questioning that makes the traditional left uncomfortable. It is likely that the seemingly inevitable will to revolutionize that was supposedly the promise of Marxism is questioned by the disorder of subjectivity. Moreover, it draws attention to autocratic and authoritarian tendencies in the left, while at the same time slipping under the relatively stable domain

---

[10] See also Miyoshi's discussion of *shutaisei* in political life and cultural debates before the 1960s (Miyoshi 1991: 97–125).

of class politics, and reaching into areas of interpersonal relations and creativity.

Rikki Kersten's work on *shutaisei* points to the larger measure of debates among Japan's progressive thinkers and intellectuals in the postwar era. In trying to rationalize the goal of collective struggle on the one hand, and the critique of authoritarianism on the other, *shutaisei* is seen not only as a reference point for these discussions, but as a way of understanding the inherent ambiguities of the new left project. For selfhood awareness, Kersten notes that individuals must become "conscious" of their "creative role" and "must factor within (this) humanity the freedom to determine the values that... inform the world" (Kersten 1996: 79). In rethinking democracy in Japan, Kirsten draws attention to radical attempts to redefine the political space and *shutaisei* makes more visible the inherent struggle between idealism and historical determinism.

Eric Cazdyn's work on Japanese cinema also proposes a commentary on the broader context of *shutaisei* noting how selfhood gives rise to questions about: "the degree to which active human agents shape themselves and their social environment" (Cazdyn 2002: 236). Thinking in this way offers individuals the possibility of rejecting the collective assumptions of the immediate postwar left in Japan. As for the wartime organization of society, where the needs of the nation are imagined not as a class transformation, but in terms of imperial destiny, one might come to reject, through selfhood consciousness, the expectation that one's subjectivity must always be sublimated to the ideological dictates of a movement. The same thinking could equally apply to the postwar economic reconstruction of Japan, where historians have noted how company workers in the 1950s were urged to work long hours and endure poor working conditions for the "good" of the nation. Thus, *shutaisei* is a formation that tries to be critical of authoritarian modes of collectivization such as the military, while also trying to rethink class politics and the problematic relationship and exploitation inherent in processes of collective action.

Cazdyn, moreover, notes the shift from questions of alternatives at the local level, to those that prefigure an awareness of the global. In essence, he argues that in respect of cyborg images in recent Japanese cinema (he discusses the example of Tsukamoto Shinya's "Tetsuo", 1989), subjectivity traverses across historical and cultural frames via the representation of the body. In modernity, the body's autonomy struggles with history and society. In the globalized postmodern society, the body is exceeded (Cazdyn 2002: 242). This is an insightful observation and one that anticipates discussions about theatre and globalisation. The degree to which the body in *angura*, for example, was trans-historical and liminal in ways similar to the cyborg imagination is striking. As will be discussed in the following chapter, *angura* worked at the representational limits of the body and exceeded them. Like *shutaisei* politics, the body became ambiguous in *angura*.[11] And, as will be seen, *angura's* interest in the body eventually takes on its own cyborg dimensions.

In each of the ways discussed above, we see that *shutaisei* is a discourse that was helpful to the new left in rethinking ideology and political action as something more individuated, participatory, spontaneous and experiential.

Shutaisei *and the new left*

The first evidence of *shutaisei* in the *Zengakuren* context lies in the following 1960 statement by *bund* leader and *Zengakuren* Secretary-General, Kitakoji Satoshi:

> Both as youth and as nascent intelligentsia we are strongly inclined to search for ways to connect personal ways of life with social modes of existence. It is therefore extremely important to recognise the student movement as a process of the formulation of selfhood (*shutaisei*), which might solve this problem of intelligentsia, while at the same time, as it exists as a political movement. (Tsurumi 1975: 200)

Kitakoji's comments summarize what is arguably the core philosophy of the new left student movement in terms that connect this core centrally to the politics of *shutaisei*. This is no mere philosophical discussion though; his statement seeks the rationalization of individual and radical collectivist identity within an overriding framework of liberation consciousness, and thereby proposes the dynamics of a

---

[11] One could argue that postmodern theories of politics and identity, which arose in 1980s cyberculture theory, are prefigured in the 1960s avant-garde. The most influential reading of the cyborg as politically progressive is Donna Haraway's "Cyborg Manifesto." By imagining a feminist cyborg, Haraway asks that we consider the cyborg as creative, multiple and multi-coupling, offering new political and personal possibilities, and subjective realities hitherto unimagined. See (Haraway 1991).

new political movement. Although not at all concerned with details, Kitakoji stresses the importance of somehow translating ideas into action and actions into ideas. A circular or fluid formation of embodiment and experience is therefore suggested.

Given the inherent factionalism of 1960s activism, generalized doctrines like *selfhood* were flexible and allowed the contemplation of a great number of counter-culture issues. In other words, the *shutaisei* discourse could be applied across factions among *Zengakuren* membership and be a common point of experience.

In contrast to classical Marxist theory and postwar political norms, the "search for selfhood," promised a re-examination of Japanese society and its wartime history, as well as (and relating to) the postwar democracy movement. Questions of national identity and individualism, the interplay between the dynamics of collective action and independence, sexual liberation, and exploration of subversive potentials in creative expression, all played their part in the critical domain of *shutaisei*. Over and above everything, however, was an abiding emphasis on the positive, dynamic, performative effects of direct participation, visceral experience, and spontaneous action. Henceforth, to be is to act, as one student activist commented: "I never try to confirm whether another's view is the same as mine in order to establish solidarity between him and me. I feel solidarity with anyone who struggles hard to do something" (Tsurumi 1975: 216–7). In other words, a political awareness akin to a "revolution of consciousness" is suggested. The following statement by a University of Tokyo student during the occupation of the campus in 1968, further develops the connection between personal and political modes of transformation:

> Our struggle to seek a fully human way of life of course avoids "political revolution" which attempts to change only institutions and systems without touching the issue of what man's life should be in the modern age . . . Thus, what we aim at is spiritual revolution." (Nakazawa 1984: 41)

By this we see that the *Zengakuren* new left conception of *shutaisei* dramatically and irrevocably shifts from an orthodox leftist political identity to the search for a new activist one that is sustained by liberated (although self-critical) variations of personal and national consciousness and experience. It suggests that we might think about activist identity in its performative dimensions: a radical self that exists mainly through embodied experiences—marches, struggles, occupations, and sit ins. Self-expression as a form of revolutionary consciousness was the goal of 1960s *shutaisei*. In the words of another activist: "Rather than question whether a thing can be done or not, the essential thing is to give full expression to oneself" (Fukashiro 1970: 33).

Mapping the critical space of early postwar Japan

In mapping this critical space we can see that a number of important pathways are coming into view. First, in the immediate postwar space there is a period of optimism and activity among leftist groups. A parallel sense of achievement is evident in *shingeki*, which has regrouped in the aftermath of its virtual exclusion in the wartime cultural space. Moreover, the growth of political institutions to agitate on behalf of working people and cultural institutions to advance postwar progressive values, quickly develops momentum until at least 1950. Into the next decade, we see the consolidation of these forces as they become built into Japan's postwar landscape. But we also observe their moderation and the curtailment of some of their activities in response to a more censorial and antagonistic political environment. During the 1950s authoritarian tendencies reappear as a geo-political reality. Externally, Japan is drawn into the American cold war mentality, while in the domestic sphere resurgent corporate interests strongly agitate against workers rights and *keiretsu* reform in the process of economic reconstruction and postwar recovery. By the late 1950s university students, only just born in wartime, come to reject the increasingly ineffectual actions of the communist and socialist parties and related groups. Meanwhile in the theatre world, the progressive rhetoric of *shingeki* no longer matches reality, yet nor does it seem ready to be completely subsumed into a postmodern culture industry formation. Rather, theatre sits uneasy and is unsure. Never before, from the early days of Tsukiji through wartime silence and postwar growth, has a more powerful sense of pessimism been seen in the modern theatre. A fundamental questioning of the modern theatre project is about to begin. And in the end, everything is ready for change.

CHAPTER TWO

PERFORMING POLITICS AND THE *SHUTAISEI* EFFECT

The cultural space of the 1960s continues to haunt contemporary performance in Japan even though the era itself has turned to nostalgia. Indeed, the originality of 1960s theatre and its turbulent, spirited conditions of production remain as an echo in the collective memory of Japan's cultural landscape. Alongside the wholesale rejection of alternatives to capitalism and the gradual incorporation of our theatres into a culture industry of ever-increasing commodification, we might find it difficult to understand but are nonetheless drawn to this last era of rebellion. In this respect, inventions of utopia and the impossible revolution underscore a nuanced reading of 1960s Japanese theatre.

The dispersed and yet fundamentally transformational politics born in 1960s society—which Suga Hidemi (2003: 6–7) goes so far as to call the only true revolution in the modern era—and the interrelationship of this politics with performance in rethinking the Japanese avant-garde are the focus of this chapter. In this and the following chapter, we will try to show how 1960s theatre and culture in Japan was a transformational moment: a *shutaisei* effect intersecting across history, postwar formations of politics and art, and optimistic expectations for a better world. Performances by newly formed *angura* groups, the subject of the following chapter, mirrored a rising sense of performativity in political life that aimed to discover a radical selfhood (*shutaisei*) among young Japanese. During this decade, social models and creative systems of production were established that are still in play today. Perhaps especially for those of us who came to the theatre in the 1980s, we have a faint but, nevertheless, compelling memory of the 1960s as the era of possibility and unique creativity.[1]

---

[1] As discussed in the following chapters, I have come to understand in retrospect the *shutaisei* effect as not so much a praxis of radical politics, but one of individualized politics. While therefore substantiating aspects of progressive change such as advances in identity, sexual, and ecological political movements, for example, *shutaisei* also evidenced a radical realignment within capitalism.

Shutaisei's influence on 1960s Japan requires further analysis, not only to examine its share of nostalgia, but more importantly in order to give critical space to the radical experiences of the times. Just as we are concerned with how to remember the 1960s, that generation of artists and activists were struggling with the recent past of their social reality. As seen in the preceding chapter, bitterly divisive experiences of wartime imperial aggression, occupation and postwar capitalism all factored in the construction of the 1960s space. In this chapter, I am motivated from a sense of trying to better understand this space and its potentials. In one way, this can be read as a corrective to the contemporaneous moment where neo-conservative critiques of alternative 1960s spaces are often heard. The subsequent diminution of global cultures into narrowly conceived polarities and singular perspectives is a complete contrast to the subtle nuances and fluid, albeit, messy politics of 1960s counter-culture movements. The problem for radical history is, moreover, not only one of changing social values; it is one of forgetting the significance of the past altogether. On this point Terry Eagleton argues that discussions that engage with idealism, socialism or communitarian forms of social change have become unfashionable with the effect that these debates are increasingly marginalized or silenced. Thus, a comprehensive history of alternatives has consequently gone missing in contemporary readings of 1960s cultural production (Eagleton 1996). Although with the benefit of hindsight, one might be sceptical about the possibility for theatre to effect social change this was the only period in recent memory when such change seemed at all possible. Hence, one of my objectives is to highlight a period of theatre culture during which theatre artists and political activists were more closely aligned, albeit factionalized and sometimes split by debates about the politics and dynamics of performance. I am interested in the question of how theatre might serve, or resist, various new left ideologies as they were formulated in the shifting patterns of student new left political factions.

This is not to ignore the problems of arguing for a radical 1960s theatre culture, only to point out that the dismissal or conservative reappraisal of the 1960s space disavows the significant innovations that the era produced. Such a stance is expedient and aims to erase from our collective memory an understanding of the degree to which radical culture came to challenge and undermine vested political and economic ruling forces in Japan and elsewhere. At the same time,

one cannot ignore critical appraisals of the movement that point to
its flaws. Briefly mentioned in the previous chapter, for example,
were company structures that evidenced blindness to sexual and gender politics, and the formation of eccentric top-down systems of rule.
It is also a valid point that *angura* was blind to class issues. As the
aforementioned elder-leftist of the *shingeki* movement, Senda Koreya,
pointed out in an interview with the young "radicals" of the Theatre
Centre 68/70 (later Black Tent), *angura* was often removed from the
working class and the daily concerns, political struggles, or hardships
of Japanese people (Senda 1970).

The 1960s space was nonetheless radically optimistic. It wanted
to throw off seemingly predestined shackles of modern history and
attempted to relativize ideas of self-identity in relation to the collective pressure of conformity. Even though it was in conception a
kind of uniquely Japanese invention, it also aspired to alternative
modes of social organization that could resist banal jingoism and
overt forms of cultural imperialism. In this sense, the 1960s space
was about the reappraisal of history in order to condemn militarism
and simultaneously challenge the dominance and seeming inevitabil-
ity of capitalism. Thus, we might come to more readily accept Suga's
claims, noted above, regarding the unique properties of the 1960s
space in Japan. During this period, Japan experienced political, ideological and cultural paradigm shifts of the first order. The 1960s
movement diluted the power of the JCP and put an end to anticipation among Marxists—always more hopeful than actual—that the
revolution would arrive soon.

Here, we will consider how performing arts were prefigured in
the political space in a discussion of *politics as performance*, in the sense
that politics during this era displayed strong performative tendencies.
As we shall see, to be political in the 1960s required action and a
willingness to put one's body at the line of confrontation. It is in
this heady mix of experiencing the body and politics in motion that
we come to understand the *shutaisei* effect.

May and June 1960

Mass demonstrations in the streets of Tokyo were a common event
in Japan in 1960. Culminating in June, angry crowds surrounded
the Diet and the central government area of Kasumigaseki. Nearby,

long columns of people marched through Ginza, Tokyo's most expensive shopping district. These mass demonstrations protesting the
renewal of the US-Japan mutual security treaty (*Anzen Hoshō Jōyaku*
or Ampo)[2] were some of the largest in Japan's postwar experience.
Participation in the protest movement became a life changing experience for many people. High profile media attention reporting the
dramas of the lockouts, strikes, formation marching and battles with
police; even the fact that the protests soon produced their first mar-
tyr when the university student Kamba Michiko was killed in a
melee, worked to ensure that Ampo was a protest movement of high
drama and apocryphal intensity. Before considering the performative qualities of this protest, it is necessary to understand some wider
issues relating to the security treaty.

The US-Japan mutual security treaty that was first signed following the allied occupation of Japan has been widely discussed, not
least for its relevance to Article Nine, the "no war" clause of the
postwar Japanese Constitution. Negotiated in a context of renewed
American strategic interest in Asia and cold war, anti-communist
political rhetoric, the treaty required the US to ensure Japan's international security. In return, the US retained a significant military
presence in Japan and continuing influence over Japan's foreign policy. Wherever domestic policy could be interpreted to have implications for American interests in the region, US interests were also
said to predominate. Scholars agree that the first treaty was extremely
unfavourable to Japan.

The treaty was to be revised in 1960 and some hoped for better
outcomes. What these outcomes might be revolved around two issues:
the wish that Okinawa be returned to Japanese sovereignty (this
eventually happened on May 15, 1972), and the issue of Japan's self-
defence forces (JSDF, *Jieitai*). Many supporters of the government
wanted some kind of rearmament and an external defence role for
the SDF. By the 1960s, American policy accorded with this aim as
well. Such a view, however, faced strong resistance from opposition
parties and among the Japanese public for whom memories of the
war remained strong. Postwar Japanese society had elided a critique

---

[2] For the complete text of the Ampo Treaty in English, see (Packard 1966: 364).

of militarism into an uncritical, yet stubbornly pacifist stance. In this context, Prime Minister Kishi Nobusuke attempted to have the new security treaty ratified by parliament. Opposition members blocked the parliamentary speaker's entrance to the chamber: without the speaker of the house being present, Kishi's security bill could not to be passed. On May 19, 1960, Kishi ordered 200 police to forcibly remove the opposition and the security bills were passed in their absence. Kishi's forceful, anti-democratic tactics shocked the public. For many observers, the subsequent political showdown was construed as a re-awakening of authoritarianism and reminiscent of the wartime parliament of which Kishi himself was a member. As Igarashi Yoshikuni notes: "Kishi represented in an easy-to-recognize form the dark forces in Japanese politics that challenged the postwar democratic order." An ex-war criminal, he was sometimes called "*yōkai*," a term meaning a monstrous creature from Japan's premodern imagination (Igarashi 2000: 136). This reference to the premodern is interesting in the light of discussion soon to follow about the premodern in *angura*.

Kishi's actions have been interpreted as making Ampo into a struggle of absolute terms, between democracy and a return to prewar totalitarianism (Igarashi 2000: 137). Although the 1960 renegotiation of the treaty might sympathetically be read as an attempt to gain equality for Japan in its relationship with the US, it also drew Japan into a deeper entanglement in US military campaigns. While the concept of a mutually acceptable defence policy was stated, Igarashi notes that this was undermined by the fact that Japan did not have an army. Moreover, the 1960 treaty restated the right of the US military to continue to occupy Japanese territory (Igarashi 2000: 134). The resigning of the treaty dismayed many Japanese people. Not only were the military ramifications of the treaty unacceptable, but the roughshod treatment of the political process was a sign of its failing.

Takahashi Yasunari (Takahashi 1992) has been concerned with debating the political culture of democracy and its problematic integration in Japanese society. Postwar Japan, Takahashi asserts, had been cast with an alien 'democratic' institution that is not clearly understood and sits uncomfortably with the history of Japan's political culture. He argues that the political ideals of democracy, as defined by the Japanese constitution, are not systematic; the drafting of the constitution was hurried and then imposed on a political culture that few of the constitutional authors understood. As a result, it has been easily manipulated by conservative groups in Japan and was therefore unable to give voice to oppositional views. For these reasons, Takahashi asserts that by the 1960s, the political and cultural effectiveness of parliamentary democracy was in decline. Changing notions of political order, from initial idealism to the gradual marginalisation of acts of broad participation, not to mention the unconscionable acts of Kishi's government in overriding parliamentary convention, together with perceptions of American political interference, eroded public support for the constitution and created a sense of anxiety and disquiet about the status of democracy. Notions of democracy were supposed to be shaping the reformation of culture in 'new' Japan. However, in inverse proportions to postwar economic growth, the decline of political freedoms culminating in the 1960 Ampo struggle symbolized the decline of democracy in Japan.

This observation gives rise to another factor helping to delineate the 1960s space; the irony that mass opposition to the treaty and to conservative politics was unfolding in a context of rising wealth and prosperity. It is often stated that the double income promises realized by Ikeda Hayato's administration (Ikeda replaced Kishi in an attempt to smooth over the latter's tainted legacy) ushered in an "age of light . . . of peace, prosperity and modern living" (Igarashi 2000: 131–2). Scholars note how the 1960s space was transforming from an ideological one to that defined by economy and materialism. It is not surprising then, that radical politics in the time of rising standards of living were set to produce some peculiar mixes; the hybrid politics of popular cultures and of youth movements were rising to contest with the older forms of ideological firmness. This produced a kind of critical breakdown, a fragmentation of the political and cultural landscape; not in the sense that the city or state was crumbling, but from the perspective that people were unable to understand the meaning of the changes and were not sure what it meant for Japan. Takahashi, for example, writes that: "while people were just beginning to enjoy new affluence, they were at the same time searching the national conscience, ardently discussing what lay behind the material prosperity" (Takahashi 1992: 3). This was not simply a crisis brought on by material wealth then, but one that was taken to have both personal and national perspectives.

It is interesting to consider playwright-director Kawamura Takeshi's thinking about the 1960s national space in the 2000 version[3] of his play *Hamletclone* (*Hamuretto Kurōn*, 2000), a scathing critique of post-war Japan:

> Responsibility? What is this responsibility?
> Writing a new constitution.
> Rebuilding the city.
> Hosting the Olympics.
> A world fair, an Expo.
> Happiness for the people!
> Is this responsibility? (Kawamura 2000a)

Kawamura's play references symbolic events marking 1960s prosperity and Japan's re-entry into world affairs. The 1964 Tokyo Olympic Games was preceded by massive transformations in the urban spaces of Tokyo spreading across the nation. Modern, notably avant-garde public buildings were constructed; visible memories of wartime ruin were finally erased from the city landscape. The first bullet trains and expressways were built. Traditional cultural activities on prominent display during the Olympics were successfully decoupled from wartime associations with imperial propaganda. Instead, they might be read as hoping to stand for the birthright of a successfully modern nation with a timeless, enduring history. Meanwhile, the search for a "happy life" (*ureshii seikatsu*) prompted further integration of the *shutaisei* effect, as happiness itself became more individual and was linked to material prosperity. The games were widely seen as a great success. Meanwhile, closing the decade, the Osaka World Expo was once again a site for remaking Japan's image as futuristic, productive and global; a cumulative representation of "the bright sanitised space" of the 1960s (Igarashi 2000: 164). Alongside these remarkable successes, however, we should also think about the nature of change and its impact beyond the material level. Kawamura's play looks below the surface of prosperity and asks questions about what was lost or elided in the shift from the apparent

---

[3] My translation of the 2002 version of *Hamletclone* is featured in the final section of this book. In revising the play, Kawamura removed this scene. The above citation is from the Japanese text of 2000. It remains relevant here for its clever synthesis of key moments in the 1960s.

authoritarian over-coding of the Kishi era and moving towards the
safe and regulated sanitized comfort of the everyday in Ikeda's prosperity drive. In fact, Kawamura's play is a commentary on the social
unease found in the apparently comfortable and peaceful domain of
contemporary Japanese society (Moriyama 2004); his method references historical events and makes connections between themes and
cultural practices from the past as a way of prefiguring the present.
In this sense, his play can be understood to be concerned with historicizing euphoric tendencies that underlie the construction of modern day social reality and paste over contemporary dystopia. Perhaps
Kawamura is wondering if all this euphoria is a responsible path
given subsequent events.

   While we will return to a more detailed discussion of Kawamura
Takeshi's work in later chapters, what is interesting here is the fact
that his play aims at wider concerns about the direction of society.
Such issues were already fermenting around the treaty and voicing
a darker apocalyptic tone. Political groups emanating from both the
left and right of the political spectrum articulated warnings of the
social consequences of rapid economic development and its associated materialist culture. The condemnation of the continued US military presence in Japan was coupled with broader concerns about
the decline of Japanese cultural values and the Americanization of
Japanese identity. Questions about ideology, cultural production,
authority and identity, already deeply ingrained in Japanese intellectual traditions since the Meiji era, were given renewed presence.

Performativity and action

Maruyama Masao's philosophical writing on postwar democracy in
Japan underscores the fact that when it came to debates about *shutaisei*, action was everything. Thus, he writes: "Freedom is not something that is like an object, but rather something that can only be
protected by action in the present; in other words, something is free
for the first time through trying day by day to become free" (Kersten
1996: 104). As Rikki Kersten's study of Maruyama and the postwar
democracy movement shows, individuals developed the capacity to
act and participate in political processes. The individual came to
"formulate values which would propel him [*sic*] to act, as a subjective, motivated entity, to realise and legitimise reform" (Kersten 1996:

104). This emphasis on the momentum of participation in political action is helpful to understanding the experience of 1960s protest as a performed experience of the *shutaisei* effect. Demonstrations and related activities such as occupations and political meetings were spaces where *shutaisei* sensibilities were formed and resistance to the old order enacted. Beyond ideological forums of debate, what is important in *shutaisei* politics is the recourse to action. In other words, the intensities of the body moving in and through the social space determined the radical sensibility.

Anti-security treaty protests culminated when, on June 15–16, 1960, an estimated three hundred thousand people surrounded the parliament and attempted to overrun the legislature. Although the treaty was already sanctioned by the state, the protestors loudly voiced their opposition. They were given succour when later, in July, they successfully halted the planned state visit by President Eisenhower to celebrate the treaty's resigning. Despite occasional violence, the protests were described as festive and theatrical:

> The more radical mainstream Zengakuren favoured the 'snake dance' (*Jigu-Jagu*) . . . ranks of six abreast locked arms and careered from side to side down the street in long columns; the flanks brushing aside all obstacles, causing skirmishes with the police . . . other demos were more relaxed, with long columns of workers or students simply walking or jogging shouting slogans. (Packard 1966: 262–3)[4]

The enactment of dissent described bears comparison with the style of *angura*; both were chaotic, dynamic events. The description of the protest expresses an atmosphere of vitality, fluidity and spontaneity; the demonstrators formed seemingly abstract patterns pushing through the city. Similarities to village *matsuri* (festivals), where a *mikoshi* or portable shrine is marched through the town carried by a phalanx of jostling bodies chanting in unison, means that the protests super-imposed the imagery of notionally traditional culture onto the indus-trial, corporate and political landscape of modern Tokyo. In this

---

[4] Further documentation of "*demo*" (demonstrations) can be gained from docu-mentary records including important cinema works from the era. One such source is the emergent youth cinema movement or 'Sun Tribe' genre. Oshima Nagisa's 1960 film *Cruel Story of Youth* (*Seishun zankoku monogatari*), for example, features some striking footage of *demo* and, in general, is an important document of social atti-tudes inherent in the new youth culture.

sense, the protests shared with *angura* an interest in making use of images drawn from village culture and folklore. As will be noted, *angura* was steeped in nostalgia for premodern Japanese aesthetic symbols (Goodman 1988). In this way, the demonstrations and the images developed in the theatre have a ritual significance as expressions of the problematic quest for nationhood and identity.

Moreover, symbolic gestures and rehearsed performative actions can be seen to be put to good effect on the protest marches. Close formation groups, unison chants, signs painted with calligraphic slogans, arm bands and head bands identifying collective membership or espousing a cause, and in many cases, handkerchiefs covering the mouth and nose (a feeble protection against tear gas, but also to preserve anonymity) also mark the participants as opponents to state policy. These symbols of opposition—a carefully prepared semiotics of resistance—are signs of defiance that have historical precedence and signify a long history of marginalized protest in Japan, records of which go back at least until the early Tokugawa era where peasant uprisings utilized similar symbolic gestures (headbands, slogans, painted signs) in their protest. This, and the emphasis on group participation, points to the fact that in opposing the state, the participants do so in defence of the state, at least as the state is conceived of in terms of radical ideas of nationhood. Gestures that symbolize Japan and Japanese identity were therefore used to assert the idea that Japan was compromized and had somehow lost its way. Recourse to symbols associated with the premodern recall a less problematic construction of Japanese identity. In this way, the demonstrations were not simply oppositional performances to one or two government policies, but were narratives outlining a deep prevailing confusion about, and opposition to, the mainstream constructions of postwar nationhood and identity.

Ideological rendering of space and a subsequent dramatic reordering of the political geography is evident in Ampo. In considering a famous photograph of demonstrators massed in front of the *Diet* Stephen Barber writes:

> (T)he mass of converging bodies forms an immense and distinctive 'X' shape, with its centre located precisely at the gates of the parliament building, as though in the act of inflicting its own mark of summary negation upon the political power of the country. (Barber 2002: 171)

Especially in 1968 and 1969, when the protest movement reached a peak, the physical incursions into city spaces by the *Zengakuren* mass became a kind of spectacle. Stuart Dowsey, for example, describes how people gathered on the pedestrian walkways to watch skirmishes with riot police:

> The time is April 28, 1969, and in Japan, it is Okinawa Day. Tokyo is an armed camp; police are guarding all the government buildings . . . Unable to get near the Diet House . . . the revolutionary students of Zengakuren have turned on the Ginza to vent their spleen. . . . On the elevated expressways above us (is) the audience, thousands of bystanders craning to get a better view. (Dowsey 1970: 1)

Student tactics included blocking city streets, storming railway stations, and forcing the suspension of railway services. Well-known in 1968, too, was the occupation of the universities, most notoriously Waseda University and the University of Tokyo, both traditionally centres for educating the Japan's ruling elites. When Sawara Yukiko describes the battle for the occupation of Yasuda Hall at the Hongo campus of the University of Tokyo on the January 18–20, 1969 the tone of her description is performative and emphasis is placed on set pieces of sloganeering, ritualized gestures of protest, and wilful and excessive destruction. The students placed great emphasis on the collective experience of hardship; cold, hunger, fear and pain all figured prominently as modes of experience directly felt on the body. Eroticism was also deep in the *shutaisei* mix. Sawara notes, for example, that the poems and slogans painted on the walls of the Yasuda Hall were a mix of revolutionary, romantic, and sentimental sentiments. One protestor wrote poems to his girlfriend (Sawara 1970: 160).

The students stressed solidarity and the narrative of physical occupation by placing their collective bodies on the line of confrontation. The purpose of occupying Yasuda Hall was never quite clear, the fact of occupation seemed most important in the minds of the activists. According to Sawara, ideology was downplayed and more spontaneous, possibly unquestioned acts of protest celebrated. Moreover, the students became actors in a more literal sense when the occupation dramas were shown on television nationwide. On Sunday January 19, six of the seven television stations suspended normal programs and carried the occupations final battle with police live-to-air. Ironically, and coincidentally, the coverage unfolded as if

directed for television, at 5:45 p.m.—just before people might be
going to make dinner—the occupation was over (Sawara 1970:
155–59). When one considers the wanton destruction of research
materials such as books and notes (academic staff had their offices
raided and notes were strewn across the campus), the damage to
university buildings and the broken bodies of participants on both
sides of the action, given that there seemed so little change after the
occupation and so few reasons for it, one cannot help thinking that
this was a kind of star tantrum by unruly actors playing out their
imaginary version of Paris in 1968. This was a protest of raw energy,
the *shutaisei* effect unbounded and chaotically embodied.

The protests became media material in other ways as well.
Advertisements used images from demonstrations, student activists
were fictionalized in television dramas and comedy shows. Nakanishi
Masahiro notes how one comic magazine coined the phrase "*Zenpa-
karen*" to mean the National Federation of Fools as a way of sati-
rizing the protest movement (Nakanishi 1970: 215). Also widely noted
is the fact that until around the time of the 1968 university campaign, financial and trading companies working in an aggressively
competitive environment, sought to recruit *Zengakuren* activists. Chants
against capitalism clearly did not shake the foundations of these cor-
nerstone institutions of the capitalist state; rather, the students' actions
and their commitment to causes were celebrated. Such willingness
to act was deemed a measure of one's guts and fighting spirit![5]

How radical sects organized themselves gives further insight into
the performative and embodied experience of 1960s political life. As
the following richly detailed description of a meeting by the ultra-
radical sect *Kakumaru* shows, various ritualized practices of the meeting help to ensure an overall sense of embodied collective solidarity.

> A typical Kakumaru meeting for the public is arranged as follows. The
> hall is divided into four sections; for students, workers, high school stu-

---

[5] As Kan Takayuki notes, this practice ceased around 1968, a time of rising
ultra-radical sects. Major companies who generally recruit from the graduates of
leading universities announced that they would no longer employ former student
radicals (Kan 1982). It is suggested that the changes in recruitment policy led to a
polarization within the protest movement. Many students left the movement, likely
unwilling to risk their future career prospects. On the other hand, the magnanim-
ity of the decision to participate likely hardened the resolve of radical activists who
stayed and pushed them further from mainstream society.

dents and citizens. The active members come in proudly wearing their helmets and sit in the front rows, or if it gets too crowded, they will sit on the stage at the feet of the speakers. Flags from each university and local chapter are unhooked from their poles and are pinned to the walls, deep ruby red rectangles of cloth emblazoned with the Kakumaru 'Z' across the middle. The name of the meeting and the slogans chosen have been painted onto long paper or cloth banners which stretch across the top of the stage and down the sides. When everyone is seated, having paid a contribution in the form of an entrance fee, the proceedings can begin. A spokesperson gets up to start the meeting with the calling of slogans. The audience stands and shouts the phrases in unison, and with the last two syllables of each slogan, everyone punches the air in the clenched fist salute. The styles of the speakers vary somewhat, with the younger speakers shouting harshly and the older speakers using a quieter style with more humour and balance. The meeting ends with a second round of slogans and the singing of the 'Internationale' as the whole mass of people link arms and sway rhythmically to and fro. (Nakanishi 1970: 197)

The performative dynamics of the space and the dramaturgy of the meeting are striking for their ritualized forceful sense of embodiment and of collective, subtly coercive identity formation. Various signs mark the participants as actors for their cause; their roles and their histories as members of the cause are further defined in the spatial dynamics of the meeting. A hierarchy of performative practices is therefore established in the coding of space. The political substance of the meeting is then inscribed on the space through the chanting of slogans and use of banners. This kind of ritualized protest can be now seen at any demonstration around the world, as a kind of formula for performing the *shutaisei* effect.

Indeed, Nakanishi's eyewitness account helps us to conclude that an important aspect of the protest movement was its performance of the *shutaisei* effect. He notes that: "It is the trappings of the student activist that have captured the imagination. The life-style of the students has become a sub-culture within postwar Japanese society" (Nakanishi 1970: 212). The subculture of action underscored a pursuit of *shutaisei*. As the decade progressed this search for selfhood became more ritualized in such symbols of rebellion. Thus, as one student remarked: "When you face the struggle unarmed, you feel weak, but with a *gebabo* (fighting stick) in your hands, you become strong" (Nakanishi 1970: 214).

Conclusion

In closing, we note how the sensibility of performing politics in the 1960s space evolved. By 1968 the creative chaotic atmosphere present in some of the earlier demonstrations had evolved into one characterized by planned confrontation, anger and hardened resolve. Lines of stick wielding protestors faced lines of police. The public face of *Zengakuren* was taken over by the confrontationist *Sanpa Rengō* (Three Faction Alliance). Gathered around the *Sanpa Rengō* alliance were ultra radical students who favoured violent tactics. Their bloody battles with riot police, and attempts to cede control of the activist agenda were their witness to a performance of the radical. Thus, *Sanpa Rengō* exhibited a more violent counter-culture sensibility and expression of the activist identity.[6] They played out roles as radical warriors; demonstrations were organized as dramatic performances staged for an avid, if somewhat anxious audience of press and onlookers. As Richard Schechner notes in respect of American counter-culture protest: "By the 1960s, these actions constituted a distinct liminoid-celebratory-political-theatrical ritual genre" (Schechner 1993: 50). In other words, a theatre of collective disorder symbolically designed to combat the hegemony of the Japanese state comes into play. Participation was also an act of self-discovery as one sought to overcome fear and discover one's own selfhood nature, by now necessarily extremist. It is therefore not surprising that student activists spoke of the struggle to conquer their fear, and overcome their social conditioning in terms akin to actors displaying commitment to their role as they engaged the State in a series of violent battles (Nakazawa 1984).

Tactical aggression of *Sanpa Rengō* laid the groundwork for the rise of ultra radical groups such as *Sekigun* (the Red Army Faction) whose objective was to undermine and eventually destroy the 'capitalist-militarist State' using campaigns of assassination, community violence

---

[6] The alliance was large and well-organized. In March 1968, for example, *Sanpa Rengō* were instrumental in organizing major campaigns opposing the planned Narita airport, large protests at the opening of a US military hospital in Oji, Tokyo, and 'solidarity' involvement in the student strike and developing siege undertaken by medical students at The University of Tokyo. For each campaign, Three Faction participation numbered from anywhere between fifty or so students up to several thousand (these figures are taken from *Asahi Shinbun* reporting of the protests).

and terror. Latter forms of protest rejected the plural notion of the counter-culture and substituted an ethics of selfhood for ideological rigidity. More like sects than political groups, they became more intolerant of dissent than the mainstream that they sought to attack. Red Army members turned on their own membership executing 'dissenting' cadres in a 1972 siege (Farrell 1990).

We have seen how the *shutaisei* effect as an embodied search for political answers to Japan's evolving capitalist modernity is a key ingredient of the 1960s space. *Gebabo* and crash helmets were the symbols of a pure spirit that stood against tear gas and water cannons and the aesthetics of violence and chaos permeated the movement.

While critics have sometimes dismissed 1960s radical protest precisely as a kind of performance or playful mood enjoyed principally among Japan's young elite[7] this overlooks the degree to which the project as a whole was an avant-garde act. Acts of interruption and chaos were strategic interventions applied against the State. While this was by no means a cohesive or well-formed theorization of political alternatives, such protest actions display a sympathy for a new political mode of expression: one that is fluid, counter-hegemonic, nihilist and revolutionary in its speed and intensity. Nineteen sixties protest had no respect for the city that was evolving in the clean seamless invention of peace and prosperity in postwar Japan.

Setting the scene for the following chapter is a well-known photograph of Hijikata Tatsumi, co-creator of the transgressive dance-performance genre *butō*, taken by Fukase Masahisa (Fukase 1969). With the 1969 demonstrations as a backdrop, Hijikata walks across the frame dressed in a torn red kimono and knee-high white stockings, with wild hair, and carrying a watermelon in a string bag. He is a singular, defiant and unruly figure passing a phalanx of youthful, anxious looking riot police who are walking the other way. In the moment of passing, a critical space between two experiences of humanity is opened and two versions of history become visible and intersect. It is the inherent complexity, social tension and sense of possibility of this moment that invites our acknowledgment. Sitting between these worlds, the image is hybrid and contested; an overwhelming moment of performance is born.

---

[7] See for example, (Havens 1987).

CHAPTER THREE

ANGURA AND PROTEST

> Throw Away Your Books: Let's Go into the Streets
> Terayama Shūji

Having discussed 1960s politics and the experiences of protest as an embodied expression of *shutaisei*, we can now look at avant-garde theatre more closely. In this chapter, I will outline some of the most distinctive characteristics of *angura* and discuss particular themes and issues that have been identified with *angura* by other scholars. I will begin to consider how the experience of 1960s politics was first explored in *angura* in an analysis of two key works, one from 1960 and contemporaneous to the Ampo *demo*, and another arising amidst the turbulence of 1968. Finally, as a way of leading into further discussion in the next chapter, I will begin to explain how *angura* not only reflected politics, but came to directly embody experiences of radical subjectivity.

Characteristics of *angura* will be identified and discussed in terms that show how the avant-garde in Japan came to be redefined and localized through the making of what has been termed the *angura* paradigm. This frame of analysis rests on a methodology that explores an awareness of Japanese history in relation to the present day world and assumes a capacity for dramatic intervention. Accordingly, in a quickly shifting cultural scene described by the *angura* critic and intellectual figure Tsuno Kaitarō as "the immediate rupture of that continuity which damns us" (Tsuno 1970: 143), *angura* seemingly broke from *shingeki* and became a paradigmatic site for the avant-garde transformation of culture.

To briefly explain this point further we need to remember that political ideologies and groundbreaking events of the 1960s have often been related to aesthetic and formalistic innovations in theatre. Studies focusing on theatre and culture often more broadly comment on the appearance of new social flows just as dichotomous relations of power were increasingly and successfully contested. Thomas Crow calls the emergent relationship between the arts and the counter-culture an "energising congruence", wherein dissenting experiments

of artists coupled with the most exciting and successful forms of dissenting politics (Crow 1996: 11). In the case of the Japanese, this
coupling of the often indeterminate, anti-narrative concerns of *angura*
with the *shutaisei* effect opens interpretive possibilities for theatre to
function as a site of cultural subversion and social change. In fact,
a circularity of cultural flows will become evident; relating to the
avant-garde formation of *angura* was the fact that it arose as an
important site of cultural displacement and political activism. And
as I have already shown in the previous chapter in relation to the
politics of selfhood, the 1960s space was performative.

Terayama Shūji (1939–83), Kara Jūrō (1940–), Satoh Makoto
(1943–), Suzuki Tadashi (1939–) and the *butō* performers Hijikata
Tatsumi (1928–86) and Ōno Kazuo (1906–)[1] are names most often
associated with 1960s *angura*. While many artists participated in the
development of *angura*, those mentioned above were of overriding
importance to the movement as whole. Their works and the theatre
groups they established and led, mark the origins of the movement
and its development. Satoh, Kara and Suzuki continue to have prolific
careers in the theatre. Meanwhile, Terayama and Hijikata died in
the midst of reaching fame as artists of extraordinary invention. All
have been discussed in scholarly texts and have written commentaries about their own work. But while scholarship has often concentrated on the work of these artists and their philosophical outlooks,
my aim is to further develop our understanding of the movement
as a whole through a consideration of the politics evident in contrasting examples of performances by these radical theatre makers.
Before discussing these connections, it is necessary to outline a theory of *angura* as a theatrical form and to identify its most distinctive
dramaturgical elements.

---

[1] Discussion of the contemporary dance/performance art genre *butō* lies outside
the specific concerns of this study although many aspects of the art developed in
sympathy with, if not out of the same cultural concerns, as *angura*. It is certain that
butō is an interrelated phenomenon, part of the emergent radical performance culture in 1960s Japan. For the purpose of this discussion, however, I will focus on
avant-garde theatre, a form that in the 1960s grappled with text and physicality.

The angura *paradigm*

Angura artists rebelled against the ideological and artistic shackles of the conservative *shingeki* theatre and their work was a decisive unravelling of Japanese modernity. The foundations of this schism lay in an aesthetic and dramaturgical rebellion that saw many of the artistic practices of *shingeki* turned on their head. If *shingeki* was concerned with faithfully interpreting the play on the stage, *angura* took the stage up to the play and transformed it. As noted in the introduction, *angura* connected with forms and practices from traditional Japanese theatre worlds alongside influences carried over from contemporary transnational avant-garde movements. Vigorous exploration of historical theatre forms including *kabuki* and *nō*, but also vaudeville, folk plays, and lowbrow culture sat easily with an interest in Antonin Artaud, Samuel Beckett (whose works likewise display an interest in comic and folk arts) and the chaotic, anti-conformist spirit and inventiveness of the dada movement. This combination of premodern and avant-garde dramaturgy in dramatic contrast to the ordered aesthetic mechanisms of *shingeki* production is one aspect of what Nishidō Kōjin calls the *angura* paradigm (Nishidō 1996).

As will be shown, other common principles of the new drama included the fact that to a significant degree, *angura* was a university-based movement. Companies often began as student theatre groups who later moved off campus and into small alternative spaces. *Angura* groups not only recruited members from universities, but attracted younger student audiences who were upwardly mobile, educated and had free time; they wanted new experiences that the theatre offered. Some people became enthusiasts for particular groups and followed their work over years of productions. A number of *angura* critics' circles developed in this way and the wider support network for companies (sometimes extending to financial patronage) was important for their long-term survival.

The repudiation of psychological realism and the consequent de-privileging of text in relation to form and theatricality is another significant characteristic of *angura* dramaturgy. *Angura* artists criticized the formal sequential construction of conventional drama. Their works moved away from neat logocentric developments of plot, narrative and character and sought something more fluid. In this way, *angura* rejected the sacred heart of *shingeki*. The overriding success of *angura*, however, lay also in the artists' capacities to rethink the play form.

Angura artists were distinguished, pioneering dramatists as well as theatre makers. What is perhaps distinctive is the emphasis they placed
on creating an idiosyncratic theatrical environment connected to, but
not dictated by, the representation of their dramatic writing. In other
words, *angura* evidences a growing recognition of performance dramaturgy over and above the textual dramaturgical models favoured
in the *shingeki* world.

The inventive uses of space in *angura* helped to consolidate this
trend. Techniques of deconstruction, alienation and interrogation of
conventional creative spaces and their normal uses were commonplace. For one, this gave rise to the term *shōgekijō* in reference to the
small theatres that were set-up in coffee houses and basements. Tent
theatres, outdoor performance events and experimental performance
'happenings' that disoriented audiences in a philosophical and political critique of theatrical space, are further examples of how *angura*
developed avant-garde spatial dynamics.

These dynamic qualities of space were extended and enhanced
through a particular emphasis on actor physicality and the exploration of bodies in relation to theatrical space. *Angura* sought ways
to develop the capacities of the body as an expressive instrument.
As a result, spontaneous and sometimes chaotic sensibilities that
embody the dynamic characteristics of the *shutaisei* effect can be
observed. Later, artists began to train the body more systematically
and developed distinct and unique corporeal aesthetics.

As *angura* grew, it became an event in some ways comparable to
the ways that rock bands in the 1960s promised a kind of underground spectacle. At the same time, *angura's* complex sensibilities and
abstraction perhaps lend more of a comparison to subcultures associated with contemporary art of the period. Everything was mixed
though and the arts mingled and influenced each other. As a result,
we see that *angura* crossed between the traditional borders of discreet
art forms, and at one time or another encompassed music, dance,
visual arts, cinema, contemporary writing, and so on.

Audiences were also part of the *angura* paradigm. Theatre began
to question and transform stage-audience relations and explore new
notions of communication and theatrical experience. Paradoxically,
in some respects, this saw a move away from politics in the sense
that *angura* artists rejected what they saw as the didactic strictness of
shingeki. *Angura* held no such lofty ideals for art and was more often

than not unwilling to explain its role in logically consistent terms. It was suspicious of trends in theatrical realism to 'preach to its audience.' For the *angura* generation, *shingeki* staging made audiences passive receptors of information. This was code for 'dead theatre,' a kind of preaching theatre that was devoid of any sense of life and empty of any true meaning. But *angura* was not apolitical and formations of artistic practice often aimed to develop human and or cultural sensibilities and speak to everyday experience. *Angura* spoke to confrontation, communication and experiential approaches, thereby, drawing audiences into a greater sense of participation.

Alongside the critique of didactic forms of political expression, *angura* also tried to transform *shingeki* style organizational structures. Certainly, this was a complex process: a balance of democratizing trends on the one hand, and reinscribing notionally traditional power relations on the other. Some *angura* groups maintain open door policies and recruit people from all walks of life. Such groups signal their ideological preference for enthusiasm and commitment to the group ethos over and above the professional actor training that one might bring to the company's work. On the other hand, as previously noted, some of the conventions of the *angura* system recast older mechanisms of power. *Angura* is also both emboldened and problematized by its semi-professional status. Few people are paid for their work in *angura* and working conditions are poor and often unsafe compared to other types of theatre. Here we see a connection to the ethos of the radical protest movement; commitment and solidarity are stressed over and above organized structural processes, the amateur status of *angura* artists—as with the bold commitment of student protestors—was a sign of their purity. Such rhetoric can become one dimensional, however, and has probably been over fetishized and romanticized. As will be noted, a "cult" of *angura* sometimes falls into the trap of essentializing cultural relations at the theatre company level as well as within the national cultural space.

Finally, the *angura* paradigm has all of these elements working in tandem, to radically disarticulate standard conventional theatrical forms and their accepted or established relationships to cultural totality. The *angura* paradigm is a complex fluid formation and by no means consistent. It is also one that responds to changes around it. As an avant-garde practice, *angura* only finds its complete shape in relation to wider cultural space. It is this capacity—to interweave

levels of social and cultural interaction and critique into *angura* performance—that defines its reputation as an important site of radical
avant-garde performance.

I will return to the discussion of the *angura* paradigm in the next
chapter where performances will be analysed in relation to political
dimensions of *shutaisei*. For now, it is important to have a sense of
angura's dramaturgical features. We also need to consider how scholars have interpreted *angura* and what aspects of the form have been
regarded as most important.

Discussing angura

Senda Akihiko's historical perspective on *angura* notes that in comparison to traditional Japanese theatre and *shingeki*, contemporary
performance featured a different schema of motifs and images. Senda
observes that *angura* playwrights were concerned with "new worlds."
Consequently, Senda argues that the motif of departure was a constant theme in their work (Senda 1988: 49–51).

Senda also argues that the history of *angura* exhibits two culturally distinctive eras. The first dates from the early 1960s, covering
the beginning of the rebellion in theatre, ends with the death of
Terayama in 1983. This phase was characterized by a rapid expansion of new theatre culture and many diverse experiments in form.
During this era, the theatre seemed to be perpetually questioning
and discovering new ways to approach performance. Debates about
style and content were evident in the innovative rediscovery of corporeal modes of acting and an expanded *mise-en-scène*. Senda notes
that the spirit of innovation was also popular with audiences who
developed strong opinions about the structure and culture of theatre
and were generally motivated to investigate new ways to make theatre address social issues. As we shall see, audiences were sometimes
keen to debate these issues alongside theatre artists and could be
critical of theatre productions on political grounds. Thus, while new
theatre was enjoyed for its spirit of experimentation and adventure,
it was also widely viewed as a form of political expression and debate.

The number of people who participated as artists and theatre-
goers remained a small minority of the Japanese population. Even
so, *angura's* reach extended into influential political and cultural fields
such as fine art, popular art, television, popular music, publishing,

and the like. Also noteworthy is the fact that small theatre arose on University campuses and were influential to a generation of Japanese intellectuals. Stylistically, however, the first generation of *angura* remained a genre cast in the mould of "poor theatre" (Grotowski 1968) emphasizing space and body; it lacked the sophisticated technologies and marketing strategies of the second phase. This era, from around 1983 until the end of the century, is characterized by a shift to less emphasis on avant-garde debates about textuality and towards a more visual and playful *mise-en-scène*. Senda notes how the movement become more dispersed and popular. According to some, the new generation rejected the term avant-garde as heavy and too intellectual. They were more concerned with creating increasingly sophisticated and technologically complex works of spectacle that were often comic and stressed entertainment value over and above sociocultural and political debate.

A trend that continued from the 1960s was theatre as an outgrowth of student theatre. This was the case with Noda Hideki, for example, who founded his theatre group at The University of Tokyo, and later made the shift to the public stage. Likewise, the performance art company dumb type emerged from the Kyoto Art College and Kawamura Takeshi's Daisan Erotica began its life at Meiji University. Indeed, it remains a common ambition of many young artists who begin working in theatre at university to take their companies into the wider theatre scene. This also means that *angura* artist were generally not trained in drama schools of which there are few in Japan and, until recently, none offered the kind of intensive training to be found in arts training schools elsewhere. Meanwhile, separating the generations were contrasting attitudes regarding the social role of theatre. In the university drama societies of the 1960s, theatre was discussed as a problem of culture. Students of the 1980s, with some notable exceptions, generally expressed far less political thinking and were more sympathetic to material culture than student theatre artists of the former era. For 1980s students, theatre was a form of play. Compounding this was the fact that by this time remnants of the radical student protest movement were small, and even ostracized by the main student body.

The new generation's subsequent rejection of the term 'avant-garde' is an important marker of the second phase of *angura*. This rejection is not due to the fact that avant-garde art has been undermined by contemporary cultural and political developments (as discussed in chapter 5, the postmodern avant-garde was a prominent and successful form of theatre in the 1980s). Rather, the rejection seems to have resulted from the fact that 1980s artists perceived the work of the former generation to be excessively intellectual, even boring. This points to a political backlash against the radicalism of the 1960s generation; even attempts to disparage and trivialize their work are evident in the work of 1980s artists. Many of the eighties generation of theatre makers did not seek to position themselves in opposition to the status quo. Rather, the sense of playfulness evident in their work, together with an abiding interest in the nostalgia of childhood, suggests they were seeking a more broadly popular theatre culture, and were especially attuned to mainstream media and new technologies. Debates concerning the progress of second-generation *angura* will be addressed later. I draw attention to them here, however, to indicate the degrees of revisionism that is evident in Japanese theatre culture with regard to the sixties. The way that this decade has come to be read, in conservative circles at least, has tended to down play or otherwise dismiss its importance.

Senda's categorization of *angura* into two eras is, perhaps, too tightly drawn. Although this is an influential and helpful proposition that furthers our understanding of *angura* history, many factors come into play in his attempt to historicize the genre. As will be argued in later chapters, *angura* has been swallowed by a postmodern capitalist matrix of the kind loosely identified by Senda, but there are also persuasive examples of groups that seek to resist this cultural-ideological event. Accordingly, the linear, historical, and cultural division of *angura* that Senda's work proposes requires further nuancing to the considerable overlap between the first and second phases. As Japanese culture has changed, the sites and possibilities for radical cultural intervention and avant-garde expression have also changed; a multi-dimensional site of interaction/intervention must be theorized instead.

Senda's thinking about *angura* is encapsulated by the way that he uses the image of a journey and the theme of departure to describe the movement in overall terms. This captures well the sense that artists were seeking new directions and were broadly inquisitive. Yet, although he has written extensively on the movement as a whole, Senda generally addresses such overarching questions only in the broadest sense. Writing as a newspaper critic, Senda is mainly concerned with the record of performance. While his detailed accounts of performances are insightful, he avoids detailed discussion of the surrounding culture of radicalism.

In contrast to Senda, David Goodman's work on *angura* is philosophical in outlook and scholarly. While Senda captures a sense of the everyday vitality of *angura*, Goodman's work is important for understanding the critical spaces that the movement uncovered and explored. Goodman's involvement in *angura* includes artistic affiliation with Theatre 68/79–Black Tent (BT). With the help of his BT colleagues, he published the extraordinary theatre journal *Concerned Theatre Japan* (CTJ), an English language companion journal to *Dōjidai Engeki*. CTJ featured up to the minute commentaries on plays, *angura* politics, and also explored the wider developments in the 1960s space. A unique historical resource, the essays and plays in CTJ, complimented by documentation and original artwork convey a powerful sense of the era and it concerns (Goodman 2001).

Goodman's *angura* scholarship remains almost singularly influential. He argues for an "eschatological" presence in 1960s drama and points to the reappearance of premodern phantasmic images in *angura*. This finds its clearest expression in the poetic notion of the "return of the gods" a thematic that is exemplified in the title of his major work on the era (Goodman 1988). Accordingly, *angura* saw the awakening of a collective unconscious in Japan and had the possibility to heal a rift in Japanese theatre and culture wrought by *shingeki* and the history of Japanese modernity. As Goodman argues, ghosts and shamans once more inhabited the stage. His thesis is that *angura* texts feature premodern, taboo and shamanic elements in their conceptualizations of characterization and narrative form. Concomitant with a crisis in modernity, he argues that the premodern fixation of *angura* was, in part, a response to the failure of the protest movement. This in turn, relates to a postwar identity crisis, where the past has been massively interrupted; its sense of darkness and turmoil, but also its sense of vitality has been elided by postwar prosperity. *Angura* is also in part a response to the terrifying images and memory of nuclear-fuelled annihilation that inhabit the postwar Japanese psyche. For Goodman, such memories of death cannot be washed away by material prosperity; they remain ghostly presences in the Japanese landscape. Goodman's work shows that the premodern imagination of *angura* displaces the assumption of continual progress and social improvement that underlies more positive postwar assessments of Japanese cultural history.

Like Goodman, Nishidō's approach to *angura* is characterized by a comprehensive critique of the new wave in terms of its rejection of the modern. For Nishidō, the privileging and display of the raw, expressive premodern body in the theatrical space signify this (Nishidō 1987: 25). This action also exemplifies the distrust and repudiation of modernist intellectual and dialectical approaches to performance making in general. Interestingly, in Japanese Zen philosophy the intellect has traditionally been located physically in the stomach region (*hara*). In this regard, the constant presence of a "centre" in much of the physical work in *angura* (clearly articulated in Suzuki Tadashi's performance method, for example, also often explored in *butō*) can be seen as a contrasting philosophical centre, a physical intellect that arguably brings to light alternative forms of knowledge in performance. This perspective lies in marked contrast to the preceptively intellectual mode of *shingeki*, where an action is though about, rationalized and meticulously planned. Brechtian theories of acting that gave expression to *shingeki's* Marxist dialectical side are similarly intellectually based. The physical repositioning and fundamental reappraisal of what constitutes the intellect can therefore be read as a counter strategy of *angura* to remake knowledge and experience in theatre. The reorientation of the actor's body had the effect of revitalizing theatre; from this perspective, new and independent notions of subjectivity and identity can be theorized. Thus, some Japanese artists have maintained that the corporeal knowledge inherent in physical acting is expressive of deeper Japanese relationships to the physical elements. In the context of the 1960s, this might be considered a radical stance, an epistemological break from the overdetermined modern stage. We should also note that this influential reading of *angura* has been problematized. Instead of liberated bodies, some critics point to the performing body's re-essentialisation. The extension of this argument is that in tantalisingly abstract performance such as *butō,* Japanese identity has tended to become essentialized and tinged with possible neo-nationalist rendering (Eckersall 2004a; Marotti 1997; Uchino 1999).

Brian Powell calls *angura* a "radical anti-*shingeki* drama" that explores the "darker quarters of human experience" (Powell 2002: 177). He notes, for example, how Kara Jūrō wanted to make the audience experience "terrifying situations" and anti-reality. *Angura's* salient absurdism broke the logical sequence of modern dramaturgy, what Powell calls a "vertical axis of memory." This in turn, undermined a belief system structured by orderly and explainable progressions of history as the axis of understanding and orienting oneself in the contemporary world. In the context of a discussion of Terayama Shūji, Powell notes how *angura* questioned all conventional expectations and assumptions about theatre:

> The right of the audience to see a whole play after having bought a ticket, the right of the audience to watch a performance rather than being involved in it, even the expectation of an audience that drama would be brought to them rather than them having to go in search of it—over the course of the next decade all this and much more was challenged by Terayama and Tenjō Sajiki. (Powell 2002: 185)

Nishidō (2002) has also recently discussed *angura's* anti-*shingeki* stance suggesting that the split was a mix of generational and social issues alongside aesthetic rebellion. On the one hand, *shingeki* leaders like Senda Koreya rejected the chaos and lack of discipline in *angura*. On the other, Nishidō points to the fact that "it simply became impossible for *shingeki* to respond to changes in contemporary society" (Nishidō 2002: 17). Whatever the truth of the matter, the principle that the older generation was dead to the realities of the 1960s space became an influential discourse among 1960s theatre makers in Japan.

Kan Takayuki (Kan 1991), whose prior scholarly work was on the *Zengakuren*, makes explicit connections between *angura* and the protest movement, suggesting that both were engaged in defining the symbolic cultural status of the term 'underground'. As Kan argues, membership of the protest groups appealed to many as a way of signalling their rejection of the expectations and morality cast on them by their parents and the state. Protestors' actions realized in a tangible and visceral sense the reality of another space, that of counter-culture. This, notionally "free space" was essential to the development of support networks and audience bases for *angura*, and to the dissemination and subsequent popularization of its anti-establishment ideas and values. Kan points to the powerful informal connections and networks that arose between theatre and politics during the 1960s and argues that the anti-establishment space of *angura* was an extension of the protest sensibility. *Angura's* rapport with the *shutai-sei* effect was ensured by its frequent common membership among new left groups and theatre companies, university drama societies and radical activist audiences. In response to contemporary cultural experience, a powerful angst that harboured feelings of alienation, anti-establishment rebelliousness, nihilism, and a search for identity further united theatrical and political groups and underlined the common call for change. *Angura* sought to awaken human imagination and reaffirm the theatre's former essential role in cultural experience.

Suga Hidemi also considers the question of how *angura* came to relate to the protest movement when he writes: "Underground theatre was the first cultural genre that the new left (*bund*) was able to come to terms with. (*Angura*) lacked the relatively extant method of belonging to a theatrical training system and company structure. They were independent from such things" (Suga 2003: 144). Independence and lack of precedence, notes Suga, gave *angura* the freedom to work outside Communist Party interference, something that was not the case in *shingeki*. As *angura* experienced gradual dispersion, it was able to move away from collective control mechanisms that were still common in left-wing theatre circles. This move from the organized left, in some ways, defines *angura*. As playwright Hirata Oriza suggests: "The history of Japanese modern theatre is a history of how one relates to and is released from the political aspect, including propaganda. . . . (In the 1960s) every playwright had to think about how to relate their work to communism and leftist orthodoxy" (Hirata 2003).

Angura *and protest*

Angura's split from *shingeki* and the beginnings of the new theatrical paradigm are first evident in the theatre's struggle to come to terms with wider events in the protest movement of the sixties. Among *shingeki* members, philosophical debates arose concerning the responsibility of the artist and the role of *shingeki* in the political crisis. Scholars note the rising tensions in *shingeki* circles as artists struggled to rationalize its success as a large-scale theatre industry, with calls for *shingeki* to respond to the rapidly shifting cultural space. *Shingeki* had become unwieldy and, according to some at least, had lost its *raison d'être*. Powell notes how the general picture of *shingeki* was one of a genre "increasingly concerned with stability" and frightened of change (Powell 2002: 168). In this environment of intransigence and confusion, mainly younger artists began to question how their political and artistic beliefs were compromized by the *shingeki* system. As a result, many artists left *shingeki* and formed new companies. Even more importantly in the long term was the fact that *shingeki* was no longer the first port of call for younger theatre makers, in fact they avoided *shingeki* circles for the next forty years.

Document Number One (*Kiroku Nambaa Ichi*, 1960) by Fukuda Yoshiyuki was the first performance directly inspired by the protest movement. A former member of Mingei and co-founder of Seinen Geijitsu Gekijō (Youth Arts Theatre or *Seiji*), Fukuda was one of the younger generation of theatre artists who came to reject the *shingeki* system. As the name suggests, *Document Number One* 'documented' a group of actors' involvement in, and reaction to, the protest events as they unfolded around them. The content of the play drew on the daily lived experience of the artists, a kind of *sprechtchör* theatre, where speaking about contemporary events was woven into the performance (Powell 2002: 171). Fukuda described the play as: "scenes for free discussion and for ensemble movement; the content of the play alternated between fantasy and documentary plays-within-the play" (Goodman 1988: 38). Put simply, *Document Number One* played as a parallel discourse to simultaneously occurring events of the protest struggle.

In contrast to conventional forms of dramaturgy this performance was directly shaped by personal experience, thus, representing a changed approach to the relationship contemporary theatre articulated between politics and cultural life. As discussed previously, politically inspired *shingeki* employed Marxist dialectical approaches to theatre that tended to highlight particular issues and themes in epic form. In *Document Number One*, this kind of ideological determinism begins to break down. Nor are the symbolic dimensions of psychological realism, *shingeki's* other familial relations, evident here. Instead, *Document Number One* explored spontaneous and intimate experiences of contemporary political and social life. In cultural terms, this process was both personal and political, representing in some ways a distillation of the two genres as well as the rejection of the pigeonholing that genre categorisation affirmed. The belief in the importance of direct and unmediated actions informed the work's construction as well as its reception: all participants related to the work within an axis of their own experience. As a process of making theatre from protest, the gap between the human and political dimensions of reality was reduced, and protest activity ideally and symbolically became a form of art and vice versa. In this respect, the student movements' claim "to give full expression to oneself" and to give oneself over the unpredictable experimental politics of the *shutaisei* effect is the

rhetorical counterpart to the message of the play. Both ideally come
to share a similar sense of radical consciousness validating personal
politics and experience through participation and action.

Moreover, the shifting variety of experiences drawn from daily
events meant that stylistically the performance changed. This was an
example of work responding to the immediate context of its production and not buried by the closed and slow moving production
system of *shingeki*. This, too, is reflective of the protest experience,
where dynamics of protest and specific issues changed quickly and
were even obscured by the resolve to action. As an idealized expression of a committed activist experience, *Document Number One* was also
sensual and embodied as theatre. It explored politics through an
avant-garde form of expression.

Referencing protest movements either literally or symbolically
became a characteristic feature of the 1960s theatre, as for cinema,
literature, and popular culture. By 1968, when student protests peaked,
theatre was often dealing in protest themes and participating, agit-
prop-style, in public demonstrations and confrontations with state
mechanisms of authority and power. Such ideas as immediacy, inde-
terminacy, and spontaneity—even chaos—came to underlie the *angura*
approach and in turn, the theatre promoted and validated like-minded
cultural practices of protest movements. In this sense, *angura* 'documented' one's own view of the world; one's personal experience
became a point of mediation around which theatre and culture were
given meaning and sense of purpose. But what could be said about
this experience? Already in the 1960s, protest was also a fashionable
wave. How could theatre continue to travel an activist path? How
to resist deadening and soulless forms of modern culture that surrounded them preoccupied the ablest political and artistic minds of
the 1960s generation.

Terayama's work *Throw Away Your Books: Let's Go Into The Streets*
(*Sho o suteyo machi e deyō*) throws light onto the dramaturgical space
of protest theatre in the latter part of the decade. The play comes
across as a psychedelic collage of political speeches, dream-states, sex
and sports, all woven into the everyday world of the 1960s space
and loosely held together by the restless wandering of a young male
protagonist. In fact, there are three works authored by Terayama
with this name; a book of collected essays published in 1967, the
above mentioned theatre work in 1968, and a film directed by
Terayama in 1971 (Terayama 1971). The essay, stage and film ver-

sions differ markedly in form and content, although not surprisingly each is characterized by intertextuality and—in the case of the two art works—a kind of strategic narrative confusion. The film offers a remarkable play of images of rebellion and uncertainty in its fragmentary portrayal of contemporary life largely set in the rapidly transforming urban society of Tokyo. A Korean-Japanese family live in a poor neighbourhood and a young man of the family and his autistic sister are the focus of the story that meanders along. Texts by Terayama and other favoured authors are painted on the walls of the city like political slogans. In light of these visually stunning texts, Morita Nori argues that Terayama hoped to make a film of the city as if it were a book that might be read (Morita 2005). Meanwhile, the stage version of *Throw Away Your Books*, draws on poems previously written by Terayama under the title *High Tea Poems*. A CD recording also features protest songs and psychedelic music composed by J. A. Seazer, Terayama's long time musical collaborator. From viewing productions stills and revivals, the work seems to display a gothic ambience of cruelty and an eerie nostalgia. Goodman describes the play as a ' "docudrama" consisting of poems read on stage by their teenage authors (articulating) Terayama's "recommendation to run away from home" ' (Goodman 1999: 54). Both film and stage versions develop from a system of montage. Polemics, images, sounds and actions are layered to make a journey of self-discovery and a critical representation of socialisation pressures experienced by young people. As the young man is adrift, he encounters the world around him as a place that is familiar and also strange. He is unsure of his world and his memories are unreliable. Hence, the works are abstract and illogical. Overall, the two works are preoccupied with youth culture and the *shutaisei* effect, the frequently nihilist tone symbolically references the protest movement. In this sense, existentialism is a key reference point for understanding *Throw Away Your Books*. Such a force is sensed in the atmosphere of uncertainty, and through the ongoing questioning of how one might come to accept the emptiness inside with equanimity. It is a study of how one might transcend this world through imagination and action.

The title itself seems to present a double message. In the context of university occupations in 1968, *Throw Away Your Books* calls for rebellion and exhorts protestors to greater actions. From another perspective, it validates a sense of nihilism and inaction that is commonly explored in 1960s artworks: what is the point of learning when all it has seemingly produced is such apathy and cruelty? In the end, to go into the streets is the only thing left: of course to protest, but also to mark them with subjectivity and presence, simply to enter the stream of the everyday. Contact in the alienated space of the everyday is no simple matter. Neither, however, is the alternative. Long scenes in the film record many of the slogans questioning the possibility of freedom. The themes of failure and emptiness are chalked on walls of the city. The recurring image of a soccer club suggesting the collective rite of passage of healthy young Japanese men is undercut by a gang rape they commit on the autistic girl in the clubroom showers. Other hippy-like images of sexual liberation, for example, the burning of the American flag to reveal a couple having intercourse, can be read, perhaps, as a corrective to sexual violence. In the final analysis though, the collective is viewed with a sense of uncertainty; these dissolute soccer players share male bonding rituals with radical sect protestors, and both put their bodies on the line. But they commit crimes and atrocities. For Terayama, the question seems to be not so much how to belong to society, or escape from it, but how to avoid its drive towards annihilation. Thus, the work acknowledges the regular, increasingly volatile actions of the protests, but is also sceptical of the protesters' revolutionary stance. As discussed in the previous chapter, the 1968 occupation of the University of Tokyo was an ambiguous site of resistance. While it was a playful space accorded to a privileged elite, the widespread coverage and indeed historical memory of these events affords them a certain radical symbolic value as well. The high level of chaos they caused, both symbolically and in actual terms, was instructive and, perhaps, a gesture towards freedom. *Throw Away Your Books* arose from this spirit of dissent and questioning. It attacked education on the grounds that educational systems merely extended and replicated the values of the State. In Foucault's terms, education was seen as a technology of power controlled by ruling interests. But the critique was double-edged.

Conclusion

One recurring image in Terayama's work is of an old-fashioned paper and wood biplane. Actors run across the fields trying to catch the wind and take off, gliding above the ground as if powered by human invention.[2] There is a scene in the film version showing this biplane burning on a bonfire at night. This footage seems to be taken from an outdoor performance by Terayama's company in Holland in 1970. Does this image suggest the end of freedom, or, is it a Hindu-like fire-ritual of rebirth? Perhaps the confusion and sense of slippage between the two possibilities is deliberate. Terayama's works are intended to fire the imagination and they must be made in the mind of the viewer. As will be discussed in the next chapter, the same might be said for *angura's* wider paradigmatic encounter with the *shutaisei* effect.

---

[2] The "human powered aeroplane" was one of the many contraptions featuring in Terayama's group. These machines were often a cross between Victorian era torture implements, sadomasochist play machines and early cybernetic systems. For illustrations see (Terayama 1978).

CHAPTER FOUR

THE *ANGURA* PARADIGM AND THE END OF
THE 1960s SPACE

Take power with imagination
Tenjō Sajiki Manifesto/new leftist graffiti in Paris,
1968

In the preceding chapter, we considered the theme of protest and
its expression in *angura*. We examined performances that referenced
protest culture through direct citation and polemic forms of expression. While this work is important to understanding the sense of cor-
relation between protest and radical performance, the implicit and
rhetorical expression of politics in *angura* must also be considered. As
has been suggested, *angura* in the 1960s space was for the most part
complex and nuanced; reading the politics of this avant-garde requires
a broad analysis of the effects of its representation in and on the
social world. Hence, discussion will now identify how *angura* maps a
less visible, although perhaps more fundamental political mode in
the form of radical subjectivity. This subjectivity—or what I have
called the *shutaisei* effect—was an expression of cultural rebellion. It
was a movement towards defining modes of cultural politics, agency
and personal intervention that might lead to progressive outcomes
in the wider political landscape of Japan. Thus, in contrast to the
visible politics of performance already discussed, *angura* will be shown
here to be developing oblique and sideways strategies as the 1960s
progressed. As a result, the politics of subjectivity that came to define
the *angura* experience perhaps rested deeper in the contemporary setting and cast an eye to wider questions about human experience,
history and autonomy.

The prefacing comment points to the fact that *angura* anticipated
a fluid and constantly changing understanding of the interrelationship of politics and creativity. The slogan "Take power with imagination" was not only associated with the expressionistic theatricality
of Terayama Shūji, it was also the catch-cry of the French new left
in 1968. Both sources of expression proposed a new political order
designed to undermine the binary-cultural mechanisms of established

modes of power in their respective national and political spaces. Instead, a boundless politics of ceaseless movement and relational experiences, alongside on-going forms of experimentation was proposed. This appeared at times as a unique combination of utopia and violence. As *angura* attempted to banish the distinctions between life and art and realize a kind of Artaudian avant-garde vision of theatre and life reordered and inseparable, it came to embody, if not define outright, the transformation of cultural politics of the 1960s space.

In order to gain a better understanding of *angura* in its wider setting, this chapter returns to a more detailed consideration of significant aspects of the *angura* paradigm. It will be remembered that I broadly identified the key aspects of this model in the previous chapter. Here, I will consider the model in relation to analysis of groundbreaking artistic styles and key productions from the period. The question of how *angura* brings into play the field of premodern theatre and culture will be considered, as will *angura's* formation of an expression of radical corporeality. New approaches to performance space and text will also be discussed. We can then examine precisely how the rethinking of primary dramaturgical forms in *angura* worked to construct a radical politics of anti-realism: in other words, how *angura* brought to life a utopian politics borne of the imagination and aiming for a reconsideration of the political boundaries of self-expression and identity.

Two 'performance' events signalling a kind of closure on the 1960s will be discussed in the final section of the chapter: the gory suicide of Mishima Yukio in 1970; and the play *The Dance of Angels Who Burn Their Own Wings* (*Tsubasa o Moyasu Tenshi-Tachi no Butō*, 1970) by leading *angura* company Theatre 68/70–Black Tent (Satoh, Yamamoto et al. 1988). Despite continued political dramas into the next decade and the eventual consolidation of *angura*, it will be argued that these events signal the resurgent power of capitalism in shaping politics and culture in Japan. Following on the heels of the counter culture were forces that reified the sense of possibility that it created.

Tradition and the making of history

As previously noted, one of the most important concerns for *angura* was the overthrow of *shingeki*. In the process, an amalgam of transnational avant-gardism and local theatrical expression arose in works by *angura* artists. The rejection of *shingeki*, the subsequent reappraisal of indigenous performance traditions and an abiding interest in contemporary culture imbued *angura* with an historical consciousness. The ensuing imbrication of aesthetic and cultural references, seemingly taken from everywhere as contemporary artists revisited theatre traditions, resulted in an array of remarkable new images in theatre and even gave rise to new genres. As will be seen, stage environments emphasizing iconic design and stylized movement patterns alongside myth-like narrative forms was the result of this trend. Each part of the design did not sit alone, rather *angura* sought to effect the total synthesis of theatrical elements and create a theatre where music and design—not to mention movement and bodies—might be as important to the overall effect as the text. The dramaturgical frame of *angura* was composite, intertextual and meta-theatrical.

As might be expected, hybridity is a prominent aspect of this process and *angura* is characterized by a hybrid *mise-en-scène* of premodern and contemporary popular cultural signs drawn seemingly without discrimination from eastern and western sources. And while critiques of hybridity and appropriation in theatre offer complex political problems for scholars, it is also clear that *angura's* use of hybrid forms has a radical political context. For example, *angura's* interest in exploring elements of Japanese tradition represents an aspect of continuity in the fractured historical experience of Japan. By their move to consider Japanese cultural memory from a sense of interconnectedness rather than breech, *angura* artists expressed a willingness to reconsider Japanese cultural totality including factors such as the war and Japanese aggression that had been excised from the more fragmented historical view. Hence, in exploring tradition, *angura* promised a theatre that was more complete in cultural terms than *shingeki*, but also more problematic and harder to explain.

As scholars such as Brandon have shown, *nō, kyōgen, bunraku* and *kabuki*—singularly and in combination—within their histories have a vivid store of imagery and techniques that the avant-garde has drawn from (Brandon 1985). Goodman's work on the Japanese theatre in the 1960s space also explores this connection and shows how *angura* drew on elements of animism and shamanic mythology; elements that are centrally and manifestly alluded to in these premodern theatres. Goodman argues that *angura's* interest in premodern folklore was a "grotesque abstraction of the subliminal impulses of the modern Japanese imagination" (Ōzaza in Goodman 1988: 15). His reading of Satoh Makoto and the post-*shingeki* movement (as he terms 1960s theatre) explores the ways that contemporary Japanese theatre worked to transcend the closure of modern Japan to its troubled past. Goodman shows how such theatre worked to awaken a sense of past trauma. From this perspective, it is clear that neo-traditionalism and hybridity in *angura* are not only to be associated with structural and stylistic concerns, or the surface dimensions of performance, but with the wider socio-political latitudes of cultural experience. In Goodman's terms, such theatre works to confront trauma and examine violence and horror. Meanwhile, related questions about identity and Japan's modern history also arise.

The perpetual dialogue between reality and unreality, mimesis and ritual, and the apparent illogical states of premodern theatre were also an enduring source of relativity and freedom on the *angura* stage. Specifically, *nō* and *kyōgen*—to the extent that these genres bring to mind notions of the uncanny and sublime—were sources of a premodern consciousness and a collective unconscious in *angura*. The basis in collective myth, the influence of Zen Buddhism, non-linear concepts of time, and the combination of music, dance and narrative are all important aesthetic–cultural dimensions of traditional theatre from which *angura* derived its abstraction and subliminal premodern sensibility.

Body and history in Suzuki Tadashi's theatre

Suzuki Tadashi's innovative physical theatre and training system for actors helps explain these points by showing how hybridity shaped the *angura* space and informed its politics. Suzuki began working in the early 1960s initially at the Waseda Little Theatre (*Waseda Shōgekijō*) and then, from 1976, with the Suzuki Company of Toga (SCOT). Like a modern day Zeami, Suzuki's writings on theatre (e.g. Suzuki 1986) explore theories of theatre and corporeality that are in essence archetypal and elemental: his work bears hallmarks of *nō* and *kyōgen*, but also classical Greek theatre. According to Suzuki, the actor as a central visible agent in the theatre is connected to the ground, and is grounded in and by this powerful essence. In other words, the actor operates inside a field of spatial and cultural dynamics that this observation implies. In this regard, Suzuki delineates a space of collective consciousness commonly associated with the ritual dimensions of traditional theatres. His essay on his theatre in the remote Toga Village, for example, evokes a memory of theatre as an antimodern community ritual and a form of shared celebration; the "public space" in "the middle of nature" (Suzuki 1986: 81).

Also of relevance is Suga's view that Waseda Shōgekijō "can be said to have been a student intelligentsia group that bore (the brunt of) the cultural disputes of the new left" (Suga 2003: 142). Suga argues that in splintering from the famed Jū Butai (Free Stage), a JCP affiliated social realist theatre in 1966, Waseda Shōgekijō signalled their opposition to the *shingeki* system. In other words, their rejection of modern theatre processes led to a revival of tradition as a political standpoint, even if this fact was not explicitly stated as the motivation for the company's restructure. Later, SCOT evolved into a training and performance community in Toga with the aim to reconnect the work of the company with a sense of history, culture, and the rhythms of village life. A path away from old style politics towards iconoclastic communitarian and local identity oriented new left politics is apparent.

Suzuki's theorization of historical consciousness is further evident in his *nō*-like stylization of the performing body. SCOT performances typically display formal movement patterns and *kata*—fully voiced delivery of texts, use of chants and stylized front-on—or flat, two dimensional modes of presentation that are suggestive of premodern theatricality and staging. His stage wavers between postmodern and premodern sensibilities as a result; the epic mystery of *nō* is heightened through a rigorous stylization of the body and echoed in classically informed stage design and spatial dynamics. This in turn is layered with popular culture references and farce. Uchino, for example, notes how the potpourri of intensified body elements and *karaoke* in Suzuki's work came to explore the dynamics of Japanese mass culture in extreme states (Uchino 1996: 76–97). Overall, Suzuki's ideal theatre memorializes the neo-traditional and collective sense of prehistorical consciousness, while simultaneously referencing the contemporaneous world, often through a surreal, existential humour that is part *kyōgen* part Samuel Beckett in style.

Suzuki's training method aims to free the actor of physical and mental blocks and make them available to creative possibilities and is now widely known in acting communities around the world. Ironically, for a program that is designed to create freedom for the actor, the training is a disciplined and challenging amalgam of classical and modern sources that form the basis of physical exercises. This is combined with a seemingly authoritarian master-disciple method of practice. Beginning with walks, marches, and modal *kata*-like physical forms, the basic training works from a sense of locating the body in space and achieving and controlling a high level of performance energy, thereby intensifying the performance dynamic overall. Hence, the scholar and Suzuki-trained actor Paul Allain writes that Suzuki's training: "attempts to integrate physical and mental systems, to create a 'mind-body'." Through exploring otherwise esoteric Japanese performance traditions and Asian philosophy, Allain suggests that Suzuki's method "acts as a functional bridge between East and West, and traditional and contemporary models" of theatre (Allain 2002: 96). The organizing principles of the training are the feet and the actor's centre, which in turn, locate the body as it moves through space or remains dynamically still. Like traditional Japanese theatres, processes of acting are almost archetypal; the dynamics of a scene develop through the *mise-en-scène* of bodies interacting on the stage. The mythological dimensions of narrative often subsume individual details of character. Unlike traditional theatre worlds, however, where learning to perform is a process slowly absorbed, Suzuki's training system has a modern pedagogy. The emphasis is on efficiency and transplanting ill-defined religious— aesthetic concepts such as *yūgen* (mysterious depth) into secular forms; for example, "the grammar of the feet," suggestive of *yūgen* transformed into the visceral dynamic excitement of well-trained bodies performing collective actions. The practice of repetitive training rituals, the precise correction of techniques, and group exercizes overseen by a senior company member who often strikes a bamboo *kendo* sword on the floor, bear comparison to dance training and military drills.

Accordingly, it might be argued that while Suzuki's theatre is concerned with the interrogation of cultural history, it is not concerned with the creative expression of individual actors and their personal histories, motivations that might be seen in the psychological drama of *shingeki*. This is an important point, not only in respect of *angura's* rebellion against *shingeki*, but for the ongoing political project of theatre as well. Attenuated psychodramatic responses that form a system of representation such as psychological realism risk reverting to a kind of individuated capitalist narrative. In this narrative, the oppressed and sublimated individual relives their traumatic experience as a form catharsis. While staunchly defended in many western theatre cultures, psychological realism is also criticized as a primary expression of theatre's imbrication inside capitalism and the culture industry.

From the perspective of staging theatre, realism is also outside history. By intensely focusing on an acting method of being in the present moment—even with an awareness of previous circumstances—realism is unable to realize historicity in the actors' body and can only explore historical themes through narrative. Suzuki's training system, on the other hand, suggests an actual embodiment of history. It draws on examples of physicality from the past. In this way, social and cultural aspects of Japan's history enter the staging of theatre in *angura*; they are inside the mechanisms of production.

However, this is not to say that *angura* solved the theatre's complex dialectical issues in total—a problem for the politics of *angura* is also evident. The kinds of subjective experiences framing and legitimating *angura* expression might also fall into the psychodramatic trap of art as an individuated bourgeois system where experience is personalized and owned. Resisting this trend, however, is the collective dimension in Suzuki's work that attenuates the sense of closure and internalization that is the private world of naturalism. Instead, the sense of a collective is clearly seen in the chorus of bodies and unity of the stylized modes of acting that constitute the Suzuki method in performance. Consequently, a contest of history and tradition can be observed in Suzuki's productions. By giving attention to the contest of disparate performance forms and the abrasive application of cultural references that are inside the aesthetic system of the Suzuki method, one can see how a study of culture from the perspective of history is an overriding theme in Suzuki's work. Suzuki is interested in questions of how narratives come into everyday life and, by extension, he is concerned with the social effects of power.

We see this when after working with playwright Betsuyaku Minoru between 1961 and 1969 (after which Betsuyaku left the company), Suzuki came to question Betusyaku's characteristically absurd and existential mode of theatre. Suzuki's breakthrough piece that explored a different sense of theatre *On Dramatic Passions* (*Geki teki naru mono o magute*, 1969–72) was a collage of texts on the theme of dramatic passion, taken from classical Greek, *nō*, Shakespeare, *kabuki*, and so on, and featuring the powerful acting of Shiraishi Kayoko. A second version of *On Dramatic Passions* about "wronged women" was sourced from *kabuki*, *shinpa* and gothic fiction by Izumi Kyōka. Dramaturgically, *On Dramatic Passions* curates a field of historical experience on the theme of emotion and contemporaneously embodies this through the vortex of Shiraishi's performance. In this sense, her depiction of extreme states of madness in *On Dramatic Passions*—often talked about as a form of possession—draws not on the madness of catharsis, principally the dramaturgy of classical Greek theatre—but on the revelation of history.

Later works by Suzuki have been adapted in similar fashion from the western canon, for example: *The Trojan Women* (1977), *The Bacchae* (1978), *King Lear* (1984) and *The Tale of Lear* (1988). In 1992, Suzuki made *The Chronicle of Macbeth* in association with Playbox Theatre in Melbourne (Carruthers 2001). All of these works feature a dramaturgic system of mixing premodern and modern worlds with processes that explicitly interrogate history as a mode of power. In *The Chronicle of Macbeth* and *The Tale of Lear*, for example, the act of remembering a past event or experience is staged as history that is remembered and made into drama. Thus, in *The Tale of Lear* a nurse reading from a book that has fallen from the lap of a dying old man recounts the vision of the man who sees himself as Lear. As Takahashi Yasunari points out: "The continual presence of the Nurse leads us to suspect that the dramatic action going on onstage is not only a figment of the Old Man's fantasy but also a representation in 'real time' of what she is reading" (Takahashi 2001: 113). In the opening moments of *The Chronicle of Macbeth*, a chorus of men read from books and chant: "Today we shall do *Macbeth*. Begin Reading!" (Carruthers 2001: 122). In similar fashion to the dramaturgy of *nō*, one that typically returns to events from the past and reanimates them as an act of collective memory, Suzuki's work is both an object of tradition and a critical exploration of that tradition in the form of history and memory. The abiding intertextualism works to explore the ways that memory and history are constructed, and the disjunctions that might lie between the act and its reconstruction in the social space of theatre.

As a further marker of contesting traditions in *angura*, the sensibilities of *kabuki* in revised form have been influential alongside the *nō*. Kara Jūrō's tent theatres (Situation Theatre, Red Tent, *Kara Gumi*) are known for their evocation of a proto-*kabuki* atmosphere. Performances written and directed by Kara and usually featuring him in a lead role suggest the spectacle-like and chaotic collusion of imagined premodern *kabuki*-style. This invention of low class, lively and anti-establishment entertainment points to a sense of nostalgia for a spontaneous, community oriented theatre; one reminiscent of the popular and provincial *taishū engeki* (marginalized semi-*kabuki* performance popular among poorer people) that was performed in the working class neighbourhoods of Tokyo, where Kara was born and lived (Kara 1997). Scholars have commented on Kara's references to his theatre as a place of self-styled "river beggars" (*kawa kojiki*), a name given to those early-day *kabuki* groups performing in the dry riverbeds, and in the licensed entertainment and pleasure districts of Tokugawa Japan (Powell 2002: 178). Thus, Kara's theatre evokes imagined pre-Meiji sensibilities of *kabuki*, a form of theatre known to be ribald, spontaneous, and extravagantly poetic. The idea of theatre for the common people and the distain for authority associated with the Edo period *kabuki* is mythologized in performances of Kara's troupe, and in the lifestyle of its members who spent their earlier years travelling around Japan. They wanted to rediscover *kabuki's* spirit of radicalism and experience life as an outsider.

While Kara's theatre is further discussed below, for the present we can note how neo-traditional aesthetics in *angura* are cultural and historical. They arise from the delayed and troubled manifestation of modern art in Japan and sit in relation to the difficult history of Japanese nationhood and identity formation. What grows from the *shutaisei* effect then is an attempt to understand radical subjectivity in relation to history. Because the sources of *shutaisei* were cultural, *shutaisei* debates were essentially debates about culture. The concerns of *angura* also validated a discussion of links between tradition, culture, identity and political activism. While in one sense this was a new paradigm suggestive of radical prospects in the 1960s cultural space, it also returned to debates that arose at the beginning of Japan's modernity. In turning away from the theatre as a site of meaningful indigenous cultural formation in the late nineteenth century, Japanese society came to regard premodern theatre as a source of propaganda or quaintness. Against this, Tsubouchi Shōyō called for a theatre that was uniquely an expression of Japanese cultural identity—both modern and long established at the same time. Thus, in the same way that *angura* moved against *shingeki*, we find an earlier precedent in Tsubouchi's hopes that theatre move against western aesthetics (Marra 1999: 38). *Angura's* subsequent fascination with history and premodern theatre is therefore of central importance. It proposed a radical project that might be capable of looking forward from a groundswell of cultural history. In this regard, *angura's* invention of tradition is also an act of historicism; it is an attempt to resolve the inherent contradictions that arize in Japan's modern history.

Radical corporeality

We have already begun to discuss the concentrated physicality that characterized *angura* bodies in performance. By appropriating aspects of the premodern theatre—especially those grotesque, subconscious forms of embodiment mentioned by Goodman—the body and its expressive possibilities were brought to the centre of theatrical investigations and became a site of radical corporeality with political dimensions. Thus, Suzuki, Kara, Terayama, Ōta Shōgo and, of course the *butō* world, created distinctive, often extraordinary and extreme physical modes of performance, and *angura* began a theorization of the body in theatre that has grown in complexity up to the present day. Central to this was the realization that the body was the crucial and intrinsic factor in the performance process. For example, Suzuki makes the statement that:

> Behind all of these words (in the theatre) is a body. . . . Theatre is made from a physical body in space, speaking words, and resulting in the transformation of that space. It is a cultural activity wherein the body utilizes space and language and is able to transform the space into something unfamiliar and changed. If a director has actors with good bodies then any space in the world can be a theatre. (Suzuki 1996)

The expressive body, in one form or another, has been accorded the highest value in the avant-garde's far-reaching confrontation with the social world.

Suzuki's mention of transformation is important to understanding *angura*. Transformation is an enduring metaphor that relates actor physicality to the *shutaisei* effect. During the 1960s, "pre-expressive," subjective and spontaneous transformational qualities of the actor's body in space were important concerns for artists. Avant-garde theories developed by Antonin Artaud in *The Theatre and its Double* (Artaud 1970)—available in Japanese translation from 1963—privileged the body's subjective, transformative potential as transgressive. *Angura* came to view the body as a less inhibited expressive instrument, a spontaneously radical site, and perhaps not clouded by intellectual thought. An example of this way of thinking is Kara's notion of the actors' essential "privileged physical being" (*tokken-teki nikutai*), relating in other words to an idea akin to a visceral embodiment of the flesh. According to Powell, actors in Kara's theatre aim to acquire a force of presence: "that would work on conventional views of reality with the object of exploding them" (Powell 2002: 179).

Contemporary debates regarding body politics have often been a counteractive response to the idea that the body is a pristine site that is capable of expressing in movement and dance the untamed or less mediated aspects of social reality. Even so, these nominally post-structural readings of the body as a surface for inscription, for example, (discussed in chapter 9) developed out of critical theorizations of the body during the 1960s era, and an awareness of the idea that the body "speaks" in ways around and beyond the limited schemata of spoken word and text, was a powerful realisation for *angura*. In keeping with the spirit of the *shutaisei* effect, that life experience and cultural debates should be voiced in the theatre, the *angura* body was presented as a surface of authentic life experience and as evidence of the selfhood struggle in motion. That *angura* should come to utilize the body and attempt to liberate the body was an effective counter to the physiological and moral constraints placed on the body in naturalistic acting. Obviously, this was also a comment on society-at-large. As has been argued in preceding chapters, the body in action, in demonstrations and other modes of political expression, and in the arts shared a common dynamic goal of selfhood revelation. To be in motion, or to be moved by events, and to have those events flow through the corporal space of performance was seen as a vigorous act of cultural awakening.

Igarashi's work on the body in postwar history notes that: "By the late 1960s, bright images of progress overshadowed the ghost of the war in Japanese society. . . . The hardship and starvation suffered by Japanese people during and immediately after the war became an integral part of the narrative that everyone knew had a happy ending" (Igarashi 2000: 165). The question for theatre became one of how to challenge "the national space of remembrance" (ibid: 167) and the glib postwar narrative of peace and prosperity. Kawamura writes in the aforementioned play *Hamletclone*: "The main point is to overthrow the happy ending" (Kawamura 2000a). When seen in this light, sensualism and grotesque abstraction found in the innovative physical expression of *angura* worked to liberate the senses and feed the imagination. It also aimed to explore Japan's darkness; to summarise the thoughts of the *butō* performer Min Tanaka, these are the ugly fragments of Japan's history (Tanaka 1986). In the clean space of the 1960s, radical corporeality was born in mud and dirt.

This principle was extended to incorporate wider aspects of the performative frame, notably the inventive and playful use of space and overt use of design.

The experiential mise-en-scène *in the 1960s space*

Theatrical space and the combined aspects of theatrical presentation (staging, lighting, sound effects, etc.) that comprise the performance *mise-en-scène* are representational and symbolic of the social environment. The *mise-en-scène* can therefore be read as a metaphor for social space, and according to the theory of semiotics, as utilizing signs and signifiers that draw attention to the investigation of culture. In line with thinking that characterizes the *mise-en-scène* as a cultural signifier, the *mise-en-scène* of *angura* represents a radical interrogation of the cultural space of 1960s Japan.

As we have seen, *mise-en-scène* in 1960s *angura* tends to be eclectic and atmospheric. Examples from this period point to the fact that *angura* theatrics stressed the imaginary, transhistorical, and experiential over-and-above the logical, realistic depiction of a social reality. Hence, theatre design was radically expanded and theatricalized, its customary silence in the background shattered and instead, design elements were bought into the foreground. In conjunction with an interest in the performing body, experiments with staging created opportunities for new ways of seeing the world. Rather than represent social reality with a stable, cohesive *mise-en-scène, angura* can be seen to undermine the smooth veneer of an unchanging world by the presentation of multiple, even contrary spaces and states of awareness.

I've already noted that theatre companies sometimes developed work in unconventional spaces—as was the case with Kara's tent shows. Even more nonconformist was Terayama's company Tenjō

Sajiki and their radical disarticulation of theatrical space. In some instances, these performances were designed in such a manner that sections of the audience could experience only a portion of the stage action. People seated in one area might have a completely different perspective to those seated elsewhere and thereby gained a different understanding of the work, one that was relative to their context and viewpoint. We see this intention signalled in the prefacing remarks to the 1969 production of Tenjō Sajiki's *Dr Garigari's Crime* (*Garigari Hakasei no Hanzai*) in which Terayama wrote: "The various parts of the drama begin simultaneously in the various rooms. Members of the audience are only able to come in contact with it in a subjective manner. This drama resembles the world" (Terayama 1984: 9). Carol Sorgenfrei describes how audience perceptions were distorted and made almost virtual in this production by employing:

> (A) concept of private rooms in which portions of the audience were segregated, making it impossible for any member of the audience to view the action in all the rooms. Fragmented perceptions and simultaneous action combined with group improvisations forced the audience to imaginatively create the missing parts of the action. (Sorgenfrei 1978: 209)

Terayama's company was also well-known for placing audiences in extreme conditions of light, darkness and noise, as well as being placed among all manner of staging inventions and unexpected environments. Actors were shackled in sculptural machinery and restraints such as hybrid human-machine centrifugal devices and noise making instruments.

Although a work from the 1970s, Terayama's production of *Knock* (*Noku*, 1976), co-written with Kishida Rio, illustrates just how fragmented and experiential the avant-garde would become in Japan. *Knock*—which owes more of a debt to performance art and happenings associated with early 1960s groups like High Red Centre (*Haireddo Senta*) than to theatre—was staged at multiple sites across the city of Tokyo over one seventy-two hour period, including a widely discussed scene that took place in a public bathhouse. Senda's description of attending the performance includes the observation that once in the bathhouse "nobody could be sure who were the spectators and who were the actors" (Senda 1986: 6).[1] By extension

---

[1] Although photographic documentation of *Knock* housed in the Terayama Museum

of this ambiguity, the larger and more fundamental question of what might constitute a performance is also broached. In other words, the question of what is live in the singular moment and what is mediated comes to be a question about the nature of social reality. The performance explores wider issues: are social outcomes predetermined by history, or perhaps by disciplinary mechanisms embedded in cultural practices, or are they truly and momentarily liberated from external control? Certainly, the ambiguous space with its shifting borders and meanings explored in *Knock* challenge audiences to question their assumptions and reconsider the foundations of their social reality.

Discussions about the politics of theatrical space were also evident among theoreticians aligned with the 1960s movement. They argued that the shift to performing in non-traditional spaces was not simply a matter of creating new sensations for audiences; it was predicated on a new economics of production and the rejection of the *shingeki* system. In supporting this view, Tsuno Kaitaro argued that staging conventions in the modern theatre could be seen to uphold dominant ideologies and worked to silence alternative forms of expression. Brecht's essay on the "smoking theatre"—an essay that proposes a theatre where the audience sits apart from the action and measures its messages in relation to their experience of the social world—was the starting point for Tsuno's influential discussion on the politics of theatrical space. For Tsuno, theatre space and the conventions that were built into the space—the proscenium arch, the seating configuration, and so on—worked to inculcate systems of authoritarian power. The systemic presence of these production elements in modern theatres was rarely questioned. As Tusno writes: "The theatre is not merely a concept or an ideology. In the theatre a single sheet of cloth guarantees a special form of dramatic imagination, and that piece of cloth survives not only by virtue of modern social custom, but also because it enjoys the protection of legally codified, coercive force" (Tsuno 1970a: 94). Tsuno makes a case that while theatre remains in legally sanctioned, modern theatre build-

---

in Aomori seems to refute this point. In one image, we seem to see members of the company in the baths and fully dressed audience members looking on. For a brief discussion of this work and a translation of the bathhouse section, see also (Rolf and Gillespie 1992: 225–248).

ings it is effectively controlled. Even the most radically motivated performance is consequently limited by theatrical space and associated conventions. The single sheet of cloth—a Brecht-like reference to the stage curtain—means that the imagination is already bound by orthodoxy. The reach of such theatre is also conditioned by the fact that few people regularly attend theatre. Theatre buildings have their own cultures that tend to put-off working class people, for example. It is also likely that even the most authoritarian society will tolerate a small anti-establishment theatre culture while it remains marginalized and safely out of view. On the other hand, artists can fall prey to shifting attitudes of government authorities, especially once their theatres begin to attract a greater degree of attention. For example, in 1969, Kara was arrested for pitching his tent in Shinjuku, but only after his tent theatre had previously performed elsewhere for some time. There seems little doubt that the reason for his arrest was the fact that, as Yamamoto Kiyokazu writes: "Setting up his red tent there was an act of provocation, an assault upon the most thriving section of Tokyo – the embodiment of Japan's postwar economic growth" (Yamamoto 1970: 217).

Influenced by Tsuno's essay, Black Tent-Theatre 68/70 planned a theatre company that was "capable of continuous performance anywhere in Japan for periods from six months to a year at a time" (Saito and Nakamura 1971: 8). Named the Mobile Theatre, it hoped to escape the tyranny of the legally tolerated, modern theatre building. By doing away with the curtain, the Mobile Theatre in their prospectus stated that their intention was:

> To flee the walls of theatre and make the theatre move. Rather, to make motion itself theatre. Since we began our Theatre Centre, we seem to have been fascinated by the idea of motion. But this is the jet age. Well-tailored businessmen, attaché cases in hand, mount planes and bullet-trains to cover hundreds of miles in minutes. Mobility is a hallmark of our age. Nevertheless, the freedom to move remains a selective freedom. (Saito and Nakamura 1971: 8)

When the Mobile Theatre sought to present performances in a tent, they met institutional challenges that impinged on their movement and free expression. "We were talking about politics in terms of park ordinances, fire laws and public sanitation codes" (Saito and Nakamura 1971: 12) they wrote; the geographical spaces and local ordinances, like the curtain, became for the Mobile Theatre coercive forces designed to confine expression. Theatre 68/70 director Satoh Makoto, one of the instigators of the Mobile Theatre, also thought that the touring had the effect of strengthening links with the student movement:

> Because we were going to places that we had never been before and the fact that we had the tent meant that we had the problem of where to put it up. Universities were an obvious place, as all the public spaces in Japan usually said no. The people on the university campuses who invited us were mostly people involved in the student movement, so links were coming from the practical necessity of having to use a space. Asking questions about why we were denied the use of public space also started to feed into a debate about the restriction on public space and freedom. (Satoh 1996)

Mobility, therefore, becomes a political statement, even a revolutionary strategy as it confronts social systems and geographical constraints that directly impinge on the free expression of the activist agenda. Confirming the radical selfhood of the mobile theatre is a comment made by Tsuno about the tour: "Theatre is more than theatre because the most theatrical thing of all is the manner in which one forces theatre in upon the world" (Tsuno and Senda 1971: 49).

Finally, we have noted briefly that the use of symbols from Japanese folklore juxtaposed with representative signs of western popular culture in *angura mise-en-scène* constitutes a style of design that ironically comments on history and the East-West amalgam that constitutes postwar Japanese cultural experience. The mix of kimono and American cigarette advertizements, wheel chairs and Groucho Marx comic glasses with *enka* music in Suzuki's work, for example, is described by James Brandon as "a collage of times and places" (Brandon 1985: 74). Such a playful mix delimits axiomatic design codes and breaks with convention. It popularizes the *mise-en-scène* and engages the audience in a critical dialogue about popular culture. Our attention is drawn to the uses of various symbols to define and limit notions of Japanese culture and identity. The question of the significant Americanization of Japan, together with emblematic representations of the hybrid mix that ultimately signifies Japanese identity, are consequently placed under investigation in the work. To this end, Suzuki's dramaturgy always emphasizes the constructed nature of the world. As noted above, his radical disarticulation of texts often features a central protagonist who dreams multiple narratives of their past existence; the subsequent subjectification and disarticulation of reality is vindicated in a polymorphic and surreal *mise-en-scène*, where symbols of Japanese history and contemporary experience collide and unravel.[2]

Thinking again about text

In radically rethinking the values of the text, *angura* arguably finds its most symbiotic connection to the culture of activism and *shutai-sei*. Remembering how *shingeki* was tied to an implicit faith in the authority of the text, *angura's* polysemic approach had the opposite effect. *Angura* employed a number of devices that undermined the centrality of conventional narrative form. This subsequently blurred, or made relative to context and experience, the customary notion of making intent and meaning crystal clear in the theatre.

Improvized and hybrid dramaturgical functions seen in many of the plays that have already been discussed point to one such device. In works such as *Document Number One, Throw Away Your Books: Let's Go into the Streets* and *Knock*, we have seen that text was displaced from being the foremost representational focus of the performance. During improvized moments in each of these works, the text might serve as a guide only for performers in the unfolding of the work. Several companies including Terayama's used this device on many projects.

Artaud's theory of the avant-garde might once again be said to inform this approach. His model for the theatre of cruelty proposed a total theatre that immersed the text inside the full range of expressive devices; he often suggested that the vocalization of text should be treated as pure sound and, consequently, open to endless interpretive possibilities. Premodern theatres offer somewhat comparable grounds for *angura's* textual rebellion. The composite variety of theatrical experience in *nō* and *kabuki*—combining elements of performance, music,

---

[2] Suzuki's beautiful theatres in Toga, the first of which were converted from old farm buildings designed by Arata Isoyaki, demonstrated the fusion of premodern Japanese elements and late twentieth century culture. They were multifunctional and interactive spaces. The memory of place seemed to have been absorbed atmospherically in the old beams and wooden flooring of the structures. Meanwhile, they contained the latest in theatre equipment and were the site for some memorable performances that consciously played in the gaps between modern and premodern theatrics.

chorus, and dance—demonstrates both a rarefied polysemy and moments of fluid improvization. Students of *nō* might notice the sense of tension and spontaneity that is generated in the interplay between actor (*shite*) and musical and chorus accompaniments. In a different sense, the improvization and satire—not to mention the constant punning and clever use of contemporary references in *kabuki*—are highly regarded by audiences and offer a fresh, spontaneous and even anarchic flavour to the form as a whole. Perhaps in contrast to these arts, however, that are often thought of as primarily focusing on the skills of the actor, in *angura*, the director-*auteur* is more often celebrated. The work of the director and company leader is measured by an adventurous and original staging of the total theatrical experience. Kara Jūrō might be said to be the exception; as the creator and usually star player in his works, he is typical of an *angura* director and yet also a gifted actor.

A second assault on conventional language was the distinctive speeding up of textual delivery to the point where meaning becomes imprecise and listening becomes somehow an embodied, visceral experience. Thus, Yamamoto compared texts by Kara to the "pop-art language of cartoons . . . direct and rapid fire . . . almost violent" (Yamamoto 1970: 216). Experiencing this in performance, one can only absorb portions of the text at the level of comprehension and is thereby encouraged to experience text as sound, for its wider expressive qualities. Other common devices included playing loud music over text, or employing physical acting styles that distorted the delivery of text. This process often began in the writing, which as we have seen tended to employ intertextual strategies. The style was sometimes abstract and many texts reworked older sources. Some plays also feature a high level of self-referentialism or meta-theatrical commentary on the arbitrary presence of textuality. This acts as a constant reminder to treat the text as a performance document, one that requires the inclusion of non-textual elements of performance and the theatricality of *mise-en-scène*.

These developments point to a rejection of modernist theatre and the linear logo-centric narrative form. Audiences were rather invited to participate in the experience of theatre on other, perhaps deeper and sometimes more disturbing levels. As meaning becomes less clear in conventional terms, responses to the work become more subjective, an effect of *shutaisei*. Just as the new left had rejected the dialectic of orthodox Marxist discourse, so too *angura* rejected the narrative base of orthodox leftist, didactic theatre. And in each instance, the spirit of refusal implies an identical rationale: protest politics and *angura* envisaged a new culture; one that experience had shown could not be attained through previous models of resistance. The textual rebellion in *angura* was therefore an attack on the culture of power that had taken language for its very own, to serve its own ends, and depict and describe the world of its own making. Critiques of narrative utilized the deferral of logo-centric meaning as a strategy to engage in a debate about language and the depiction of social reality. This analysis of dramaturgy suggests a philosophical base for theorizing the *angura* paradigm in relation to the politics of subjectivity. To radically disarticulate the text in this manner not only presupposes a determination to overturn *shingeki's* literariness but suggests a further critique of the functions of literature, in particular, its authority as the privileged marker of cultural experience, and as a narrow, intellectual system of representation.

Dreams, reality and being

As we have seen, the question of identity—of ways of being—was a key issue in the 1960s space, manifestly at the very centre of the *shutaisei* effect. For this reason, investigations of history and the experience of nihilism in theatre were accompanied by a powerful dissidence and sense of identity crisis. By recalling the war and Japanese imperialism in Asia, Kara's *John Silver The Beggar of Love* (*Jon Shiruba: Ai no Kojiki*, 1965) (Kara 1970, 1988) exemplifies this kind of interpretive critique. In this well-known play—one of a handful of representative texts from the 1960s era—the character of John Silver is a spectral presence. He is a pirate, a figure of myth and history, preying on the flesh of young Asian bodies in the hunt for sex and pleasure. His spectre, moreover, is like an effect of the plague and brings death wherever it goes; John Silver kills his victims and removes their gold teeth as bounty. It should be clear from these allusions that the themes of occupation, exploitation and outright fascism are key motifs in the play. Hence, *John Silver* can be read as a symbolic critique of Japan's colonisation of East Asia during the Pacific War. Kara's play reminds us of Japanese war profiteering, the existence of state organized prostitution rings, enforced labour camps, the puppet state in Manchuria, relocation of Japanese to the region, and so on. The play also references imperialism in the wider sense, where statehood and identity are forged from a sense of empire, and one where the notion of imperial racial destiny informs the colonial mindset. Accordingly, to lead and occupy is a duty of race, when in fact, this mindset conceals the reality of exploitation and profiting. In this sense, the play also comments on the tangible interrelationship between capitalism and military conflict evident in Japan's wartime experience, also a factor in the account of contemporary conflicts. The 'peg-leg' pirate is an icon symbolic of a kind of 'piracy' throughout the world. In *John Silver*, the dreams of the new world that imperial forces offer to their subjects are revealed as illusions that hide an inner core of contempt.

But *John Silver* is not as a straightforward critique of war. Rather, the play focuses on characters grappling with their own sense of being defeated by history. The question—as it always is in *angura*—is not such much about the past, but what to do with the past in the present. The opening scenes of *John Silver* are set in a public toilet amid the partially reconstructed landscape of Japan. The scene soon transforms into a Korean cabaret patronized by soldiers, and later, a dock in Manchuria. As is typical of *angura*, the characters in *John Silver* exist in multiple historical dimensions and shifts between remembered events and present events, although the latter has a sense that it is no more real than the memory of the former. In other words, *John Silver* might signify a null and void existence. Unable to resolve the sense of history, John Silver's world is powerless to intercede in the future. The past collides with the present, and in his critique of Japanese history, Kara seems to assert that little has changed, that the 'new Japan' has been built on the ill-gotten spoils of war and is as corrupted and eschatological as its former identity.

On another level of analysis the play is at least, in some sense, alive to hope. To dream of a life of vigour, intensity and worth is the aspiration that lies at the heart of *angura-shutaisei* experience. Kara reasserts the powerful need to dream in all its beauty and horror. But herein lies the dilemma. We can dream up our own destruction the play reminds us. Or, we can become conscious and aware and fight the seemingly inevitable desolation that surrounds us, thereby engaging the *shutaisei* effect. A 1996 revival of *John Silver*, directed by Suzuki Tadashi helps develop this point.[3] In Suzuki's production,

---

[3] *Jon Shiruba*, adapted from the text by Kara Jūrō and directed by Suzuki Tadashi, premiered at the Toga Festival in August 1996.

Kara's play was not a statement about the 1960s, nor about the state of Japan following the war, but about the struggle for meaningful existence and human sensation in the contemporary world. Like many of Suzuki's plays, the central metaphor is once again the figurative dimensions of disease. Throughout the production, the character of John Silver is ill. A crowd of nurses care for him and yet they are unable to diagnose his condition, reduced as they are to speaking rapid-fire, gibberish. The doctor is also unable to diagnose any illness and an ambience of disease seeps through the work. The noise of the peg leg walking down imagined pathways and corridors backstage resonates throughout the production, seemingly a reminder of the ghostly presence of John Silver in his former incarnation. The echoes of his power suggest a comparison to his present day tenuous grip on reality—a force without presence of mind. Or alternatively, it may have symbolized the inescapable and ruinous forces of industrial and technological capitalism and its effects on the body. Program notes stated that Suzuki hoped to "depict the wishful illusions of a human being in an inescapable situation, thus, dramatically illustrating the relationship between an imaginary world and an unchangeable situation." This was a radical departure from the Kara text, and no doubt, a commentary on the declining living standards and political and cultural stagnation evident in Japan in the 1990s, nevertheless, at its core, the production continued to explore the dystopic politics of the imaginary. A disjunction between the past and the present—a yet to be resolved wartime psyche combined with a sense of incomplete modernity imposing systems and outside forces—are perhaps the dystopic experiences of John Silver's world. Hence, enduring confusion and ambiguity in the intersecting fields of identity politics and cultural formation in Japan are explored in this work.

The Dance of Angels Who Burn Their Own Wings

The Dance of Angels Who Burn Their Own Wings (*Tsubasa o moyasu tenshi-tachi no butō*), written by Satoh Makoto and others in 1970 for Black Tent/Theatre 68/70 explores the sense of closure entering the 1960s space at the turn of the decade. Described as "a dream within a dream within a dream," *Dance of Angels* seeks to reflect on and evaluate a decade of progress. As Darko Suvin suggests, this play is "the strongest Japanese repudiation of *shingeki* until now" and a compelling critique of 1960s political experience (Suvin 1990: 134). The work, adapted from Peter Weiss' *Marat Sade* was a multi-media performance designed for the travelling Black Tent mobile theatre. According to Suvin, it critically reviewed the Weiss play, condemning the original for its bourgeois naivety and rewrote the text "in terms of a Japanese youth rebellion" (Suvin 1990: 131).[4] As Goodman notes, the Japanese revision of the text removed "those devices Weiss had employed to give his play a coherent structure" (Goodman 1988: 287), thus *Dance of Angels* is consequently a difficult work to summarize, but also typically *angura*. Mythical characters blend with figures from popular culture; the Angels, seekers of liberation and redemption, ride into the space on motorbikes. They dream of freedom and revolution and are perhaps symbolic of the student protesters. Grey Wind and Red Wind, who represent the twin political forces of revolution (i.e. the collective/social and the personal dimensions), derived from the characters of Marat and Sade from the original work, mingle with a rock band on one of the three playing areas. The play uses youth cultural symbols throughout with symbolic intent. As Goodman suggests: "Just as the Beatles were the communal fantasy of contemporary youth, the Winds are the Angels communal fantasy of the French revolution" (Goodman 1988: 289). There is also a third ensemble of actors called 'the birds'. They occupy the heavens, signified by the fact that they perform on an elevated platform in the tent theatre. Throughout the play we learn that the Winds and the Angels are phantasms, existing only in the dreams of the birds. The birds dream the play's events, thus, we have a concentrically structured dramaturgy of dreams dreaming dreams, dreaming dreams. As dreamers of all other dreams, the birds are understood to be transcendent and god-like.

Taking the idea of dreaming as a form of ideological resistance, this complicated work employs a discontinuous narrative and non-naturalistic performance style and constitutes a celebration of counter-culture life. Thus, the Angels wear contemporary youth fashions and are emblematic of the 1960s generation. The counter-cultural quality was reinforced by the fact that the piece was "on the road" and

---

[4] See also Satoh's comments about the adaptation being in response to the members of 68/70 reading the original as ineffectual and bourgeois (Goodman 1988: 288).

touring for much of its life, while the artists were negotiating a collective working model as they went (Tsuno and Senda 1971: 40–52).

But even as the piece might have continued to investigate new forms of cultural production and espouse the progressive outlook of the 1960s space, *Dance of Angels* explores the abject failure of the protest generation to bring about lasting change. Goodman suggests that Satoh intended *Dance of Angels* to express "the fragmentation of bourgeois class consciousness [and] its understanding of history" (Goodman 1988: 288). As might be expected of 1960s culture, an implicit criticism of the Marxist dialectic and the failure of the old guard are suggested here, but there is also alarm at the loss of experimentation and progressive politics in the 1960s space. It is as if the symbols of the counter-culture are memorialized as empty promises. As Goodman notes, "by defining revolution as 'a dream' *Dance of Angels* brings the entire concept of the revolution into question" (Goodman 1988: 291).

In interview, Satoh's comments regarding *Dance of Angels* point to the fact that the piece was a critical assessment of the 1960s space. His comments are noteworthy in drawing together a number of threads discussed here and they warrant a longer citation:

> From a personal point of view, from 1967 to 1970 was the period that I was most intensely committed to political debate and to the political movement. The reason for that was that the movement at that time was not just a political movement, it had a cultural dimension as well. I participated frequently in direct action. At the time there were many independent study groups set up at universities especially at arts universities and I went to speak to these groups around the country. *In The Dance of Angels Who Burn Their Own Wings* I wanted to dramatize my experiences of those years. In the play, I was writing about the limitations of political revolution.
>
> One thing that you could compare it to is the work of Peter Weiss who was using Sade to talk about emotional revolution, or maybe its better to say, artistic revolution. Peter Weiss' intention was probably to criticize Sade, but in spite of that no matter how you read Weiss' play and no matter how you perform the play, the tragedy of Sade's life is always going to be more significant, more impressive than the life of Marat. However, in my interpretation, just as political revolution has its limitations so too does artistic revolution. And it would be good if people could reconsider Weiss' play in those terms rather than saying that personal revolution is more important than political revolution or vice versa.
>
> So I wished to consider those ideas (political, personal and artistic revolution). I wanted to look at human imagination and how it relates

to these issues. The personal experiences that I drew on were the Ampo demonstrations of the 1960s and the *Zenkyōtō* (student union) of 1970. The 1970 student movement had a much stronger cultural aspect to it. . . . The actual difference between the Ampo student movement and the 1970 movement is that in 1970 each university had its own *Zenkyō* group. Each was operating independently and pursued common goals without the overarching dominance of an outside group such as *Zengakuren*. . . . Then we saw the emergence of *Zenkoku* (another national student body), and the idea to link up all the student organisations into one structure. I did not go to the mass meeting where they decided to do this because I felt that by doing this they were simply setting up hierarchical and rigid, organizational mechanisms as had previously emerged in the *Zengakuren*. The development of such an organization concentrates power in one place and destroyed the communality and communication that existed before.

Looking back on that process it seemed to mirror what had happened in the 1960s where the various groups had tried to gain some independence from the Communist Party but in setting up their organizations they actually mirrored what they had tried to get away from. Looking at that process made me want to bring up these issues of repetition and circularity in my work. . . . What we wanted to do was get people together and collectively come up with fragments of structure and dialogue, then take those fragments into rehearsal with the actors and create a unified play. So the piece would come together theatrically rather than in a literary fashion, it would be a product of theatrical rather than literary imagination. The methodology was to bring together various elements which we had been aware of and various problems that we had been working with since the *Jiyūgekijō* (Free Theatre) days and bring them together with the events of the *Zenkyō*, and the failure of the student movement. (Satoh 1996)

Satoh's judgement of the *Zenkyōtō* seems correct. As Koschmann points out "some of present-day Japan's leading neoconservative ideologues were student leaders in the radical *Zenkyōtō* movement of the early 1970s" (Koschmann 1996: 247). The tendency for some *angura* groups to pattern themselves on traditional theatre and establish hierarchical systems of organization reflects a similar reality for Japanese culture at large. The play is therefore suspicious of cries for political revolution. By 1970, even the new left had hardened into political orthodoxy. As the play notes:

The first revolution: revolution within the
revolution
To turn oneself from inside out. (Satoh, Yamamoto et al. 1988: 303)

Thus, *Dance of Angels* proposes that theatre is only as revolutionary as its audience. The first revolution is the revolution of society. In a tone notable for its similarity, Guy Debord writes in his militant 1967 work *The Society of the Spectacle*: "So long as the realm of necessity remains a social dream, dreaming will remain a social necessity" (Debord 1995: 18).[5] The *Dance of Angels* challenges the 1960s generation to once more consider its political identity and think about the social necessity of dreaming. Later in the play, the writers propose a new transcendental order in which dreaming will no longer be a necessary cultural act. Even while they also acknowledge the improbability of this and reassert the need to dream on. But dreaming has limits. Real world events seemed to overrun such creative militant dreamscapes; the initial hope and joyful enthusiasm of the counter-culture is replaced in the play by a sense of hopelessness and nihilism. *The Dance of Angels Who Burn Their Own Wings* thereby marks the end of the 1960s space.

The end of the 1960s space?

As we move to considering the closing stages of the 1960s, we should acknowledge the many accomplishments of this generation. If measured, for example, in terms of wider political participation, a community sense of pride and purpose, improved rights for minorities, ecological awareness, and improved relationships with Japan's neighbours—not to mention the astounding achievements of experimental theatre over the next three decades—the 1960s project was of immense and lasting significance. At the same time, by the end of this decade it was becoming increasingly clear just how complex and difficult it would be to realize a truly radical project in Japan. In fact, the very vagueness of the *shutaisei* effect—so much about participation and experience—compounded the problem; while it anticipated a cultural revolution that was partially realized, exactly what effect selfhood realization was able to affirm in political terms remained a difficult question.

A number of events in Japan pointed to a sense of closure on the cultural aspirations of the 1960s space. Kersten and Suga, for example,

---

[5] So similar are these sentiments that perhaps Debord's work influenced the political sensibilities of the play.

both identify the constant and rising sense of infighting among radical sects (*uchi geba*) that came to preoccupy the protest movement
and further remove them from mainstream political processes. Kersten
suggests that the movement was imperilled by a failure of intellectual
leadership and lack of debate (1996: 227). Suga notes a debilitating
sense of impotence and inwardness; protesters were exhausted by
infighting and had no energy for anything else. We also noted previously how this sense of unreality culminated in the shocking Mt
Asano incident in 1972, when members of *Sekigun* were executed.
On the other hand, one source of hope perhaps lay in the massive
demonstrations organized to protest the resigning of the security
treaty. On June 23, 1970, more than one million people marched
in the streets of Tokyo (police estimated 774,000 whereas the *Mainichi
Shinbun* put the figure at 1.5 million (see Havens 1987: 206–7). Yet,
a sense of futility also seemed to pervade this movement and the
treaty was signed with little actual obstruction or difficulty from protestors. In other words, it seems that protest had become legitimate,
but also ineffectual.

Mishima Yukio's bizarre ritual suicide—an appallingly misguided
act of political protest—is another marker of the closure of the 1960s
space. As one of Japan's leading novelists and playwrights, Mishima's
turn towards extremist neo-nationalist politics and the unreal world
of his private army (*tate no kai*), mirrored the more fanatical cult-like
political formations on the left. The events of his suicide are well-known.
On November 25, 1970, after taking the commander of the Setagaya
unit of the self-defence forces hostage, his insistent speech to the
massed troops calling them to join in a military coup (reportedly
drowned out by press helicopters, Mishima, self-indulgent to the end,
had tipped-off the press), and his final disembowelment, has even
been the subject of a film (Paul Schrader's *Mishima: a Life in Four
Parts*). The response to his suicide was one of perhaps confusion and
disgust. How could the discourse of radical selfhood embodiment
come to such a prima donna-like end—or, as Suga puts it: "a performance that parodied underground theatre itself" (Suga 2003: 142).
For Igarashi, Mishima's death was an impossible, "farcical desire of
remembering war in the clean space" and had no impact on the
"peaceful everyday" world of the late 1960s (Igarashi 2000: 181–97).

Whatever the response, the idea of political protest in Japan had
changed. Suga's observation is correct, Mishima's garbled speech and
urgent posturing parodied the pure spirit of *angura*. Henceforth, the

radical imaginary of the *shutaisei* effect—the almost always potential critical space of 1960s politics—was so distorted that it would never recover.

Conclusion

To dream of the world is to subjectify and particularize human experience. In Japan in the 1960s, as was the case elsewhere, a new generation fought for a new ideal: one in which each person could fully experience life in all its force and splendour. Once reconciled with society, the generation hoped to resolve a strong sense of cultural dislocation and identity crisis.

Through a startling and powerful theatrical vision of disarticulation and cultural displacement, *angura* can be seen to have undertaken similar investigations and manifestly embodies the ideas of the *shutaisei* effect. As with the protesters, *angura* aimed through its actions to search for what Tsurumi calls "new modes of existence" (Tsurumi 1975: 22) to replace the repudiated *shingeki* culture and ideology. Life, art, and politics were re-examined as composite aspects of *shutaisei*. A Tenjō Sajiki manifesto arguably encapsulates the first wave of *angura* best where it states:

> We consider the theatre to be a crime. We are not working towards the revolution of theatre but we will whip the world with our imagination and theatricalize revolution. Tenjō Sajiki has gone beyond all drama of the past. We as a group will reform the world through poetry and imagination. Take power with imagination. (Mellen 1975: 275)

This statement is an inspiring expression of the subversive intent of *angura* and expressive of the uniquely ineffable qualities of the *shutaisei* effect.

PART TWO

CULTURE AFTER THE BUBBLE:
PERFORMANCE AND PERFORMATIVITY

CHAPTER FIVE

THEATRE IN THE BUBBLE ECONOMY

> Ultimately theatre is an economic commodity.
> (Bennett 1990: 126)

By the end of the 1970s, the momentum of *angura* as a manifestly radical political experience had been lost. A sense of uncertainty and a lack of confidence in the capacity of theatre to make meaningful political interventions was becoming more evident, and the critique of the avant-garde as an alternative form of expression was underway. In light of these factors, I argue that the experiential politics of the *shutaisei* effect was dulled by the emergent commodification of the 1960s space.

This transition is most visible during the 1980s—an age of overt consumption, speculative capitalism and generous spending on the arts and fashion. Sometimes called the era of the bubble economy (*babaru keizai*) and peaking in the second half of the 1980s, it is also associated with Japan's momentary "number one" global economic standing, the so-called East-Asian "economic miracle" and nasty trade wars with the US.[1] During this period, Senda Akihiko points to the emergence of a new entrepreneurial generation of theatre makers around this time (Senda 1991: 4–7). And it is around this occurrence—new forms of artistic production in the context of a concentration of consumer and speculative capitalism—that debates about politics and anxiety about the future of contemporary theatre culture in Japan come to rest.

The case of Tsuka Kōhei, leader of the first *angura* style company to enjoy popular commercial success, illustrates the point. Figures show that the final production of his company before its dissolution in 1980 "ran for three months at Kinokuniya Hall in Tokyo and attracted a total of 100,000 spectators" (Tonooka 1990: 43). As

---

[1] The period of economic expansion characterized by inflated stock market and land prices from February 1986 to 1990 is officially referred to as *Heisei Keiki*, as the period spans the transition from the *Showa* to *Heisei* eras. The term bubble economy was popularized by the Japanese media.

Naomi Tonooka notes, this factor alone raises the question of whether or not it is "appropriate to give the name 'little' to a theatre group that can attract such a huge audience" (1990: 43). In other words, the idea of *angura* was transformed: the question being, in what ways and to what ends?

Changes wrought in the 1980s era—including the acute effects of the collapse of the bubble economy after 1990—continue to influence trends in Japanese society, politics and culture. They have had lasting consequences for theatre and the arts in general. Most relevant to our discussion is the fact that events and experiences from this era have been said to display postmodern characteristics. As will be shown, the 1980s was a postmodern time. Although postmodern theory has been been overlooked in recent times and globalization studies have moved into many of the relevant sites of inquiry, postmodernism was an influential paradigm of cultural production of the bubble era. Postmodernism described political, economic, social and cultural trends in the bubble era. Indeed, the bubble economy itself might be said to exemplify a postmodern space in critical terms.

Hence, I will introduce notions of postmodernism as they pertain to Japan and theatre culture in the 1980s. Further, I will identify socio-political and economic changes in the Japanese case that shifted the grounds for *angura* and undermined its sense of activism. I will argue that a considerable part of the new wave theatre withdrew from counter-culture debates during the 1980s. Dissident outsider notions of *angura* gave way to the celebration of play, hyper-cuteness (*kawaii*), and an aversion to the problems of history. In fact, the degree to which *angura* vacated the oppositional ground in late twentieth century Japan is an indication of the significant decline of alternative politics in general. As will be shown, the ways in which *angura* is waylaid and diverted from sites of cultural resistance is itself a spectacular act of cultural revision. Most evident in this respect are the cultural capacities and creative energies of capitalism to draw within its ambit even the most oppositional and marginal forms of expression. In the following chapters not only was the 1980s theatre changed as a result, but, the avant-garde was necessarily reconceptualized and oriented towards theoretical debates and cultural politics.

Theatre in the 1980s was a kind of intense version of 1960s *angura* style; a distillation of *angura's* avant-garde dramaturgy and the subsequent attainment of an extremely accomplished, popular, commercially successful, contemporary theatre scene. It is interesting, therefore, to consider not only the political crisis for the avant-garde that develops, but also to think about how theatre in the bubble was able to interact with, and to a significant degree embody, the hyper playful intensities of Japanese society in the period under discussion. In the longer term, one can predict the blurring of popular and underground theatre systems.

Japan, postmodernism and the avant-garde

By now postmodernism has been widely debated and in many respects is an historical formation—one mainly associated with capitalist societies during the 1980s and 1990s. My intention is not to debate this point, but rather to map the critical space for an *angura* sensibility and resistant political outlook in performance in Japan after the 1970s in relation to postmodern theory. Key among postmodernism's early theorists are the philosophers Jean-Francois Lyotard (Lyotard 1993) and Jean Baudrillard (Baudrillard 1983).

Postmodernism is often described both in terms that highlight a diverse range of operative practices and in contrast to what it is not. Thus, postmodernism is an open system and seeks hybridity. It affords the sensibilities of play, *bricollage*, simulation, juxtaposition, contingency, interruption, and appropriation. It is counter to and seeks to theorize resistance to totalising perspectives such as those observed by postmodernists in relation to their critique of modern history as a continuum and the constantly rising, progressive construction of the post enlightenment worldview.

Lyotard, although dissatisfied with the term avant-garde, was one of first to theorize the obsolescence of the avant-garde in the face of postmodernity. He writes: "There seems to be general agreement about laughing at the avant-gardes, considered as the expression of an obsolete modernity" (Lyotard 1993: 173). Moreover, as Fredric Jameson demonstrates, the challenge that postmodernism makes to the avant-garde lies in postmodernism's characteristic twinning of the "logic" or imperatives of postmodern capitalism with aesthetic commodification and the corporatization of the cultural space (Jameson 1991). Jameson's influential study of postmodernism as the *cultural logic* of late capitalism builds its claim around the visible and rapid imbrication of political, economic and cultural spheres. A manifestly apolitical stance associated with postmodernism—or at the other extreme, what might be termed the progressive side of postmodernism's promise of cultural plurality and endless permutations of freedom—are both contested by the Jameson's critique. Jameson outlines a model of capitalism that inculcates at every opportunity, and seeks to naturalize the powerful cultural presence of the corporate state across cultures and at global levels of rhizomatic diversity.[2] In this respect, another important critic of postmodernism, Terry Eagleton, explores the almost narcissistic proliferation of postmodern modes. Postmodernist culture, he writes: "is both radical and conservative, iconoclastic and incorporated, in the same breath" (Eagleton 1990: 373). Eagleton is of course unsympathetic to postmodernism and is a foremost critic of its seemingly hidden political agenda. He measures the optimistic claim that postmodernism "represents the latest iconoclastic upsurge of the avant-garde" against:

> postmodernism's consumerist hedonism and philistine anti-historicism, its wholesale abandonment of critique and commitment, its cynical erasure of truth, meaning and subjectivity, its blank, reified technologism. (Eagleton 1990: 373)

Hence, we see the case for postmodernism's dystopic relationship to economy, and through economy, to politics and aesthetics.

The idea of postmodernism in Japan was widely debated among scholars of Japanese Studies in the 1980s. In an influential collection of essays titled *Postmodernism and Japan*, the editors note that: "Playfulness, gaming, spectacle, tentativeness, alterity, reproduction and pastiche are offered to guide the new age (of postmodernism)" (Miyoshi and Harootunian 1989: vii). We can say that the postmodern space centrally informs new modes of production and economy in Japanese society, proscribes some forms of expression while promoting others, suggests new relationships between formerly discrete activities—between the individual and the state, for example— and most important, makes problematic the idea of dissidence, and hence the manifestly avant-garde idea of resistance is lost. This then begs the question, what is the future for *angura* if not to be resistant?

---

[2] For evidence of the relationship between postmodernism and globalization, Hardt and Negri discuss global fields of power and cultural production in terms markedly similar to Jameson's, above. For example, they define globalization as a "a *decentred* and *deterritorializing* apparatus of rule that progressively incorporates the entire global realm within its open, expanding frontiers" (Hardt and Negri 2000: xii).

While Japan has often been said to evidence many postmodern attributes, the euphoria of the bubble era has for sometime elided critique. All the more important then is work by Japanese Studies' specialists such as Harootunian and Miyoshi (Miyoshi and Harootunian 1989), Clammer (Clammer 1997, 2000), and Mouer and Sugimoto (Mouer and Sugimoto 1986) that opens up an important critical space interrogating the relationship between postmodernism and Japanese society. These scholars are inclined to view postmodernism as an aspect of cultural domination consequent to the dysfunctions of capitalism. As their works variously show, historicizing the post-modern space and establishing a kind of local temporality is impor-tant if we are to gain an appreciation of the wider consequences of postmodern society. Hence, the problem that I will discuss here is not the question of postmodern theatre in isolation, with it charac-teristics of *bricollage*, sense of dislocation and meta-theatricalism (Aus-lander 1997; Kaye 1994), but the politics of contemporary theatre in Japan as a result of the postmodern political economy.

In this regard, the question of the aforementioned pluralities, the possibilities of emancipation sometimes connected with progressive modes of postmodernism, ought to be discussed further. Some caveats need to be drawn as well. Progressive postmodernism has given renewed impetus to the left, promising outcomes of greater freedom of expression by avoiding essentialism and false totality. Critical analy-sis of the literary canon, for example, when applying postmodern deconstructive reading practices—not to mention postmodernism's radical critique of established historical norms—have helped to show how authority and power circulate in the world and how cultural outcomes favouring power elites have been determined. However, we need to assess the extent to which this critical space is dimin-ished by the overwhelming context of corporatization and cultural commodification. For theatre, this means that the socio-political con-text of the event is crucial when attempting to identify the cultural position and ideological dimension of a theatre work, especially one that might be characterized as postmodern.

Most postmodern theatre exhibits liminal qualities, or liminoid characteristics. Like postmodernism, the liminoid is playful and open to chance. According to the performance theorist Marvin Carlson, the potential for liminoid activity to provide a site for social and cul-tural resistance is great. He suggests that:

> Liminoid, like liminal, activities mark sites where conventional struc-
> ture is no longer honoured, but being more playful and open to chance,
> they are also much more likely to be subversive, consciously or by
> accident introducing or exploring different structures that may develop
> into real alternatives to the status quo. (Carlson 1996: 24)

This is an influential viewpoint, indeed, a key methodological principle in performance studies. At the same time, the emphasis on the
characteristics of play have a somewhat different resonance in Japan,
one that puts into the contention the substance of Carlson's view.

The cultural environment of Japan changed fundamentally in the
1980s and few possible contexts for playful, anti-establishment performance remain as a result. Scholars observe the extent to which
commodity culture and the products of Jamesonian late capitalism
are the manifest socio-cultural reality of urban Japan. In this regard,
John Clammer suggests that developments in Japanese society that
have brought about the most changes in recent times are the interrelated forces of consumerism, urbanization, and the expansion of
the media. As a result, he argues, consumption became integrated
with the production of popular culture (Clammer 1997: 24–53). And
it is precisely around the point of how he defines consumption that
a critique of the liminal space as an alternative arises. Importantly,
Clammer argues that consumption is a site of subjectivity (Clammer
2000: 212). It is "a response to desire . . . it is *asobi*" (play) (Clammer
1997: 7). In other words culture has become, at least to a significant
degree, a process aligned with, if not moulded outright by, consumption with an identity quotient attached. Subjectivity, that may
have once been manifest in the *shutaisei* effect, has now been taken
over by material culture. Hence, while in some respects, Carlson's
notion of the liminoid as an anti-establishment strategy is an apt
description of similar rebellious strategies associated with first generation *angura*, its assurances of cultural liberation become increasing problematic as contemporary theatre developed as a culture
industry in parallel with advanced capitalism and the rise of the postmodern, corporate state in Japan.

That fashionable department stores became, in the 1980s, some
of the main producers of popular new wave theatre, is an indication of this trend. In one view, the 1980s new wave theatre can be
read as an emergent source of popular culture. Consumed by large
numbers of young people in Japan and featuring regular tie-ins with
popular magazines such as PIA, the leading entertainment and leisure-

lifestyle magazine with an extensive 'what's on' section, the popular new wave shares popular culture associations with other facets of a sophisticated entertainment industry.[3] To a degree, it has become a lifestyle commodity and part of a system of commodity production that includes "independent" cinema, art, fashion, and contemporary music. In other words, if the postmodern theatre is to be seen as a site of resistance then we should also keep in mind the controversial relationship that popular cultures have with contemporary manifestations of the culture industry and power.

This is precisely the point made by Marilyn Ivy when she suggests that: '"Popular Culture" must be carefully distinguished from the culture industry's productions, if the popular is to retain any critical force or resistant grass-roots connection to the "people"' (Ivy 1995: 195). Ivy argues that marginal cultural practices in Japan that survive, despite pressures to consolidate cultural assets, can be read as sites of resistance to hegemony, nationalism and capitalism. She shows how outsider and premodern practices such as shamanism and *taishū engeki*, convey a sense of unease about the transmission and stability of culture and express unstable and phantasmic representations of identity. The very endurance of these marginal cultures in the face of modernity indicates a compulsion towards a diversity of cultural practice. The very same might be said for the avant-garde, as indeed we have seen how this was also a goal of 1960s performance. *Angura's* interest in the premodern and *taishū* worlds predicates a similar sense of resistance. But if department stores sell the transgressive acts of a dysfunctional culture, what are the consequences for performance as a mode of cultural critique? Can we expect radical performance to move from the margins into the cultural mainstream and still hope to affect some kind of *angura* sensibility, some kind of *shutaisei* effect? And if we cannot, then is this still *angura*?

Theatre in the bubble

Theatre in the bubble shows a decoupling of performance from politics, an appropriation of style and its reconstitution as a commodity.

---

[3] PIA was first launched on July 10, 1972. PIA Corporation was incorporated on December 20, 1974.

Its very ubiquity and intensity, however, can also be read as an uncompromising representation of the 1980s space, and in its own way, 1980s theatre might unconsciously bring to light some critical points. Thus, for example, Senda recalls that from the time PIA began to give coverage to *angura* in 1984, the new wave was well on the way to becoming incorporated into a fashionable event culture (Senda 1991: 5). Senda coined the phase "*Shōgekijō* boom" to describe contemporary theatres increasing popularity and declining dissident status. PIA's apparent lack of coverage of the Japanese underground until the 1980s points to its continuing dissident status until the era of "*Shōgekijō* boom." Despite this fact, Senda continued to review contemporary performance often by referencing suggested social and political comments arising from the works. Tonooka also notes the evolving commercialization of *angura*. Her analysis of the impact of the introduction, in 1984, of a computerized ticketing system called "Ticket PIA" shows how easier access to ticketing, and increased marketing through magazine cross-promotion combined to feed the boom (Tonooka 1990: 44–46).

PIA shareholders include advertising and media companies—Densu being principal among them. As Japan's largest advertising agency, Densu was reported to control more than one quarter of all advertising business in Japan during the 1980s (Wolferen 1989: 177). Meanwhile the Seibu department store and leisure conglomerate became the major sponsor of contemporary theatre and arts during the same period. Hence, while the expansion of theatre activities helped create Tokyo's diverse contemporary scene, it is also the case that theatre in the bubble was becoming increasingly defined as an adjunct to fashion and modes of corporate spectacle. As Callas observes, with the building of the *Bunkamura* culture village in trendy Shibuya by the Saison group, corporations began to discover how contemporary art could be "good for business" (Callas 1991: 19). Viewed in this light, theatre in the bubble can be interpreted as aligning itself with the dominant values of postmodern capitalism, the affluent space of the 1980s.

Yume no Yūminsha

The most innovative and successful *angura*-style group associated with this time was Noda Hideki's Yume no Yūminsha (Dream Wanderers

Company). From the outset, when Yume no Yūminsha began in 1976 at the Komaba Shōgekijō, a theatre on the Komaba campus of the University of Tokyo where Noda and other group members were students, the company was characterized by a wild *angura* theatricality and an equally resolute avoidance of politics. Originally called the Komaba Circus Theatre, according to founding member and company manager Takahagi Hiroshi, Yume no Yūminsha was motivated by the aspiration "to make a different world" and "to reconstruct the environment of theatre" (Takahagi 1996). The playful sensibility suggested by the circus theatre name was carried forward in Yume no Yūminsha, a name that suggests a sense of wandering players or dreamers of an alternate reality. The motif of escaping into a fantasy-like space or an alternative playful dimension that might be compared to *Alice in Wonderland* is an enduring obsession in Noda's plays of the 1980s.

While the themes of departure and alternative realities are enduring concerns of *angura* as well, Noda's work can be seen as a move away from the *angura* paradigm. On seeing his first production by Yume no Yūminsha, a play called *Phantom Thief Ranma* (*Kai to Ranma*, 1978),[4] Nishidō Kōjin remembers how the sense of space was a marked contrast to the narrow and dark spaces of *angura*. His comments point to the ways that Noda's company differed from *angura* style; there was no darkness intended in Noda's theatrical world. Nishidō notes how the "space had a sense of freedom that the tent theatres do . . . you could say that this fact alone bought into the university situation the outlaw feeling of tent theatre, in spite of which there was not even the slightest whiff of any political message or intent or political consciousness" (Nishidō 2002: 126). Perhaps similar thoughts have led Robert Rolf to describe 1980s theatre in Japan as "the ludic conspiracy" (Rolf 1992a). Rolf is likely alluding to the fact that the utopian style of eighties performance was, in reality, an invention of advanced capitalism—the excitement of *angura* without the pain.

On the other hand, Yume no Yūminsha has been described as a "surreal kaleidoscope." Margaret Shewring points to the international

---

[4] The full title is: *Phantom Thief Ranma: In search of a family system in which husband and wife can coexist* (*Kaito Ranma-Teishu to Maotoko no Kyozon Dekiru Kazoku Seido o Motomete*, 1978).

popularity of the group and their clever imbrication of popular cul-
ture worlds in surreal performances. From her perspective, Yume no
Yūminsha is of the moment and she compares viewing Yume no
Yūminsha with the experience of channel hopping and surfing the
Internet (Shewring 1998: 95).

From 1976 until 1981, Yume no Yūminsha performed to student
audiences at *Komaba Shōgekijō*. Then, during the 1980s the company
began to develop increasingly commercial and large-scale activities.
The company moved into more financially rewarding markets motivated by the desire to realise a full-time acting ensemble. To achieve
this, Yume no Yūminsha successfully attracted corporate sponsorship, developed innovative marketing aimed extensively at young
audiences, engaged in widespread touring, and played to larger venues
for longer runs. Of these production activities, only touring had been
associated with the *angura* system; the other aspects were an effect
of Yume no Yūminsha 's willingness to rethink the *angura* paradigm.
After winning the prestigious Kinokuniya Prize in 1986, the company celebrated their ten-year anniversary with a season of their
work *The Stonehenge Trilogy* at the Yoyogi National Stadium. Tickets
for this huge sports venue were sold out one month in advance
(Shewring 1998: 94) and the production was seen as a coming of
age for *angura*—a new level of professionalism was evident. From the
late 1980s to 1992 when the company disbanded, Yume no Yūminsha
were playing to large auditoriums of 1,000 seats or more, running
programs for a month at a time. This compares to a more typical
situation where even acclaimed *angura* groups such as SCOT and
Red Tent, usually played in 300 to 500 seat spaces for three or four
nights only. Despite apparent reservations from Noda, Yume no
Yūminsha established a larger audience base and developed economies
of scale much greater than any other contemporary Japanese theatre. At the same time, the company worked to attract corporate
sponsorship and their marketing techniques were now adopted by
other companies—even those resolutely underground in spirit.

Such heights of popularity suggest that Yume no Yūminsha tran-
scended the small theatre mould, although popularity alone (or the
lack of it) should not be viewed as a defining feature of the genre.
In fact, Yume no Yūminsha is interesting precisely because many of
its aesthetic hallmarks are drawn from innovations of the 1960s avant-
garde. What is also interesting is the degree of continuity with earlier generations of artists and most importantly, the degree to which

this company can be seen to exemplify the appropriation of such theatrical techniques or aesthetics, and the consequences of this in political terms.

Yume no Yūminsha typifies the processes by which forms and elements of the former generation are transformed by a new generation who at the same time are reluctant to acknowledge—or explicitly deny—any sense of political context for their work. In this respect, the most immediately apparent lineage of 1960s theatre to Noda's style can be observed in his appropriation of non-narrative dramaturgical forms and an endlessly transformative theatrical space, combined with the hyperactive corporeal presence of the actor. Noda's theatricality has been described as: "light physical movement, jumping into the sky, fast dialogue, stories that don't go anywhere, no theme or message, making Noda seem like someone from outer space" (Nishidō 2002: 126).

The sense of speed is the most visible of dramaturgical elements in Yume no Yūminsha and is a condition that governs other modes of theatrical expression. Thus, velocity and forward momentum propel Noda's theatrical style, with the result that all other dramaturgical elements propel and enhance the sensibility of speed. As Hasebe Hiroshi writes, "Noda Hideki is . . . speed" (Hasebe 1993a: 477). In a memorable description of a three-minute sequence (twenty-seven lines of text) of stage business in the above-mentioned play *Phantom Thief Ranma* that is typical of Noda's acting style, Hasebe writes:

> (Noda) jumped off (a stage-prop cauldron). Then, he engaged in a choreographed fight. Leapt. Ran up the stairs. Skipped around. Jumped off. Knelt formally. Bowed. Clasped hands in front of his body. Leant back. Walked around busily. Kicked. Sat down. Clung to another actor's hand. Hopped on one foot. Bent backwards. Pointed. Drew his hand back. Turned his back to us. Stretched up. Leaned and whispered. Covered his mouth. Stuck out his chest. And he sat down. (Hasebe 1993a: 478)

Speed not only gives an atmosphere of constant activity on Noda's stage but also propels the textual narrative. The pace of dialogue is extremely rapid and sometimes beyond comprehension. Hasebe comments: "Noda drives his play almost into the realm of no-meaning" (Hasebe 1993a: 478). Design and musical elements also serve the absolute alacrity of form.

Noda's plays typically jump historical periods and geographical locations within the time it takes to change a lighting state. In one of his most popular works *Descent of the Brutes* (*Nokemono Kitarite*, 1984), for example, the actors begin the play dressed as astronauts landing on the moon, then they are depicted as children playing games, then singing and dancing as in a main stage musical number (shades of *Takurazuka*), and only a few scenes later, they find themselves in medieval Japan. The performance includes references to Jules Verne, the Kon Tiki boating expedition, and the rabbit in the moon legend from Japanese folklore. The motif of exploration provides a loose framework for a series of rapid fire and multi-layered concentrically evolving stories. The excitement of the 'quick change' of costume and make-up (*hayagawari*) that denotes the shift from one role to the next when performed by the actor in *kabuki* is suggested. In *kabuki* this is a demonstration of the skill of the actor. Here, we can read the *hayagawari* sensibility in kinetic terms. In Noda's theatre, there is rarely any logical reason for these kinds of shifts, nor for the often equally disjointed dialogue. It is about the thrill of speed and the momentum of the story as its transports the audience to new fantasy worlds. As Hasebe observes: "We cannot keep up with the speed of the story jumping over time" (Hasebe 1993a: 480). Nishidō suggests that this leaping back and forward between and across space and time, is a form of anti-relativity that does not have conventional links with the past (Nishidō 2002: 218). Instead, Noda seems to combine history and non-history, to collapse history and fantasy in an urgent moment of hyper-reality.

This seems to be as a very postmodern way of thinking. Noda's theatre is not an assault on reality designed to foster a spirit of cultural critique. Noda's works are akin to fantasy novels, populated with talking animals and other non-humans, gods, giants and dwarfs; they are escapist rather than challenging, child-like and cute (*kawaii*) rather than disturbing or grotesque. Hasebe makes a comparison with the simple-minded innocence of infancy and suggests that the fun lies in "eluding attempts by adults to decode it" (Hasebe 1993a: 479). Rolf considers Yume no Yūminsha's work "morally neutral" and emphasizes the sense of escapism while stressing that no social or cultural attack is intended or present in the work (Rolf 1992a: 127–9). If anything, Yume no Yūminsha's appropriation of 1960s theatre takes the form of pastiche.

According to Jameson, pastiche is "blank parody," a neutral practice of mimicry somewhat akin to Rolf's notion of moral neutrality. Thus, pastiche is without ulterior motive, without the "satirical impulse" and is consequently uncritical (Jameson 1984: 114). It is not without ideological significance, however, if one accepts Jameson's argument that the postmodern (and pastiche is a defining postmodern cultural practice) "is closely related to the emergence of this new moment of late, consumer or multinational capitalism" (Jameson 1984: 125).

In a relevant move, Rolf mounts a sustained critique of 1980s theatre in Japan and many of his observations correlate with such critical assessments of the postmodern space. Rolf argues that 1980s theatre in Japan exhibits four major characteristics: socio-political relativism; the preoccupation with childhood and fantasy; a ludic spirit, that is to say a theatre of play, surprise and humour; and a self conscious awareness of dramatic form, or the meta-theatre (Rolf 1992a). He notes, as I have above, the mindset among 1980s theatre makers who have little interest in making political statements. Their unintellectual simplicity, however, belies the fact that these artists are without exception graduates of elite, competitively ranked universities. Rolf extends this point in his comparison of eighties theatre to the aesthetics of *manga*:

> Not only is a cartoon world created on stage, but also programs and promotional materials are similarly marked by cartoons, cutely posed photos, bright colours, and the absence of critical and bibliographical commentary found in the material for older artists. The artists of the 1980s cultivate an unintellectual image that belies their obvious intelligence. (Rolf 1992a: 129)

Looking at the program for Yume no Yūminsha's farewell season, a production of *The Prisoner of Zenda: The Night of our Moss-Covered Infants (Zenda Jō no Toriko: Kokemusu Bokura ga Midorigo no Yoru*, 1992), we see ample evidence for Rolf's conclusion. The cover of the program (the poster or handbill was the same) depicts a journey-like board game (as with 'snakes and ladders' the player travels according to the roll of a dice) that narrates aspects of the performance. The page is divided into cartoon frame segments around a circular motif depicting the curtains of a theatre and the name of the show. Slightly above this appears the main sponsors name; Japan Rail is the sponsor of what it calls "JR express theatre" (*JR ekusupuresu shiataa*). Below is the play's title. All the typography is a boldly colourful but simple naive style and announces the fact that this, the 43rd season of Yume no Yūminsha, is the last. This is described as a 'last run' (*rasuto ran*), once again utilizing innocent and childlike loan-word

Yume no Yūminsha theatre program, author copy.

phrases. Dice are printed along with a cartoon-esque journey of cute characters, and short comments about the progress of the game or story. The program also came in a cellophane bag that contained a Yume no Yūminsha pencil and a JR paper lantern.

Turning the page of the program, one reads the credits of the production, followed by a photo of a ceramic sculpture of a sand castle; the game motif is continued in a picture of a spinning arrow that points to numbers. The next pages are a double spread featuring a Chinese chequers board and farewell messages from the company: "*Jaa ne bai bai* (bye bye) from Noda Hideki," and the tone is familiar and warm, humorous and nostalgic. Moving further in, we see some cute, purposefully naive childlike drawings of set designs and short pieces of text about the company, then large pin-up style photographs of each of the main actors and brief biographical details. These details are mainly about where the actor was born or went to school (primary school in some cases!), where they studied at university, and how long they have been in the company. Other comments reveal company members' enjoyment of the rehearsal process, or how they learned to speak fast-paced dialogue, respond to direction, and so on. The tone is forever winsome, breezy and light. Following this are three pages of rehearsal photographs heavily favouring Noda surrounded by smiling members of his company, usually going hard at some physical activity. In the centre of each page is a cartoon figure representation of a character from the play. In the back half of the program, there are five pages of advertizements including one featuring Noda. There is also an advertizement for Yume no Yūminsha videotapes of previous shows and some final childlike designed messages from Japan Rail and the theatre company, to the effect of "so long, see you around, thank you for your support." The tone is light, uncomplicated, and tinged with the nostalgic sadness of loss. The board game motif, the textual familiarity, and the happy energy of the cast photos all work to construct a picture of life that is a simulacra; like a playground, an amusement, a fun-filled adventure, a city of cuteness, a self-proclaimed commodity. In other words, a composite that confirms Rolf's observation that "the ludic spirit of today's theatre (like its apoliticalization and absorption in childhood fantasy) points to a certain mentality: indifferent, self-absorbed, comfortable" (Rolf 1992a: 129). Noda's company is presented almost like a wholesome youth club, an image that is conveyed through pictures of smiling and conservatively dressed young actors doing warm-ups and generally enjoying the Noda experience. This depiction of a young persons' theatre company is far removed from the dark and anti-social image of *angura*.

Making the link between Noda's sense of pastiche and channel-surfing, however, points to how the company's work draws on experiences of contemporary society, or in Shewring's words is "rooted in the youth culture of a generation brought up in a global village where everything is accessible" (Shewring 1998: 106). In this sense, Yume no Yūminsha might be interpreted as a site for the critical display—and hence interrogation—of the ludic space. Postmodern theorists might suggest that the act of critique lies within the act of representation here. In other words, the manic energy and aesthetic frenzy of Noda's theatre mirrors the spectacular, dizzying spiral of bubble capitalism. Capitalist abundance and cultural desensitization are expressed through the hyper-endurance and playful bodies on

Noda's stage, which subsequently enacts a world in which everything is fluid—a stage that is a microcosm of a city that is playfully transformed overnight. But there remains a question about the way that Yume no Yūminsha display their generational bond. For me, the lack of intervention remains a sticking point. For theatre to respond to the dialectic of late capitalism, it needs to factor an awareness of its own functions inside the system of production. It needs to explore processes of interpretation and share this insight among its viewers. Thus, a sense of self-referencing or deconstruction might be developed. Without this factor, Yume no Yūminsha risk replicating the postmodern feel—the smooth apolitical space of 1980s Japan.

Miyagi Satoshi's Transmission Book

A discussion of Miyagi Satoshi's solo *rakugo*-style performance *Transmission Book* (*Shosetsu Den*, 1992–3) offers a further point of comparison for discussing the avant-garde in the postmodern space of the late 1980s and early 1990s in Japan.

Miyagi is the director of Ku Na'uka and his performances often draw on traditional Japanese theatre styles with an additional comparative theatrical dimension. Miyagi began working in theatre after graduating from The University of Tokyo in the late 1980s. Atypically for a young, student theatre maker, Miyagi was not actually engaged in student theatre, but in student activism and was involved with issues relating to discrimination against Korean minorities in Japan. Miyagi's political activity continued despite an avowed interest in art, but he states that he was uncomfortable with the idea of attempting to bring the two activities closer together. While at university, Miyagi felt that art had no place in student activist circles, and was of the view that: "Art was separate from political issues and the world of politics" (Miyagi 1996). Miyagi has continued to speak about the separation of art and politics, arguing: "Currently in the developed world there are few people who believe that the arts can change things" (Miyagi 1996). Miyagi is consequently an interesting artist in the context of the present discussion as he is an articulate former activist with a well-developed political consciousness who, nevertheless, has explicitly sought to separate politics and art.

Arguably such pragmatism seems directly related to Miyagi's student experience. Like many of the post-1960s generation of student activists, he experienced the decline of idealism. Many of his generation became disillusioned, seeing how little the world had changed, even after the cultural upheavals of the 1960s. They experienced the trivialisation of the activist identity. Miyagi's disappointment in student politics rests in the feeling that "it was impossible to come together to do something productive" (Miyagi 1996). In his experience, political issues could only bring people together temporarily; soon political differences and struggles for power would manifest. With respect to politics, Miyagi seems to have become cynical.

Miyagi's theatre, however, does not show any degree of cynicism or bitterness. One reading of his company is that it remains concerned with political questions albeit in the form of continued experiments with modes of social collectivization. Thus, despite Miyagi's scepticism about the political, his theatre exhibits a determination to resolve the question of community, even if this means putting political problems and challenges into the background. Regarding his motivation for working in theatre Miyagi seems optimistically communal:

> Even though I realised that people could not form a true collective I thought is there not some way that people can accept other people's differences, come together, and work to do something? If this is impossible, then surely it is true that humans will be alone. (Miyagi 1996)

These sentiments can be seen as both the source of politics in Miyagi's theatre and the source of his subsequent avoidance of political subjects in his work. We see that he is motivated to work in collective enterprizes and negotiate individual participation in order to achieve a communal outcome. At the same time, he acknowledges how little support there is for this synthesis of the social and the creative, with the result (confirmed by his experience) that people seem less able to conceive of communitarian production models. A subsequent attitude of despondency is evident in the withdrawal from communitarian production modes into more hierarchical, director-centred ones. Perhaps ironically too, Miyagi has possibly become more fully integrated into sites of popular culture, postmodernism, and fashion cliques than any theatre artist of his generation. While this entanglement may be founded on an in principle concern to separate politics from art, one inevitably returns to political gesturing—despite the fact that this might be unintentional. Accordingly, we might ask to what extent is Miyagi's theatre able to offer a sense of critical distance to Japanese cultural reality, and to what extent is it caught up in a process of endorsing the politics of the postmodern space?

Written, directed and performed by Miyagi, *Transmission Book* was a kind of science fiction theatre, described by Miyagi as the story of a novel written by a 108-year-old man. The man writes in a future era somewhere in the mid-twenty-first century and depicts a world in which the whole genre of the novel has been in decline. Called *The Last Novel* and written over thirty years, it comprises "stories with-in stories with-in stories," with at least five hundred parts. The novel in question has become a powerful weapon in the hands of the mass media who now rule the world (in the story the media and the government are seemingly one and the same) and has the effect of brainwashing those who are exposed to it (Miyagi 1992).

Miyagi's narrative freely blended portions of the imagined novel with descriptions of its effects. The latter were often comic moments comprising details of the imagined day-to-day events of the future. A *fin de siècle*-like atmosphere was also conveyed by topical references to known behaviors, objects and locations. These were given quirky postmodern twists as they blended the familiar and everyday into the science fiction narrative; the fashion shopping district of Harajuku, for example, found its way into the sci-fi narrative. Like films such as *Blade Runner* (1982) and *Akira* (1990) or William Gibson's description of Chiba in the Cyber-punk novel *Neuromancer* (1986), part of the appeal of this genre lies in how familiar the terrain looks—how estranged the normal has become. Norma Field observes a similar manifestation in Tanaka Yasuo's *Somewhere Crystal* (*Nantoaku Kurisutaru*, 1980) in which urban life is characterized by its relationship to commodity, human relations are portrayed as increasingly streamlined into a kind of corporatist matrix, and the narrative comprises a list of consumer items and a description of shopping (Field 1989). The segue into science fiction depicts futures that we live in and slightly off-centre descriptions of everyday life in the near future of Tokyo; descriptions of what we eat, what we wear, family relations, the urban spaces, new products and new fashions, were all well received by the audience. In one sense, for all its clever parody, this is a play about shopping.

Miyagi's use of *rakugo* (a postmodern *rakugo* was one description of the performance) also draws attention to Japan's history. Typically, *rakugo* is a performance medium immersed in nostalgic depictions of the everyday world. Traditional *rakugo* tends to feature humorous descriptions of local communities and the characters that populate its friendly environment: the noodle seller, the local identity, the police officer, the bar hostess, the schoolteacher, and so on. Miyagi enacts a clever inversion of the tendency in *rakugo* to evoke nostalgic memories of the past, especially in depictions of images of *shitamachi*, an overtly mythologized space of working-class old Tokyo. Miyagi's sentimental celebration is for the opposite culture of *Yamanote*; not noodle sellers and craft-workshops or small local drinking places, but fashion boutiques, expensive cafes, and glassy department stores.

A more dramatic turn of events was a nuclear war scenario that was woven into Miyagi's narrative. This was not treated as a highly significant event, however, merely one of the many. Miyagi's story does not depict Armageddon. In this sense, it was very similar in sensibility to the opening scene of the animated science fiction feature *Akira*. The film begins with a nuclear explosion in "Tokyo 1992", but rather than dwell on the horror aesthetics of post-apocalypse, the very next scene is identified as "neo-Tokyo" in the early twenty-first century—completely reconstructed, gleaming and bright. The image signals that the nuclear future promises spectacle, not horror and in fact is euphoric. This overtly playful aesthetic overlay working on such a key image in the Japanese psyche surely distances Japanese cultural memory from history, especially the problem of atomic bomb victims (*hibakusha*). Certainly, Uchino makes a strong case that Japanese theatre in the 1980s expressed an overwhelming "urge to erase history" (Uchino 2000: 93). Such an impulse makes an historical reality seem distant, playful and without substance, while at the same time underlining the sense of historical amnesia regarding unpleasant realities of war and Japan's past.

The construction of *Transmission Book's* narrative was decentred, comic book-like, sketched out, uncomplicated, ingenious: as the performance proceeded it became increasingly difficult to distinguish between the portions that were descriptions of *The Last Novel* and description of the imaginary future world. The basic premise appeared to be the message that all information and all understanding was fictive, like a novel, but nevertheless retained powerful functions as an agency of mind control, and an instigator of disciplinary actions on society at large. This suggests, from Miyagi, a critical commentary on the nature of contemporary Japanese society.

However, the vexed question of popular culture in relation to such theatre events complicates this conclusion. *Transmission Book* draws on images of mass media and urban consumption. Miyagi has tapped into a 1980s economy *par excellence*. But is *Transmission Book* itself a product of the same world? While it might be argued that a sense of parody offers the promise of social commentary, in *Transmission Book* there is confusion between the satirical and critical investigation of commodity culture. Such a critical perspective is difficult to separate from the work's reified tone of celebration. This makes for a blurred and undefinable critical position. In depicting consumption as culture, *Transmission Book* manages to both tease and embrace the aesthetics of the controlling order. Hence, Miyagi's work seems to depart from the *angura* space in the sense that it ultimately refuses to take seriously the political function of theatre and art. Instead of critique, a process of reification is evident; we are absorbed by the jokes and reminded centrally of the playful varieties of capitalism. Thus, while the potential for subversion and critique is strong in this work, so too is the counterpoint argument. In Walter Benjamin's terms, not the protest but the reality of commodity culture comes to centrally occupy our minds. In this respect, Miyagi might be correct in saying that theatre and politics are different. The ironic stance of *Transmission Book*, even though keenly observed and brilliantly performed, cannot bring about political alternatives.

Conclusion

We have seen in this chapter how the *angura* space was transformed in 1980s Japan. The contemporary theatre scene grew in magnitude and crossed over into popular and commercial sites of production. Still based on a charismatic writer-director and a semi-professional company structure, the *angura* system nevertheless developed along professional lines. Marketing and corporate support are more visible and contemporary theatre groups proliferated in the age of the *shōgekijō* boom. Moreover, postmodern characteristics that were said to emerge in 1980s society were reflected in the theatre world. As Japanese society was observed as being liminal, playful and commodity-oriented, the contemporary theatre came to share these characteristics.

Concurrently 1980s theatre can also be said to have extended and developed the *angura* project. It demonstrates a pleasing and successful negotiation of theatrical tradition alongside the influence of modern styles of theatre and skilfully blends a proliferation of sources. It can be said that such theatre came to realise the *angura* ideal of interwoven and comparative dramaturgical themes co-existing in the one moment. Moreover, theatrical space and the performing body are explored in ways also evidently related to the *angura* world. In these ways, we can say that *angura's* originality and inventiveness came to fruition in a maturing and sophisticated 1980s theatre culture.

In respect of politics, however, we see the opposite situation emerge. The theatre seems to reflect a widespread anxiety about politics in 1980s Japan. Can it be that during the era of the bubble, a generation of theatre makers arose who resisted political positioning in their work as a matter of course? Instead, they seemed to create a theatre that was a closed system of aesthetic forms. The evidence shows that 1980s artists were either despairing about the possibilities for theatre to be a site of political commentary, or were hostile to the notion of linking theatre and politics altogether. There might be good reasons for this. For people coming to theatre in the 1980s, the protest generation's obsession with theatre and politics may have appeared nostalgic—if not a discourse intended to silence the younger generation.

On the other hand, it might be argued that the very absence of politics in these works might show a sense of longing for something more, some dissident or critical sensation. This raises the possibility that 1980s theatre artists might be ironically drawing our attention to absence and loss. The hyper-intensities of Noda's theatre, for example, might be an accurate reflection of the ambient euphoria and speed of capitalim; the subsequent intervention of showing the body in such volatile states might be the only form of effective critique possible in the postmodern age. However, because his works do not consciously address this point, nor direct our attention to this strategy, the existence of intentional critical positions in the work becomes less likely. Likewise, Miyagi's work might fetishize, rather than criticize commodity culture, and consequently reify dissent.

In other words, although 1980s bubble theatre can satirize and may attempt to evaluate systems of commodity power, such statements may simply have the effect of drawing our attention to the apparent immutability of the culture industry. In this situation, even the most outlandish or extreme works from the theatrical avant-garde come to be appropriated by the inexhaustible demands of postmodern capitalism and the culture industry. On the one hand, the avant-garde space in Japan was transformed into a diverse, compelling theatre industry in the 1980s. On the other, the postmodern space in Japan disallowed the latent possibilities for the contemporary theatre to function as a mode of political action: lacking a critical function, the avant-garde risks irrelevance.

PART THREE

RETHINKING RADICAL SPACES IN
THE JAPANESE AVANT-GARDE THEATRE

CHAPTER SIX

THEATRE AND POLITICS AFTER THE 1960s:
KISHIDA RIO'S *WOVEN HELL*

In the previous chapter, we discussed the decline of the political
avant-garde as symptomatic of the effects of postmodern capitalism
in Japan. We saw how this cultural turn paved the way for the
appropriation of the aesthetics of radical theatre production and their
subsequent repositioning as forms of commodity, play and leisure.
In short, postmodern society put to rest the idea of capitalism's overthrow, at least for now. At the same time as this was evident we
saw the widespread popularity of theatre, the "*shōgekijō* boom," and
its subsequent fusion with urban mainstream social trends, while also
continuing to espouse various sub-cultural associations and effects.
Thus, an expanded sense of the *angura* paradigm was evident as its
influences were seen in an increasing variety of theatrical contexts.
This development was accompanied by a rising professionalism in
the arts. We saw how production processes were interwoven or imbri-
cated within the entirety of the culture industry; as cultural production became circumscribed by economics, then the political space
for theatre and art became more difficult to analyse. Indeed, it is
surprising that a flourishing and dynamic aspect of the culture industry—keeping in mind that it is also a measure of its control—is the
degree to which modes of dissidence and critique have arisen in contemporary performance practices over the last twenty years. Various
contradictory forces promoted the ideology of materialism and consumption. Concurrently, however, the other side of this process was
the gradual fragmentation and diversification of cultural forms. Thus,
while the 1980s marked the reification of art it also gave rise to the
beginnings of a many sided contemporary theatre scene.

One result of the changing situation was a rethinking of politics
and theatre in light of the above factors. Although valuing the memory of radical dissent of the kinds seen in 1960s *angura*, such modes
of political intervention were now historical. People came to an
awareness that 1960s models were no longer effective or even desirable in the contemporary age. As we have seen, in the bubble era,

such art was likely to become commodified rather than radical, as Richard Schechner puts it: "soaked-up by the society it hates . . . co-opted and made fashionable" (Schechner 1991: 15).

I have noted that important achievements with a lasting impact on society grew from the 1960s space in Japan—many at a grass-roots level of political participation. At the same time, scholars and activists began to identify limitations and ideological divisions within *shutaisei* practices. Unequal power relations in *angura* groups, for example, have already been discussed. Here, I will begin to investigate how artists began to review the 1960s space and reappraise political conditions associated with *angura*. In particular, the absence of race, sexual, gender and class politics is evident in the 1960s and, in response, a new cultural doctrine associated with postmodernism can be observed. In contrast to the former sense of organic spontaneity and validity of experience as a marker of truth that was manifestly a part of the *shutaisei* effect, postmodern politics revolved around questions of one positioning in respect of the world. Such nuancing of the political space tends to favour provisional and discursive relationships alongside a growing sense of identity politics as a negotiated, nominally collective project.

Moreover, the arts—especially theatre and performance art—came to stress the fact that they were constructed and volatile events, capable of diversely imagined political interventions into the cultural landscape. Henceforth, art tended to foster a sense of positional meaning in order to invite provisional transactions. In an ideal setting, fluid and wide-ranging responses from audiences might be encouraged in such work. As everything on the stage came to be available to be read as a sign, theatre makers assumed that there would be diverse responses to their productions as a matter of course. In other words, the space of contemporary art was emerging as one of interpretive possibilities, semiotic analysis and not, it should emphasized, unmediated or woolly experiences. As a result, people began to argue that theatre and art functioned not so much as a mode of intervention *in* social reality, but as a method of critique *of* social reality. In the following case studies, I will outline how artists and groups came to explore the range of new perspectives for theatre in an age of cultural politics as opposed to revolution.

Brief acknowledgement should be given to the widespread social changes in Japan in the 1990s. The period from 1989 until the end of the century was marked by adversity and an emergent sense of crisis in Japanese society. In 1989, the long and troubled reign of the *Shōwa* Emperor ended. Controversial questions about his role in wartime Japan were broached and his relevance in the postwar era was debated more vigorously after his death. Subsequently, the historical record of Japan as an imperial power that carried out numerous unacceptable acts of exploitation was more widely discussed. Issues such as the use of Asian women as military sex slaves (*jūgun ianfu*), Chinese prisoners as test subjects in medical experiments and the cult of emperor worship—all manifestations of Japan at war— were becoming a subject of vigorous debate. Meanwhile, the fall of the Berlin Wall signalled declining fortunes of communism and a geo-political shift towards America becoming the sole superpower— the first US Gulf War of 1991 saw Japan contributing billions of Yen in lieu of direct military support. Also, in 1991 Japan entered a long period of economic recession. Numerous financial scandals, political intrigues, and resurgent neo-nationalism cast a pall over the decade as a whole and put an end to the superficial euphoria of the 1980s. Events including the Hanshin earthquake (January 17, 1995) in Kobe, the visible tides of unemployed and homeless people living in parks, school bullying and seemingly inexplicably violent acts by young people, and the March 20, 1995 releasing of Sarin Gas into the Tokyo subway system by the Aum Supreme Truth Sect (*Aum Shinrikyo*) were deeply disturbing. Such events were markers of a society at the edge of a more dystopic social reality. The clean space that became the euphoric space was suddenly sinking into a quagmire.

We will now consider the example of performance in relation to questions of gender politics in a discussion of work by Kishida Rio (1946–2003) and the company Kishida Jimusho + Rakutendan. In particular, Kishida's play *Woven Hell* (*Ito Jigoku*, 1984, 1992) in a production by Kishida Jimusho + Rakutendan in 1992 will form the basis of discussion that will highlight aspects of material feminism in relation to Kishida's feminist history.

Kishida Jimusho + Rakutendan

Kishida Jimusho + Rakutendan opened a link between first generation *angura* and the political reawakening of experimental theatre. Founded in 1983, this joint company came into existence when the

Kishida Office (*Kishida Jimusho*) merged with Rakutendan. Kishida began working in theatre with Terayama Shūji in 1971 and Terayama remained one of her most enduring influences. Kishida co-wrote prominent avant-garde Tenjō Sajiki works, including *Knock* and the remarkable, characteristically *angura* style film, *Le labyrinthe d'herbes* (Kusa Meikyu, Grass Labyrinth, Terayama and Kishida 2003).[1] In 1984, Kishida wrote the award winning play *Woven Hell* (*Ito Jigoku*) for performance by the Kishida Jimusho + Rakutendan theatre group.[2] Along with Kisaragi Koharu (1956–2000), Kishida was one of two best-known, contemporary women playwrights working in a field dominated by male writers and directors.

Director Wada Yoshio established Rakutendan in 1976, while Kishida founded her company in 1981. In 1982, Rakutendan performed Kishida's text *The Butcher of Hanover* (*Hanover no Nikuya*) directed by Wada and this production bought the two groups together. Kishida Jimusho + Rakutendan evolved as a company staging texts written exclusively by Kishida, offering performances that in some ways bore the hallmarks of Terayama's theatrical style; a baroque and dark atmosphere, for example. One observes stage craft reminiscent of Tenjō Sajiki including the use of ghoulish bodies in performance, pop-vaudeville surrealism, and references to premodern Japan. As in many Terayama productions, Kishida Jimusho + Rakutendan used fire as a kinaesthetic effect and played music at cinematic levels of intensity.

However, Kishida Jimusho + Rakutendan differed from other companies working under the influence of Terayama, notably Ban'yu Inryoku, the theatre group headed by former Tenjō Sajiki composer

---

[1] In the film based on a story by Izumi Kyōka, a young man tries to find the lyrics to a half-remembered tune from his childhood. His journey takes him into a surreal world of imagination and hallucination. The film is therefore characteristic of Terayama's surreal, labyrinth of the mind approach. Such strangely haunting and beautiful images sometimes recur in Terayama's theatre from one play to the next, and are remembered in the mind's eye long after they have gone.

[2] *Woven Hell* was awarded the 29th Kishida Prize in 1984. Named after the *shingeki* playwright, Kishida Kunio, the Kishida Prize is an annual award given to a play judged by a panel of experts to be the best, modern Japanese play for the year. A translation of the play's title as *Thread Hell* appears in Sorgenfrei and Tonooka's translation (Kishida 2002). The title *Woven Hell* is taken from an unpublished translation authored by writer Paddy O'Reilly for the company's 1992 tour to Perth and the January and February 1992 Adelaide Arts Festivals in Australia. With Kishida's approval, the play was billed as *Woven Hell*.

J. A. Seazer. Seazer's work often followed a distinctive Terayama
style and the company usually performed Terayama authored plays.
In contrast to Ban'yu Inroyku and others reviving Terayama plays,
however, Kishida Jimusho + Rakutendan was more motivated to
critically engage with issues in contemporary society. In particular,
Kishida's evolving concern with interpersonal relations, intercultural
politics and material feminism came to characterize her work and
the work of other groups she was involved with.

Kishida was an early advocate of collaborative performance and
came to view intercultural performance as a way of building bridges
with Japan's neighbours. She made a joint Japanese-Korean production called *The Blessing of the Passing of Time* (*Seiori Chotta*, 1992)
and later *Flower* (*Hana*, 1994), a work that featured multiple texts,
song and dance and was reminiscent of *madung* performance from
Korea. For *Bird, Bird, Blue Bird* (1994), Kishida devised vignettes
investigating the Japanese occupation of Korea from the point of
view of Koreans. Nishidō Kōjin confirms that Kishida was a key
figure in theatre exchange with Korean artists: "Although these days
theatre exchange with Asia is being promoted by public arts organizations, Kishida was one of the people who made the connections
for the program to happen" (Nishidō 2002: 106). More recently,
Kishida was the playwright for the Singapore-based Theatreworks-
Flying Circus intercultural collaborative productions of *Lear* and
Desdemona. Both works were directed by Ong Ken Seng and featured
performers from various Asian cultures performing in their own language and using their own performance traditions. *Lear* highlighted
diverse performance traditions from the Asian region; *nō* and Beijing
opera featured centrally in the performance, which was applauded
by critics and popular among audiences. On the other hand, *Desdemona*
was considered by the artists as a work-in-progress to "deconstruct
the politics of intercultural theatre" and very interesting for this fact,
but less popular with audiences, and perhaps less developed as a
project overall. Much has been written about these innovative productions (e.g. Grehan 2000; Nishidō 2002: 102–4) and this is not
the place for further discussion. Suffice to say that a feminist poetics manifestly realized in *Woven Hell* endures in Kishida's *Lear*. As
Nishidō writes: a "critique of the father figure in *Lear* signified a critical perspective that straddles Asia. The colonialism of the original
was rewritten to show Asian women strangling the Western father/ruler
figure" (Nishidō 2002: 104). Hence, while Kishida was involved in

many aspects of theatre production in Japan, her exploration of feminist poetics extending to a deep awareness of history might be said to be representative of her dramaturgical style. Certainly, qualities associated with material feminism and social feminism are evident in informing her political convictions and creative expression.

Woven Hell, *history and feminist poetics*

Writing on the theme of the relationship between feminism and modernity, historian Janet Wolff comments:

> Women, unable to articulate their specific experiences and perspective in the world in a language formed and moulded by the dominant group, men, might now have the opportunity to speak for themselves, working with these new, barely formulated literary and linguistic tools. (Wolff 1990: 78)

Kishida's work can be understood in light of this statement. Her work develops new languages and tells women's stories. Her theatre is precisely about finding a social voice for women so that they might speak for themselves and about their social and political condition.

Woven Hell is set in 1939 in the Kameido silk spinning and weaving factory. Twelve women spin thread by day in the mill that transforms into a brothel each night. In the play, once inside the "Weaving House" (*Itoya*), the women no longer remember their outside lives. The master of *Itoya* has given them new identities. Only two are allowed: factory worker and prostitute. The women have been programmed to accept these identity frames to serve the demands of prewar industrial capitalism and men's demanding sexual urges, without protest. A young woman named Mayu (literally meaning 'cocoon' and made of silk) arrives at the factory bringing with her memories and visions of the world beyond. Her presence unsettles the women and the power of memory, carried along by seasonal winds, gives the women the strength to challenge their ruler-captors. Finally, regaining a sense of their former identities these women's histories come alive once more.

The play refers to the common historical practice of indentured labour in Japan. Poor farmers were sometimes forced to sell their daughters as indentured labour for factories and brothels in cities. Before World War II, people from poor regions could only hope to break a cycle of poverty over generations, if at all. As is typical of such situations, the poor only have bodies to trade; in Japan, work in mines, factories and brothels was typically harsh and conditions of employment little better than a prison. Women's debt to their owners was sometimes sexual as well as menial, and thus, was particularly hard felt.

Surprisingly, however, although *Woven Hell* depicts the downcast social history of prewar Japan, Kishida said that she finds the early *Shōwa* period of the 1930s to be one of the most important and even optimistic in Japanese history (Kishida 1992). It was the first era of consolidated economic and political development and despite the above mentioned practices, Kishida considers this a time during which a stronger sense of independence was especially evident for women. Even though early modernization and the increasing presence of militarism made particular demands on women's freedom and their bodies; there was also a latent, cosmopolitan women's rights movement and, in wartime, women were able to work in places and activities otherwise denied them. Growing from these contradictory trends, Kishida finds inspiration from the small suffragist movement of the 1920s on the one hand, but also identifies the tools of women's oppression on the other. And while women were often in difficult and oppressive situations in the prewar period, Kishida suggests that in some ways postwar Japan is even worse. The possibilities for feminist activism, she argued, have been blunted by materialism and the pursuit of a culture of consumption (Kishida 1992). Hence, the setting of the play in 1939 is a crucial moment; a time when women were strongly denied their rights, but in this play at least they were able to gain an awareness of selfhood and take control of their lives. Perhaps Kishida is suggesting that in contemporary Japanese society, the realisation of oppression has become less visible, less felt, and consequently there is less resistance.

As noted above, the presentation of *Woven Hell* reprised many of the distinctive forms seen in early *angura* and is a window into 1960s theatre. In the opening moments of the play, male figures—the recruiters of indentured labour—are portrayed as grotesque gangsters lit by the flicking of bundles of matches (a device developed by Terayama and used on many occasions). As they called out the terms and conditions of employment, large size picture cards from the traditional Japanese card game *hanafude*, featuring depictions of flowers and plants, were seen at the back of the space. Each woman in the factory was known by the name of a flower; as their names were called, cards, each with an image of a flower, were revealed. This too incorporated a Terayama-like motif and *hanafude* images that recall the prewar Japanese social under class of gangsters are also seen in designs for earlier Terayama works. The spinning wheels of *Itoya* were used to particularly good effect. In tableau, the women on stage dressed in white kimonos—changing in to red kimonos at night to signify the brothel—were seen spinning in unison. Lit by shafts of pure white backlight they cried out the daily sequence of events. In one sequence the women reported to the master how happy they were, thus, signifying their loss of memory for any other place or time. "*Ii asa deshita*" (it's been a fine morning), they replied in chorus to the masters' questions, thereby reinforcing their deep social conditioning to the needs and wants of the factory enterprize. A tangling thread that interrupted the women's spinning work in another scene in the performance was a sign to them that a new arrival would come to *Itoya*; it would be Mayu searching for her mother. The moment when Mayu finally confronts her mother was staged by having the two actors tangled in the red twine of the spinning wheel, drawing each other closer together—Mayu trying to cut them free from the entanglement. Looking like *butō* performers, ghoulish male figures intruded during the scene snapping at the tangles with scissors.

From these images we can begin to see how *Woven Hell* is a dystopic feminist text tracing parallel histories of generations of women in Japan. Exploited for their labour and sexuality, they are also without identity. They are both hidden and marginalized by their forced employment in sweatshop spinning factories and literally without identity as the family register in Japan follows the male lineage. If a woman marries, then her name will be listed on her husband's family register and her lineage terminated. If she does not marry, then her lineage will end upon her death. Kishida explores these twin dimensions of absence—the institutional and material denial of women's identity—against a background of overpowering images of capitalist–militarist oppression.

The threads representing tangled family and social relations are an enduring symbol in *Woven Hell*. The motion of spinning wheels binds the women of *Itoya*. Winds of the four seasons carry their story. Knots in a Peruvian rope hold memories from the past. Regarding these images in her work, Kishida commented:

In *Woven Hell*, there are two major kinds of thread. The first is the kind of thread between a mother and daughter, the thread of blood. The second is the kind of thread that binds us in various ways within society. As for the wind, it is a wind that awakens the women of *Itoya*. It opens their eyes, it brings alive the happiness of their childhood. Through the blowing of the various season winds: summer, autumn, winter and spring, the women start to remember. It is a wind that gives them power. They are winds that awaken emotion. (Kishida 1992)

Thus, the threads are woven into an image of oppression and family, a composite image that is also on the point of splitting apart. By extension of the image of family, the authority mechanism of patriarchy is also explored. With the wind comes the possibility of release—a release into emotion. This gives the women power, but it might also return the women of *Itoya* to a sense of their own entrapment. This unsettled way of thinking about the play has been noted by Nishidō who writes: "The women who appear in Kishida's play are blown around by the powers of the times and are sacrificed to these powers" (Nishidō 2002: 108).

Tonooka explores the duality of domination and self-control that is suggested in her extensive discussion of *Woven Hell*. For Tonooka, it is not so much emotion that is problematic, but the related question of subjectivity: how the women in *Itoya* might be seen to construct their world in feelings and through the senses. Subjectivity also explores notions of autonomy. Under the right circumstances, it might undermine proscriptive reality and, thereby place feminist discourse in an equal contest with patriarchal social reality. Tonooka writes that Kishida: "Believes that subjectivity is a socially constructed narrative, and that history is also an arbitrary narrative created by those in a position of power" (Tonooka 1990: 174). In *Woven Hell* she adds, "the playwright seems to search for a bonding between women as a possible way to redefine a relatively autonomous mode of subjectivity for women" (Tonooka 1990: 194). As Tonooka points out, Kishida proposes a strategy of deconstruction that challenges more simplistic notions of subjectivity as a site of liberation and instead "emphasises that both history and subjectivity are narratives controlled by men" (Tonooka 1990: 194). Her stance raises the question of subjectivity as a political issue in a way that the *shutaisei* debates of the 1960s did not. Nineteen sixties versions of subjectivity have been criticized for their extreme individualist turn and core assumption that subjectivity was universally shared among all members of society. For Kishida, subjectivity must be recast as a feminist strategy. Yet, Tonooka notes that at the end of the play "what we see is the endless repetition of the same love-hate relationship between mothers and daughters" and concludes that the work "underscores the hierarchical structure which reinforces a women's effacement of self with men on a higher level" (Tonooka 1990: 201–3). According to this reading, the attempt to discover an "autonomous mode of subjectivity for women" has failed. There is no possibility for escape from external subjugation and subjectification. Even the notion that women are by nature somehow subjective (in a way that male power is not) is a self-replicating closure for women, a circular self-limiting trap.

Feminism and history

Conversely, if we consider the discussion of history in *Woven Hell*, then perhaps a more affirming political intervention can be read in the work. As Tonooka shows, in Kishida's plays not only subjectivity but also history was the providence of male power. Hence, there is a recurrent need to realign history and make the memory of the past more nuanced and inclusive, to make history work as a critical space for the advance of women specifically and the analysis of power in general. In reference to *Woven Hell* there are a number of interrelating points to consider.

First, is the importance that Kishida Jimusho + Rakutendan attached to the idea of *dekigoto*—meaning an event or a happening. As *Woven Hell* director Wada Yoshio said:

> When we are thinking about the play, one of the words that Kishida often uses is *dekigoto*. For us, words are not the only factor of the play, and our performance is not just technique . . . (it is witness to life). Each time an actor stands up and gives life to a part is a *dekigoto*. (Wada 1992)

I argue that the notion of *dekigoto* is a factor in creating the sense of a multidimensional feminist poetics that is present throughout *Woven Hell* as a whole. Moreover, processes of history alongside personal narratives that might constitute a feminist poetics if imagined within a feminist political frame have bearing on this point as well. As the actor brings their historical experience to the stage and gives life to a part, in the context of *Woven Hell*, it might be understood as aiming to realize a kind of feminist historicity and materialism. That is to say, to connect the moment of acting to the experience of the actor is a political unity that rests on material feminism and feminist interpretations of history. While personal and intimate, this moment also forms a relationship with the social world beyond the theatre. It makes the idea of presence on the stage become imbued with a history of embodiment and a history of theatrical signs that audiences might read in order to perceive a feminist sensibility of the world. This is perhaps similar to Bertolt Brecht's notion of *gestus*. Brecht used the idea of *gestus* to describe a political aesthetic through which incidents of life are illustrated in a political manner on the stage. "A language is gestic when it is grounded in a gest and conveys particular attitudes adopted by the speaker towards other(s)" (Brecht 1974: 282). Such attitudes when adopted by the actor are unavoidably informed by the actors' experience. Their history, and the historical and social dimensions of theatrical signs combine; together these are primary sources of determining meaning in theatre.

In *Woven Hell*, two forms of *dekigoto* or gestic performance seem to standout—both relating to history. The first is philosophical and construed from the absence of history and memory, literally in the play the vanishing past. This is in contrast with the desire to know oneself, to know the past and therefore to have a sense of one's place and identity. The broken threads of history are the threads of entrapment that condition the women's existence and ensure their domination. Hence, the women of *Itoya* live in an endless present of routine captivity, their every moment and life-event is conditioned by their lack of awareness of existence over time. When Mayu arrives, she brings with her a wind carrying memory and history. Consequently, the women become alive to the entrapment that the momentary *dekigoto* has thus far established as the norm.

A second appearance of the *dekigoto* has a more affirming tone and stresses the importance of placing actors, empowered with feminist presence, in the social space that theatre defines. In other words, the overwhelming presence of women and their own concerns come to dominate the *mise-en-scène* in *Woven Hell*. This reaffirms the need for an overwhelming presence of women in society. The former understanding of *dekigoto* relates to the internal narrative logic of the piece, while the latter connects with social and political contexts. At this level, actors connote a series of gestic feminist moments or events that contest that which is presented as the inevitable outcome of history. By extension, the gestures of performance—the actors tied up in threads and endlessly turning their spinning wheels—have an historical dimension aimed at referencing wider cultural experience.

From the perspective of history, we also note that theatre has concentrated on the male quest and depicts a gestic world construed from male points of view. Kishida inverts this and a feminist sense of *dekigoto* or *gestus* imbued with feminist poetics is the result. By reading the *dekigoto* back through Brecht, we can see how it might begin to proliferate feminist qualities. In each moment of performance, one might observe a continually renewed feminist presence that exposes and explores the relations of gender inequality and power. The construction of meaning in the space should resonate back through history as well as reflect present day experiences of women in Japanese society—a task that the narrative of the play and the central position of the female actors well supports. *Woven Hell* therefore presents moments of *dekigoto-gestus* that are constructed to convey feminist attitudes to an audience.

Another significant quality of *Woven Hell* in its articulation of feminist poetics is the fact that Kishida's play depicts ruling forces—economic, military and sexual—as essential components of a male capitalist–military order. The play suggests that unless this factor is addressed, women's autonomy—subjective or otherwise—will never be achieved. This means that the notion of subjectivity as a site of power must be read in relation to the systems of power that underscore Japanese society and have made it oppressive to women. Accordingly, much more can be made of the factory as the site of women's containment in *Woven Hell* and the appearance of soldiers that the women must service as prostitutes each night. The former image evokes the domination of capitalism and modernity, while the latter suggests a reference to militarism and, as a source of Japanese patriarchy, a site of violence perpetuated against women. Perhaps also implied is the issue of comfort women. Given Kishida's deep knowledge of Korean history and her desire to criticize the history of Japan–Korea relations, a connection between the fact of mainly Korean women being forced into prostitution during Japan's occupation of Korea and the image of the brothel in its prewar Japan setting is suggested. In total effect, both prewar and postwar domains of power are represented as constituent dominating forces made from military and corporate agents. Hence, faceless authoritarian images of soldiers, factory bosses, and recruiters in the play are presented as inextricably bound up with mechanisms of capitalism and militarism, while they are also presented as predominant agents of women's oppression.

By considering these factors, it becomes apparent that *Woven Hell* places the question of women's autonomy in relation to a reading of Japan's history. In this sense, Kishida seems to argue that the question of women's subjectivity should be read within an understanding of history and material politics. Thus, women's absence is doubled. It is understood because of the reality of male power that is manifest in Japan's military past and simultaneously in the contemporary era of capitalism. Women are absent in the public space for this reason and the recuperation of women's autonomy will only occur when the social boundaries that make women absent are addressed and ultimately collapse. The play therefore warns that gendered authority determines social space and class.

Conclusion

Subjectivity is a useful strategy in the task to expose patriarchal capitalism. It is an acknowledged position from which women can speak and a powerful tool in the destabilization of proscriptive reality. Nevertheless, the ultimate goal of shifting the dystopic political and social space is not addressed at this level. Kishida states that: "since *Woven Hell* is a play about the restoration of female rights, I want women in the audience to think about what they are being bound by, to become more aware of that" (Kishida 1992). She suggests that advancement is possible only when memory is restored: a memory of the institutional oppression of women and women's consequent absence, and a history of institutions that manufacture absence and containment. *Woven Hell* is such a history, an investigation of the history of modernity and capitalism in twentieth century Japan. The twin images of factory and soldier represent the two dimensions of this historical trajectory. They are the forces that have shaped the institutions and agencies that silence the experience of women in Japan. In other words, by their feminist reading of Japanese history in the modern era, Kishida Jimusho + Rakutendan expose a network of relationships built upon the necessary strategy of women's effacement.

CHAPTER SEVEN

KAWAMURA TAKESHI AND DAISAN EROTICA:
THE 1990s DYSTOPIAN SPACE

> Japan as a nation is well on the way to eradicating his-
> tory. As long as we stay within Japanese society, this will
> induce a pseudo-utopian euphoria. The moment we step
> outside and look around, we will see our own condition
> for what it is: deformed, distressed, and unnatural.
> (Yomota 1991: 47)

Even while the aesthetics of *angura* became absorbed by bubble capitalism, more critical assessments of Japanese society were also emerging. In this chapter I will examine how some of these responses were
attempting to make Japan's sense of decline more visible. Thus, while
even the open-minded Senda Akihiko was moved to comment that
during the 1980s "the relentless logic of capitalism . . . unified us all"
(Senda 1997: 10) others were determined to present another more
dystopic picture of the contemporary world. This markedly radical
theatre push was often critical of the 1960s and was in no way nostalgic for a return to the old ways of protest. It was not moved by
what Senda calls hung over "phantom concepts of revolt" (Senda
1997: 8). Instead, this movement took several paths that we will consider in these final chapters. While each of the examples discussed
are distinctive in their creative forms and ideas, all arise in the context of new trends in society and new forms of power. Hence, important events and experiences from the 1980s and 1990s including
Japan's recession, new and omnipresent forms of media and technology, the rise of globalization, America's first Gulf War, and a
flourishing international market for Japan's contemporary arts are
addressed in the work of these artists.

Kawamura Takeshi (b. 1959) and his group Daisan Erotica are
one of the best examples of this trend. The group explores a vision
of Japan as one conditioned by an ongoing state of "pseudo-utopian
euphoria"—a condition akin to Senda's observations regarding the
above trend towards homogenization. This observation correlates
with my negative assessment, in political terms, of Japanese postmodernism in previous chapters. Daisan Erotica expresses the opposite

view to bubble theatre's playful style and it is this ludic view that
Kawamura's group comprehensively rejects. Hence, it is a composite picture of Japan as "deformed, distressed, and unnatural" that
the group is concerned to expose. The theme of a theatricalized and
at the same time imminent sense of dystopia in Japan is therefore
an appropriate theme to frame a discussion of Daisan Erotica, while
also providing an important context for reading contemporary Japanese
theatre as a whole.

Daisan Erotica

Daisan Erotica was founded while Kawamura was a student at Meiji
University in Tokyo in 1980. All their productions are created and
directed by Kawamura who, on occasion, also takes on acting roles.
With regard to production systems and company organization, Daisan
Erotica began as a typical *angura* group. Its first production was the
apocalyptically titled *Fin de Siècle Love* (*Seikimatsu Rabu*, 1980) and the
company has since produced one or two new productions each year.
Daisan Erotica's best known productions include: *Nippon Wars* (*Nippon
Woozu*, 1984), *Last Frankenstein* (*Rasuto Furakensutein*, 1986), *Freaks* (*Furikusu*,
1987), *A Man Called Macbeth* (*Macbeth to yu na no Otoko* 1990), *Tokyo
Trauma* (*Tokyo Torauma*, 1995), and *Obsession Sight/Site* (*Obuseshon Saitto*,
1996). In 1985, Kawamura received the Kishida drama prize for his
play *Shinjuku Dogs #1* (*Shinjuku Hakkenden, Dai-ichikan Inu no Tanjo*). In
1997, he received an Asia Culture Council award allowing him to
observe theatre in New York, to where he returned in 1998 to direct
two plays from Mishima Yukio's *Modern Noh Plays* (*Kindai Nōgaku Shu*)
at New York University's Department of Drama, Tisch School of
Arts. The Mishima plays—*Yoroboshi* and *Sotobakomachi*—had been performed by Daisan Erotica in 1989. In 1999, the company performed
Kawamura's *The Lost Babylon* (Rosuto Babiron, Kawamura 2000b)
and in 2000, the first version of *Hamletclone* (Hamuretto Kuron,
Kawamura 2000a); a complex intertextual work, taking contemporary social issues as its base, and loosely inspired by Heiner Müller's
HamletMachine. Daisan Erotica have been described as depicting "sci-
ence-fiction world(s) with *fin-de-siècle* ambience" (Mori, Nishidō et al.
1993: 20); and praised for its raw energy and violence in performance (Senda 1997: 192). Nishidō remembers the "electrified energy"
of Daisan Erotica's early work: "The trembling actors appeared on

stage with ropes in their mouths. Rather than making people wonder where this movement came from . . . people wondered how long
the work could continue. (Daisan Erotica) had an overwhelming smell
of danger" (Nishidō 2002: 190).

Kawamura "seeks out observations and events from popular culture, film, *manga*, TV, newspapers and daily incidents" to inform the
ambience and politics of his work (Kawamura 1998b). During the
1980s, Daisan Erotica become popular among university student
audiences who enjoyed Kawamura's use of antibourgeois "low culture"—pro-wrestling, freaks, porn shows and news' stories of violent
crimes—combined with the dystopian themes of science fiction. From
an ideological perspective, Daisan Erotica represents suburban dystopia
while also reminding us of how these media "entertainments" are
consumed without irony. This was a provocation issued to the 1960s
generation of *angura* artists, whose Artuadian sense of theatre rejected
mass culture and was linked to the new left counter-culture.[1] Kawamura
sees revolution as an impossible and ultimately authoritarian form
of social coercion that limited the imagination of 1980s generation
theatre makers who worked in the wake of the first generation of
angura artists. Daisan Erotica rejected the optimism of the *shutaisei*
effect and liberation politics in order to criticize late twentieth century capitalism. Kawamura's plays also move between time and
explore Japanese history; they often piece together fragmentary references to controversial figures and events from the past. Thus, a
sense of historical critique informs Kawamura's dramaturgical method
and ensures that his work is closely connected to the public con-
troversies of Japanese history. Daisan Erotica offers complex readings of Japan's political and cultural development. The theatre that
they felt was appropriate to the 1980s was called *kaibutsu engeki*—
monster or freak show theatre. *Kaibutsu engeki* captures the sense of
gothic cartoon sensibilities associated with the rising dystopia and
nihilism evident in punk movements and in *manga* stories of post-
apocalyptic worlds.

---

[1] Suzuki Tadashi might be the exception here although his highly selective use
of popular culture iconography tends to be selective and retro-nostalgic or, in other
words, aestheticized with an irony associated with high culture intellectualism. Where
Suzuki references *enka* music and Marlboro cigarettes, Kawamura appropriates pro-
wrestling and *manga*.

In 2001, Kawamura formed a second company called *T Factory* with the aim of creating more flexible production systems and working on a wider variety of theatrical projects. Intercultural collaborations, Kawamura's own modern *nō* plays *Aoi and Komachi* (2003), and even writing for *shingeki* are examples of recent *T Factory* activities. While these examples suggest new directions for Kawamura's work in the theatre, it is too early to comment comprehensively on the outcomes of this direction. Thus, this chapter will concentrate on the work of Daisan Erotica in the 1980s and 1990s and will explore Kawamura's analysis of Japan's dystopic space after the bubble.

Dystopia and the politics of kaibutsu engeki

Dystopia is a position expressed by Walter Benjamin's prophetic observation (made in the context of rising Nazism) that humankind's "self alienation has reached such a degree that it can experience its own destruction as an aesthetic pleasure of the first order" (Benjamin 1969: 242). A fatalistic attraction to the underground—aberrant or monstrous—seen in *kaibutsu* performances suggests dystopia. Many examples of 1980s and 1990s Japanese experimental theatre are dystopic. According to Kawamura, *kaibutsu engeki* enabled him to "look beneath the skin" of humanity and gain a clearer picture of the subconscious violence and disharmony that characterizes Japanese history and culture (Kawamura 1996).

Japanese theatre must come to grips with dystopic social realities or what Kawamura describes as "fake culture and surface euphoria layered over deep-seated problems in Japan" (Kawamura 1998b; Murakami 1984). Daisan Erotica stresses connections to actual—if hidden—power relations and the fears of lived-experience—making dystopia visible.

Since the decline of 1960s aesthetics, avant-garde theatre has moved towards personal narrative—the politics of identity, sexuality and postmodern abstraction. This theatre appeals more to the middle-aged (who are nostalgic about the 1960s and 1970s) than to the young, who instead flock to clubs and raves. The audience for Daisan Erotica is mostly young; the kind of people who like film, new media, science fiction and the latest music. What has developed is a sub-cultural world with its own languages and styles—including a range of socially dystopic "new-humans" (*shinjinrui*), pimps and gangsters, soldiers, street gangs, schoolkids, mutant beings, and cyborgs. These are the stock-in-trade of Kawamura's imagination. Add to that a Gothic horror pastiche of white painted faces with black lips: reminding me of the ultra-violent *manga* art of Maruō Suehiro.[2] Both Maruō and Kawamura explore the abject and amoral, the authoritarian underbelly of Japanese society.

Kawamura uses the abject to criticize authoritarianism and the cultural complexities of the *shutaisei* effect. He critically investigates social relations, examining the political nexus of self and society and questions the prospect of reaching a state of autonomy. He looks behind ordinary social reality to discover the workings of power:

> Suspicion and distrust of the self is one of my basic theatrical stances. This is the starting point for me. Distrust can be directed towards society and you can ask why is society like this. Beyond this the same thought can be directed at oneself and you ask why am I like this, why have I come to behave in this manner? . . . Theatre should be suspicious and casting doubts on society. (Kawamura 1996)

The critic Murakami Katsue (1984) suggests that Daisan Erotica perform the surface gloss and lack of interiority—the emptiness associated with the society of the bubble era. But unlike many theatre companies that were active during this period, Daisan Erotica was not apolitical. Still, Murakami makes an important point: From the 1980s onwards, former strategies of resistance were appropriated and disarmed by the postmodernists. The ensuring commodification of the avant-garde meant that a new way of expressing socio-political concerns had to be found.

Kawamura toyed with the idea that only "indifference" could offer an escape from the feelings of predetermination and closure that by 1980 were self-evident in organized protest movements. Kawamura was cited as saying that "this is the best time not to care and to do nothing in particular, just enjoy the sensation of life" (Murakami 1984: 206). Murakami reads this statement as a provocation. Underneath the cynicism and nihilism, he detects in Daisan Erotica, a strong desire to "wake up" the apathetic culture of Japan (Murakami

---

[2] Maruō Suehiro is a *manga* artist who depicts ultra-violent and abject imagery in his work that often features extreme forms of school bullying, sexual assault and torture in the Japanese family. While controversial and distasteful, some assert that his intention is to point to latent fascism in Japanese society. Stanley Kubrick's *Clockwork Orange* is another good point of reference for *kaibutsu engeki*.

1984: 206–7). Kawamura, likewise, is keen to clarify his attitude towards political involvement. When asked about his position in the Japanese theatre world, Kawamura replied that he was an "*Onikko*" (a complainer, a demon child) (Kawamura 1996). Kawamura is, in fact, a prescient social critic who views Japan as dystopic rather than utopian, fractured rather than cohesive, violent and coercive, rather than safe and free. Kawamura's Japan sustains multiple forms of institutional compliance inscribed in language, education, the workplace, daily habits and the media.

Radical Party *and* Nippon Wars

Two works, in particular, *Radical Party* (*Radikaru Paatii* 1983) and *Nippon Wars* (*Nippon Woozu* 1984), illustrate contrasting facets of the idea of *kaibutsu engeki* in performance and, according to Kawamura, are characteristic of Daisan Erotica in the 1980s.

Radical Party depicted the lives of young members of a criminal gang who oversee an agency for male prostitutes. The production showed the nihilistic and violent lives of gang members immersed in a fatalistic, violent and transgressive environment. *Radical Party* was performed in a small, cabaret theatre venue in Shinjuku—a Tokyo district known for its seedy nightlife. The play was episodic, showing the disorder, rage, obscenity and banality that marked the gang members' lives. In a review, Senda comments that the play revealed a "teeming urban underclass . . . the unclean atmosphere . . . seems authentically of our time" (Senda 1997: 193). *Radical Party* portrays social outcasts who rebel without hope of political change. It depicts a Japan often overlooked in the rush to social harmony and prosperity: the unproductively employed biker gangs, sex workers, drug addicts, day labourers, and so on. Even the children of the middle classes—the likely audience for the production—were depicted as hopeless and lost. As one of the characters says, "We are the children of revolutionaries who do not believe in revolution" (Senda 1997: 195). The play points to the lack of social progress despite the political activism of previous generations. The title is bitterly ironic. As Senda's review comments: "The play is one of paradox: in it, 'revolution' is meaningless, and this 'party' itself so 'radical,' stands in opposition to nothing whatsoever. Yet, in all its sharpness, the play shows us a mercilessly clear outline of the author's malcontent vision" (Senda 1997: 195). From Kawamura's perspective, the promises of the former radical polemics in theatre were indefinitely deferred even as their mythical dimensions grew. In other words, a *radical poetics* had been displaced by what Japanese historian H. D. Harootunian calls a national poetics (Harootunian 1993: 216). For Kawamura, radicalism appears as an error of history and the harsher image of the apolitical society stretched over a rising sense of euphoric nationalism and capitalism gone mad, is a true reflection of Japan.

Nippon Wars carried the critique of the protest movement even further. In the style of science fiction, this production was the first of an emerging cyber-punk genre that cited such dystopic films as *Alphaville* (Jean Luc Godard, 1965), *THX 1138* (George Lucas, 1971) and, especially, Ridley Scott's *Blade Runner* (1982). Not only does *Blade Runner* draw extensively on images of the urban landscape of 1980s Japan in depicting a bleak, environmentally degraded society ruled by corporate entities, but it was also referenced directly in Kawamura's play. Interestingly, *Nippon Wars* predates the aforementioned popular, dystopic Japanese cyber-punk films, such as *Akira* (Otomo Katsuhiro, 1989) and *Tetsuo* (Tsukamoto Shinya, 1989) by five years. In *Nippon Wars*, a former radical activist known only as "O" suddenly finds himself on a gunboat called the "The Black Sea." He has no idea how he got there and knows no one else on the boat. The Black Sea is a purposefully mysterious vessel also referred to in the play as a whale. The subsequent blurring of machine and mammal is a motif extended to the characters. It gradually becomes clear that O's comrades are android soldiers programmed by "The General" with individual memories and identities. In the same way that the androids in *Blade Runner* collected old photographs, identity in *Nippon Wars* is contingent on having memories and a place in history. During the play the androids become deranged and try to smash their systems of control. Of course, technology out of control with cyborgs running wild is a common dystopic theme—almost too clichéd. But Kawamura provides a clever twist in *Nippon Wars* when it is revealed that the motivation to "smash the system" is itself programmed by The General. What is called "the final lesson of rebellion" is a socially sanctioned act of dissidence; the metaphor being that power is shown to be unapproachable and unchanging.

Senda saw the work as undermining the idealism of the 1960s as it posits 1960s activism as just another kind of top-down programming.

The play asks "whether many of the actions and sentiments so embedded in human beings, based as they are on ideas of 'love' and 'rebellion,' are indeed merely examples of programming" (Senda 1997:
210–11). *Nippon Wars* challenges the very possibility of revolution and
selfhood in a technologically advanced society. The play is a clever
deconstruction of 1980s bubble culture's ability to absorb, commodify
and even program acts of dissent. In light of this, Senda concludes
that the Japanese theatre of the 1980s era was primarily concerned
with entrapment rather than liberation (Senda 1988: 58). Another
way to read this trend is that the new generation of politically motivated theatre makers who were cognizant of the failure of the 1960s
counter-culture turned their attention to the nature of power as it
operates in society. Rather than trying to opt out of society they
begin to look at society's mechanisms.

Monstering the shutaisei *effect*

The androids in *Nippon Wars* signify the closing down of postwar
idealism in Japan. Going even further in this direction—challenging
notions of what constitutes "self" and "identity," and announcing
the presence of the monster in society is *Last Frankenstein* (1986, film
version directed by Kawamura 1992).

In this work, Tokyo is in the grip of a suicide epidemic. The character of Professor Saegusa is about to end his own life and follow
his dead wife to her grave. Saegusa lives with his psychic daughter,
Mai. Meanwhile, a former colleague, the mad Professor Aryo, has
been attempting to reanimate two cadavers—a male and a female
who will parent a new 'master-race' of emotionless beings. Mai's
psychic powers are needed to bring the cadavers back to life. In
exchange, Aryo offers a possible cure for Saegusa's sickness. When
the two beings are revived they unintentionally experience emotions;
they are repelled by each other and will not mate as planned. The
monsters wreak destruction on the city and seek revenge against their
creator.

Last Frankenstein was partly written as a response to the Chernobyl
nuclear power station meltdown. The play also featured a fictitious
cult called the *Shinokyo*—remarkably similar to the Aum Supreme
Truth (*Aum Shinrikyo*)—who sought death as the way to achieve sal-
vation. This play is also, of course, a retelling of Mary Shelley's

Frankenstein, but unlike Shelley who knows monster from creator, Kawamura asks who is the monster, the 'creator' or 'created'? He shows them symbiotically fused. Furthermore, as this is the *last* Frankenstein, Kawamura suggests that a *über*-monster has at last arrived to finally destroy the world.

Kawamura is interested in the monster as social construct. Rejecting the monster as a godlike transcendent creature—a common trope in 1960s *angura*—Kawamura argues that the *kaibutsu* sensibility: "is anything that is on the streets now, like street kids, Asahara Shoko [Aum's founder and leader] . . . such scattered monster-like pieces constitute the problems that we face and have to figure out. . . . Our monsters today might be a certain type of criminal" (Kawamura 1998a: 32). This notion of monster joins the everyday world with the extremities of human existence. The mindset of mass murderer Hannibal Lechter from Jonathan Demme's *The Silence of the Lambs* (1991) is an example that Kawamura offers of the normalization of the pathological in contemporary cultures and politics (Kawamura 1998a: 32). We are coming to see how "normal" monstrosity is, and how strong the copycat urge is, especially when it comes to murder and bizarre behavior. Kawamura hopes to stimulate resistance to the pathological turn of culture in Japan.

Daisan Erotica in the 1990s: showing the dystopian space

Early in the 1990s Daisan Erotica experienced upheaval when most of the former company departed. Kawamura suggests that the infighting and break-up of the original company was due to the hierarchical nature of the 1980s company and his own desire to ferment change. As previously discussed, it is a paradox that even radical, avant-garde Japanese theatre is very traditional in its structure, with a clearly defined hierarchy. What Kawamura terms the "queen bee syndrome," whereby each production featured the same lead actors and cast according to their place in the 'pecking order', was a system he wanted to reject. He argues that this system was rooted in 1960s social values and that the 1990s required a new systems of production with the flexibility to better respond to challenges of the era:

> In 1989, the Emperor died and it was the end of the *Shōwa* era. The Berlin Wall came down in the same era. In other words, there seemed to be many important historical events unfolding during that time. As

a result, my work began to reflect a need to face these big moments
in history. Until that era, as a theatre artist, I was known as a member
of the little theatre movement, as someone working in that tradition.
In other words, I was writing my stories and directing them with my
own company. However, I was becoming tired of making theatre in
this way, theatre based solely on one story. Given what was happening
in the world around us and the magnitude of historical events that we
saw, it seemed to me that this kind of theatre-making based on story
was no longer able to address the questions that were being asked.
Another kind of theatre making was becoming necessary. (Kawamura
2004)

Certainly events in Japan required consideration. For example, the
hierarchical Aum sect focusing obsessively on a single leader forced
a re-examination of how Daisan Erotica was operating. Kawamura
wanted to make it clear that his theatre group was not a cult. The
1990s needed a new style of company organization in which leadership was diffused and shared. Kawamura's idea was to "work more
in the style of musicians who collaborate around a musical theme
and genre" (Kawamura 1998b). As a result, his plays began to show
a marked sense of hybridity and intertextual forms; his work became
more media-based as well.

The question of dystopia and its residual capacity to work trans-
gressively also required reappraisal. Jameson notes, for example, how
the experience of apocalypse becomes absorbed in postmodern society, rapidly losing its dissident status. He calls this "postmodern muta-
tions where the apocalyptic suddenly turns into the decorative"
(Jameson 1991: xvii). Perhaps Kawamura's rebel status and use of
the abject was becoming too familiar and risked self-parody; a charge
that is asserted by Nishidō (Nishidō 2002: 192). In the new situation rather than *inventing* a dystopic space, Kawamura just needed
to *show it* as an everyday fact of life:

In the 1980s, it would have been almost embarrassing to do theatre
that dealt explicitly with social problems, whereas now, you can't afford
to think like this. The presentation of social problems in a more direct
way is what I see as part of being in a social movement after postmodernism. (Kawamura 1996)

Reflecting this thinking, the second phase of artistic development in
the company is less evident through science fiction narratives or parody of film genres and more focused on contemporary events and
the actual conditions of urban culture in Japan. Previously Kawamura

has turned to gothic images of horror; in the 1990s, however, it is Japanese society itself that has become increasingly aberrant. To this end Kawamura suggests, "actual freaks have started to disappear but at the same time reality and what is considered normal has become increasingly grotesque" (Kawamura 1996). Tokyo, in particular, is depicted as the site of social breakdown, even a war zone in his recent work.

Obsession Sight/Site

Obsession Sight/Site (Obuseshon Saitto) combines the ideas of obsession being visible and present in the 1990s urban space; sight and site are interrelated. The play was performed in a large multipurpose space on the eighth floor of a department store. Billed as the world's largest department store, the site is a testament to the property speculation boom of the bubble era. *Obsession Sight* theatricalized contemporary events in Japan, many of which can be traced to the post-bubble collapse of Japanese social fabric. A fragmented dramaturgical structure comprising glimpses of these events was used throughout. As Kawamura states, the play investigated obsession and related Japanese obsessive behaviour to the prevailing atmosphere of socio-political decline:

> In *Obsession Sight* we looked at obsession. What are Japanese obsessions and how do they define what it is to be Japanese? We wanted to theatricalise and dramatise certain obsessions that Japanese people will not confront directly. (Kawamura 1996)

Brechtian-style slogans and video projections used to indicate the sequence of scenes read: this is "the city in our time." The fact that various obsessive behaviours were identified in the piece as a reflection of the "here and now" rather than any future or past time, meant that the viewer was faced with questions of self-recognition and complicity.

The darkened stage was littered with strewn newspapers; the decorated box-shelter of a homeless person sat to one side. The performance began with a video tour of the artworks painted on the side of boxes and interviews with homeless men. Kawamura reminds us that in the 1990s a series of art events were held among homeless people, including a project to decorate their cardboard shelters. At the same time, the performance took place in the month when

the City of Tokyo controversially installed "art works" in the underground west entrance of Shinjuku Station. Formerly, this was one
of the first sites where the homeless gathered. A garden of small,
ugly plastic posts with tops sheared at sharp angles was installed; no
place for sitting, no space between them for boxes. Loud techno
music began and white-faced actors—not clowns, but gothic and
death like—popped up from behind each monitor and barked at the
audience. This is a world of dogs. A man emerged from his box
home, a young girl dressed in white shirt and pleats; the innocent
schoolgirl entered and without speaking, drew a gun and shot the
homeless man. This is a simple, if not brutal image of callous disregard for so-called good and civilized people when confronted with
the dysfunction of capitalism and their intolerance of difference.
Obsession Sight began at the point of social destitution and chaos.
Kawamura depicted a world in which everyone was on the verge
of a totalitarian abyss. Lying just beneath the surface of our present
time is a future Japan of porno-kings, ethnic gangs, neo-nationalism,
failed revolutionary despots, and decay. Kawamura's images of Tokyo
are not the commodified images of a neon lit salaryman-ville, nor
the nostalgic reverie of *shitamachi*, but ugly images of Sanya—the
Tokyo East End—where life is dirty, dangerous and short. The production asks us to dwell on the fact that the corporate army daily
walks past the human waste products of their own system; over sen-
sitive and enamoured with fleeting *kawaii*-consciousness they com-
plain about the smell!

Obsession Sight emerged from a "group devised" dramaturgical
method—a direct result of newer modes of production, discussed
above. There were some advantages to realising such a political work
in this way. Actors were given the opportunity to suggest and discuss themes, and the piece displays multiple subject positions and
strands of polemical investigation. Already mentioned is the innovative use of video; a device that extended to several documentary
style interviews with controversial right-wing activists and a porno-
grapher that were interspersed with scenes of live action. These edi-
torialized and complicated dystopic political views.

A later scene showed two men repeatedly firing guns into their
own mouths—they died, fell, rose up, shot themselves again, fell,
and rose-up again. . . . A resurgent militarism in Japan that few
acknowledge was depicted by a band of rebel soldiers called the
Kanto Army (Kanto being the Tokyo region). This was in reference

to a group of right-wing students who led a violent attack on staff and students of the art department at Nihon University in November 1968. They wore grey uniforms marked with the words "*Kanto Gun*" or Kanto Army. According to Sawara, the Kanto Army was financed and equipped by a wealthy businessman and former soldier in Japan's imperial forces, named Iijima. Sawara notes that although they were all students they behaved more like an army of right-wing gangsters (Sawara 1970: 168). Sometimes depicted as imperial soldiers, armed street gangs, sometimes as doomsday cultists or as corporate warriors, the Kanto Army in Kawamura's play made associations with various nationalistic movements in Japan. In each case, the ceaseless activity and violence suggested the obsessive domination of the military and capitalism.

Obsession Sight is a good example of the success of the group devised method and shows how a non-linear, hybrid and participatory theatre that embodies multiple responses to the political critique of Japan, can enliven theatre culture and offer a source of renewal for the avant-garde.

The Lost Babylon

It appears ironic that in a society noted for low levels of street violence guns are ever present in Kawamura's work. Guns are used as fetishes, as cinematic parody. Not surprisingly, Kawamura cites the shoot out films of Sam Peckinpah (1925–1984) as an early influence. As Kawamura notes:

> Because Japanese society frowns upon guns and outlaws them, people think that Japan is not a violent society. But I think that Japan is violent. This is expressed in different ways, through discrimination and people's attitudes towards others. A sense of violence is always present; it is just not being expressed through guns and weapons. When I want to depict the violence in Japanese society, it is very easy to use the gun as an unequivocal image of violence. (Kawamura 1996)

This proliferation of guns reaches its zenith in Daisan Erotica's production, *The Lost Babylon* (1999).

In some respects, this work seems to revisit a theme first explored in *Nippon Wars*. But *Babylon* goes further than the earlier work in showing the seductive and self-destructive urge towards accepting the aesthetics of violence in everyday life. *The Lost Babylon* enacts the shredding of Japan's social fabric—an inability of the Japanese to tell the difference between what is real and what is simulated. As with films like *Westworld* (Michael Crichton, 1973) and *Jurassic Park* (Steven Spielberg, 1993), *The Lost Babylon* is set in an amusement or theme park where people can experience the "real thing" as simulacra. At the beginning of the play "The Boss"—yet another of Kawamura's distant and depersonalized figures of authority—is interviewing job applicants to work as live targets in an interactive shooting gallery. The applicants are *furosha*, homeless and marginalized illegal workers, who are required to die realistic deaths when shot by paying visitors to the park. The meaning is clear: *furosha* are disposable people and in the play they eventually die as the levels of violence intensify in the search for more realistic confrontations. The *furosha* are people who pay for Japan's increasingly hyper-capitalist and escapist lifestyle. As might be expected, real bullets and high-powered guns are brought into the park and it is no longer possible to distinguish between simulated and actual murder. Jameson's comments seem appropriate: "The world . . . momentarily loses its depth and threatens to become a glossy skin, a stereoscopic illusion, a rush of filmic images without density. But is this now a terrifying or an exhilarating experience?" (Jameson 1991: 34). Kawamura says that "as the play shifts between virtual reality and reality with little discernible difference between the two, Japanese society has likewise only a thin line between the virtual and the real" (Kawamura 1998b). The intentional blurring of realities reiterates Daisan Erotica's earlier theme of Japanese society as pseudo-euphoric, while actually being extremely repressive.

Although the prototype theme park is not yet open, street-smart youths dressed in American gangster-rap fashions arrive to preview the shooting gallery. They succumb to the thrill of blood sports and the place descends into chaos. Kawamura introduces two film writers into this narrative, reminding his audience that a virtual reality is written right in front of their faces. One writer is a man chosen for his reputation for including a record number of gun fights in a single film; the other is a woman known for her work in romantic fiction. The boss requires them to write "a film so good that it will become a part of cinema history" for the theme park. Much of the drama concerns the relationship between the writers. The complex weave of the developing film scenario as a play-within-a-play gradually make it impossible for any spectator to separate out the discrete components. Of the two writers, only the woman survives. Initially she refuses to participate in gun play, but finally takes up a weapon and shoots the murderer of the male film writer: perhaps their former love for each other gives her a hold on what is real in the face of so many competing simulations. Her murder of the murderer parodies the romantic fiction she writes—a world in which emotion binds people to a nostalgic sense of reality.

The Lost Babylon may be read as a parody of action movies staged with the slap-dash violence of video games. The intensity of the hypervisceral and fetishized clips of cinema violence are evident. In staging *Babylon*, Kawamura was not only influenced by American cinema and video games, but also by his experience of living in the US. But America per se is not the subject of this work. He asserts that it will only be a matter of time before violence of this type will dominate Japan. Kawamura knows where there is a black-market for guns in Japan—anyone can buy a gun from a street punk in the Tokyo suburb of Takadanobaba—where the Daisan Erotica office was located for many years. "The gun is a symbol of modern fear and emblematic of the fact that Japanese streets have become increasingly dangerous" (Kawamura 1998b).

Who or what the woman scenario writer represents is not resolved. Kawamura suggests that the character is a critique of representations of women in Japanese popular culture, where women gaining power are often depicted as women with guns. Kawamura cites *Thelma and Louise* (Ridely Scott, 1991) as a work widely viewed in Japan as a commentary on women's self-empowerment. But, as he argues, "even if women have guns this does not mean that they have power" (Kawamura 1998b). The screenwriter in *Babylon* remains disempowered, guns and all. She belongs to the romantic fiction that she writes; her behavior is conventionally feminine. She is presented rather than critically investigated. Her underdevelopment as a character is evidence (and much more could be cited beyond Kawamura's work) that Japan's feminist politics lags behind that of many other economically developed societies. Kawamura's character reveals considerable confusion about feminism. Whether or not this is another of Kawamura's critiques of Japanese culture, or that his own thoughts on these matters are in need of development, remains to be seen.

At the end of the century: Hamletclone

Kawamura is now an established artist and a professor of theatre at the Kyoto University of Fine Arts and Design.[3] It is appropriate to conclude, however, with a discussion of his work, *Hamletclone* (2000). Arguably, one of the most important plays in Japan's recent theatrical experience, *Hamletclone* ponders the fate of the avant-garde and considers potential outcomes in the encounter between theatre and politics. We also have the rare experience of play and commentary being included in the same volume as a translation of *Hamletclone* follows in chapter 10.

Hamletclone like its namesake, Heiner Müller's *HamletMachine*, is a loose rewriting and metacritique of Shakespeare's *Hamlet*. All three plays describe a ruling family in crisis. In Kawamura's version, Hamlet's split personality and dysfunctional rebellious family represent Japan's postwar experience. As Kawamura says (with all the darkness around): "it was a good time for Hamlet to be produced in Japan" (Nishidō 2002: 204). The critique of idealism and revolution in this play are forefront in the mind. Kawamura adopts *HamletMachine's* fragmented, appropriative dramaturgy and, like Müller's text, explores history, politics, and the failure of the left. Kawamura's play *clones* various Hamlet-like dramatic situations, placing them alongside parallel narratives that are loosely about the fall of communism in Eastern Europe, Japan's political inertia and cultural malaise, and rising violence. Despite everything there is nothing, or so the play suggests.

Intertextuality and hybridity are the dramaturgical foundations of *Hamletclone*. The play begins with the audience standing on the stage trapped behind barbed wire and looking into the auditorium. In the prologue, a thief wandering among the audience describes in jumbled, unconnected sentences the chaos of civil war and his desire to play Hamlet. Allusions to Japanese political radicalism and extremism become intermingled. In the first short scene "Colony," the Japanese national anthem (*Kimigayo*) plays while the Japanese flag of the red sun (*Hinomaru*) blows in the breeze. This sets the tone for an investigation into resurgent nationalism in Japan. As many critics have argued, the political landscape of the post-bubble era has

---

[3] For discussion of some recent works by Kawamura including Moriyama's excellent essay on *Hamletclone*, see (Eckersall 2003; Moriyama 2004).

been characterized by rising neo-nationalist sentiments that have seen former imperial symbols of Japan, such as the flag and national anthem, almost deified. Kawamura hopes to remind people of nationalism's negative and warlike consequences. Hence, in the play, people come to realise that the wire is electrified and the colony is a prison or concentration camp.

A mysterious figure known as "The Gay" lords over the story that unfolds and provides narration and commentary via a series of projected texts. Hamlet and the other characters in the play are facets of the composite figure of The Gay; the point being that a degree of uncertainty is encouraged by the characters' fluid identity and the play's mutable style. Kawamura stated that he was not thinking about gay issues here, but wanted to explore a situation of gender fluidity and the effect this might have on society, and asks: "What would society be like if it were without such divisions?" (Kawamura 2004). It is important to note that the psychology of the character of Hamlet is not central to reading this play, rather it is Hamlet's pathological nature and fragmented being that determine the play's sense of drama. Thus, in the second scene of *Hamletclone*, called "Autobiography," Hamlet is introduced as a composite of three characters; one played by a male actor, the second cross-dressed, and the third played by a woman. They soon take on additional personalities and name historical locations where they witness crimes and genocide. Countering Müller's negation of the subject (expressed in the statement from his play, "I am not Hamlet. I don't take part anymore"), Kawamura's text proposes a proliferation of subjects. The characters split into a multiplication of subjectivities as they recite the lines: "I was Hamlet. . . . I was Mishima Yukio, . . . I was Hiroshima," and so on. In other words, the play presents a critical image of Japanese identity, one measured in relation to politics, current affairs and the Emperor system, but also strategically woven into an awareness of larger historical events and general sense of disorder.

In the following scene the thief hopes to find security in a normal family environment and instructs the gathered cast to perform the story *Hamlet*, a family drama, or so the thief thinks. Claudius, Polonius, Horatio, Gertrude and Ophelia are simultaneously depicted as members of the Japanese imperial family and the 'family of Japan,' who are living in a commuter suburb. Both counter-readings in the play explore neo-nationalist tendencies. In the ideology of prewar Japanese imperialism, the figure of the Emperor was literally seen as the embodiment of Japan—a living God and symbolic father figure of the Japanese race. Kawamura cleverly uses the image of an over-lord and blends it with a critique of contemporary society. The foot soldiers of imperial rule—in line with Japan's status as an economic power—no longer live in the castle, but in the Japanese suburbs. This is one of Japan's famed commuter towns in which children are born and bred and to which Japan's corporate class nightly return. The tone of the scene is nihilist, as The Gay comments: "I am nowhere. The sound of breath at birth and its absence at death is the only truth." In reference to this, Moriyama Naoto has concluded that the site of the suburbs in Japan is a signifier of violence and the violent disorder hidden below the surface of the suburban calm is a central metaphor in *Hamletclone* (Moriyama 2004). Kawamura's reading of the family is actively disturbed and yet everyday. The violence that is suggested is even more shocking for its banality and lack of explanation.

Over the next few scenes, recent troubling events from Japanese society unfold. Suicide, rape, murder, attacks on homeless people, bullying, schoolgirl prostitution, and the Aum cult's attempt to stage a coup by gassing the subway are somehow linked as interconnected consequences of the Japanese historical condition. As the family tells the story the events unfold as a record of contemporary Japan. At the same time The Gay, using words lifted from real right-wing pro-paganda texts, proposes a systematic analysis of the steps needed to bring on a military takeover. This is explored in a series of lurid, violent dreamscapes that are perhaps reminiscent of a Mishima-like millennial fantasy of conjoining blood, race and sex in an ideologi-cal fusion. Rival groups—among them neo-nationalists and school-girl gangs—vie for power.

The recurring image of schoolgirls and the wider question of sex-ual politics in *Hamletclone* is a complex problem to analyse. In the scene "Training Brides for Homemaking Duties," Ophelia is liter-ally wrapped in bandages—her repression is so complete. Later on, when she removes the bandages, she is dressed as a schoolgirl. This is an ambiguous image, simultaneously a symbol of exploitation and—as the women discuss organizing their escape from patriarchy—insur-rection. Kawamura presents a complex and shifting analysis of gender and sex that is more ambitious than in *The Lost Babylon*. On the one hand, his representation of gender politics is shown to be a source of capitalist aggression. On the other, the potential for gender fluidity and of acting outside the boundaries of social norms might be seen as invigorating. However, neither is fully realized. In the final analysis, the overwhelming tone of this and other scenes is of disappointment and failure: failure to act and an inability to experience human sensation. As the coup comes to life, ironically, people are unable to experience it in meaningful terms. Hence, the girls come to lament: "Therefore I thought about my life but nothing happened." In other words, the family are deeply troubled, but frustrated by this sense of inertia.

In the closing scenes of *Hamletclone*, the uprising is staged and then quashed. Coalitions of rival forces form the new government, but as always, the politics seem to remain inside the same old system. The play ends on a note of despair. While normality is restored, nothing has improved. The Gay is shot. His dream of transmutation into a hybrid-figure of possibilities and potentials, of political and personal transcendence, is over. Hamlet is not free to act, but remains a puppet—a tool enmeshed in the ugly foreboding history of Japan's modernity.

Hamletclone mirrors contemporary events in Japan in that it captures the strong sense of political lethargy, lack of opportunity for political participation, and the continuing sense of social unrest lying beneath the smooth surface of the Japanese suburban everyday. All of Kawamura's interests reappear in this play; the omnipresent authority figure, the street gangs, the neo-nationalists, the guns, the violent schoolgirls, Tokyo as a city on the edge. *Hamletclone* examines the failure of capitalism and the need for a new cultural system to evolve in Japan: above all, the need to develop a critically aware and mature historical consciousness. In asking the question, what is the family now in and of Japan? Kawamura's answer is bleak and cutting. The breakdown of the family is the failure of postwar Japan to address the past and create an alternative space for the future.

Conclusion

Kawamura asserts:

> Daisan Erotica's plays do not have neat conclusions . . . I don't like this kind of simplistic humanistic way of telling stories. Instead, I want to leave things open in my theatre so that that audience can think about the different issues that I put on the stage. (Kawamura 2004)

Shinjuku west exit "art works" where homeless people had gathered.
Photo: Peter Eckersall.

The revelation of dystopia is the central factor in understanding
Daisan Erotica. As Kawamura suggests: "It is absolutely necessary
for an age of monsters to put in an appearance.... In actual fact
such an age has already come very close to us" (Kawamura 1998a:
38). Beyond this point, the audience has to decide where they stand.

CHAPTER EIGHT

1990s PERFORMANCES OF DUMB TYPE: TOWARDS A NEW HUMANITY

> The times demand an evolution in our humanity.
> (Furuhashi 1995a: 2)

In the 1990s, the Kyoto based, media performance art group, dumb type[1] was one of the best known performance art groups worldwide, constituting an artistic and intellectual force within contemporary art, dance, and sub-cultural performance scenes. Dumb type's investigations of technology and capitalism—as well as the body and sexuality—were like a mirror reflecting the cultural politics of the era. Their work moved between discourse and composite sites of artistic expression, always blurring the boundaries. They aimed to theorize notions of globalization, explore the effects of media and diverse cultural flows and open spaces of difference that might serves as effective modes of resistance to capitalism and other dominating forms of power. Through artistic activities that included performance, art installations, music and nightclub events and publishing, dumb type aimed to forge new forms of community and explore new possibilities for selfhood. The company's work might be understood as a creative application of 1990s cultural politics insomuch as their avantgarde performances presented personal experience as political reality, while functioning inside a collective process. Hence, the marginal status of many dumb type members in respect of their sexuality, race and lifestyle choices meant that they sought a politics that was contingent and inclusive, spontaneous and fluid. It is interesting to reflect on the 1990s cultural mood, when ideas such as globalization and cyberculture were being discussed in a form that was different to our current understanding of these forces. While enthusiastically promoting life's diversity—and even utopian in contrast to Daisan Erotica's essential dystopia, for example—this is not to say that dumb type were blind to rising forces of authoritarianism either. They explored new forms of power, especially the rising effects of the information

---

[1] The name dumb type appears in lowercase by company preference.

economy as a form of biopower and an agency of cultural imperialism. As dumb type claimed in their prescient 1989 work *pH*, the so-called "new world order" of the post-Berlin wall era equals "new world border." We can only reflect on how perceptive such observations have become in the present age and how difficult it is to comprehend the magnitude of their effects.

Dumb type's performances and artworks offer a critical assessment of the 1990s fetish of technology and, at the same time, they demonstrate a distain for technophobia. Like the influential theorist Donna Haraway—whose work was influential during the 1990s—they accept the beauties of the microprocessor, but acknowledge the need for new politics to oppose the technodystopic future it is causing. Their stance has much in common with the arguments of Haraway: that given the certainty of technological progress, we ought to theorize new spaces for negotiating its socio-political, scientific, ecological, and human dimensions (Haraway 1997). Haraway's *A Cyborg Manifesto: Science Technology, and Socialist-Feminism in the Late Twentieth Century* (Haraway 1991) resonates in the work of dumb type. In an often-quoted section of the manifesto, Haraway writes:

> By the late twentieth century, our time, a mythic time, we are all chimeras, theorized and fabricated hybrids of machine and organism; in short, we are cyborgs. The cyborg is our ontology; it gives us our politics. (Haraway 1991: 150)

Haraway's work includes a dialectic chart contrasting forms and practices associated with "white capitalist patriarchy" on the one hand, and the "informatics of domination" on the other (Haraway 1991: 162–63). As Zoë Sofoulis writes, "Haraway situates the cyborg within the context of postmodern technoscience, especially biology, in which comforting modern dualisms . . . such as organism versus machine, reality versus representation, self versus other, subject versus object, culture versus nature—are broken down" (Sofoulis 2002: 87). Dumb type appear to address these ideas in *S/N* (1994) where we see a comparable dialectic exercise conducted over the possible meanings of concepts associated with "Signal" (perhaps relating to informatics) and "Noise" (relating to white capitalist patriarchy). In *S/N*, dumb type seems to be constantly searching for points between the extremities—moments where the dialectic breaks. In this sense, dumb type and Haraway share a political interest in blurring the boundaries. Proposals for new and inclusive models of community and new "intimate couplings," to use Haraway's term, are suggested in these ideas: cyberfeminism for Haraway, and, for dumb type, an imaginative, playful cyberfeminist–queer notion of the social collective. Dumb type imagines as normal postmodern, transnational and transgendered spaces. Perhaps, they dream of a world so accepting of difference that one's power to protect oneself, or one's need to fight in order to achieve participation and equality is no longer necessary. As a phrase from their performance *S/N* says: "I dream my power will disappear" (dumb type 1995: 9).

The 1990s work by dumb type will also be remembered for pioneering multimedia performance technologies. In particular, their use of emergent, digital recording technologies and projection systems broke new ground and this has become a seminal influence on hybrid media, dance, and performance genres worldwide. Moreover, the practice of sampling, where a number of different moments—be they in the form of music, text, or image—are rapidly and precisely lifted from their source and re-assembled is uniquely associated with digital technologies of the 1990s. Subsequently, forms of expression as diverse as rap and techno music, and video and film production have become fragmentary, layered and sequenced. Sampling is an apt phrase for dumb type. It communicates a sense of their dramaturgical approach and philosophical outlook. As Koyamada Toru, a former company spokesperson states, "dumb type's philosophy is to sample the source" (Koyamada 1996). This example helps to explain how dumb type are able to accommodate potentially opposing forces in their work; the humanist and the technological dimensions, for example. Everything is possible in a montage of layered and interwoven moments of image, sound and performance.

At the same time, the nominal status of the original source and ways that we have traditionally understood creative practice have been challenged because of techniques such as sampling and montage and their use in postmodern performance. Henceforth, processes of compilation become an original form of expression. In this respect, dumb type's manipulation of media technologies reflected a sense that the identity of the artist and the meaning of the arts in cultural terms was changing. The consequences of this are significant. Film theorist, Adrian Martin, makes the observation that in the 1990s, artists became agents for the transmission and critique of culture, while at the same time their identity and social role as artists became less clearly defined. In other words, their *authenticity* was no longer clear. Martin compares the historical identity of the artist, who he suggests was uniquely independent and struggled to express him or herself from a distanced and reflective perspective on society. In contrast, "stood the artist as invaded, divided, decentred—self as pure surface crossed by cultural flows, a mere effect of everything around him or her" (Marsh 1993: 188). As we will see, this observation meshes neatly with dumb type's 1990s performances, which often included sequences of bodies over-coded by projected images and controlled by technological forces.

Jean Baudrillard's theory of simulacra was associated with this moment as well. Simulacra no longer distinguish between knowing what is real and unreal in the world. A literal copy of the real, in Baudrillard's terms, is a second order simulation; in other words, a direct transfer from one to the other. But Baudrillard argues that we live in a world of third order simulations where we loose a link to the original object and the *hyperreal* becomes our only point of reference. In an often-quoted piece Baudrillard writes about the hyperreal nature of America:

> Disneyland is there to conceal the fact that it is the 'real' country, all of the 'real' America which is Disneyland . . . Disneyland is presented as imaginary in order to make us believe that the rest is real, when in fact all of Los Angles and the America surrounding it are no longer real, but of the order of the hyperreal and of simulation. (Baudrillard 1983: 25)

Dumb type explores the consequential politics of hyperreality (a quintessentially 1990s idea) especially in their work *pH*, discussed below.

The company also shows another face in which an active commitment to community arts come together with dumb type's technological bent. A discussion of the ways that dumb type worked in communities during the 1990s has been overlooked and consequently we lack a fuller understanding of the company's work at this time. While dumb type is not a community theatre group in the conventional sense, events devised over the 1990s, for example, a monthly cafe forum for gays and lesbians in Kyoto, and their alliance with the community arts organization Art-Scape, show dumb type to be a community activist organization with grass-roots connections. This is further evident in the public positions that many dumb type members were taking on issues of gender, sexuality and disability, for example. While they are international in performance style, their politics of a certain 1990s phase were often directed to interventions in their local community. This mix of notionally postmodern, globalist, and local communitarian perspectives ultimately sustains the artistic and political success of this company, and define their singular occurrence in the 1990s scene. Although discussing recent activities of dumb type is beyond the scope of this study, we should note how members of the group continue to build on this practice, including recent explorations of contemporary arts in community settings and grass-roots community festivals around Japan.

Dumb type came from outside theatre and *angura* circles. The company was founded by a diverse group of art students at the Kyoto Fine Arts University (*Kyoto Shiritsu Geijutsu Daigaku*) in 1984. Koyamada recalls how they moved from installation work to performance:

> We started doing art installations and then video art. The combination of these led to an idea for performance. . . . But our performance was very simple. We had no training as performers or dancers. In fact, we did not like the dance world or dance training, we did not like the dance body. Rather, we were interested in personal experience and our own everyday life. We wanted to make dance and performance from our own personal worlds. For these reasons we used simple things, the patterns and movement of everyday life influenced us. (Koyamada 1996)

According to Koyamada, the company's first works were more influenced by Terayama Shūji and his imaginative world than anything else (Koyamada 1996). Hence, *The Order of the Square* (1985), a little-known early work, bears comparison to Terayama's *Knock*. Like *Knock*, *The Order of the Square* was made from events that moved from site to site. Instead of being performed over seventy-two hours though this performance took place over one year. Furuhashi Teiji, a key figure in dumb type until his death in 1995, recalled that performance sites included the street, a department store and the garden of a Temple (dumb type 1991). Debates about the nature of personal existence were also seen in dumb type's early work. *Plan for Sleep*, first performed in 1984, was "about the nature of self and existence." Koyamada suggests that, for the 1990s membership of dump type at least, all their work was connected to this theme in someway or another (Koyamada 1996).

O36-Pleasure Life *and* Pleasure Life

The works *O36-Pleasure Life* (1987) and the final version of this piece, *Pleasure Life* (1988) were the first qualified results of dumb type's investigations into the information economy and its consequences for society and the individual. Kumakura notes that the "seeds of the plastic and thematic language" of dumb type can be seen in these works (Kumakura 1995: 25). It is interesting to note how a number of aspects of this performance were extended in later works. In particular, we can see the developing use of aesthetic and performative elements such as parody, video art and visual explorations of bodies in performance, and a dramaturgical premise whereby these bodies are incorporated within the technological environment.

O36-Pleasure Life began with the performers looking cold and lifeless and laid out on a white geometrically patterned floor (dumb type 1991). Four monitors were installed in the rear wall of the space together with a large digital clock. As the piece progressed, the clock marked time and the performers enacted figures from everyday life: images of the middle-class salary man, homemaker, and so on. As with many dumb type representations of life, however, these images were notionally out of kilter, slightly surreal perhaps, too sharp in their details. In other words, they were queer images that suggested parody and satire. The performers moved in mechanized patterns that gradually began to make shapes and forms; a "life formation game" as it was called in the piece. At the same time as the bodies became regulated by the environment, video cameras filmed various angles and close-up images of the performers, transmitting them onto the monitors in the background. Their images were presented as a form of measurement—an aesthetic gesture signalling a selection and categorisation process—a representational device that was extended in later shows. The bodies attempting to mimic a sense of mechanical order were slightly out of synch and jarred, as if experiencing programming glitches. In this respect, *O36-Pleasure Life-Pleasure Life* explored a dehumanizing, clinical environment of surveillance and technology. As the performers were forced into a set of interactions with the environment, the environment modified their behaviour. Furuhashi stated that "the performers don't act, they just react. They react to the various signals and the circumstances that develop" (Durland 1990: 37).

Koyamada explains that in *036-Pleasure Life* the company explored a growing awareness of the information economy: "In this project we started to investigate information, the basis of information as it shapes our notions of reality, and how we accept that digital informational reality" (Koyamada 1996). Hence, the sense in *036-Pleasure Life-Pleasure Life* of regulated, rationalistic environments in which human agents are governed by technological presence. As Koyamada suggests, these works are immersed in the context of the bubble era in Japan in which the information revolution and postmodern capitalism were conspicuous features.

Cultural critic, Mark Dery, described the informational space as a "fatal seduction . . . distracting us from the devastation of nature, the unravelling of the social fabric, and the widening chasm between the technocratic elite and the minimum-wage masses (Dery 1996: 17). In light of this well-known criticism of globalization, a provocative and artistically compelling analysis of the information economy is a chief concern of the works following *036-Pleasure Life-Pleasure Life*, especially, *pH* and *S/N*.

The body as love vehicle/information capitalism: pH and S/N

In his essay *The Performance Art of 'dumb type': The Body as Love Vehicle*, Kumakura Taka'aki claims that: "The contemporary body is exposed to at least two threats, informationalization and AIDS" (Kumakura 1995: 22). The comment is noteworthy not least for its positioning of the body as being under threat of invasion. There is a sense that the body is operating in hostile territory and has become compromized, invaded, and less able to 'defend' its autonomy. Doubtless influenced by developments in critical theory, Kumakura sees the contemporary body as possessing at least three aspects: the personal space of subjectivity, the social-collective dimensions of bodies in community, and—as a result of developments in science and technocapitalism—the body as medicalized and technocratic. The subsequent interplay between autonomy and the social space comes into critical focus as a result. Under the rubric of techno-capitalism and the postmodern economy of information, social factors categorize and limit the political and human dimensions of the body. In accordance with the needs of social power the body might be labelled in various ways; as a worker, as hetero or homosexual, as sick, attractive, redundant, as a client, a consumer, a slave, or a combination, and any other classifications that one might imagine. Capitalism has historically made great demands on the body—be they on its physical strength, mental capacities, or the requirement that it become more fully integrated into corporate or military systems. And for capitalism, there are no limits to the re-categorization of the body, therefore, the requirement that it adapt to new systems is unbounded. This is made more complex in present day society, where forms of social engineering are enforced through media and workplace regimes. Moreover, images of bodily consumption are at levels unprecedented in history. The body is now expected to work in fully integrated modes: with technology, with corporate systems (it must smile on demand, perform automated service functions, remake its physicality so as to interface with computers), and do all of this over long hours with constant threats of termination. Its thinking, habitual tendencies and leisure times are monitored by surveillance and data, its social interactions are increasing described in pseudo-corporate-speak terms: 'quality time', performance optimums, slogans from the latest television show . . . all this has the capacity to overrun and transform the personal body. We can only conclude that mechanisms of informationalization—highlighted in Kumakura's essay as a new mode of power—are an invasive transformation of the social body that leaves the body empty and under command.

036-Pleasure Life-Pleasure Life began investigating the information economy and its effects on personal and social states of embodiment. Subsequent works, *pH* and *S/N*, developed this theme considerably. *pH* considered the implications of such modes of informationalization in a global context as they impinge on questions of identity and selfhood. *S/N*, arguably the widest ranging and personal of dumb type's works, modified the critique of the social body and, in addition, addressed issues of sexuality and HIV-AIDS. The direct motivation for *S/N* was the fact that several members of dumb type chose to politicize the issue of their own sexuality in a public space. Furuhashi also publicly announced that he was HIV-positive and *S/N* was strongly influenced by his status. Knowing this, Kumakura's notion of 'the body as love vehicle' can be read as an attempt to proactively position the body in response to these dystopic themes.

The use of technology and design in *pH* was spectacularly impressive. As the audience stood on platforms running around three sides at the upper edges of a rectangular pit they looked down on the performance space. This space was a bright cold surface reminiscent of a "clean room" of a hospital or a computer component manufacturer. Two beams silently sliding back and forth in perpetual motion, traversed the ground floor level. One was approximately 50 centimetres from the floor; the other beam passed above the heads of the performers, but was situated below the audience. Both swept back and forth, replicating the movement of the scanning beam in a photocopy machine. The lower beam, in particular, conjured the photocopy image with its thin band of white light and automated "prowling" up and down the space, as it scanned the performers' bodies and the shiny surfaces of the floor. The upper beam supported slide projectors that projected images of maps, timetables, statistics, and corporate logos onto the bodies and the floor. At the far end of the space, video images were projected onto a wall while at the other end, hidden underneath the audience, an automatic serving machine lobbed tennis balls into the space at random intervals. Like projectiles, they were unpredictable—aiming, yet not aiming at performers.

John Coulborn's review of *pH* describes how all human movements were forced to respond to the gliding mechanisms of the machinery: "the company members integrate their movements with those of the mechanised set, creating a civilisation that is not only at home with the relentless machinery, but too often dominated by it" (Coulborn 1995). The choreography during most of the piece was built around the encumbrance of the mechanical arms and the need for the performers to lie under or jump over the lower arm at each passing phase. Hence, a literal and visible sense of the autonomy of the performers was overrun as they were forced to respond to the ceaselessly smooth running, silent machinery. Overall, the design of the space and the effect of the machinery were intended to distance the viewer and objectify their gaze (Koyamada 1996).

The content of *pH* comprised thirteen scenes or "phases" that were in no sense linear or connected as a narrative. Phase one featured three women (Sunayama Noriko, Tanaka Mayumi, Yabuuchi Misako) with white folding chairs. They alternately danced, sat, and lay down (collapsing their chairs) as the beam passed over their prostrate forms. Peter Golightly (whose evidently multiracial body aides in the complex reading of identity in the piece) walked around pushing a shopping trolley. The text "pH: A media-theatre of global consequences registered in our nerve circuits" and other catch-phrases—like protest slogans and advertising—were projected onto the wall and sometimes onto the floor. In phase two, the womens' bodies were laid out on the floor and scanned by light. In other phases, images, bar codes and numerical data patterns were pro-jected around the space. Corporate symbols, flags, charts, satellite images, maps from street directories; all forms of coding and map-ping were variously projected onto the rear wall and onto the floor, and the bodies of performers via the moving array of projectors installed in the top beam. "Latest Findings," phase six, showed a series of retro-women's fashion images accompanied by a humorous parodied commentary and playful camp gestures; the images were listed as "sporty, tropical, snobbish, active, casual", and so on. Furuhashi modelled some of the costumes in drag. Phase nine was a "Global Village Mambo," developed as a humorous counterpoint to Marshall McLuhan's influential 1960s concept of the "global vil-lage." "Marshall McLuhan what are you doin?" they ask. "Marshall McLuhan, the place is a ruin" (dumb type 1993). Meanwhile, bat-tery operated pink pigs lumbered around the space in the next phase. Some critics suggested that this image symbolised Japanese indus-trial growth (Alvarez-Basso 1993; Hasegawa 1993) although surely this was dumb type's parody of the bubble era. Phases eleven ("pass-port-control"), twelve ("Are you lonesome tonight?") and thirteen ("Do you have some form of identification?") shifted between inter-rogations of identity and informational branding. Numbers outlined in white light seemed to burn onto the skin of the performers' bod-ies; like cattle, they were freshly branded with an owner's seal. The sequence where bodies were shown spinning on a table onto which images of a terrestrial globe were projected to the tune of "Are you lonesome tonight?" seemed to convey the message that the human subject is lost in the world.

Wide ranging critical responses to *pH* (which toured to many places) come together around a common focus on the themes of commodity capitalism, information, and the body. Thus, Onitsuka Tetsuro summed-up *pH* as ". . . various human activities, consumerism, war, even gender differences . . . expressed as conflicts between advanced system technologies and the (human) characters" (Onitsuka 1993: 29). Coulborn stated that *pH* "defies analysis and order as it bom-bards its audience with a series of images of a conformist consumer society that mows down all individuality" (Coulborn 1995). Carlota

Alvarez-Basso concludes, "The entire piece serves as a criticism of global consumer society" (Alvarez-Basso 1993). Koyamada, who was involved in making *pH*, agrees that investigating issues of autonomy and politics were important aims of the work as a whole. But more than this, the work sought to explore the question of existence.

> In the 1980s, we began to face many social problems. We wanted to look at the effect of these changes on the surrounding culture and on ourselves. Once again, we questioned social reality. Reality is an English word also used in Japanese. We played with ideas of realism. What is our reality and how does it compare with other notions of Japanese reality? (Koyamada 1996)

PH broaches philosophical questions about the nature of social reality. It questions how reality is constructed for Japanese people and how alternative forms of selfhood can be explored.

The site of this debate in the work is the body itself. As we have seen, the body is automated in *pH* and bodies are written on and controlled. The Japanese subject presented here concedes to a stereotype of conformity and technological integration—a dystopic, corporate, post-human scenario. As Hasegawa argues, in *pH* dumb type examines a "hierarchy of values (and) experiences of self" (Hasegawa 1993). Each phase of *pH* presents a particular hierarchy of practices that constitute identity as something that is external and learnt. Each encounter with the machinery leads us to ask what factors are important in the construction of self image; thus, the recourse to brand logos, the physical force of the beams, the projectiles, and the rituals of scanning and marking the bodies with numbers and maps. Rather than Japanese, we might ask if this is a globalized body and consider the broader implications of this question. Alternately, *pH* reflects precisely on the question of how globalized information and commodity structures have been internalized by individuals in Japan. It recalls the 1990s world of superbrands and, harking back to John Clammer's work on consumption, it reinforces the fact that "consumer capitalism creates new subjectivities," (Clammer 2000: 212). It regulates and disciplines the body in this way and becomes a substantive base for subjectivity of a particular materialist, apolitical kind. By operating through media and advertising, it "profoundly influences emotions" (Clammer 2000: 212).

Towards the end of *pH* the following text is played to suggest the act of being questioned by an immigration officer:

Do you have some form of identification?
Is this trip for business or pleasure?
And how long do you expect to be staying here? . . .
What is special about your personality?
What happiness do you dream of?
Have you ever wanted to be president? . . .
What mistakes can you tolerate?
Would you die for your country?
What do you think heaven is like?
(dumb type 1993: 55)

Alternate possibilities for subjectivity are included in this matrix of border policing and interrogation procedures. It is about discovering where the borders lie and where they might be broken.

> *pH* was about borders, the main borders being political borders and identity borders. The political centred on the borders of nation, society, and the political body. The identity borders were concerned with nationality and gender. What is Japanese (and by implication what is nation and ethnicity) was one of the questions we were concerned with. We were concerned with how society develops notions of gender and thereby defines identities within society. The notion of the New World Order also influenced our thinking: "the new world order (equals) new world border." There was a new political situation being discussed, the Berlin Wall came down, many things seemed to be challenging the notion of borders. West-East dichotomies too, both in Berlin, and between Japan and the West, changing borders, changing situations. (Koyamada 1996)

PH does not just look at the singular issues of power but considers their social context and co-dependency. Mostly the conclusions are pessimistic, as in Kumakura's assessment: "information and technology: they act to combine the logic of advanced capitalism" (Kumakura 1995: 27). Furuhashi concurs: "*pH* expressed an '80s view of life—a chill despair camouflaged in seductive images" (Furuhashi 1995a: 5). Nevertheless, by ironically turning our attention to the notion of borders, *pH* is not without optimism. The margins of technology are the mechanism of subjugation for the human subject, but also the source of our rescue. Hence, during the performance of *pH*, Furuhashi says:

> If only that, the sole contribution—
> The blow Technology can deal to Art
> If only that, our one means of escape from the jail
> Then Technology's good for something (dumb type 1993: 23)

Likewise, fellow dumb type member Fujimoto Takayuki in another section of the performance states that: "thought-patterns and actions come to set dominant world models . . . Still there are no grounds for believing them to be immutable" (dumb type 1993: 43).

S/N *and the new subjectivity*

For Koyamada, *pH* was concerned with social and political borders, while *S/N* was about individual reality, sexuality and one's personal boundaries.

> (*S/N*) was about localism, communication and the performance of self. We were getting closer to answering the questions posed by this overarching statement (and thematic concern of dumb type): what is this thing called self? (Koyamada 1996)

S/N or signal to noise ratio is a term that measures the relative amount of noise that accompanies a given signal. It is the ratio between unwanted signal (e.g. tape hiss, component noise, etc.) and wanted signal (e.g. music). Furuhashi takes a more social inspiration from the formula: "The noise embodied in the actor is a reflection of that person's own life" (dumb type 1995: 2). *S/N* drew on stories from dumb type members' experiences of HIV-AIDS, sexuality, disability and identity politics. In a culture that is known for silence and even aversion to these subjects, dumb type sought to make them noisy and normative.

The performance version of *S/N* that premiered in 1994 comprised six scenes (in English throughout the performance): "Evolution/Invention," "Love Song," "Censor Me," "Hysteria," "Coming Out," and "Blood Exchange/Amapola." Most combined rapidly changing video images with music compositions, monologues, dance, critical texts, and a complex lighting design. The idea for *S/N* grew from a smaller performance and seminar on the politics of HIV-AIDS held in 1993. There were also two exhibition formats of *S/N* devised in 1992. In subsequent performances content changed and an *S/N* performance text was published in 1995 (dumb type 1995). The stage design featured a raised platform extending across the up-stage area furthermost from the audience perspective with performers sometimes working on a moving walkway. The face of the platform served as a screen for video projections. Below this was a second performance space. In the first scene "Evolution/Invention," music combined with video and strobe lighting effects accompanied a dance in which the performers moved across the platform; sometimes meeting, sometimes passing, sometimes free-falling off into darkness. Texts such as "I dream my gender will disappear/I dream my nationality will disappear/I dream my blood will disappear," were rapidly projected onto the surface below the walkway. Scrutinizing images of the naked bodies of company members framed by cross hairs like an x-ray machine were intermittently seen running across several circular projection areas. A series of texts based on opposite configurations of *S/N*; for example, "signal/noise, some/none, soma/noos, south/north," also blended with the aforementioned images. Many such images recurred throughout the performance. Remembering that the scene is called "evolution/invention" whereby the question of societal effects on the construction of gender and identity is bought to the fore and the body's autonomy is presented as a dream—an essence that requires imagination.

As in *pH*, labelling and forms of social categorization were used. In the next scene "Love Song," for example, Furuhashi wore placards on his suit: "male," "Japanese," "HIV+," and "homosexual." Others performers also wore signs: "deaf," "Japanese," "homosexual," and so on. Furuhashi asserts the scene shows that: "We are what we are labelled" and not actors (Furuhashi 1995b). Later he applied make-up and dressed in drag—another label, another self. The commentary: "Can you see which is the person with AIDS? Who cares if we all have safe sex" was projected along with a selection of commentaries on HIV-AIDS taken from the worlds' press and medical journals. The question of the playing out of HIV-AIDS in the 1990s as a way of targeting gays and the profound consequences of labelling are explored, as is the proactive strategy of wearing and expressing labels of choice. To quote Laura Trippi, "as the performance builds, the categories of risk proliferate" (Trippi 1996: 32).

In "Censor Me" a "foreigner" was interrogated at passport control. Once again, labels were highlighted. Here, governmental and geopolitical rules of citizenship and nationality were subjected to ridicule. When an imaginary customs and immigration officer refused to believe a woman when she said she truly was Japanese, the woman inserted a fibre-optic camera into her vagina as if to cite some form of authentic identity; the body was both demystified and invaded. As if her sex organs define nationality: in this performative gesture the actor viciously parodied images of good wife-good mother (*ryōsai kenbo*) as an enduring stereotype of Japanese womanhood.

At a certain point, the labelling of bodies and their interrogation began to be positioned even more strongly. In the scene "Coming out," the following is projected:

> I do not depend on your love. I invent my own love . . .
> I do not depend on your sex. I invent my own sex . . .
> I do not depend on your death. I invent my own death . . .
> I do not depend on your life. I invent my own life . . . (dumb type 1995: 19)

In the final scene, "LIFE/LOVE/SEX/MONEY/DEATH" cycled rapidly in sequence. Previous actions were repeated. Two dozen miniature flags of the world were on a string pulled from her vagina by unseen hands and trained across the space like a mini United Nation's summit. This image suggests a new age of invention and a celebration of creative, personal-political difference.

Conclusion

New couplings and social relations are proposed in *S/N*. Furuhashi asserts: "the possibilities of sexual experience have to be invented in a new way. We have to reinvent the idea of sex and human bonding, otherwise we can't survive in the next century" (Trippi 1996: 33). *S/N* is positing an evolution of the social space.

Love equals communication. . . . The body, the information body, AIDS . . . it is actually impossible to know my body by myself. We need other people to know ourselves. Communication and relationships, these are very important. . . . Ultimately, it is the dream everyone (in the company) shares that we call reality. (Koyamada 1996)

After *pH*, the meaning of the performing body changed. From alienated reactive and passive, the body came to be displayed explicitly and vulnerably in *S/N*. Its sense of personal space was reimagined. In this regard, "the body as love vehicle" is a desire to see the body reintegrated into communitarian, rather than corporate spaces. *pH* is predominantly dystopic, but *S/N* finds hope in resiting technological imperatives by countering these with personal desires, alternate histories, and newfound community. When compared to the backward steps taken since, this is even more provocative to consider.

CHAPTER NINE

RETHINKING THE *ANGURA* BODY
IN GEKIDAN KAITAISHA

> Contemporary theatre is divided into two cate-
> gories; one is where humans are ill, therefore, we
> should do something to cure or awaken them. The
> other is the violence that is endemic to society. I
> wish to criticize this.
>
> Shimizu Shinjin (Nishidō 2002: 182)

Angura's far-reaching rethinking of the performing body—a factor
that has resulted in numerous compelling aesthetic developments—
has been a recurrent theme of this study. And unlike some other
aesthetic innovations, such as surreal experiences of theatrical space
or the utilization of material drawn from traditional theatres, the
body's importance to vanguard theatre culture has grown in stature.
To this end, the body as a medium for the investigation of performance theory came to dominate the work of the 1990s. In previous
chapters we considered the critique of *angura* from diverse perspectives, but we have not yet focused on defining this radical sense of
physical being. How can *angura's* sense of corporeality work as a
mode of cultural expression without replicating, or falling into, the
political endgame of postmodernity? Alternatively, is there an activist
and militant system of cultural representation experienced in the
body that can affect the evolving sensibility and cultural significance
of the Japanese avant-garde?

These questions will be considered in a discussion of Gekidan
Kaitaisha (Theatre of Deconstruction) and their seminal work about
the politics of embodiment from the late 1990s, *Tokyo Ghetto: Hard
Core* (*Tōkyō Ghetto: Haado Koa*, 1996). *Tokyo Ghetto* was a decisive work
for the company—many of Kaitaisha's concerns with the body and
society ferment in this production. In speaking about *Tokyo Ghetto*,
Kaitaisha artistic director, Shimizu Shinjin, comments:

> In today's society, there is coercion at work, but in terms of what
> people say and do, that coercion is hidden. Physical theatre is no
> exception to this situation. We want to reveal this fact in our theatre.
> Our solution is not to stage a confrontation between the controlled

and the controller and not to make theatre into tales about resistance and freedom. (Nishidō 2002: 177)

The evident concern with disciplinary regimes here, that calls to mind the work of Michel Foucault, suggests that Kaitaisha's work has been invigorated by the creative exploration of cultural politics and the analysis of power.[1] In fact, as I have argued, the rise of theory as a factor that shaped the production and reception of the contemporary arts of the 1990s was widespread. As we have already seen in the discussion of dumb type, the potential for a reinvigorated performance scene in Japan was evidenced by their work on media technologies and identity politics. An increased awareness of the possibilities of critique enabled the performing arts to begin to reclaim ground that the avant-garde had ceded to bubble theatre.[2] In Kaitaisha's work the body, as a political aesthetic site of experience, is one of the ways in which the purpose of theatre culture in the 1990s differed from the generic, playful genre of the former decade. Recognition of the influence of cultural politics in the work of Kaitaisha was a fundamental aspect of this paradigm shift. Insomuch as current debates about the avant-garde stem from those in the 1990s, these factors also call for further analysis that might cast light on the present-day art scene.

Body politics

Some of the questions to be addressed arise in response to William Marotti's 1997 essay in *Shiataa Aatsu* (Theatre Arts), a journal published in Tokyo. Marotti investigates political readings of the body in the history of *butō*. He concludes that recent experience shows a paradigm shift away from viewing the *butō* body in performance as a site for opening up forms of social or cultural inquiry and toward the body, signifying increasingly immobile representations of Japanese identity.

---

[1] In recent works, Kaitaisha have focused on themes and issues that have predominately arisen in cultural politics, themes such as: globalisation, cross-cultural performance, the body and war, and the body as refugee. For writing dealing with these issues see: (Barber 2002; Broinowski 2003; Eckersall 2005; Eckersall, Uchino et al. 2004b; Kaitaisha 2001).

[2] Nishidō suggests that the 1990s saw a "paradigm shift" in the Japanese new wave, arguing that groups associated with the shift displayed a tendency to develop less binary and more conditional responses to social and critical issues (Nishidō 1996).

It is . . . a tremendous tragedy that the richness of *Butō's* complex development and experimental content has tended to fall victim to approaches
that displace this historicity, obscure its problematics, and dull its crit-
icality. In the worst instance this can amount to a reading of *Butō* that
sees in it merely an instance of the signification of the eternally identical,
based on an idealized conception of racio-cultural essence. (Marotti 1997)

Thus, Marotti argues that *butō* has been displaced from historical
context and made into an issue of race and nationalism. What militant critical possibilities remain for the body in the *angura* space,
given that even *butō*—the most radical site of disarticulation of the
social body in the Japanese theatre world since the 1960s—has
become aligned with dominant modes of racial signification? Such
embodiment of approved and legislated cultural practices favours the
maintenance of a monocultural tradition in Japan. At the same time,
divergent spaces and possibilities for individuals and groups in Japanese
society that might not fit the mould are closed down. Are there other
sites and strategies for performing arts and body politics and, if so,
what might they be? Is the critical placement of the body as a culturally determined entity—a hallmark of *angura*—still seen as a useful strategy among contemporary theatre practitioners in Japan?

In the forms of physical and spatial abstraction marking Kaitaisha's
work one observes a sense of dislocation or slippage from fixed
notions of the body, fixed concepts of performance, and, by impli-
cation, fixed ideas and assumptions about the nature of Japanese
cultural representation in the 1990s. The central importance of the
body and its simultaneous interrogation in Kaitaisha's work, can be
read as a return to a theatre that offers strategies that resist the surrender of body politics to service mainstream and status quo interests in society alone. I argue that the body is presented as a socially
constructed subject in Kaitaisha's work while, at the same time, it
is a site for showing the body's extension into social space. The body
as sign—and the marks of its simultaneous encounter with the social
world—are two modes of corporeal expression in Kaitaisha's work
that hold political significance. In a powerful statement exploring this
dual sense of body politics, Francesca Alfano Miglietti writing on the
role of the body in art since the 1960s notes:

There is an insistence on the anguish of the vanishing of meaning,
there is a discussion of legitimacy of all power, isolated contorted bodies are shown torn in half, frightened, a precipitous sentimentality, and
the anguished surfaces, in the images of works that declare their own
will, their determination not to condescend. (Miglietti 2003: 41)

To understand the performing body in such a manner—grappling with meanings of the body that coincidently insist on signifying representation and validating phenomenological experience—opens new spaces within which a radical sense of questioning of society and culture is again possible.

Gekidan Kaitaisha

Gekidan Kaitaisha began as a loose-knit gathering of university students who wanted to work on a project with Shimizu Shinjin in the mid-1980s. According to the director, the group had no particular artistic formula in mind though members held in common a desire to "change the world around them through art" (Shimizu 1996). As it turned out, the resulting artwork utilized performance as a way of giving expression to the "student dancers, visual artists, performers and musicians" who had come together. Although there was no presumption that performance would be the outcome, Shimizu has said that he began to "realise that performance art was at the core of (his) being" (Shimizu 1996). Indicating that he regards performance making as a social art form, and an ideal forum for the investigation of struggles between individual and collective rights, Shimizu says:

> There are many ways of changing the world: dance, filmmaking, art, etc. But these are all personal art forms whereas theatre is a communal thing. The basis for the collective (of theatre) is recognizing that each member is an individual and even though all the members are Japanese, we need to recognize the possibility that each member can be different from each other. (Shimizu 1996)

This statement shows the importance that Shimizu places on the principle of negotiation as a possible way of resolving political conflicts that are manifest in Japanese culture. It points to an awareness of political forces in society that might shift between the extremities of social coercion on the one hand, and isolation and individualism on the other. As was also stressed in reference to dumb type, questions of difference and how difference might be negotiated in society are now paramount. This understanding is implicit in Shimizu's thinking.

Evidently, the company regards art to be an effective alternative aesthetic and political agency. Through the example of the performing body, Kaitaisha operates at a point of intense debate and social criticism. The company therefore has a role to play in monitoring and interpreting what they perceive to be the destructive realities of contemporary Japanese life. Hence, Kaitaisha proposes that in the 1990s Japan wound back the progressive advances of the 1960s and 1970s and came to display disturbing revisionist, authoritarian, political and cultural tendencies. As will be argued, a "national poetics" that combines the imperatives of global capitalism with an intensification of the rigid binary of Japan–Other, so as to counter the possible weakening or dispersal of "Japanese values" when faced with the forces of internationalization and the global economy, has been wrought. In drawing attention to the possible reification of Japanese culture along racially essentialist lines Kaitaisha is an example of a resistant and rebellious political avant-garde, the antecedent of which lies in the nexus between new left politics and new theatre groups from the 1960s era. However, the difference for Kaitaisha lies in the changed political environment: not Ampo, the Vietnam War and America; but globalisation, war bodies and the disciplinary exigencies of power. In reference to art and politics in the 1990s, Shimizu writes:

> I regard theatre as "war." It's truly war, in the sense that a human body is indiscriminately consumed (in war). However, there was no body in the Gulf War. It was such a shock for theatre, that a war without bodies had raised the curtain of the 1990s. (Otori and Shimizu 2001)

Kaitaisha are alive to questions of performance methodology and processes of creating theatre in a social context. This extends to evaluating their own processes and connecting them to practice. To a large degree this means that what Kaitaisha *is* in its social and organizational structures, Kaitaisha *does* in performance. For example, their commitment to an alternative politics extends to an open door membership policy and members' life experience is often drawn upon in the making of a performance. In performance, a fragile membrane of physical representations and memories of lived experience seems to intermingle with ideological perspectives and statements on the nature of power. Like Kawamura Takeshi, Shimizu has been critical of leadership issues in *angura*. His criticism stems from his belief that one should view theatre as a microcosm of social reality, and notes that: "a sense of coercion has not been made clear to group members; it's the way Japanese society has worked until now" (Shimizu 1996). For Kaitaisha this is a complex issue. While Shimizu is critical of power issues in the domain of small theatre companies, he does not attempt to deny their impact in his own work. A potentially ambiguous, double sense of criticism is played out in the work as a result. Kaitaisha aim to show that theatre is complicit in acts of social coercion and is authoritarian, hence a kind of warfare ensues. But at the same time, the group is an outlet for self-expression and militant creative dissent. In this respect, Kaitaisha is perhaps uniquely self-reflexive among Japanese theatre groups and views its own processes of making work—as well as the works' presentation—as sites of political action.

In fact, Kaitaisha propose a radical rethinking of performance. The difficulty of creative expression and the wider political problems faced by artists in an age when moments of artistic representation are clouded by media saturation and materialism are central considerations in their work. Although the ability to represent something in the theatre is fundamental to theatrical language, *Kaitaisha* have come to question the meaning of this when society is so saturated by representational forms. In responding to this sense of inertia, performance is not seen as an isolated or singular function, or the outcome of a singular and modular creative process. Instead, performance arises from the lives of the company members. There is no distinction between rehearsal and preparation for work, and the presentation of that work for audiences. In other words, the work of *Kaitaisha* accumulates through the experience of performers and designers and their interactions with and responses to the expanding vision of Shimizu and other company members. They also seek involvement with political and social groups such as NGO's and activists. Hence, in keeping with the spirit of 1960s groups, performance is a total reality and a consuming life experience; the theatre is understood as a social practice and a way of being in the world. Shimizu does not work with metaphor or dramaturgical complexity in his work; rather he aims to show things as they are: "The only thing that can be done is exposing the body to the audience" (Nishidō 2002: 178), he says. As will be seen, this is an important point especially in respect of *Tokyo Ghetto*, a performance where performers' bodies were displayed in controversial circumstances.

Tokyo Ghetto: Hard Core *and the experience of violence on the body*

Tokyo Ghetto: Hard Core was a compilation of thematically linked scenes that were not sequential and did not constitute parts of a cohesive narrative. Comprising dance, music and performance art, each scene was typically long (some twenty or thirty minutes), often involving the repetition of one core action that slowly developed into a pattern. However, we cannot easily read these moments as straightforward acts of representation. Instead, their *presentation* suggests an overwhelming atmosphere of effect that gradually accumulates from the disciplining control and troubling, enigmatic physical presence of bodies in the space. All the performers display excellent physical skills and are deeply absorbed by their internalized sense of physicality. In fact, Kaitaisha members draw inspiration from Hijikata Tatsumi's *ankoku butō* and have a strong sense of the mechanisms and energies of performance—they are endurance performers with exceptional body awareness. The themes themselves remained obscure, although systems of power, processes of socialization, the body politic and occasional references to contemporary events, were thematically present throughout the work. Kaitaisha's 1996 tour to Croatia, for example, and the complex political and ethnic tensions that have dominated that region were referred to and used as a point of analysis with the view to making broader comments on the nature of power. An analysis of power and its inscriptions on the body is a core concern of the piece as a whole.

In the first scene a woman (Hino Hiruko) in a white backless dress, carefully carrying a stool, slowly walked to the centre of the stage and sat with her back to the audience. Her face was expressionless and her eyes were focused directly ahead, suggesting a state of disengaged compliance that she maintained throughout the scene. A man (Kumamoto Kenjiro) dressed in a black suit entered. The space was silent. He walked the length of the space and stood to one side of the woman. His composure was also expressionless. He carefully reached out to touch her shoulder with one hand. He then touched her back with a caress that was both tender and detached, and then moved behind her and placed a hand on each shoulder, before lowering his body into a crouch. Squatting, he reached up and began to slap the woman's right shoulder in a regular rhythm. Occasional slaps on the woman's left shoulder provided a counter

rhythm. After a short time of regular, emotionally disassociated slapping, the woman's skin turned red. As the slapping continued, one
was forced to watch the skin bruise and then become bright red.
The cumulative effects of several performances were evident. This
scene continued for a long time.

The man finally stopped and carefully stood to one side of the
woman, slightly behind her. He walked around to face her, lifted
her feet and rotated her body so that she faced the audience. Once
more, we observed the impassive face of the woman as the man
quickly spread her knees apart. The man then rapped out the same
rhythm on the woman's knees. After a time, the man transferred
the slapping to his own knees, gradually moving away from the
woman, bending low, as he eventually sank to the floor, exhausted.

Following a pause during which the only sound was the laboured
breathing of the exhausted man, the woman slowly got up and walked
to the man, picking him up and carrying him like a baby, returning to her place. She placed him so that he was standing on the
floor and then resumed her first position, with her back to the audience. He returned to his position, squatting below the woman, and
began to slap her back once more. After awhile he stopped and the
woman turned of her own volition, presenting her knees. The man
slapped her knees before retreating and continuing to violently slap
his own knees, finally collapsing.

The performers show a cycle of small, intense, private violence
on their own and their partners' bodies. There was no reason given,
nor did any form of expression or response mark the slapping action.
Both seemed to be in a state of deep conditioning: to inflict and
receive this localized pain, accepted without comment. The audience
was also wounded; by our own conditioning that views the bruising
with empathy, and by the length of the scene, which lasted about
twenty-five minutes. This meant that the scene became progressively
harder to watch. At the same time audiences seemed to experience
a growing sense of detachment to the violence as a result of the
mechanical repetition. During one showing a member of the audience called for the action to be stopped, but was ignored. The scene
concluded with the man removing his shoes and placing them on
his hands; he writhed on the floor like an animal as he crawled off
stage. The woman carefully picked up the stool and slowly exited.

Only during one performance in Croatia an audience member
attempted to physically intervene and stop the slapping; he twice

attempted to physically stop the man, only to be brushed aside by Kumamoto who then continued the slapping action. Later, a speech inserted into the middle of the Tokyo performance by Onuki Takashi (a former Kaitaisha dramaturgical advisor) discussed the reaction of the Zagreb audiences. Nishidō notes, however, that the violence in Tokyo caused none of the consternation that it received in Zagreb. "In the case of Japanese audiences there is only a lukewarm reaction to the work. Their confusion and hesitation is sublimated and the problem (of violence) concealed" (Nishidō 2002: 180–1). When variations of the scene were performed in Melbourne in 1999, having two of the male performers slap their own thighs perhaps lessened the overtly confrontational experience. To witness real pain, seemingly without justification or contextual framing, was nonetheless challenging and confusing for some audience members.

In Kaitaisha productions, performers are often shown to be without individual will and seemingly locked into coercive practices and situations. The question of replicating or naturalizing coercive states and their presentation for the purpose of critical commentary comes into play in this and other scenes in their work. The performers obviously consent to subject their bodies to a performance that in some ways objectifies and dehumanises them. However, ironically for Kaitaisha, this might be understood as a step towards the artist achieving autonomy and a sense of control over their experience of the world. Kaitaisha performers experience a powerful sense of release through their work, a point that is evident in their processes of training and creative practices as a group (Eckersall 2005).

The work is also prescient at the level of a more generalized sense of social criticism. Thus, if Japanese society is rudely coercive, Shimizu works within a long tradition of artists in Japan who address this fact in their work. Hence, confronting audiences with the violence of their own culture and perhaps their own compliance with regimes of power is a valid and tested strategy of the avant-garde.[3] Even more important than this artistic legacy in the current work is Shimizu's evident use of cultural theory as a way of informing his

---

[3] For example, writing on the relationship between theatre and politics, Baz Kershaw argues: "A theatrical attack on the oppressions of the state, say, gains in political stature by demonstrating that the nature of its opposition may invoke processes of oppression almost identical to those it sets out to attack" (Kershaw 1996: 139).

creative process. As Uchino Tadashi points out: "The space in Shimizu's theatre is filled with various 'political bodies' whose theoretical background we can find in Michel Foucault's notion of archaeology, or in feminism's theorization of the 'male gaze'" (Uchino 1999: 49). In fact, Kaitaisha affect a rare double act of performative praxis; the bodies both express a sense of authentic experience *and* present images as manifestations of power. Thus, the body "speaks" to a reordering of the sensorium (in the Artaudian sense of atmospheres and curative essence), but also has an eye to showing its disciplinary functions—the instructional procedures that are enacted on the body in the social world are visible in this work as well.

Two predominant aspects of *Tokyo Ghetto* are the crisis in representation, as seen in and on the body, and in relation to the reality of Japanese cultural identity; the work addresses the sense that coercive forces are evidently at play in order to perpetuate a national cultural project.

Tokyo Ghetto *and the "empty" body*

I argue that the slapping scene at the outset of Kaitaisha's performance puts on display and critically engages with the notion of the social body. In this scene, there is no avoiding the body; the slow precision of its placement in space and the physical violence enacted on the body demands our total attention. No other action, character or narrative that might be a source of distraction or comfort to the audience is available. There is no explanation for the deep conditioning of the body, or the performance of a closed circle of seemingly preordained, violent co-dependency. In particular, the sight of reddening skin and the regular slapping sound that shocks our sensibilities. "The skin turning red is a kind of actuality," says Shimizu (Shimizu 1996). The fact that the slapping results in a surface inscription on the body that is without interiority, without pain, meaning, comment or explanation, is profoundly disturbing. Our discomfort in viewing this act perhaps stems from a purposeful problematization of the body's presentation in this performance. Human qualities and any sense of social stability from which we may recognize or, indeed, empathize with the performer are undermined by the fact that in this scene there is no interiority, no determinacy or logic, only the exterior conditioning of a surface inscription. We are therefore confronted with an experience of the body that is empty.

For Shimizu, the body is the primary mode of investigation in this performance precisely because of its problematic status. He says: "My basic premise is that the body is now unable to say anything—that it is impossible to say anything through the body . . . Instead the body exposes something, brings something to light. The body . . . reveals something, some other condition" (Shimizu 1996).[4]

The work of feminist scholar Elizabeth Grosz on the theme of the body sheds light on this condition and will be referred to extensively in the following discussion. To relate Grosz's terminology to *Tokyo Ghetto*: "the body becomes a book of instruction, a moral lesson to be learned" (Grosz 1994: 151) and "a medium, on which power operates and through which it functions" (1994: 146). Grosz applies Foucaultian criticism to argue that the body is indelibly marked with inscriptions that occur because of coercive and corrective social institutions: hospitals, prisons, psychiatric institutions, educational institutions and the like. She also points to the coercive inscriptions of more or less daily life experience—inscriptions that occur because of our work, personal values, relationships, gender, fashion, class, and ethnicity. Grosz argues:

> There is nothing natural or ahistorical about these modes of corporeal inscription. Through them, bodies are made amenable to the prevailing exigencies of power. They make the flesh into a particular type of body- pagan, primitive, medieval, capitalist, Italian, American, Australian. What is sometimes loosely called body language is a not inappropriate description of the ways in which culturally specific grids of power, regulation, and force condition and provide techniques for the formation of particular bodies. (Grosz 1994: 142)

Grosz is therefore in agreement with Shimizu in arguing that the contemporary body has no interiority, no natural human comfort zone, and that we are left with only the surface of the body that

---

[4] Also relevant is Kaitaisha's idea of theatre as "sur-documentalism." In replying to a question of clarification about the term, Shimizu comments: "In this era, representation is no longer possible; the methodology that emerges is documentation" (Shimizu 1996). The notion of sur-documentalism is first explored in program notes for Kaitaisha's 1992 outdoor performance art event, *The Drifting View*. Meanwhile, its likely precursor, Documentary Theatre, was a revolutionary theatre first associated with Erwin Piscator. Murayama Tomoyoshi had explored Documentary Theatre in Japan in the 1920s. However, Shimizu's adaptation of the term arises from this aforementioned crisis of representation. Kaitaisha tries to show things as they are without the framing of a documentary genre, in other words, the sur-documentation is almost by chance and evident by the presence of these bodies in the space and their actions.

exposes something or brings something to light. In the opening scene and throughout *Tokyo Ghetto* body language is complicit, preordained, and able to respond only to what Grosz observes as prevailing exigencies of power.

Shedding further light on the slapping sequence is Foucault's writing on punishment. Accordingly, punishment can be seen as "procedures for the subjugation, manipulation and control of the body." Punishment in this guise is what Foucault terms a "political technology" of the body (Grosz 1994: 151). This reading sees the body in Shimizu's work as a medium for showing the experience of social coercion, and the presentation of these images confront us with the experience of power in actual terms.

Many scenes in *Tokyo Ghetto* contain images of social conditioning designed to demonstrate how political technologies work on and through the body. In the second scene, for example, which is structured around a dance improvization, the accumulation of movements gradually transmute until each actor performs in synchronization. It is an effective demonstration of "procedures for the subjugation, manipulation and control" of the body as in the first scene, although less graphic.

The scene also featured a woman being periodically frisked by a mysterious male in a black suit, wearing a sinister black hood to cover his features. Disturbing repetitions of a series of gestures: patting down the body and searching through the hair, increased in intensity over time. The scene culminated in the woman automatically and repetitiously frisking herself, as if interrogating her own body for concealed abnormality. This is a feminist statement about the invasion of womens' bodies by the patriarchy and exposes political technologies (sexual, medical, ideas of feminine beauty, etc.) of domination and control. It suggests the conditioning effect of social and educational institutions and gender relations wherein one is searched or subjected to surveillance so often, and in so many ways, that the body learns to enact its own, ultimately more extreme self-surveillance. In other words, we begin to regulate and condition ourselves in relation to dominant and acceptable forms of behavior through voluntary self-censorship, thought modification, and self-punishment.

Only Kumamoto, who we see in scene four singing the words of the punk-rocker anthem *All Power* (performed at bone-jarring intensity by Iggy Pop) might be seen as a solo agent and a seemingly independent force. The sentiments of the song might suggest access to power or at least an understanding of its mechanisms. But no matter what the intent, nor one's relationship to power and place in the 'pecking order', the suggestion is that power is totalizing in its intensity. As the auditory assault of the accompanying soundtrack increases its volume, drowning out the rasping voice of the performer—who continues his ineffectual performance regardless—personal autonomy is shown to be futile and defeated by exhaustion. As extreme as this action is in aesthetic terms, he is allowed to make the statement precisely because it exhausts and diverts him and damages his vocal cords. Consequently, as much as his speech is already reduced to banal and empty slogans, he is silenced by his own actions.

In each of these instances the performing body is inscribed with a semiotics of power. It is given over to patterns of performance that escalate in their intensity and culminate in regimented moments, where human agency is defeated by the accumulation of external signs and forces. The empty body, inscribed with such instruments of power is designed to draw attention to how authoritarian and monolithic forms of enculturation might work in Japanese society. Moreover, the lack of resistance to the body's makeover—especially evident in the slapping scene—and the first two moments described above, suggest that we are conditioned to accept our socialization and might not be fully aware of ways in which power might overtake our lives and our being.

While these intense images unfold, however, a parallel and alternate critique of the body is also evident. The argument that the body has no interiority and is readily inscribed with outside cultural forces in *Tokyo Ghetto* is balanced by the human presence of the performers. Indeed, as I have already suggested, much depends on their awareness of their bodies as self-sufficient inside the performance environment. In discussing the slapping scene, Shimizu acknowledges that the performance is mediated by the fact that "the performers have feelings for each other" (Shimizu 1996). A paradox emerges from the fact that the body is given autonomous status in order to devise a performance that denies autonomy. Although Shimizu states that the body is empty and unable to have interiority, the company also seems to work toward a return of the fulsome body of sensation and experience. Thus, as Elaine Scarry writes: "Though the capacity to experience physical pain is as primal a fact about the human being as is the capacity to hear, to touch, to desire . . . (pain differs) from every other bodily and physic event, by not having an

object in the external world" (Scarry 1985: 161). Perhaps this perspective is most expressive in the sensations of release and transformation that are almost privately experienced by group members
inside their performance process. This means that the notion of the
empty body both is presentational and actual, creative and provocative in the same moment. *Tokyo Ghetto* is a vehicle for the company
to explore and agitate about the poor state of affairs in present-day
Japan; it is also a way of activating sensation. In marking experiences in the world and responding to these conditions on their own
terms, Kaitaisha seems to revive a politics of action.

Empty self/empty other: "National Poetics"

If the body is "empty" of interiority; so too is the condition of
Japanese culture. A question that emerges then is the notional position of the Japanese subject. Shimizu suggests that Japanese people
are like zombies: "their actions are zombie-like as they move toward
the new wave of culture . . . like empty vessels ready to be filled with
the newest imported ideas" (Shimizu 1996). This point concurs with
Grosz's notion of the body lacking interiority and being inscribed
with the social and political agents of culture and identity. But can
the body be inscribed with national–racial political essence and, if
so, what does it mean?

Both inside Japan and in the international field of image production, the Japanese body as a reflection of society has been classified
in stereotypic ways. Popular images of Japan include humbleness,
bushidō and harmony (*wa*); at the other extreme, violence, complicity and infantilism are commonplace images of social reality. Japanese
bodies are sometimes seen as overly commodified with their designer
brand loyalty and conspicuous consumption. Scholars also point to
the prevailing sense of intensely gendered behavior that construes
males as dynamic and mobile, and women as self-regulating and self-
censoring. In the early 1990s, the French Minister for Foreign Affairs
caused a diplomatic incident when it was suggested that Japanese
people were like rabbits—so complete was their conditioned accep-
tance of living in small spaces. By contrast, the memory of Mishima
Yukio's fetishized Japanese body as erotic, masculine and mystical is
also with us.

Most disturbing is the trend toward theories of an essentialized Japanese body and by extension, the notion of an ideologically laden, imaginary community of bodies. This provides the material for H. D. Harootunian's persuasive critique of "national poetics" and gives rise to an idealized ethnocentrism, involving a particular notion of the body as the embodiment of Japan. Although Harootunian is writing about the occupation era, his observations extend to the rise of globalization in the 1990s. As the author suggests, a national poetics results from Japan's engagement with America and postwar capitalism. While Japanese society develops a poetics of difference, it actually serves the interests of Japanese and multinational corporate elites and not, as promised, some kind of unique Japanese essence. From Harootunian, a sense of "cultural holism" is suggested that is naturalized through culture as the ceaseless and enduring reality of the uniqueness of Japanese existence. To relate this theme to Kaitaisha in *Tokyo Ghetto*, the body is brutalized into sameness. To adopt Harootunian's phrasing, it is inscribed with "the ideological force of continuity and value integration" and a national poetics "which are ceaselessly promoted as enduring presences in contemporary Japan," and the "'common-sensical' means for differentiating Japanese from others" (Harootunian 1993: 216–7). The intensely mediated Japanese social body as it is explored in *Tokyo Ghetto* exists in counterpoint to the body of national poetics. According to Harootunian, the latter exists "to remind Japanese that this cultural uniqueness and difference accounts for the nation's vast economic and technological successes" (Harootunian 1993: 216–7). Meanwhile, the theatrical image remonstrates against national poetics by its presentation of inscriptions of complicity and violence. *Tokyo Ghetto* shows that different cultural movements co-exist in Japan by its presentation of coercive social practice that would condition and supplant variation.

Conclusion

In closing, we might ask what are the chances for a militant corporeal theatre when the body has been so thoroughly expropriated as a social condition? "At best such a subject remains indeterminate, nonfunctional, as incapable of social resistance as of social compliance" (Grosz 1994: 144). In these circumstances, the body is enmeshed in disciplinary regimes that result in a complete repudiation of a sense of self-autonomy. Shimizu argues that this is how the new social reality of Japan has come about, and says that: "People are not aware that they are individuals and no longer members of the community. This is how the idea of being all-similar or like-minded Japanese continues to exist" (Shimizu 1996).

Tokyo Ghetto: Hard Core shows how Japanese culture has historically evidenced ideals of commonality and unity, perhaps to a greater degree than many other nations; ideals that infuse institutions and subcultures more completely than was commonly experienced in the west, for example. However, we should also question these thinly marked distinctions in the present age. The focus on national poetics in this reading of *Tokyo Ghetto* applies to contemporary, social–political processes concomitant to and fundamentally inside of processes of globalization. Subsequently, such forms of national cultural essentialism are widely experienced across the globe. And while social cohesion and community values are desirable in society, so too is a critical eye and a lively debate about their effect. In *Tokyo Ghetto*, Kaitaisha theorizes the body and the cultural space as interrelated, and in so doing, have made some deeply disturbing theatrical images; images that comment critically on the uncertainty surrounding the status of the individual subject in the contemporary world. Such investigations inevitably ask explicit questions about society, economy, and the state. The company's use of the body should also be read as a critique of history and of the operations of power from wider perspectives than the Japanese context alone. They remind us of how much Foucault's notions of discipline and biopower have been realized under the rubric of globalization. Hence, the critical assessment of Japanese society in the 1990s seen through iconic presentational and expressive signs of the performing body, not only place Japan in the national context, but point to the global space as well. This is above all a prescient gesturing towards refugee bodies, bodies at war, and the regimes of compliance and dissent that figure in our present day, tumultuous world.

CHAPTER TEN

PERFORMANCE AS HISTORY: *HAMLETCLONE* BY KAWAMURA TAKESHI, AN ANNOTATED PLAY TRANSLATION[1]

Translator's Note

This translation of *Hamletclone* is from the Japanese publication of the play *Hamuretto Kurōn* (Tokyo: Ronsōsha, 2000) and undertaken in consultation with the playwright Kawamura Takeshi. Kawamura subsequently made changes to the playscript in February 2002 and again in 2003, prior to a German tour of the work. These changes have been incorporated in this translation. *Hamletclone* responds, in part, to Heiner Müller's work *HamletMachine*. Throughout, I have referenced the English translation from Müller's *HamletMachine and other texts for the stage*, edited and translated by Carl Weber (New York: Performing Arts Journal Publications, 1984). I have also consulted the Japanese publication of *HamletMachine* translated by Iwabuchi Tatsuji and Tanigawa Michiko (Tokyo: Orion Literary Agency 1992). Excerpts from Shakespeare's *Hamlet* and *Macbeth* are also included in this play.

Cast
Thief
Soldier A
Soldier B
Prince A
Prince B
Prince C
Old Gay Prince/Man
Girl A
Girl B

---

[1] I would like to acknowledge translation assistance and give thanks to Nishida Mariko and Don Kenny. Inquiries about performing rights for *Hamletclone* in English should be forwarded to Kawamura Takeshi and T factory.

Girl C
Gertrude
Claudius
Polonius
Horatio
Ophelia
Young Man
Tramp
Laertes
Fortinbras
Man

Prologue

Large gates covered with barbed wire are strung across the stage apron. The image suggests a concentration camp. When the audience enters, they discover they are on the stage proper, looking out through the wire into the auditorium.

A dog is barking at a man.

Thief Who do you think you are, asking me who I am? If either one of us lets on then it's civil war for sure. Is that a revolution? No! How can it be Hamlet, unless everyone in the family kills each other?

The dream of total ruin is like a shining moon in the winter sky.

With the force of a heart attack, somewhere a Vampire chants.

How could it be?

Long Live the Emperor of Japan! Banzai!

Politics! I fought in the anti-Narita airport struggle, became active in the People's Party. I hid in Osaka and on the western side of Japan. I voted for Yokoyama Knock.[2] Then I came back to Tokyo.

Dreaming of the day when we can say who we are.

---

[2] Yokoyama Knock is an outspoken, right-wing nationalist politician who was a TV comedian before embarking on a controversial political career. In the 1990s he was elected Mayor of Osaka, only to be found guilty of sexual harassment against a female campaign worker.

Abandoned by family and company. . . . Hah! The word abandoned has a tiny seed of hope. The hope that you're not going to lose anything else.

Stop! Who are you! A friend of Japan.

Bring on the civil war, I demand to play Hamlet!

Can you understand? At the dawn of the new century the curtain is drawn. But only melodrama plays.

I am Hamlet. Rough hewn and beautiful, all actors want to be me.

To dream of acting Hamlet. I will not die before playing Hamlet!

I am the prince. I am the prince who lives in the age of late capitalism. To be in this age or not to be . . . that is the question.

To be or not to be . . . that is the question. How good it is to feel this way.

The pleasure of speech . . . the critical mass of the play bubbles over into civil war.

Let us go and look for Ophelia now . . . Let us look among the mass of refugees trying to cross the border.

Let me find a menstruating virgin, innocent and beguiling, one who will drown in the Sumida River.

That's how I will finish my civil war!

1. Colony

Night scene in Shinjuku. A Thief riding a stolen bicycle moves among the audience singing the Japanese National Anthem (Kimigayo). An image of the 'Red Sun' Japanese National Flag (Hinomaru) is projected on to a wall. It mutates into lurid colours as it sways in the breeze.

Two soldiers have rifles at ready. People are lined up behind the barbed wire fence. When they touch it, they realize that it is electrified.

A solder points his gun and shouts, "stop"!
The Thief loses his balance and falls. As he falls his clothes catch on the barbed wire.

2. *Autobiography*

Prince A, B, and C and Girl A, B, and C appear as a rotating array of figures among the seats in the auditorium. Prince A is played by a male actor. Prince B is a male actor cross-dressed as female. Prince C is a female actor. All are standing, but fall at the end of each line as if shot. Their dialogue is punctuated by gunshots.

Prince A   I am Hamlet.

Prince B   I might be Hamlet.

Prince C   I was Hamlet.

Prince A   I was Mishima Yukio.

Prince B   I was Peidro Paulo Passolini.

Prince C   I was Riener Weiner Fassbinder.

Prince A   I was Adolf Hitler.

Prince B   I was Joseph Stalin.

Prince C   I was Pol Pot.

Prince A   I raped Korean women. I cut off the heads of the Chinese.

Soldier B fires his gun and Girl A reacts.

Prince B   I sent Jews to the gas chambers. I sentenced a political prisoner to death by firing squad.

Soldier A fires his gun and Girl B reacts.

Prince C   In Los Alamos I finished making 'Little Boy' and 'Fat Man'.

Soldier A fires his gun and Girl C reacts.

Prince A   I was the woman who killed my best friend.

Prince B   I was the woman who killed my neighbours with poisoned curry rice.[3]

---

[3] In the summer of 1998 at festival in Wakayama Prefecture, local housewife Hayashi Masumi served curry rice laced with arsenic to passers-by. Four people died and 63 others suffered the effects of the poison. Hayashi was convicted and sentenced to death. Her subsequent appeal was rejected by the courts in June 2005 and she is now on death row.

Prince C   I was the woman who killed my own child.

Soldier B fires his gun and Girls A, B, and C react.

Prince A   I was a bullet.

Prince B   I was mustard gas.

Prince C   I was Sarin Gas.

Prince B   As the top floors of the building collapse, the reverse course of communism is like an after image playing on my eyelids.

Soldier B fires his gun and Girls A, B, and C react.

Prince A   Banzai. For the Mt Fuji Geisha Girl, Banzai.

Prince C   Banzai. For the economic animal, Banzai.

Prince B   Banzai. For the animation and TV games, Banzai.

Prince A   The ruins of Japan in the midst of the world. Bravo!

Prince B   I was Hiroshima.

Prince A   I was Nanking.

Prince C   I was Auschwitz.

Prince B   I forced my way into the State funeral procession while shouting the name of the ruined city.[4] And even in the midst of all the fervour, the government gave out poisoned human flesh to the citizens.

Soldier A fires his gun and Girls A, B, and C react.

Prince C   The roast sirloin for the Marxists. The karebi joints for neo-Nationalists. To which one should I add the sanchu sauce?[5]

Prince B   In Shinjuku Park the homeless who ate the flesh send-up smoke signals. An uprising by the homeless people.

---

[4] Perhaps a reference to: "Something is rotten in the state of Denmark", from Shakespeare's *Hamlet* (Act 1, Scene 4).

[5] From Korean barbecue-style eating. The Roast and Karebi are different cuts of meat, while the Sanchu is lettuce and sauce that is used to roll the meat in before eating.

I was arrested. Meanwhile, what they saw was an empty coffin where the King was supposed to be.

Prince A   I took a video of my uncle and mother having sex and sold it as part of the amateur housewives porno collection. Thank you mother for not raping me.

Prince B   I looked up at the sky and saw several, low flying passenger jets. What will they blast into next?

Soldier A fires his gun and Girl A falls down.

Prince A   I was in the World Trade Centre.

Soldier B fires his gun and Girl B falls down.

Prince C   I lay in the empty coffin masturbating in rhythm with the world scraping against itself. I listened to the creaking squeaking world.

Soldier A fires his gun and Girl C falls down.

The sound of a plane exploding. Two soldiers climb over the barbed wire and approach Prince B. They force his arms behind his back, tie his hands, and lead him away. Prince A and C run away.

Soldier A   Banzai to happiness in the home!

Soldier B   Banzai to a healthy spirit!

Prince B   Without doubt, Hamlet's story made me Gay. In the Palace, my first experience, with the buffoon Yorrick. My flower bud. . . . He dribbled his saliva into my arsehole and entered me. Later, a threesome with Rosencrantz and Gildenstern. As I expected, run-of-the-mill guys with mediocre technique. Oh, but distinguished Horatio. Horatio that I loved. When Ophelia found out her menstruations went awry. That crazy old man Polonius told her. As for me though, I was determined to have a pseudo-family.

To be sure, Polonius did not want his daughter taken. I know this to be true. The father who never stopped wanting to commit incest.

> Ah, Fortinbras my long-distance lover in a faraway land. Polish men always cry tears from only one eye.[6] In my country that is full of empty laughter and complicity, Fortinbras taught us such ways of crying. A Latin man who loves pigs' trotters.

Soldier A   I don't want this story any more.

Prince B   Well then, what do you want?

Soldier A   Punishment and execution.

Soldier B   Hail Disney!

Soldier A   Hail McDonalds!

Suddenly, people surround Prince B and try to cut him into small pieces.

A voice calls from a tower surrounded by barbed wire. It is Hamlet as an Old Gay Prince dressed in drag. Standing below is a political party leader/woman and Prince C.

Old Gay Prince

> Unhealthy, unsound. A life that is finished should always be beautiful. This scene is obviously different from reality. Hatred is always lovely and the uprising is beautiful. Torture is like the cosmetics that cover a dirty body. It is always the murders on the streets that angels envy.

Party Leader

> That's exactly right, Prince.

Old Gay Prince

> I am the only one, a Prince who conquered AIDS and continued to live a long life. My story is the drama of the people. Alone, I'm a vast nothing. I haven't any dialogue or story at all. Everything has been left up to the people. Only the people play out the drama.

Party Leader

> To read the drama as a history of drama.

---

[6] A reference to Poland, as a Soviet satellite State during the cold war. The condition of Poland is a pain that is unable to be expressed.

Old Gay Prince

> Let the visitors through to this side.

Party Leader

> Yes. You, the masses. Now our country is unified.

The barbed wire gates across the front of the stage are opened. The audience moves to the auditorium. The following texts by Old Gay Prince are projected as <surtitles>. Each time a text is projected in this manner, it signifies the voice of the Old Gay Prince.

> <This border was built as a lesson to the people of a country without borders. This lesson was unexpectedly successful. People managed to find a seed of racial discrimination even though they share the same coloured skin. The unification of the country. Western Tokyo and Eastern Tokyo, communism or capitalism? Which blessing is suitable for Tokyo people to receive?>

The last sentence of the previous dialogue echoes with the voice of Prince C. The Party Leader and Women A, B and C stand. They are dressed in black.

Woman A   This is Electra speaking.

Woman B   This is Juliet speaking.

Woman C   This is Ophelia speaking.

Woman A   This is Joan of Arc.

Woman C   This is Rosa Luxembourg.

Woman B   This is Marilyn Monroe.

Woman C   This is Scarlet O'Hara.

Woman A   A woman is a woman.

Woman B   She buries ideology in her wet crotch.

Woman C   Once fucked, such things no longer work.

Woman B   I will not wash such things as the underpants of the men of the national parliament.

Woman A   I know no such thing as family happiness.

Woman C   I will not make anything like a gentleman's agreement.

Woman B   Long live hate and contempt, violence and death.

Prince C joins the women.

Prince C   I want to become a man.

The Party Leader slaps Prince C's cheek.

<(*Surtitles*) My brain is a scar that tempts destruction. Only a jumbled memory is a guide to the truth. Consciousness conspires with confusion. Half of my life is strutted on the stage, playing at the Imperial Theatre. The last emperor of the new century. At the heart of the people's consciousness is always the desire for the last emperor. Autobiography is constantly inclined towards utopia. The turbulence of my mind gives rise to visions of civil war. I am punished for my self-loathing.>

Party Leader
                Why?

Prince C   I want to ask the same question.

Party Leader
                Communism is invalid.

Prince C   Who are you to talk? You haven't even experienced it.

Party Leader
                I hate words like "proletariat."

Prince C   What would you know! The lowly daughter of a tonkatsu man.[7]

Party Leader
                I got to where I am today by myself.

Prince C   Don't you realize that unless you can give the people dreams, they aren't content.

---

[7] Tonkatsu: pork cutlet dish, often cheap and eaten quickly.

Party Leader
But you can't just say "communism" now—it's not so simple.

Prince C   I'm not saying that!

Party Leader
Well then, do you have any other bright ideas?

Prince C   We must tell the people how fortunate they are not to be bothered by visions and dreams.

Party Leader
Prince.

Prince C   What?

Party Leader
Nothing, I just felt like speaking your name. Prince, Prince, Prince. . . .

3. Family Portrait
A godlike and mythical photographic tableau of the emperor's family doubles as Shakespeare's characters. Claudius/first son. Polonius/second son. Horatio/third son. Gertrude/mother. Ophelia/first daughter.

Old Gay Prince reflects on his life.
<The age of hope is coming to the suburbs. Happy thoughts grow inside me and wipe out the memory of bad dreams. Trees grow and the leaves spread thickly. The scent of the forest fills my senses encasing my entire consciousness. I am the Prince of the suburbs. In the city that was built after the bomb, I lost my father. At a wild orgy, mother got-it-on with my uncle.>

Claudius   It is the privilege of a young man to have a gloomy face.

Gertrude   Do you think I brought him up badly?

Horatio   Mothers always speak like that because they are animals wanting to affirm their own identity.

Claudius   The problem is that he (Hamlet) doesn't even look for work.

Polonius	It's the fault of society.
Claudius	How about him training at your company, Polonius?
Polonius	If you don't mind a girl like this. What do you think Ophelia?
Ophelia	(*Sitting in a wheelchair, her whole body wrapped in bandages*) I won't be able to get married.
Polonius	That's why I am telling you to get married.
Ophelia	But I won't be able to get married.
Gertrude	What's so funny Horatio?
Horatio	One can live without working. Look at me. I am living and I don't work.
Polonius	What is going to happen to this country?
Horatio	Sometimes I talk about this with the Prince.
Claudius	I'd like to listen-in on that.
Horatio	The main point is to overthrow all existing conditions.
Ophelia	Ha, Ha. I won't be able to get married.
Claudius	Education. The problem lies with school education.

The Thief appears reading Shakespeare's 'Hamlet'

Gertrude	Here he comes.
Horatio	Shush!
Thief	Then I gave roles to the family. The reason that the family is so divided is that everyone was demanding they be given a role to play. I finally realized that. I am Hamlet. My wife is Gertrude, the eldest boy is Claudius, the second is Polonius, the third is Horatio, and the eldest girl is Ophelia. Just now, I went to a lecture on Shakespeare at my local public theatre. The lecturer, who is also a theatre director, was arguing that theatre contributes to the recovery of the human spirit. "In the world of today everything is out of alignment. This is a gloomy story but I was born to make things right! So let's get going."

Ophelia	Where are you going?
Polonius	To "Hello Work," the job centre of course.[8]
Gertrude	Do you have your lunchbox? You know you can't afford to eat out when you don't have a job.
Thief	I only had a bowl of plain soba noodles at the train station.
Gertrude	So you can save money.
Thief	Denmark is a prison.
Claudius	This house is a prison.
Gertrude	So why don't you go then?
Claudius	It will cost me too much money.
Gertrude	Well, if everyone is going to speak so plainly. . . .
Claudius	It's because you brought so many of us in to the world. This is the age of one child per family, you know. But this household always wants to go against the norm.
Thief	That's not what it's about.
Polonius	What isn't?
Thief	Hamlet.
Polonius	Hello Work, right?
Thief	To be or not to be, that is the question.
Gertrude	That's exactly right. It is pitiful.
Thief	Um, somehow, I think we are being too realistic here.
Polonius	Don't you think that's good?
Thief	No, it's not good!
Ophelia	What isn't? And don't talk so loud.
Claudius	*Opening a book and reading.*

---

[8] *Haroowaku* (Hello Work) is the name of a chain of employment agencies in Japan.

If it were done when 'tis done, then 'twere well
It were done quickly: if the assassination
Could trammel up the consequence, and catch
With his surcease success; that but this blow
Might be the be-all and the end-all here,
But here, upon this bank and shoal of time,
We'ld jump the life to come. But in these cases
We still have judgment here; that we but teach
Bloody instructions, which, being taught, return
To plague the inventor: this even-handed justice
Commends the ingredients of our poison'd chalice
To our own lips.[9]

Unnoticed, the Thief walks behind Claudius and stabs him with a knife. Claudius falls to the ground.

Thief   Those lines are not written here.

The Thief hits Ophelia over her head with a golf club. He hits Polonius with a baseball bat. Ophelia and Polonius fall down.

Gertrude   What! A baseball bat?

Thief   Dumb sow! You probably didn't notice, but I knew. The moment they realized this bat was a weapon . . . (*swish with the bat*).

Gertrude   Is that your memory?

Thief   Yes.

Gertrude   It's so sad . . .

Thief   Because I am a father.

The Thief removes the leather belt from his pants, puts it around Gertrude's neck, and begins to choke her. Gertrude goes limp.

<Inside my consciousness, a forest sways in the wind. I become a featureless person. I am bored with the pleasures of being seen and speaking. To be socialised is to become bland and nothing. I am nowhere. The

---

[9] From Shakespeare's *Macbeth* (Act 1, Scene 7).

sound of breath at birth and its absence at death is the only truth.>

Thief   The play was a failure.

The Thief runs away. Everyone who was killed by the Thief stands again.

Claudius   Then what happened?

Polonius   Then what happened?

Ophelia   Then what happened?

Gertrude   Then what happened?

Horatio   The people left.

4. Leadership Studies: How to be a Successful Imperialist

Enter Prince A and Horatio. Various photographs are projected on to the wall.

Horatio starts to put make-up on Prince A's face. The Thief rides by on a bicycle.

Old Gay Prince:

<I become a woman, amidst the destruction of war, the US occupation forces behind me.

The taste of Hershey bars remains as a memory on my gums. Mickey Mouse raped me. My cock wet by McDonald's hamburger ketchup, Donald Duck sucked me.

Wearing a suit and tie, my father worked in the public service built from the ruins. The country prospered from public works. There is little doubt that the first images seen by the children who flooded the subways with Sarin Gas, were images of the Nazi gas chambers.>

Horatio   What a mess contemporary history is.

Prince A   My drama won't happen anymore.

Horatio   True, but they're demanding that we play it out no matter what.

Prince A   Who is?

Horatio	The drama that was not part of the contemporary history of this country. A premonition of civil war.
Prince A	There was, I was there.
Horatio	Was a national boundary ever created?
Prince A	That was a bad dream.
Horatio	You just put the people to sleep, like, you drug them.
	In the midst of a peace that they didn't win by themselves, the people just want to be idle.
Prince A	They're intoxicated by a bad dream.
Horatio	More than cool headed understanding, what is needed now more than anything else is a clear ability to calculate.
Prince A	In what way?
Horatio	Well, that is what we should try to learn. I am totally disgusted with suffering this emptiness.

Horatio kisses Prince A.

Prince A goes to leave. He bumps into the Thief. The Thief picks up a piece of paper that Prince A dropped and runs after him.

Horatio	You, are you okay?
Young Man	This country is rotten.
Horatio	So tell me something that I don't know.
Young Man	I saw the Prince. . . .
Horatio	Don't worry. I let him go.
Young Man	How about me?
Horatio	I didn't say anything.
Young Man	When are you going to tell him?
Horatio	All in good time. He is still being trained.
Young Man	I wrote a project plan.

Old Gay Prince

<The metropolitan self-defence ground forces and the armoured division of the Kanto region are the main forces that are directed by the authorities to put the plans into action. The metropolitan defence forces should immediately take control of the following upon their dispatch: The police and the police communications centre, the main branches of the Bank of Japan and other banks inside Tokyo, the financial calculations centres, the Tokyo Stock Exchange and computer centre, the Tokyo electrical distribution centre, the communications and telephone company NTT, the national broadcaster NHK, Japan Rail, all private rail lines, the Tokyo underground lines and switching centre.

After the arrival of the armoured division, when the defence force has successfully taken control of the above mentioned utilities, comrades and sympathizes of the coup d'état, occupy the Imperial Palace, Nagatacho, the Prime Minister's residence and the surrounding Akasaka area, and declare the establishment of a new political order.>[10]

Horatio   Of course, I see. And then?

Old Gay Prince

<Installing the head of the opposition liberal party as the head of cabinet, who proclaims a national state of emergency and a one year suspension of the constitution. After one year, a national referendum on the rights and wrongs of the new political system is held. Drawing notice to the country's security, the dissolution of political parties is effected. The success of the coup depends on the approval of America.>

Horatio   It will cost some money.

Young Man   We need some weapons too.

---

[10] This is a quotation taken from writing by the rightist critic and neo-nationalist, Fukuda Kuzuya. A section of an imaginary overthrow of the postwar order in Japan which Fukuda published as a novel is quoted above. Nagatacho is the area where the Parliament is located.

Horatio	We'll be busy.
Young Man	Please do your best. I am relying on you and your skills of persuasion.
Horatio	This is for the good of the country. You make it sound like I'm bluffing people, the people must know they have a responsibility to pay.
Young Man	Don't worry. This is history in the making.
Horatio	The masses are like a woman.

5. Training Brides for Home-Making Duties (or Classical Arts that Every Good Woman Should Know)

The head of the political party and armed female soldiers appear late at night in a drinking club. (No speaker nominated in the text).

I dreamt that in the month of October a general election and the state funeral were held at the same time.

I dreamt in the month of October when the coup d'état and a revolution broke out at the same time.

I dreamt in the month of October when both the land war and racial purification act was discussed at the same conference table.

I dreamt in the month of October when Tokyo City separated into East and West.

I have this cunt, which is the one thing in the entire world.

I was raped.

In a coffin shaped bed. I cry out in a gasping voice that is like the level of the world's inheritance, as I smell the body of an old man.

A national treasure, I pissed on the street that is marked by the blood of a recent murder.

I plucked my pubic hair at the request of the cap-italist-male machine. I took off my underwear at the request of the Stock Market.

I was raped.

Just before the start of the rainy season on my way back from school, I was raped in the woodlands near a suburban sprawl.

I was raped as I travelled on the Chuo line in the morning.

The rapist threw himself on tracks at Kokubunji.

So, whenever the train stops because of an accident or suicide, I remember the smell of sperm.

I was raped in "Yaruki Jaya, Takanobaba shop."

I was raped in a karaoke bar in Nakano, on the Broadway side.

I got to know the word rape when I was raped.

The meaning of the word is painted on the wall that divides Tokyo into East and West.

Because you don't know the sweet taste of revenge.

Because you don't drink expensive wine with the young madams of Shiroganedai.[11]

Because you don't throw underwear stained with menstrual blood at middle-aged men at the street stalls.

Nausea, Nausea, Nausea. My nausea is the most beautiful in the world, the dirtiest thing in the world is I, and the smelliest thing is my cunt.

Inside my underwear it is even filthier than a middle-aged man who has piles.

Venereal disease or Chlamydia, which is truly the most lonely disease?

I didn't go to Egoist.[12] But I was raped and became a true egoist.

Nausea, Nausea, Nausea. My nausea, full of chocolate, the most proud.

At dusk, I buried my family in the woods near the suburbs.

There was a TV broadcast of the state funeral when I returned to my house.

The king's coffin moved along the street and passed the masses.

In the startling glare, I saw the prince . . . a memory of a group attack.

---

[11] A wealthy suburb of west Tokyo.
[12] Egoist is the name of a beauty salon franchise.

Vulgar pedigree although high born.

Prince, I want to commit adultery with the memory of your murderous desire.

There is some more time yet.

It would have been okay to stop the story.

Don't be arrogant, there was never an age when things were not out of whack. You middle-aged diabetic!

But I don't hate that smell because I was always surrounded by it, full of rotten things, and the smell of decomposing things is the normal smell for me. Being rotten is my everyday existence.

So there is no assassination or betrayal.

Here, I opened up my legs as you wished! For the happiness of the people! After burying my family there was no role left for me, except for memories. Although, I knew that the memory was already written down.

A wave of racial purification marched towards the city following the state funeral and the election. The porn video that I acted in was confiscated.

In order to erase my memory, I drew lines in the city. I formed a line that was like a border.

To escape from the kidnapping and entrapment, acts interpreted this way and that.

That was the beginning of our beautiful civil war.

I hate men . . . men who are worried about the state of the country.

For the first time I threw myself into political activities.

Ophelia, Polonius, and Gertrude enter. In a prison surrounded by barbed wire, the women change into girls' school uniforms.

Polonius   I will take care of all the expenses for the wedding.

Gertrude   Of course. It is the wedding of your own daughter.

Ophelia   Ha, Ha. I won't be a bride.

Gertrude   I was a wife, the wife of Hamlet. King Hamlet, the great masturbator. Washing, cleaning, putting out the garbage, sucking cock. I was a good wife. It was just a fancy of mine to start thinking about killing my husband.

Polonius   You just want the insurance money.

Ophelia   I won't be able to get married.

Gertrude   The only thing that men couldn't destroy is women's power to give birth to children. And the child loves the mother unconditionally. Husband. My husband. My honourable husband. All the wives in this country are slaves and chattel. But even these honourable men couldn't cut the bonds of love that slaves and chattel have. The married man soon realized that he must acquire the love of a child for himself.

Polonius   So that's how you women make men useless and vain. You say such things knowing their cruel effect.

Gertrude   I gave birth to a baby boy. I bought him up to be a real boy. Courageous and masculine. No matter what, he ran to my side whenever I faced peril.

Polonius   I feel like throwing up.

Gertrude   I have no luck with men whatsoever. My first husband was an army fanatic. He loved to play shooting games while wearing army camouflage and collected GI Joe dolls. My second husband was the younger brother of my first. He was an animation freak. He dressed me up as cartoon action characters while he wanked into his underwear and masturbated me. My partner in fidelity. . . .

Polonius   A man who wasn't a man.

Gertrude   No. A father who sexually abused his daughter.

Polonius   You misunderstood.

Gertrude   The lowest form of man, fucked up men, completely hopeless luck with men. This is the reward that I get, the so-called satisfying deal . . . cleaning, washing, cooking, and putting out the rubbish, sucking cock. . . . The only real man among you is my son!

Polonius   But that child was homosexual.

Ophelia   Ha ha, Te he.

Polonius   It's okay. I have given him extensive training in jerking off.

Gertrude and Polonius embrace each other (with sexual overtones).

Ophelia   After forty years my father said he loved me, he went into the bathroom and locked the door, he put up photographs of the children on the basin next to the black stockings and garter belts. As he looked at the photos he masturbated and then he hanged himself in the shower. It was his ultimate, final erection. And final orgasm. When my father died, a huge earthquake occurred and sarin gas was scattered in the subway. I could not hope for a better death if I tried. Because I feel guilty for having an abortion after being raped by a family member . . . you don't have to worry . . . I'm not going to say your name. The reason why my father committed suicide is that he thought I was no longer attractive.[13]

Gertrude *(to Polonius)*
                 Do you want to sleep with my husband?

Ophelia gets up from her wheelchair and removes the bandages wrapping her body. Underneath, she is wearing a Japanese schoolgirl uniform.

Women dressed as Japanese schoolgirls appear. The mobile phones of all the girls start ringing with a variety of tones. The girls leave as if haunted by some spectre. Only Ophelia and Girl A remain.

Horatio appears.

Horatio   Who are you?

6. Everlasting Suffering

The Thief opens a piece of paper dropped by Prince A. In the distance a Tramp is listening to the horse races on the radio. He has a vacant expression.

Horatio, Girl A, and Ophelia approach the Tramp. Horatio takes a video camera from his bag and films Girl A and Ophelia. (The Tramp has paid the girl to masturbate him).

---

[13] Adapted from texts by Karen Finlay with additional material by Kawamura.

Girl A	. . .
Tramp	Don't you know who I am?
Girl A	. . .
Tramp	*(To Horatio)* Why did you bring this useless prostitute along?
Girl A	Don't call me that! *(protesting)*.
Tramp	Don't act so dumb. I know that you're thinking things through, always calculating the margins. Hey *(To Ophelia)*, how about you, you know me right?
Horatio	Please forgive her, she's new around here.
Tramp	It doesn't matter. My name is Ishida. I was the Vice-Minister for self-defence. I was . . . always thinking about . . . the good . . . of the country. Those underground, left-wing scum destroyed this country. They destroyed the pride of the people of this nation. Yes, it is I, Ishida the patriot, who went to the Senkaku Island and planted the flag of the rising sun.[14]
Ophelia	*(Suddenly)* I know, I know.
Tramp	You know, ha! You *(to Ophelia)* swap with her *(Girl A)*.
Horatio	I said she's new.
Tramp	Even better.
Horatio	Now, no hitting, or punching.
Tramp	When did I ever smack anyone around?
Horatio	You know full well that you often bash people up. That's why all the girls run away from you.
Ophelia	*(Approaching the Tramp)* Phew! You stink!
Horatio	Of course he stinks.

---

[14] A reference to an event when right-wing neo-nationalists, including Tokyo Governor, Ishinha Shintaro, visited the Senkaku Islands to plant the rising sun flag and thereby claim the islands as Japanese territory. The Senkaku Islands are contested territory under claim by Japan, China and Taiwan.

Ophelia	Yes, you really smell bad.
Horatio	So what.
Ophelia	I am upset.
Horatio	About what?
Ophelia	That a person can be this smelly.
Horatio	What do you want to do?
Ophelia	I want to see the Prince.

The Tramp suddenly slaps Ophelia's face roughly. Ophelia starts to quietly weep.

Horatio	There, you've done it again!
Tramp	Don't speak of that family in front of me.
Horatio	*(To Girl A)* So get to work. Do your job.
Tramp	You think my cock is so cheap that it will get hard with this kind of stuff? Do you want to hear about my cock?
Horatio	I don't care if I listen or not.
Tramp	I was sued for sexual harassment.
Horatio	By a secretary or someone . . .
Tramp	It doesn't work unless it's in the rough hands of a labourer or soldier. You need big hands.
Horatio	Now I know. That explains it. Is that why you always gave me a hard time?
Tramp	I always feel like vomiting when I smell young women. You should praise me for having done a good job.
Horatio	Shit. Revolutions aren't easy.
Tramp	So suffer young man.
Horatio	I'll hand job you. *(Reaches for the Tramp's cock).*
Tramp	Oh no. No. Your hands are the hands of an artist, so it's no good.

Horatio	Shit. Oi, old man. *(Whispers to the Thief who was standing beside him with a blank expression on his face).* Can I borrow it?
Thief	You know I don't have any.
Horatio	Not money. Can I borrow your arse?
Thief	Oh, arse. Okay.
Horatio	Fuck wit.
Thief	*(Approaching the Tramp)* You stink.
Tramp	Too old.
Thief	But, I think he's firm enough. He's never done it before.
Tramp	Now listen here. You should value life!
Thief	Ha Ha Ha. Hey. I heard something like that before. From the sex worker. After so many times. Ha ha ha ha. . . .
Tramp	Are you kidding me?
Thief	No No No No.
Tramp	You're just a dirty old man.
Thief	That's a bit much, coming from you. God, you stink!
Horatio	Oi. Get your clothes off, quickly now!

The Thief and Tramp take off their clothes. The Tramp rapes the Thief.

Tramp	*(To Girl A)* I might get hard if you strangle me. Do it and see.

Girl A strangles him.

Tramp	Yes, more. You're really good at this. That's the spot. That's the spot.

As the sound of the horse-races stops, the Tramp falls down dead.

Horatio	Is he dead? I'll make a video. Let's take him somewhere and you can pose like you're fucking him.

Girl A   *(Pointing at the Tramp)* With him?

Horatio   Yes. While he is still warm.

Horatio carries the Tramp on his back and leaves with Girl A. Left alone, the Thief shakes the radio next to him (hoping to get some sound from it). The horse-races start again. He puts on the clothes that the Tramp earlier removed and sits calmly.

Thief   *(To Ophelia)* Stop crying. Being sorry for yourself does nothing. Come here, young lady. Don't worry I'm not going to do anything. This old man can't even get it up.

Ophelia   *(Standing)* Hey, noni noni.

Thief   Ophelia!

Ophelia   *(Reading the text in a dead flat monotone)* Oh the heart that was so kind has become so cruel! This beautiful country, the revolution of this country, the coup was a perfect war, civil war personified. All the tramps rejoiced. But everything, everything is finished! I am a very unhappy and pitiful girl. Everything, everything is finished! Ah, how sad. Everything, everything is finished! *(Repeats and exits).*

Thief   Get thee to a nunnery, to a nunnery go! *(Sees her off)*. . . . We did it, what a great scene!

Claudius enters.

Claudius   What sort of life is this?

Thief   Your Majesty!

Claudius   I am in the midst of inspecting the way in which the people live. Don't you have a job for me?

Thief   No, I'm afraid not.

Claudius   There's going to be a compulsory evacuation. I am only telling you this because it will look bad if you get hurt. You should go somewhere else. *(He looks at the Thief whose expression is uncertain, anxious)*. I understand the feelings that you have towards me. But there is no relation between the changes now and your former military associations. It is only your sexuality that is of concern. Do you understand?

Thief   What?

Claudius   Please be quiet for now. If you do, you will be able to rejoin the Party later. The people here are forgetful, in time they will forget. . . . But you won't be able to be a parliamentary vice minister like before. . . .

Thief   Sorry for all this trouble. . . .

Claudius   You have a Japanese sword, right?

Thief   What?

Claudius   Please be quiet!

Claudius finds a Japanese sword underneath the mattress in a cardboard box shelter and exchanges it for his own.

Claudius   This is good. You're neither a spy nor an informer. You just didn't know. Let's have a drink sometime soon. We can talk all night about the time when Japanese were real Japanese.

Claudius exits. The Thief picks up the sword from the mattress and removes the blade from the scabbard. He examines the blade. The Young Man enters, looking harassed.

Young Man Don't. Ishida. What are you doing?

Thief   What?

Young Man *(Snatching the Japanese sword)* There are police everywhere. *(As he speaks he swings the sword).*

Thief   You'll be seen too.

Young Man Hide it. Hide it! Don't let it go out of your sight—whatever happens. Promise me. Soon the civil war will begin. As Ishida hoped and prayed for, soon the inner city will become a battle zone. Here, this is the morning paper for you to read. I've already read it. Sell it and keep the money for yourself.

The Young Man runs away. The Thief holds the newspaper. The Thief's family is visible in the background.

Gertrude   Papa.

Claudius   Dad.

Polonius   Father.

Horatio   Old man.

Ophelia   Father, Sir.

Thief   You okay?

Gertrude   Since then I joined a new religion.

Claudius   I've joined a sect.

Polonius   I've joined the rightists.

Horatio   I became the owner of a brothel.

Ophelia   I started to appear in sex videos.

Thief   You're all wrong. It's time you all lived more morally.

Polonius   This is the right balance. The story goes more smoothly if you aren't around.

Old Gay Prince.

<Destruction is blind. I won't make you dance anymore. There is no ruin of this world. So what are you going to do? Are you going to fill up your disgusting everyday life by looking for a miracle cure that doesn't exist yet? Will you overlook the street battles as you mumble on about wanting to help and be good? How about if you make a clone? Let's give these people from the past.

No, I am not going to do this. If I am going to make a clone, I am going to make my own clone. I want to make my DNA live long. Piece by piece, I want to carve the hatred and apathy of the world into a clone.

Papa, there is no drug, no miracle cure all for this time. All that remains is the certain death of those who keep on looking. The shock of death gives people the hope for a miracle cure. It makes them feel like they have taken a wonderful medicine. I am a clone of my clone. That's it. When the time comes that's the only thing for it.>

Two soldiers appear.

Soldier A   Banzai to happiness in the home!

Soldier B   Banzai to a healthy spirit!

The soldiers beat the Thief with batons.

7. A Perfect Massage Parlour

<When I went outside the moon was hazy with a green fog. Thinking about the new century I started to reflect on a new system for society, a new political structure. I became excited by thinking about the things that can connect the loneliness of communism with the solidarity of capitalism. My fecund state was cause for caustic comments from high school girls as I walked to Kabukicho. I wanked, spraying my cum over the ruins of the wall that divided Tokyo into East and West. Two young soldiers came by and kicked my feet out from under me.>

A group of high schoolgirls are in the barbed wire prison. Ophelia moves among them.

Girls   Therefore I took a lot of sleeping tablets but nothing happened.
Therefore I slit my wrists with a cutting knife but nothing happened.
Therefore I thought about my life but nothing happened.
Therefore I fucked you for a whole night but nothing happened.
Therefore I went on a diet but nothing happened.
Hey noni noni.
Therefore I appeared in an adult video but nothing happened.

Therefore I went to the funeral of a famous rock singer who committed suicide but nothing happened.
Therefore I went to Shibuya and then went to Ikebukuro west-side park but nothing happened.
Therefore I beat up a thirty-eight year old language teacher but nothing happened,
Hey noni noni.
When I stopped going to the egoist beauty parlour, I become a true egoist.
I was raped.
Hey noni noni. Noni noni.
I live in an age of dead ends, a dead culture, and a dead end world. With a dead end job. My home is a dead end, my children's future is a dead end. A long, long street that is a dead end. Long, long street that is a dead end.
Hey noni noni.

Ophelia   I was Ophelia.

Horatio enters carrying a video camera.

Horatio   Are you ready? *(Focuses the camera on Ophelia).* Ophelia pulls down her underwear and pisses.

Party Leader
You slept with the Prince, didn't you?

The Party Leader slaps Ophelia's cheek. Girls spread out. Dropping their underpants and crouching, they each piss.

8. Overseas Research Report: From the London Study Visit

Claudius wears female underwear and talks to a female sex doll.

Claudius   I am embarrassed, don't look. This is my interpretation of the overseas research report from the London study visit.

Horatio aims the video at Claudius.

Horatio   I got you on tape. *(Runs away)*

Claudius   Stop that!

Old Gay Prince

> <Horatio goes on living thanks to the existence of the secret video tape.>

Prince B It wasn't Horatio who I gave the real instructions for dressing in drag, but Ophelia's big brother Laertes. I made him up to look like the prostitutes who hang out in St Dennis (in Paris).

Laertes *(In drag)* Do you want to eat my heart Hamlet? Ha ha ha.

Prince B That's not your line is it?

Laertes I don't hate you.

Prince B I don't blame you if you do. I made your go crazy after all.

Laertes She was a terrible anorexic before you met her. She read all these suicide manuals. And who was it that decided that such books were dangerous?

Prince B It was your father.

Laertes I see. And who was it that declared *Kimigayo* to be the national anthem?

Prince B It was my father.

Laertes Well now, let the duel begin.

(Claudius and Polonius enter carrying sword, Gertrude stands between them.)

Prince B This disagreement between these two men over my mother—it is not possible to resolve this. They refused the TV stations proposal to stage the bout and are determined to fight this battle themselves. This is the true story of Hamlet. Laertes and I have no swords, though.

Countless times I was forced to fight duels and was killed. I'm tired of being killed for the sake of people whose only sense of drama is when they're moved by the film *Titanic*. I have seen this.

Laertes   I've seen it too. Do you want to buy some popcorn?

Prince B   No I don't want any.

Claudius and Polonius begin fighting a duel. Horatio films them. At the end of the duel Claudius, Polonius and Gertrude are dead.

Prince B   And so the three of them die. Horatio sold the video for a lot of money to the TV station and used the money as a down payment for the coming civil war. It was broadcast as a special program and the ratings where high. People declared it an important record of the twentieth century. The new leader of the country was Fortinbras. A young and spirited man, and a man among men.

I retired from political life and opened a gay club with Laertes. And while it has been a rocky road, at times we've managed to make a happy life. Hamlet went on living. Even so, we never forgot politics.

Several gun shots are heard and Prince B holds a gun in the firing position.

Laertes   You shouldn't waste bullets.

Prince B   It is necessary to prepare for the civil war.

Laertes   You are so cool headed about these things.

Prince B   Yes. I can't believe it myself, it's as if I won the lottery.

Laertes   You've become a nihilist without even realizing it.

Prince B   That's absolutely necessary in terrorism.

Laertes   So let's agree on that. And reread *Das Kapital*.

Prince B   We should work to achieve a committed and full exchange with the public.

Laertes   You're going to be terribly busy, aren't you?

Prince B   We should practice. Let's go to the park.

They approach a cardboard box shelter. Inside they find the Thief, wounded and covered in bandages.

Prince B   You've suffered a bad beating. Who did this to you?

Thief . . .

Prince B Was it the Tokyo city workers? Or maybe some local toughs?

Thief . . .

Prince B Or was it a fight among yourselves?

Thief . . .

Prince B Aren't you dissatisfied with society?

Thief . . .

Prince B Let's fight!

Prince B holds out his right hand. The Thief stays silent but also holds out his right hand. They shake hands.

Prince B The working classes have lost the ability to speak.

Laertes We have to do something about that.

Prince B Yes.

They both leave. A Young Man appears. He approaches the Thief.

Young Man Mr Ishida, it's only a little longer to wait. Please be patient.

Horatio appears.

Young Man You should stop making fun of them.

Horatio Well, aren't you a man of the times.

Young Man That's me for sure.

Horatio Is that so? You were a little more uncertain before.

Young Man That was then, that was not me.

Horatio The principle of uncertainly should be strategic planning enough for this country. There's no point in deciding left or right.

Young Man Has anything changed? Do you think that there is any future to be had in Fortinbras' policy?

Horatio	It is surprising that you say such things. Although of mild temper, I think Fortinbras is a true patriot.
Young Man	It is sickening to think that he has such fame without having any proper policies. What is needed is a strong country.
Horatio	I don't think so. As long as we have a wise and adaptable nation.
Young Man	Although the target is still the same. It's you who has changed.
Horatio	Shit. It's the current political order that is the most uncertain thing. But you're thinking about re-examining the framework, aren't you?
Young Man	No way. It's business as usual.
Horatio	You sure about that?
Young Man	The glories of the past . . . give me the guns and we can overthrow all existing conditions.

Horatio hands the Boston Bag to the Young Man. Fortinbras appears.

Horatio	This is not good.

The Young Man throws the Boston Bag at the Thief.

Fortinbras	Oh dear oh dear, the video maker.
Horatio	What! You're going out without a guard?
Fortinbras	Eating at Yakitori stands and drinking Chuhai under a bridge . . . it's the best way to experience life among the common people.
Horatio	I see. I can well see the reason for your popularity.
Fortinbras	If you have any suggestions, please tell me. I would like to consider them. Have I met you before?
Young Man	No, this is the first time.
Fortinbras	What are you all doing here?

Young Man   We are a club in support of the Hinomaru and Kimigayo.

Fortinbras   I see. That is good. That is good.

Horatio   I take my leave (*leaving*).

Young Man   As do I (*leaving*).

Left alone, Fortinbras approaches the Thief.

Fortinbras   I've looked everywhere for you, Ishida san. I'm sorry that you've had such a hard time of things. Could you please come back? You're the hero of the moment, of the new regime. You were a political prisoner, a refugee in this country. You show us the inhumanity of the past. I promise to give back what was taken from you. I will guarantee to give you back your twentieth century as it should have been.

Fortinbras exits. The Thief looks in the Boston Bag. It is full of guns and hand grenades. The Thief looks surprised, closes the bag and moves away. Unable to resist, he finally takes out the weapons and arranges them in front of him.

Thief   Over here! Over here! (*as if calling his wares for sale*)

Man A enters, takes a gun and immediately starts shooting at random.

9. Premonition of Civil War

The middle of the night. Heavily armed women are talking in a lesbian club.

Women   Diabetes! Gout! High blood pressure! Cirrhosis of the liver! Enlarged liver! Stroke! Cerebral haemorrhage! Subarachnoid haemorrhage! Let's stigmatize people with these diseases of old age. Let's brand them. Carers of sick people, brand them with failure.
We are a rash. A rash and menstruation!
All power to the rash and menstruation!
Cancer, cancer, cancer. Breast cancer and cancer of the womb are the symbols of the battle.
Wait. Don't you want to add HIV-AIDS? Let's think about that.
That's what the people who are ill say. We should have discussions right away!

What shall we do? Shall we add AIDS?
Before we discuss this, I have an objection to the theory of diseases of old age. Sub-arachnoid haemorrhage happens to young women too!
Diseases of aging are diseases of discrimination! Down with discrimination!
Let's not get bogged down by incidentals and small details here!
But let's be frank and have a free discussion!
Freedom with responsibility!
Stop talking about morals and ethics. There is no freedom with responsibility. Freedom will only come when we are free of responsibility!
Let's destroy!
No, let's not! No, No, No, No, No! Smash and ruin, it's soooo phallocentric. One ejaculation and everything's over and done.
What can be done? Cut it off? Standing up to cocks just makes the cocks stand up!
Fight libido! Don't sew up yourself, don't sew your womb! But fight!
Penetration means both conquest and subordination!
Libido, libido, libido, the core is hot, even as desire cools!
There is something rotten in this age of hope!
The last pathetic jokes of capitalism!
Okay, okay, let's put AIDS into the group!

Old Gay Prince

< Hollow ringing and empty talk has never produced any grand theories, but rather such talk grows by practical means. They've *(the girls)* already stopped talking about stories of vision and hope after the revolution.>

Party Leader

Group number three to the electric company, group four to the phone company.

Old Gay Prince

<The girls stuck their thumbs in Marx's arsehole. They love reading the books of Ezra Pound. They chew off the cocks of the fascists.>

Party Leader
>   The railways control centre is group five.

Old Gay Prince
>   <The ex-high schoolgirls learnt that, when removed
>   for the determinations of history and culture, people
>   realize latent homosexual desire.>

Party Leader
>   Before anything, to gain higher approval, the new gov-
>   ernment installs as their mouth piece a collaborator
>   who has a pipeline into the White House.

Old Gay Prince
>   <Politics, politics, politics, politics and women, women
>   and politics, gays and politics, women and gays, per-
>   verts, perverts, perverts, perverts, perverts and women,
>   gays and perverts, politics and perverts, politics and
>   perverts, and women and gays.>

Party Leader
>   The emperor system should continue unchanged.

Old Gay Prince
>   <I want to be rid of my story>

*Women start to dance. When Fortinbras appears all the women freeze. Prince
B and Laertes continue dancing.*

Fortinbras   Hamlet!

Prince B   Fortinbras!

They kiss passionately.

Fortinbras   What's with the get up?

Prince B   Why? Something wrong with it?

Fortinbras   I don't like it. I told you before I don't like it. The
Joan of Arc look. The Drag King thing.

Prince B   So what?

Fortinbras   I don't like Drag Queens either.

Laertes   You shit.

Fortinbras I heard you, you queer.

Laertes Your cock is covered in shit.

Fortinbras Grab the queer.

Soldiers appear and take Laertes away.

Prince B But I don't understand?

Fortinbras Horatio has been arrested. He's been charged with hiding a camera in an official residence. He wanted to blackmail me with video pictures of my life. I heard Claudius was also being blackmailed. Claudius' weakness was also found by the same method. So they're not partners after all.

Prince B Laertes isn't part of it though?

Fortinbras Horatio confessed everything. From the plans for a coup to everything else that's happened. But you're not a part of this, right?

Prince B Let Laertes go.

Fortinbras I can't do that. If I'm going to let anyone go it will just be you, Hamlet. Only you.

Prince B That is unacceptable.

Fortinbras Why do you care what happens to Laertes? It is because you feel guilty for leaving Ophelia.

Prince B What happened to Ophelia?

Fortinbras Didn't you know. She died. Shot by a stray bullet in some drive by shooting.

Prince B Who did it?

Fortinbras A fifty-two-year old unemployed man. Ophelia just happened to be there. The women are insisting that she was assassinated. It's given them a cause, suddenly women power is on the rise.

Prince B When did it happen?

Fortinbras Just recently. On a street in the second district.

Prince B   . . . I think it might be me who shot her.

Fortinbras What makes you think that?

Prince B   In the end I don't think I am a complete woman. Ophelia has done well to extract her revenge. I am not a perfect woman yet.

Fortinbras Exactly. You are simply a man, that's all.

Prince B   Arrest me.

Fortinbras Are you sure?

Prince B   Yes.

Two soldiers take Prince B away. We see Laertes and Horatio standing with their hands tied behind their backs and their eyes blindfolded. Prince B is made to stand in a plastic, children's bathing pool. The soldiers shoot at the three of them. The Young Man—upon seeing the failure of the coup commits seppuku (ritual suicide).

10. As the Ship Sails On[15]

Old Gay Prince

<The attempted coup by the National Defence Force organized by the young man was a failure. Of course, the agitation and disruption never reached even a single soldier in the inner circle. History was repeated as comedy. Even so, his act of hara-kiri was not a meaningless death. In the confusion over the hara-kiri, the women's White Stalk Party started a civil war and occupied the seat of government. At their command I have survived and lived through the troubles. The new government planned to have the gay prince as a symbol of the people. Everyone thought it would be a combined government of women and gays. The women were not stupid, they were not a single cell of feminist separatists. They even invited Fortinbras to join them. By including a man who was popular with the public they made a pragmatic decision. That a lot

---

[15] The title of a 1983 film by Frederico Felllini.

of politicians, bureaucrats, and financial power brokers from the old system were arrested gave the people hope. The women carved lines from Shakespeare and Müller on to my body. I became a perfect woman.>

A souvenir photo of government officials is about to be taken.

Party Leader

This way Prince.

Prince C enters and joins the group for the photograph.

Fortinbras Wait a minute. Ishida's not here. He's the director of the environment agency. He's the hero of the day who stopped the coup d'état that was planned by right-wing forces. A young man tried to attack him with a sword. Director Ishida got wind of their plan and swapped the rightists' steel sword for a bamboo one.

Party Leader

So the attacker committed *seppuku* with a bamboo sword.

Fortinbras Exactly.

Party Leader

It must have hurt like hell.

The Thief enters quickly, putting a tie on as he rushes to join the group.

Thief Excuse me, I am not used to this.

The Thief joins the group and a photo is taken. They disperse as they leave.

Thief So, you're Hamlet are you?

Prince C *(Stops)* Yes.

Thief I always admired you. A cheap, proletarian fuck head like me, I always wanted to act like you. I wanted to be you.

Prince C The time for class struggle has already passed.

Thief That's not true. Throughout history there has never been a time when I could be a hero.

Prince C Do you want to act?

Thief   Oh yes. That is but a tiny hope of the people.

Prince C   What's so tiny about that?

Thief   If you say so . . .

Party Leader
                   Prince, I want to talk to you alone.

Thief   I'll take my leave.

Prince C   Wait. He's one of us.

Party Leader
                   Really?

Thief   Yes. I'll do anything for Prince Hamlet.

Party Leader
                   Really?

Thief   I'll do anything, then my name will go down in history.

Party Leader
                   You want to be a player?

Thief   Yes, yes.

Party Leader
                   Then kill Fortinbras.

Prince C   Party Leader, your beard is growing longer.

Party Leader
                   Prince, I want you to be part of this plan too.

Prince   Are you planning to make me act again?

Party Leader
                   You can't just sit back and watch. I won't let you.

Prince C   Not that boring play again!

Party Leader
                   I will give it to you *(to the Thief)*. *(He hands a gun to the Thief)*.

Prince C   At the end of the twenty-first century?

Thief	*(Receiving the gun, he announces in a clear voice)*: To be or not to be, that is the question.
Party Leader	You're doing so well. Keep up the good work.
Thief	Everyone, look at me. Your father is doing an excellent job.
Prince C	Ophelia!
Thief	Ophelia is you. Hamlet is I. Get thee to a nunnery. A nunnery.

Fortinbras enters.

Fortinbras	Well now, the Communications Intercepts Bill exists for this kind of purpose. Tapping phones, eavesdropping, it's not illegal any more.

Two soldiers appear.

Party Leader	Hamlet, shoot!

A short battle ensues. The soldiers collapse. The Party Leader runs away.

Fortinbras	*(Shot. Breathing softly)*. You repay good with evil. Although I made you one of us, on this side. The proletariat is in the end the proletariat. There is no story. *(Fortinbras dies)*.

The Thief runs away. Prince C cuts his wrists with a knife and holds his arms high in the air. Blood drips down his arms.

Prince C	This is Ophelia. I love the emptiness of the world. I love its hollowness. I love nothingness. Facing the city that has destroyed the entire world, I send out e-mail messages in the name of the victims. I bury the emptiness in my face. I bury the hollowness in my breasts. I swallow the void in my womb. I choke between my thighs the province of interpretation and stories. The main point is to overthrow the happy ending, overthrow hope and the subordination of capital. When

she walks through your bedrooms carrying butcher knives, you will know the truth.

Old Gay Prince

<Even with all this, I didn't die. I was put under house arrest. From my life in prison, my body changed back to a man.>

11. The birth of a nation[16]

The Thief appears with the Boston Bag. He takes out a gun and shoots.

Thief

Don't think I am a fool. No more am I a cheap Thief. I am the Minister. Minister! I have become a great man. I am going to trample over all the people who looked down on me. People like the company men. High schoolgirls, boys with long hair. I am going to triumph over you, I am going to triumph over you, I am going to triumph over you, I am going to triumph over you. *(Continues to shoot).*

Old Gay Prince

<This is the story of my people. Ten days that shook the land. During ten days, history sped up. The lecture on drama given in the new public theatre was the beginning of the revolution and civil war. A moment of hope for the people of the suburbs. Clear felling of the land was terminated. The leaves on the trees sway in the gentle breeze of early summer. Happiness is only born at a time when the word itself has been forgotten. Just mention the word and the suburban civil war will go on and on. I dreamt of cram school as I slept in the backyard.[17] From resting on my bare

---

[16] The title of a 1915 film by D. W. Griffith. While considered a masterpiece of the early American cinema, the film is also explicitly racist. It is based on a story called 'The Clansman' written by an anti-black rights church minister named Thomas Dickson. It has been reported that 'The Birth of a Nation' was used as a recruitment film for the Klu Klux Klan.

[17] *Juku* or cram schools specializing in preparing students for competitive entrance exams are common in Japan. Students attend *juku* in the evening after regular school and can be as young as five. Many educational specialists are critical of *juku*, where students route learn subject material and also suggest that such intense pressure on students that succeed gives rise to social problems.

feet, an ant climbed into my nose and pierced my heart. A heart that beats between the sentiments of ill will and reconciliation. I was Hamlet. A prince of depravity and corruption who was born of depravity and corruption. The ruins of Japan lay at my feet. The women reach out in anticipation. In the streets, random massacre. Having lost the ideal of politics, to take part in the massacre is to take part in history. Political asylum and refugees . . . these things won't end. But the new century will begin when the dishonest look for the hatred and love within themselves. Again, the happy ending is suspended at the end of the twenty-first century. I don't want to be cured. I don't want to be saved.>

Civil war breaks out on the street. The Thief shoots the Old Gay Prince in his tower.

Old Gay Prince

<Then I collapse. Shot by a nameless assassin. The bullet penetrates my left lung and a new emptiness is born. My autobiography is now complete. The title is *The Birth of a Nation.*>

The barbed wire cage is opened by the hands of dead people.

THE END

CONCLUSION

> It seems to be easier for us today to imagine the thoroughgoing deterioration of the earth and of nature than the breakdown of late capitalism; perhaps that is due to some weakness in our imaginations.
>
> (Jameson 1994)

The social and cultural upheavals in 1960s Japan put an end to the idea of the smooth postwar development of society despite this being a period of dramatic economic growth. Instead, vigorous criticism of the political system and opposition to America's continued influence in Japan's affairs grew. Acts of public protest escalated. It was a time of contest and possibility. Complementing these events was the formation of an *angura* space marked by revolutionary artistic inventions and widespread contemplations of alternatives to capitalism. *Angura* performance melds the politics and aesthetics of this dynamic revolutionary space and is a powerful, creative radical source of imagination.

After the 1960s, *angura* gradually transformed into a popular and extraordinary genre of performance. It marked substantial transformations in Japanese society and was changed by them. Moreover, *angura* became a distinctive aspect of wider postmodern and global trends, resulting in confusion and even a sense of crisis for the avant-garde. By the 1980s, people came to question the function of art in a society increasingly dominated by late capitalism and globalization. As art was evermore completely subsumed into the interlocking mechanisms of the culture industry, was not the "age of *angura*" well and truly finished?

In this book, I have shown how *angura* not only described and celebrated the 1960s era, but also marked some of its bitter ends. I explore the ways in which *angura* functioned in the context of the rise and fall of the bubble economy. I note how some theatres turned towards playful escapist intensities, but also the virtual collapse and subsequent rethinking of counter-culture as a way of life is evident. Relating to this, new contemporary performance groups came onto the scene in the 1980s and 1990s—groups that challenged *angura's* wholesale collapse into postmodern, apolitical reverie. Consequently, I have argued for the continuing centrality and relevance of the idea of *angura* in exploring Japan's shifting radical cultural history. In the extended history of Japan's avant-garde sensibilities, perhaps we can see the rise, fall and rise of the *angura* space.

Qualifying this perspective, however, is the fact that the contest over art and cultural space has dramatically intensified. As Clammer writes: "The difficulty of resistance in Japanese society lies primarily in the tendency for oppositional forces (whether political or cultural) to be co-opted" (Clammer 1997). Exploring resistance to dominating cultural and political formations through theatre and the arts is a primary concern of this book. Interwoven sites of resistance are highlighted as expressions of avant-garde revolutionary aesthetics and made visible in the memory of Japan's radical counter-culture. However, for reasons noted by Clammer (and other similarly informed artists and scholars cited throughout this book), exploring the space of resistance for avant-garde society necessitates a comprehensive theorization of the avant-garde in political terms. As a result, to investigate *angura* is to read the politics of *angura*. This necessitates the unravelling of parallel political events and cultural histories that sustain and interact with the Japanese avant-garde movement. This also requires careful rethinking of the notion of resistance; from being outside and contra to society in the period up to and during the 1960s to—in the theatre of the 1990s and until the present— thinking about resistance from the perspective of being inside globalizing structures of power. In a sense, the rise and fall and rise of *angura*, marks the rise and fall of counter-culture protest and the subsequent appearance of modes of counter-critique. For this reason, I note how alternative cultural formations began to create sites of cultural resistance *within* society. The very notion of resistance becomes more porous and fluid, in other words, adaptable. It is perhaps less ideological, yet also more political in understanding social and cultural orders. Perhaps more than was the case in the 1960s, theatre groups and communities since the 1980s are giving rise to counter-culture and critical trends that show the sense of political crisis in the world, but also rethink capitalism in more progressive, inclusive ways. I have tried to show how some of the most significant post-1960s performance in Japan has extended and reformed the *angura* space in these ways.

In retrospect, the period of the 1970s and 1980s when these transformations were underway is a blurred and difficult space to define.

Nonetheless, it is of great importance. As we have seen, in the early 1970s, the new left collapsed into isolationism and cultism. Although, at the same time, many of its political flavours entered the mainstream through ecological, peace and women's rights movements, for example. Opposition to building the Narita airport and the rising power of consumer groups led to greater transparency in corporate and political life in Japan. Each of these movements was made through and because of 1960s protest formations. More negative is the fact that power elites also learnt from the 1960s and resolved to prevent such revolutionary potentials rising again. So detrimental were counter-culture systems to their vested interests and beliefs that they have engaged in long campaigns to dispel and belittle the considerable advances of the protest era. Such disapproving viewpoints of the counter-culture have been widely disseminated by media and educational institutions, as well as politics. They dominate the social space to the extent that we no longer contemplate alternatives. Yet another aspect of the shift noted here is the fact that capitalism itself adapted and simply absorbed and reified many aspects of the counter-culture movement. In light of all these factors, contemporary artists in Japan and elsewhere work in the knowledge that powerful, and sometimes extremist groups and ideologies are dismissive of their efforts. But work they must and for companies like dumb type, new communities are proposed as modes of resistance, Gekidan Kaitaisha and Daisan Erotica, by contrast, aim to show the world in a critical light.

We witness in the present day an intense patterning of neo-liberalism, cultural exceptionalism, fundamentalism, and rising authoritarian forms of nationalism in Japan and elsewhere. Yet, these forces are failures of the imagination to create something better. It is precisely the arts that observe and critically analyze these trends. The avant-garde sustains imagination towards realizing ideas for progressive global change. Theatre, because it is intrinsically a social and artistic form, and culturally contingent and embodied, is a privileged marker for exploring new possibilities for the world. Through theatre one might rethink politics and society and "take power with imagination."

Chapter review

In this book, I have argued that counter-culture ideas and sites of alternative theatre production are intrinsic to a significant and lasting rethinking of Japanese society and culture. I have considered the role of the avant-garde in marking and responding to these fundamental shifts in the cultural history of Japan. Investigating the history of *angura* and exploring an activist assessment of the *angura* space are key outcomes of this work. Relating to this is a parallel investigation of the theatrical avant-garde from a broad perspective. Thus, I aim to theorize a politics of avant-garde theatre.

The first chapter addresses the early history of modern performance in Japan. We saw how aesthetics and politics joined in the *shingeki* movement making for a challenging social formation in pre-war Japan. Rising militarism and American economic and political dominance after the war were often resisted in the modern theatres, even while *shingeki* was also subjected to regular censorship, political attacks and in some instances, punishment for artists deemed transgressive to state interests. Several factors arise in the *shingeki* movement that prefigure the eventual appearance of the *angura* space. The first of these is the widespread tendency in modern art in Japan to explore notions of subjectivity and human experience. While these emergent forms of *shutaisei* go through a radical rebirth in the 1960s avant-garde, they have historical precedence. Thus, it is a matter of considering the changing effects and contexts for *shutaisei* and noting how selfhood gradually becomes intrinsic to artists' realization of an avant-garde movement.

A second aspect of the chapter addresses the history of protest in modern Japan. It outlines the historical formation of the student movement (*zengakuren*) and marks the influence of communist and socialist workers' movements in the formation of the Japanese left after World War II. As is also noted, the subsequent formation of the *angura* space in part responds to the rejection of orthodox leftist politics. I have argued that the dichotomy between old and new left politics emerged as a powerful schism in Japan's modern history—a significant factor in the rise of the avant-garde.

A further factor arising in this chapter begins a discussion about *shingeki* that continues over the following two chapters, where I explore the degree to which *shingeki* became a point of opposition for 1960s generation artists. According to many younger artists, *shingeki* had evolved in ways that made it unresponsive to new trends and ideas. Moreover, it was associated with established leftist political groups, such as unions and socialist and communist organizations. Meanwhile, the 1960s was an era that contested these political structures and established new left politics parallel to the underground theatre scene. While a sense of hubris often accompanies young artistic innovators, their criticisms of *shingeki* were also carefully considered and valid. *Shingeki* is tied to a methodology of realism and cannot radically innovate in the ways demanded by *angura*. Even today, it preserves a modern theatre tradition. What is more, this is largely a western humanist tradition and does not allow for the kinds of productive cultural hybridity displayed in *angura*. Hence, *shingeki* is both a forerunner to *angura* and a crucial point of resistance for *angura*.

Chapter 2 focused on the 1960 Ampo demonstrations—the mass protest movement of students and workers protesting the resigning of the US-Japan mutual security treaty. Ampo came to mean more than this single issue when public actions and participation in protests spread among the community. Performing politics and the *shutaisei* effect bridged old orders of resistance with counter-culture perspectives of a politics in motion. Acts of direct participation and experiencing sites of resistance through the body and its senses became the principle value of radical subjectivity. To transform the world, one had to enter the world and bring about its physical and spatial revolution. To put one's body at the line of confrontation made protest a communal and performative pastime. This overwhelming sense of radical corporeality is further discussed in chapters 3 and 4 as an intrinsic aspect of *angura* style. It is through the heady mix of experiencing the body and politics in motion that we come to understand the *shutaisei* effect in theatre.

The formation of 1960s *angura* is explored in chapters 3 and 4. I trace the aesthetic principles and political associations of the form and propose a model for an *angura* paradigm. This is outlined in terms that highlight *angura's* sensibilities of abstraction, physicality, intertextual and hybrid forms, and transhistorical foundations. Soon after the demonstrations in 1960, the connection between *angura* and protest was established in performances that explored the direct experience of political participation. The senses of spontaneity and subjectivity expressed in these works are hallmarks of *angura* and a politics of *shutaisei* subsequently came to rest in a range of extraordinary performances. I argue that the *angura* space should rightly include a realization of *shutaisei*—an effect that has revolutionary aesthetic and cultural dimensions. My analysis of notable 1960s performance stresses the influence of *shutaisei* politics in the realization of these works. Finally, Satoh Makoto's critical perspective on the 1960s is discussed in the concluding part of chapter 4. A failure of imagination is one part of Satoh's analysis of likely reasons for the dissolution of the *angura* space. This factor, alongside ultra-radical political events that seemed to be a grotesque parody of *angura*, sees the decade end in a state of confusion.

As I have also shown in these chapters, the 1960s generation of activists proposed a selfhood ideal that was subjective, relativist and individualistic. Perhaps an additional factor in the decline of 1960s counter-culture is, therefore, the rejection of class politics in relation to the pivotal new left/*angura* ethos. Arguably, selfhood risked becoming an elite or bourgeois sensibility resulting in the fragmentation of the mass protest movement. *Shingeki* artist, Senda Koreya, raised this point in relation to *angura's* inability to engage in the question of class struggle, thereby correctly predicting the absence of a class position in *angura* and subsequently making the subjective politics in new theatre vulnerable to mainstream appropriation. "Everything depends upon how you bind yourselves to the working class" Senda argued in interview (Senda 1970: 74). Under these circumstances, the possibility for a mass movement to resist dominant ideology was negated.

Finally, I have highlighted the importance of Black Tent's *The Dance of Angels Who Burn Their Own Wings*, one of the most significant and complex works from the 1960s period. I argue that this play explores the potent sense of dissolution that entered the 1960s space at the end of the decade. The play is also indirectly balanced by Kawamura Takeshi's work *Hamletclone*, discussed in chapter 7 and included in translation in chapter 10. There is no direct comparison made here, for the works are not completely analogous. At the same time, both plays rework influential avant-garde texts (by Peter Weiss and Heiner Müller, coincidently both German playwrights) and attempt to critically engage with the history of radical culture in Japan. As already discussed, the problems identified in *The Dance of Angels* are explored as a failure of the imagination. Kawamura's work, by contrast, takes in a wider perspective. While it attempts to look back on a history of radical possibilities, it also observes the dramatic and aggressive failure of alternatives to manifest in Japan. From the benefit of hindsight and forty years of *angura* production,

Kawamura seems to conclude that it is not a lack of imagination, but power and overt, lasting authoritarian tendencies in Japan that work together to preclude the possibility of progressive transformations in the social sphere. Both works are pessimistic about Japan's historical progress, but Kawamura's view is almost terminal.

Notwithstanding this assessment, the vigorous sense of negotiating the cultural politics of power in Kawamura's work, in particular, might be seen to offer positive outcomes for the play as well. Exploring cultural politics and attempting to broach a better understanding of the mechanisms of power through a revitalized political theatre become important themes in my argument for the continuing relevance of the *angura* space after the 1960s. In other words, there is a sense that cultural politics appears to begin to shape *angura* at this juncture.

Before discussing this though, the second part of the book explores the popularization and commodification of *angura* in light of the 1980s economic boom in Japan. Postmodern trends in Japanese culture are identified and analyzed in connection with the rising sense of playfulness (*asobi*) in some of the most prominent theatre productions of the period. In the theatre of the bubble era, I argue there is an absence of politics. I also maintain that this absence is political and in fact has come to define the dominant politics of our age. Central to my discussion is the hyperactive, intense theatre of speed that is evident in the work of Yume no Yūminsha. This company's vim and verve—as demonstrated in their large, enthusiastic fan base and athletic performances bordering on a perpetual state of ecstasy—transformed the small theatre movement. Their productions were also extraordinarily inventive and dexterous. In line with postmodern theory though, I suggest that it is a*ngura* techniques and not political substance that is evident in these works. Hence, while the *asobi* theatre was a theatre of brilliance and popularity it also represented postmodern capitalism. One aspect of these arguments therefore calls attention to the *asobi* theatre's lack of tension and fear of depth. I argue that this is a central factor in accounting for *angura's* decline in the 1960s.

At the same, however, the collapse of alternatives to capitalism gives rise to reconsidering alternative practices and a new generation of artists with new ideas for contesting politics and culture is seen to emerge. Postmodern trends have often been noted as contradictory. On the one hand, they give rise to an infantile space, as noted in my discussion in chapter 5, for example. Yet on another level of cultural practice postmodernism gave rise to various forms of political contest; modes of political action began to explore sub-cultures and identity politics. In the 1980s people began to notice the rising power of globalization, the media and technology's trans-forming force. Having been saturated with a politics of postmod-ernism, I argue that the avant-garde can only be revived through means that display an understanding of the totalising strategies and homogenising tendencies of this late capitalist culture in Japan. Thus, successful *angura* theatre culture since the 1980s exhibits *angura* sensibilities overcast by post-structural ways of thinking and explores intertextual and meta-theatre forms of representation. The final section of the book explores these characteristics of postmodern and globalizing society and maps various possibilities for political resistance through new styles of performance and inventive modes of production.

Chapter 6 outlines a feminist reading of Japanese history that identifies the subjugation of women as an imperative of patriarchal capitalism. Kishida Jimusho + Rakutendan's production of Kishida Rio's *Woven Hell* also stressed the sense of historical continuum evident in the momentum of Japanese culture in the twentieth century, making explicit links between militarist neo-nationalism of the wartime period and the domination of corporate culture in the postwar era. Kishida was a playwright and theatre maker of lasting importance. Her early work with Terayama Shūji was an aesthetic grounding for her later projects. These ranged in scope from intimate poetic presentations, to some of the first intercultural projects with Korean and Singaporean artists, as well as her major productions. *Woven Hell* is a window onto Kishida's *angura* influences and explores her key themes of feminism, memory, history, and human darkness.

Daisan Erotica are seen to be concerned with the sensibility of dystopia that prevails in Japan. Their pioneering use of aspects of Japanese popular culture, including *manga* and science fiction, is directed towards an investigation of the sense of dysfunction and millennial *fin de sièclism* evident in Japanese society during the 1980s and 1990s. Daisan Erotica's use of the symbols of decay seen in the collapse of the economic and social fabric of Japan—grotesque images of the homeless, youth violence, media sensationalism, right-wing ideology and death cults—present a compelling critical image of Japan that runs counter to more common representations of stability and order.

Blending styles of performance art, visual display, music and dance, dumb type pioneered multimedia and hybrid arts performance styles. Their work explores the body, technology, sexuality and globalization. These aspects of life are often considered to be at loggerheads; here, however, performance becomes a kind of between space and a place for new connections. Media and technology are coupled with witty displays of community solidarity and diverse forms of humanity. Dumb type's work rethinks the dichotomous relations of industrial capitalism and orients us towards a progressive and transforming vision of a human society. Hence, their performances are utopian but not naïve about dominant political orders. Notable as well, is the fact that their exploration of sexuality and HIV-AIDS in *S/N* was groundbreaking, both in aesthetic terms and in the context of the Japanese culture that strongly marginalized questions of sexual difference and avoided discussion of the AIDS virus in the 1990s.

Finally, Gekidan Kaitaisha seem to deconstruct the notion of performance altogether and offer challenging and bleak assessments of the state of Japanese society. Through investigations of the social and political body and their explication of the body as an inscriptive surface, the company undermines and transcends normative *angura* critiques of Japanese experience. By drawing on the theoretical work of Michel Foucault and displaying an interest in the possible relations between cultural theory and performance, Kaitaisha's production of *Tokyo Ghetto: Hard Core* explores the nature of power and its capacities to effect instant transformations of the body in space. In a radical sense, Kaitaisha have come to question the very notion of performance. These visceral, painful sensibilities seen in the work and experienced by the performers suggest uncertainty about the possibility for the codes of artistic representation to say anything in definitive terms. Instead, through exploring the act of being witness to experience in their performances, combined with their evident demonstration of complicity with power, Kaitaisha ironically seem to be returning to the perspective of phenomenology and selfhood last seen in early *angura* performance. There is a fundamental difference, however, in the emphasis on the nature of complicity in Kaitaisha's work. Accordingly, they try to show the body *in situ* and awash in a sea of disciplinary flows.

Looking at the four companies together and in relation to the earlier generation of *angura*, one of the compelling differences—and probably the most significant development in the context of Japanese avant-garde renewal—lies in their differing attitudes to power and awareness of political processes. The former generation was involved in a project to explore the boundless possibilities of a liberation ethos through subjectivity and abstraction of form. As a result, notions of intuition, personal expression and fantasy were privileged. By contrast, latter groups display a more developed sense of the coercive nature of power and the manufacture of culture. They are unable to represent liberation outright and are more concerned with displaying, exposing and investigating modes of coercion evident in their lives and in Japanese society. Rather than straightforward subjective and experiential abstraction, these companies are much more likely to engage in an investigation of the meaning of symbols, codes, patterns, images and epistemologies. Their work is fundamentally concerned with questions about the nature of power and how it circulates inside Japanese society and culture. In this regard, their work displays high levels of self-awareness and ironic self-criticism. This is an important realization for the arts and finally provides evidence for an avant-garde that is not only inside the cultural matrix, but also able to explore the terms and limits of its status. Consequently, we can conclude that *angura* was once again able to identify and maintain points of resistance, create moments in performance that undermine cultural hegemony, and discover new operative forms of aesthetic–political synthesis.

And now?

In the new century, conditions for theatre have changed yet again and we now see a proliferation of performance styles and mechanisms for their production. We can note a series of interrelated factors that have influenced this trend, principally the changing basis of arts funding, a system of state funding for contemporary arts and the rise of not for profit organizations (NPO), public theatres, and so on. A culture industry has emerged in contemporary Japanese theatre that is global in the sense that theatre is made in ways markedly similar to the ways that it is made in other developed countries. A part of this trend sees artists working freelance on a variety of projects. They become multi-skilled and work across gen-res and between cultures. This process has significant impact on the Japanese contemporary theatre scene that has historically grown from a group structure and group sensibility. While we are seeing a vast range of theatre activity in Japan, one begins to wonder how the work that was unique to *angura* will ever be made under this sys-tem. We might expect Japanese theatre to change in a multitude of ways as a result. On the one hand, artists have greater freedom and have become more widely experienced. Their work reaches wider audiences. On the other hand, those cultural locations that devel-oped distinctive and localised performing styles and dramaturgical formations seem to be in decline.

Angura *as history*

In closing, a translation of Kawamura Takeshi's play *Hamletclone* is included. In one sense, this is intended to give voice to the Japanese artists' whose extraordinary creativity has been the genesis of my research. That is not to say that Kawamura is representative of *angura* as a whole: as we have seen, a multitude of styles have emerged, although all are in some way connected to the idea of theatre as a site of cultural resistance.

Hamletclone neatly bookends the historical period of Japanese the-atre culture investigated. What began with protest and innovation in the 1960s has in some ways ended around the year 2000 when Kawamura's play was written. My deep appreciation of Kawamura's play is garnered from the way that it returns us to the experience of this period as history. It is a play about Japan's buried history; the present day social world is built from such fractured glimpses of the recent past four decades. Hopefully, I have shown that in *angura*—as with the future possible rise of alternatives—a dynamic under-standing of history is crucial. With a sense of history and continuing actions that aim to reconcile the past with the present, perhaps rev-olutionary sensibilities in art—as in the world at large—can be fos-tered and gain creative verve. And always at stake in art is an intense dialogue with the social world. *Hamletclone* offers just such a conver-sation, one that is complex, subtle and open. It is an example of the avant-garde as we need it to be.

BIBLIOGRAPHY

Allain, P. (1998). "Suzuki Training". *The Drama Review* 42(1): 66–89.
———. (2002). *The Art of Stillness: The Theatre Practices of Tadashi Suzuki*. London, Methuen.
Alvarez-Basso, C. (1993). "The Performance pH". *pHases*. Dumbtype. Tokyo, Walcoal Arts Centre: 13.
Anon. (1991). *Gendai Engeki 60s–90s*. Tokyo, Heibonsha.
———. (1991a). *Terayama Shūji no Kamem Gahō*. Tokyo, Heibonsha.
Apter, D. E. and N. Sawa (1984). *Against the State: Politics and Social Protest in Japan*. Cambridge, Massachusetts, Harvard University Press.
Artaud, A. (1970). *The Theatre and its Double*. London, Calder & Boyars.
Asada, A. (1989). "Infantile Capitalism and Japan's Postmodernism: A Fairy Tale". *Postmodernism and Japan*. M. Miyoshi and H. D. Harootunian. Durham and London, Duke University Press: 273–278.
Auslander, P. (1997). *From Acting to Performance*. London and New York, Routledge.
Balakrishnan, G. (2000). "Virgilian Visions". *New Left Review* (5 Sept.–Oct.): 142–148.
Barber, S. (2002). "Tokyo's Urban and Sexual Transformations: Performance Art and Digital Cultures". *Consuming Bodies: Sex and Contemporary Japanese Art*. F. Lloyd. London, Reaktion Books: 166–85.
———. (no date). Butoh's first images. www.poeticinhalation.com. 2004.
Baudrillard, J. (1983). *Simulacra and Simulation*. New York, Semiotest(e).
Bauman, Z. (1995). *Life in Fragments*. Oxford, Blackwell.
———. (1998). *Globalization: The Human Consequences*. Columbia, Columbia University Press.
Benjamin, W. (1969). "The Work of Art in the Age of Mechanical Reproduction". *Illuminations*. H. Arendt. New York, Shocken.
Bennett, S. (1990). *Theatre Audiences: A Theory of Production and Reception*. London & New York, Routledge.
Bharucha, R. (1990). *Theatre and the World: Performance and the Politics of Culture*. London & New York, Routledge.
———. (1996a). "Disorientations in the Cultural Politics of our Times". *The Intercultural Performance Reader*. P. Pavis. London & New York, Routledge.
Birringer, J. (1991). *Theatre, Theory, Postmodernism*. Bloomington and Indianapolis, Indiana University Press.
Brandon, J. (1978). "The Suzuki Method". *The Drama Review* 22(4): 30–42.
———. (1985). "Time and Tradition in Modern Japanese Theatre". *Asian Theatre Journal* 2(1): 71–82.
———. (1990). "Contemporary Japanese Theatre: Interculturalism and Intraculturalism". *The Dramatic Touch of Difference*. Fischer-Lichte, Riley and Gissenwehrer. Tübingen, Gunter Narr Verlag.
Brecht, B. (1974). "On Gestic Music". *Brecht on Theatre: The Development of an Aesthetic*. J. Willett. New York, Hill and Wang.
———. (1974). "A Short Organum for the Theatre". *Brecht on Theatre*. J. Willett. London, Eyre Methuen.
Brehm, M., Ed. (2002). *The Japanese Experience—Inevitable*. Ostfildern-Ruit, Hartje Cantz Verlag.
Broinowski, A. (2003). "Theatre of body in Japan: Ankoku Butoh (Dance of Darkness)-Gekidan Kaitaisha (Theatre of Deconstruction)". Melbourne, University of Melbourne. MA Thesis.

Bürger, P. (1984). *The Theory of the Avant-garde*. Illinois, University of Minnesota Press.

Callas, P. (1991). "Japan: Post-Department Store. Post-Culture". *Tension*. No 25.

Carlson, M. (1996). *Performance: a Critical Introduction*. London & New York, Routledge.

Carruthers, I. (2001). *"The Chronicle of Macbeth*: Suzuki method acting in Australia: 1992". *Performing Shakespeare in Japan*. Minami Ryuta, Ian Carruthers and J. Gilles. Cambrige, Cambrige University Press: 121–32.

Castoriadis, C. (1987-8). "The Movements of the Sixties". *Thesis Eleven* (18/19).

Cazdyn, E. (2002). *The Flash of Capital: Film and Geopolitics in Japan*. Durham and London, Duke University Press.

Chaudhuri, U. (1997). *Staging Place: The Geography of Modern Drama*. Ann Arbor, University of Michigan Press.

Clammer, J. (1997). *Contemporary Urban Japan: A Sociology of Consumption*. Oxford, Blackwell.

———. (2000). "Received Dreams: Consumer Capitalism, Social Process, and the Management of Emotions in Contemporary Japan". *Globalisation and Social Change in Contemporary Japan*. J. S. Eades, T. Gill and H. Befu. Melbourne, Trans Pacific Press: 203–223.

Coulborn, J. (1995). "pH is on a whole different level". *Toronto Sun* (25 September). Toronto.

Crow, T. (1996). *The Rise of the Sixties*. London, Harry N. Abrams Inc.

Debord, G. (1995). *The Society of the Spectacle*. New York, Zone Books.

Dery, M. (1996). *Escape Velocity*. London, Hodder & Stoughton.

Desser, D. (1988). *Eros plus Massacre: An Introduction to the Japanese New Wave Cinema*. Bloomington and Indianapolis, Indiana University Press.

Dowsey, S. J., Ed. (1970). *Zengakuren: Japan's Revolutionary Students*. Berkeley, The Ishi Press.

Dumb type (1991). *Dumb Type. Recent Works 1987–1991*. Kyoto, Dumb Type.

——— (1993). *phases*. Tokyo, Wacoal Arts Centre.

——— (1995). *S/N*. Kyoto, Dumb Type.

Durland, S. (1990). "The future is now: Kyoto's Dumb Type". *High Performance*. Summer.

Eades, J. S., T. Gill, et al., Eds. (2000). *Globalisation and Social Change in Japan*. Melbourne, Trans Pacific Press.

Eagleton, T. (1990). *The Ideology of the Aesthetic*. Oxford, Blackwell Publishers.

———. (1996). *The Illusions of Postmodernism*. Oxford, Blackwell Publishers.

Eckersall, P. (1998). "Multiculturalism and Contemporary Theatre Art in Australia and Japan". *Poetica* 50: 155–164.

———. (2000). "Japan as Dystopia: An Overview of Kawamura Takeshi's Daisan Erotica". *The Drama Review* 44(1): 97–108.

———. (2001a). "The Body and the Problematics of Representation in the Theatre of Gekidan Kaitaisha". *Japanese Theater and the International Stage*. S. Scholz-Cionca and S. Leiter. Leiden, Brill: 329–342.

———. (2003). "Surveillance Aesthetics and Theatre against 'Empire.'". *Double Dialogues* 1(4).

———. (2004a). "Trendiness and Appropriation? On Australia-Japan Contemporary Theatre Exchange". *Alternatives: Debating Theatre Culture in the Age of Confusion*. Peter Eckersall, Tadashi Uchino and N. Moriyama. Brussels, PIE Lang: 13–46.

———. (2005). "Hirata Oriza's 'Tokyo Notes' in Melbourne: conflicting expectations for theatrical naturalism". *European Association of Japanese Studies*. University of Vienna, EAJS.

———. (2005). "Theatrical Collaboration in the Age of Globalisation: The Gekidan Kaitaisha-NYID Collaboration Project". *Diasporas and Interculturalism in Asian Performing Arts*. H. Um. London, Routledge Curzon.

Eckersall, P., R. Fensham, et al. (2001b). "Tokyo Diary". *Performance Research* 6(1): 71–86.

Eckersall, P., T. Uchino, et al., Eds. (2004b). *Alternatives: Debating Theatre Culture in the Age of Confusion*. Brussels, PIE Peter Lang.

Farrell, W. (1990). *Blood and Rage: The Story of the Japanese Red Army*. Lexington, Mass. & Toronto, Lexington Books.

Fensham, R. and P. Eckersall, Eds. (1999). *Disorientations: Cultural Praxis in Theatre. Asia, Pacific, Australia*. Melbourne, Monash University.

Field, N. (1989). "The Postmodern Atmosphere". *Postmodernism and Japan*. M. Miyoshi and H. D. Harootunian. Durham and London, Duke University Press: 169–88.

———. (1991). *In the Realm of a Dying Emperor*. New York, Pantheon Books.

Foucault, M. (1977). *Discipline and Punish: The Birth of the Prison*. London, Tavistock Publications.

Fukase, M. (1969). Inauspicious (artwork). Tokyo.

Fukashiro, J. (1970). "The New Left". *Japan Quarterly* 17(1).

Furuhashi, T. (1994). Interview with author (28 February). *Arts Today*. Adelaide, Australian Broadcasting Corporation.

———. (1995a). "Interview". *S/N*. Dumbtype. Kyoto, Dumb Type.

———. (1995b). "The Conversation: Interview with Carol Luffy". *Tokyo Journal*.

Goodman, D. (1971). "Revolutionary Theatre: This is a Dream". *Concerned Theatre Japan* 1(4): 119–27.

———. (1986). *After Apocalypse: Four Japanese Plays of Hiroshima and Nagasaki*. New York, Columbia University Press.

———. (1988). *Drama and Japanese Culture in the 1960s: The Return of the Gods*. Armonk, M. E. Sharpe.

———. (1992). "Satoh Makoto and the Post-Shingeki Movement in Japanese Theatre". Ithaca, Cornell University. PhD thesis.

———. (1999). *Angura: Posters of the Japanese Avant-Garde*. New York, Princeton Architectural Press.

———. (2001). "Concerned Theatre Japan: A Personal Account". *Japanese Theatre and the International Stage*. S. Scholz-Cionca and S. Leiter. Leiden, Brill: 343–353.

Goto, Y. "Suzuki Tadashi: Innovator of Contemporary Japanese Theatre". Ann Arbour, UMI manuscript. PhD thesis.

Grehan, H. (2000). "Performed Promiscuities: Interpreting Interculturalism in the Japan Foundation Asia Centre's Lear". *Intersections Online Asian Studies Journal*. Perth, Murdoch University. 2004.

Grosz, E. (1994). *Volatile Bodies: Towards a Corporeal Feminism*. St Leonards, Allen and Unwin.

———. (2001). *Architecture from the Outside: Essays on Virtual and Real Space*. Massachusetts, MIT Press.

Grotowski, J. (1968). *Towards a Poor Theatre*. London, Methuen.

Hage, G. (2003). *Against Paranoid Nationalism: searching for hope in a shrinking society*. Sydney, Pluto Press.

Harada, H. (1970). "The Anti-Ampo Stuggle". *Zengakuren: Japan's Revolutionary Students*. S. J. Dowsey. Berkerly, The Ishi Press: 75–99.

Haraway, D. (1991). *Simians, Cyborgs, and Women: The Reinvention of Nature*. New York, Routledge.

———. (1997). *Modest Witness@Second Millennium. FemaleMan©Meets OncoMouse™: feminism and technoscience*. New York, Routledge.

Hardt, M. and A. Negri (2000). *Empire*. Cambridge Mass., Harvard University Press.

Harootunian, H. D. (1993). "America's Japan/Japan's Japan". *Japan in the World*. M. Miyoshi and H. D. Harootunian. Durham & London, Duke University Press.

Hasebe, H. (1993a). "The City of Vertigo: Hideki Noda and the Theatre of Speed". *Teihon: Noda Hideki to Yume no Yūminsha*. Noda Hideki and Hasabe Hiroshi. Tokyo, Kashu Shōbō Shinsha.

———. (1993b). *Yon Byo no Kakumei: Tokyo no Engeki 1982–1992*. Tokyo, Kawade Shōbō Shinsha.

Hasegawa, Y. (1993). "Further Comments". *pHases*. Dumbtype. Tokyo, Walcoal Arts Centre: 59.

Havens, T. (1987). *Fire Across the Sea: The Vietnam War and Japan 1965–1975*. Princeton, Princeton University Press.

Held, D. and M. Anthony (2002). *Globalization/Anti-Globalization*. Oxford, Polity Press.

Hirata, O. (2002). "Tokyo Notes". *Asian Theatre Journal* 19(1): 1–120.

———. (2003). Interview with author (November 20). P. Eckersall. Tokyo.

Horie-Weber, A. (1975). "Modernisation of the Japanese Theatre: The Shingeki Movement". *Modern Japan*. W. G. Beasley. Tokyo, Tuttle: 147–65.

Igarashi, Y. (2000). *Bodies of Memory: Narratives of War in Postwar Japanese Culture, 1945–1970*. Princeton and Oxford, Princeton University Press.

Ivy, M. (1995). *Discourses of the Vanishing: Modernity, Phantasm, Japan*. Chicago & London, The University of Chicago Press.

Iwabuchi, K. (2002). "From Western Gaze to Global Gaze: Japanese Cultural Presence in Asia". *Global Culture: Media, Arts, Policy and Globalisation*. D. Crane, N. Kawashima and K. Kawasaki. London & New York, Routledge: 256–273.

Jameson, F. (1984). "Postmodernism and the Consumer Society". *The Anti-Aesthetic: Essays on Postmodern Culture*. H. Foster. Port Townsend, Bay Press.

———. (1991). *Postmodernism or the Cultural Logic of Late Capitalism*. London & New York, Verso.

———. (1994). *The Seeds of Time*. New York, Columbia University Press.

Kaitaisha, Ed. (2001). *Theatre of Deconstruction*. Tokyo, Gekidan Kaitaisha.

Kan, T. (1982). *Zengakuren*. Tokyo, Gendai Shokan.

———. (1991). *Kaitaisuru Engeki*. Tokyo, Renga Shōbō Shinsha.

Kano, A. (2001). *Acting Like a Woman in Modern Japan: Theatre, Gender, and Nationalism*. New York, Palgrave.

Kara, J. (1970). "Jon Shiruba: Ai no Kojiki". *Umi*. March.

———. (1988). "John Silver: The Beggar of Love". *Drama and Japanese Culture in the 1960s: The Return of the Gods*. D. Goodman. Armonk, M. E. Sharpe: 237–282.

———. (1997). Interview with author (25 January). P. Eckersall. Tokyo.

———. (1997). *Tokkenteki Nikutairon*. Tokyo, Hakusuisha.

Kawamura, T. (1996). Interview with author (5 September). P. Eckersall. Tokyo.

———. (1998a). "Kaibutsu no Judaic". *Chimaera*. 1: 30–39.

———. (1998b). Interview with author (14 December). P. Eckersall. Tokyo.

———. (2000a). "Hamutettokurōn". Revised manuscript. Tokyo.

———. (2000b). "The Last Babylon". *The Drama Review* 44(1).

———. (2004). Interview with author (13 January). P. Eckersall. Tokyo.

Kaye, N. (1994). *Postmodernism and performance*. New York, St. Martin's Press.

Kershaw, B. (1996). "The Politics of Performance in a Postmodern Age". *Analysing Performance: A Critical Reader*. P. Campbell. Manchester & New York, Manchester University Press.

Kersten, R. (1996). *Democracy in Postwar Japan: Maruyama Masao and the Search for Autonomy*. London and New York, Routledge.

Kishida, R. (1992). Interview with author (23 January). P. Eckersall. Tokyo.

———. (2002). "Thread Hell". *Half a Century of Japanese Theatre Volume 4*. Japan Playwrights Asssociation. Tokyo, Kinokunya: 161–222.

Koschmann, J. V. (1996). *Revolution and Subjectivity in Postwar Japan*. Chicago, University of Chicago Press.

Kostelanetz, R. (1990). "Avant-Garde". *Avant-Garde* 3.

Koyamada, T. (1996). Interview with author (28–29 December). P. Eckersall. Kyoto.

Kumakura, T. (1995). "The Performance Art of 'Dumb Type': The Body as Love Vehicle". *S/N*. Dumptype. Kyoto, Dumb Type.

Kurihara, N. (1996). "A Critical Analysis of Hijikata Tatsumi's Butoh Dance". New York, New York University. PhD thesis.

Lingis, A. (1994). *Foreign Bodies*. New York, Routledge.

Lloyd, F., Ed. (2002). *Consuming Bodies: Sex and Contemporary Japanese Art*. London, Reaktion Books.

Lyotard, J. (1993). "Defining the postmodern". *The Cultural Studies Reader*. S. During. London and New York, Routledge.

Marotti, W. (1997). "Butoh no Mondaisei to Honshitsu Shugi Wana". *Shitaa A-tsu* (8): 88–96.

Marotti, W. A. (2001). "Simulacra and subversion in the everyday: Akasegawa Genpei's 1000-yen copy, critical art, and the State". *Postcolonial Studies* 4(2).

Marra, M. (1999). *Modern Japanese Aesthetics: A Reader*. Honolulu, University of Hawai'i Press.

Marsh, A. (1993). *Body and Self: Performance Art in Australia 1969–92*. Oxford, Oxford University Press.

Matsunami, M. (1970). "Origins of Zengakuren". *Zengakuren: Japan's Revolutionary Students*. S. J. Dowsey. Berkeley, The Ishi Press: 42–74.

Mayo, M. J., J. T. Rimer, et al., Eds. (2001). *War, Occupation, and Creativity: Japan and East Asia 1920–1960*. Honolulu, University of Hawai'i Press.

McCormack, G. and Y. Sugimoto, Eds. (1986). *Democracy in Contemporary Japan*. Sydney, Hale & Iremonger.

Mellen, J. (1975). *Voices from Japanese Cinema*. New York, Liveright.

Miglietti, F. A. (2003). *Extreme Bodies: The Use and Abuse of the Body in Art*. Milano, Skira Editore.

Minami Ryuta, Ian Carruthers, et al., Eds. (2001). *Performing Shakespeare in Japan*. Cambridge, Cambridge University Press.

Miyagi, S. (1992). "Shosetsu Den" theatre program. Tokyo,

———. (1996). Interview with author (28 September). P. Eckersall. Tokyo.

Miyoshi, M. (1991). *Off Center: Power and Culture Relations between Japan and the United States*. Cambridge, Mass., Harvard University Press.

Miyoshi, M. and H. D. Harootunian, Eds. (1989). *Postmodernism and Japan*. Durham and London, Duke University Press.

Mori, H., K. Nishidō, et al. (1993). *Theatre Japan*. Tokyo, PIA/The Japan Foundation.

Morita, N. (2005). "Avant-garde pastiche and genre-crossing: Films of Terayama Shūji". *European Association of Japanese Studies*. University of Vienna.

Moriyama, N. (2004). "A Phantom of Suburbia: Kawamura Takeshi's 'Hamletclone'". *Alternatives: Debating Theatre Culture in an Age of Confusion*. Peter Eckersall, Tadashi Uchino and N. Moriyama. Brussels, P.I.E. Peter Lang.

Mouer, R. and Y. Sugimoto (1986). *Images of Japanese society: a Study in the Social Construction of Reality*. London, KPI.

Munroe, A., Ed. (1994). *Japanese art after 1945: scream against the sky*. New York, H. N. Abrams.

Murakami, K. (1984). *Graffiti*. Tokyo, Shinsuisha.

Murayama, T. (1977). "Sukato o Haita Nero". *Gendai Nihon Gikyoku Senshū 5*. Tokyo, Kaukusui Sha: 424–444.

———. (1991). *Nippon Puroretaria Engeki Ron*. Tokyo, Yumani Shōbō.

Nakanishi, M. (1970). "Kakumaru—Analysis of an Ultra-Radical Group". *Zengakuren: Japan's Revolutionary Students*. S. J. Dowsey. Berkely, The Ishi Press: 193–225.

Nakazawa, M. (1984). "A Rhetorical Analysis of the Japanese Student Movement: University of Tokyo Struggle 1968–69", North Western University. PhD thesis.

Napier, S. J. (1996). *The Fantastic in Modern Japanese Literature: The Subversion of Modernity*. London & New York, Routledge.

Nishidō, K. (1987). *Engeki Shisō no Boken*. Tokyo, Ronsosha.

———. (1996). *Shōgekijō wa Shimetsu Shita Ka*. Tokyo, Renga Shōbō.

———. (2002). *Doramatisuto no Shōzō*. Tokyo, Renga Shōbō.

———. (2004). "The Journey to Con-Fusion: Between Australia and Japan". *Alternatives: Debating Theatre Culture in the Age of Confusion*. Peter Eckersall, Tadashi Uchino and N. Moriyama. Brussels, PIE Lang: 143–48.

Onitsuka, T. (1993). "Dumb Type in Granada". *pHases*. Dumbtype. Tokyo, Walcoal Arts Centre: 29.

Ōta, S. (1990). "The Water Station". *Asian Theatre Journal* 7(2): 150–83.

Otori, H. and S. Shimizu (2001). "The Birth of Theatre and the Besieged Body: A Strategy for Globalisation". *Theatre of Deconstruction*. Kaitaisaha. Tokyo, Gekidan Kaitaisha.

Ōzasa, Y. (1997). "Shingeki's Restless Century". *UNESCO Courier* 50(11): 19–23.

Packard, G. R. (1966). *Protest in Tokyo: The Security Treaty Crisis of 1960*. Princeton, Princeton University Press.

Pellegrini, D. (2001). "Avant-garde East and West. A Comparison of Prewar German and Japanese Avant-garde Art and Performance". Pittsburgh. University of Pittsburgh. PhD Thesis.

Powell, B. (2002). *Japan's Modern Theatre: A Century of Change and Continuity*. London, Japan Library.

Pulvers, R. (n.d.). "Terayama Shūji: Betting on Zero: An Angry Young Man in the City". *Wa-bun-ka*. (ephemera, collection of author).

Raz, J. (1992). "Self presentation and performance in the Yakuza way of life. Fieldwork with a Japanese underworld group". *Ideology and Practice in Modern Japan*. R. Goodman and K. Refsing. London and NY, Routledge: 210–234.

Rimer, J. T. (1974). *Toward a Modern Japanese Theatre: Kishida Kunio*. Princeton, Princeton University Press.

Roberts, J. G. (1979). "The Japan Crowd and the Zaibatsu Restoration". *Japan Interpreter* 12(3–4): 384–415.

Rolf, R. (1992). "Tokyo Theatre 1990". *Asian Theatre Journal* (9): 85–111.

———. (1992a). "Japanese Theatre from the 1980s: The Ludic Conspiracy". *Modern Drama* 34(1): 127–36.

Rolf, R. and J. Gillespie, Eds. (1992). *Alternative Japanese Drama: Ten Plays*. Honolulu, University of Hawai'i Press.

Saito, T. and M. Nakamura (1971). "Mobile Theatre: Prospectus". *Concerned Theatre Japan* 1(3).

Sandler, M., Ed. (1997). *The Confusion Era: Arts and Culture of Japan During the Allied Occupation, 1945–52*. Seattle and London, Arthur M. Sackler Gallery, Smithsonian Institution in association with the University of Seattle Press.

Sasaki-Uemura, W. (2001). *Organizing the Spontaneous: Citizen Protest in Postwar Japan*. Honolulu, University of Hawai'i Press.

Satoh, M. (1996). Interview with author (19 December). P. Eckersall. Tokyo.

Satoh, M., K. Yamamoto, et al. (1988). "The Dance of Angels Who Burn Their Own Wings". *Drama and Japanese Culture in the 1960s: The Return of the Gods*. D. Goodman. Armonk, M. E. Sharpe: 301–344.

Sawara, Y. (1970). "The University Struggles". *Zengakuren: Japan's Revolutionary Students*. S. J. Dowsey. Berkeley, The Ishi Press: 136–192.

Scarry, E. (1985). *The Body in Pain: The Making and Unmaking of the World*. New York, Oxford University Press.

Schechner, R. (1991). "The Decline and Fall of the Avant-Garde". *The End of Humanism: Writings on Performance*. R. Schechner. New York, Performing Arts Journal Publications.

————. (1993). *The Future of Ritual: Writings on Culture and Performance*. New York and London, Routledge.

Scholz-Cionca, S. and S. Leiter, Eds. (2001). *Japanese Theater and the International Stage*. Leiden, Brill.

Scot, Ed. (1991). *The Suzuki Company of Toga*. Tokyo, SCOT.

Senda, A. (1986). *Metamorphoses in Contemporary Japanese Theatre: Life Size and more than Life Size*. Tokyo, The Japan Foundation.

————. (1988). *Gendai Engeki no Kōkai*. Tokyo, Riburoporto.

————. (1991). "Gendai Engeki no Tenbo". *Gendai Engeki 60's–90's*. Y. Takahashi. Tokyo, Heibonsha.

————. (1997). *The Voyage of Contemporary Japanese Theatre*. Honolulu, University of Hawai'i Press.

Senda, K. (1970). "An Interview". *Concerned Theatre Japan* 1(2): 47–80.

Shea, G. T. (1964). *Leftwing Literature in Japan: A History of the Proletarian Literary Movement*. Tokyo, Hosei University Press.

Shewring, M. (1998). Hideki Noda's Shakespeare: the languages of performance. *Shakespeare and the Japanese Stage*. T. Sasayama, J. R. Mulryne and M. Shewring. Cambridge, Cambridge University Press: 94–109.

Shillony, B. (1981). *Politics and Culture in Wartime Japan*. Oxford, Clarendon University Press.

Shimizu, S. (1996). Interview with author (17 October). P. Eckersall. Tokyo: 17 October, 1996.

Smith, H. D. (1972). *Japan's First Student Radicals*. Cambridge, Mass., Harvard University Press.

Sofoulis, Z. (2002). "Cyberquake: Haraway's Manifesto". *Prefiguring Cyberculture: An Intellectual History*. D. Tofts, A. Jonson and A. Cavallaro. Sydney, Power Publications: 84–104.

Sorgenfrei, C. (1978). "Shūji Terayama: Avant-Garde Dramatist of Japan". Umi Manuscript. PhD Thesis.

Suga, H. (2003). *Kakumei teki na, amari ni kakumei teki na: '1968 Nen no Kakumei' Shiron*. Tokyo, Sakuhin Sha.

Sumitomo, F. (2004). "Out of Akihabara: Media Art in Japan and Advanced Consumer Society". *Contemporary Visual Arts and Culture*. 33: 32–3.

Suvin, D. (1990). "Satoh's 'The Dance of Angels' as Counterproject to Weiss' 'Marat/Sade': Two Dramaturgical Discourses about the Revolution in the 1960s". *The Dramatic Touch of Difference*. Fischer-Lichte, Riley and Gissenwehrer. Tübingen, Gunter Narr Verlag.

Suzuki, T. (1986). *The Way of Acting: The Theatre Writings of Suzuki Tadashi*. New York, Theatre Communications Group.

————. (1996). Public Lecture, 9 August, 1996, Toga Festival. Toga.

Takahagi, H. (1996). Interview with author (21 September). P. Eckersall. Tokyo.

Takahashi, Y. (1992). "Alternative Japanese Drama: A Brief Overview". *Alternative Japanese Drama: Ten Plays*. R. T. Rolf and J. K. Gillespie. Honolulu, University of Hawaii Press.

————. (2001). "Tragedy with laughter: Suzuki Tadashi's *The Tale of Lear*". *Performing Shakespeare in Japan*. Minami Ryuta, Ian Carruthers and J. Gillies. Cambridge, Cambridge University Press: 111–120.

Tanaka, M. (1986). "I am the avant-garde who crawls the earth". *The Drama Review* 30(2): 153–55.

Terayama, S. (1971). *Sho o suteyo machi e deyō*. Tokyo, Art Theatre Guild.

————. (1975). "Tenjō Sajiki Manifesto". *The Drama Review* 19(4).

————. (1978). *Terayama Shūji no Kamem Gahō*. Tokyo, Heibonsha.

————. (1984). "Garigari Hakasei no Hanzai". *Terayama Shūji no Gikyoku 4*. Tokyo, Shichosha.

————. (no date). Terayama Shūju Museum Program. Misawa, Terayama Shūju Museum.

Terayama, S. and R. Kishida (2003). "Le Labryrinthe d'herbes" (Sōmeikyū). DVD film recording. Tokyo, Kinokuniya.

Tomōka Kuniyuki, Kanno Sachiko, et al. (2002). "Building National Prestige: Japanese Cultural Policy and the Influence of Western Institutions". *Global Culture: Media, Arts, Policy and Globalisation*. D. Crane, N. Kawashima and K. Kawasaki. London & New York, Routledge: 49–62.

Tonooka, N. (1990). "Four contemporary Japanese Woman's theatre groups: Subjectivity-formation in performance and creative process". Honolulu, The University of Hawaii. PhD Thesis.

Trippi, L. (1996). "Smart Type". *World Art*. No. 2.

Tsubouchi, S. (1999). "What is Beauty?" *Modern Japanese Aesthetics: A Reader*. M. Marra. Honolulu, University of Hawai'i Press: 48–64.

Tsuno, K. (1969). "Biwa and Beatles: An Invitation to Modern Japanese Theatre". *Concerned Theatre Japan* Introductory issue (October): 7–32.

————. (1970). "Of Baths, Brothels and Hell". *Concerned Theatre Japan* 1(1).

————. (1970a). "The Trinity of Modern Theatre". *Concerned Theatre Japan* 1(2).

————. (1978). "The Tradition of Modern Theatre in Japan". *The Canadian Theatre Review* Fall.

Tsuno, K. and A. Senda (1971). "Conversation". *Concerned Theatre Japan* 1(4): 40–52.

Tsurumi, K. (1975). "Student Movements in 1960 and 1969 Continuity and Change". *Postwar trends in Japan*. S. Takayanagi and K. Miwa. Tokyo, University of Tokyo Press.

Uchino, T. (1996). *Merodorama no Gyakushū: Shiengeki no 80 Nendai*. Tokyo, Keisō Shōbō.

————. (1999). "Deconstructing 'Japaneseness': Towards Articulating Locality and Hybridity in Contemporary Japanese Performance". *Disorientations Cultural Praxis in Theatre: Asia, Pacific, Australia*. R. Fensham and P. Eckersall. Melbourne, Monash Theatre Papers. 1: 35–53.

————. (2000). "Images of Armageddon: Japan's 1980s Theatre Culture". *The Drama Review* 44(1): 85–96.

————. (2004). "After 9.11". *Alternatives: Debating Theatre Culture in the Age of Confusion*. Peter Eckersall, Tadashi Uchino and N. Moriyama. Brussels, PIE Peter Lang: 163–5.

Various (2004). *Tatsumi Hijikata's Butoh: Surrealism of the Flesh Ontology of the Body*. Kawasaki, Taro Okamoto Museum.

Wada, Y. (1992). Interview with author (23 January). P. Eckersall. Tokyo.

Weisenfeld, G. (2002). *Mavo: Japanese artists and the avant-garde, 1905–1931*. Berkeley, University of California Press.

Wolferen, K. V. (1989). *The Enigma of Japanese Power*. London, Macmillan.

Wolff, J. (1990). "Feminism and Modernism". *Discourse and Difference: Post-Structuralism, Feminism and the Moment of History*. A. Milner and C. Worth. Melbourne, Monash University.

Yamaguchi, S., Sankaijuku, et al. (1986). *Luna*. Tokyo, Parco.

Yamamoto, K. (1970). "The World as Public Toilet". *Concerned Theatre Japan* 1(2).

Yomota, I. (1991). "Speed and Nostalgia". *Zones of Love: Contemporary Art from Japan*. Sydney, Museum of Contemporary Art.

Yonetani, J. (2004). "The 'History Wars' in Comparative Perspective: Australia and Japan". *Cultural Studies Review* 10(2).

Yoshimoto, T. (1982). *Kyōdō gensōron*. Tokyo, Kadokawa shoten.

Yutaka, K. (1970). "The University Problem". *Zengakuren: Japan's Revolutionary Students*. S. J. Dowsey. Berkeley, The Ishi Press: 110–135.

INDEX

BRILL'S JAPANESE STUDIES LIBRARY

ISSN 0925-6512

1. Plutschow, H.E., *Chaos and Cosmos*. Ritual in Early and Medieval Japanese Literature. 1990. ISBN 90 04 08628 5
2. Leims, Th.F. *Die Entstehung des Kabuki*. Transkulturation Europa-Japan im 16. und 17. Jahrhundert. 1990. ISBN 90 04 08988 8
3. Seeley, Chr. *A History of Writing in Japan*. 1991. ISBN 90 04 09081 9
4. Vovin, A. *A Reconstruction of Proto-Ainu*. 1993. ISBN 90 04 09905 0
5. Yoda, Y. *The Foundations of Japan's Modernization*. A Comparison with China's Path Towards Modernization. Transl. by K.W. Radtke. 1996. ISBN 90 04 09999 9
6. Hardacre, H. and A.L. Kern (eds.), *New Directions in the Study of Meiji Japan*. 1997. ISBN 90 04 10735 5
7. Tucker, J.A. *Ito Jinsai's* Gomō Jigi *and the Philosophical Definition of Early Modern Japan*. 1998. ISBN 90 04 10992 7
8. Hardacre, H. (ed.) *The Postwar Development of Japanese Studies in the United States*. 1998. ISBN 90 04 10981 1
9. Hanashiro, R.S. *Thomas William Kinder and the Japanese Imperial Mint, 1868-1875*. 1999. ISBN 90 04 11345 2
10. Teitler, G. and K.W. Radtke (eds.) *A Dutch spy in China*. Reports on the First Phase of the Sino-Japanese War (1937 – 1939) 1999. ISBN 90 04 11487 4
11. Mortimer, M. *Meeting the Sensei*. The Role of the Master in Shirakaba Writers. 2000. ISBN 90 04 11655 9
12. Scholz-Cionca, S. Leiter, S.L. *Japanese Theatre and the International Stage*. 2000. ISBN 90 04 12011 4
13. Saltzman-Li, K. *Creating Kabuki Plays*. Context for *Kezairoku*, "Valuable Notes on Playwriting". 2003. ISBN 90 04 12115 3
14. Ozaki, M. *Individuum, Society, Humankind*. The Triadic Logic of Species According to Hajime Tanabe. 2001. ISBN 90 04 12118 8
15. Bentley, J.R. *A Descriptive Grammar of Early Old Japanese Prose*. 2001. ISBN 90 04 123083
16. Higashibaba, I. *Christianity in Early Modern Japan*. Kirishitan Belief and Practice. 2001. ISBN 90 04 12290 7
17. Schmidt, P. *Capital Punishment in Japan*. 2001. ISBN 90 04 12421 7
18. Foljanty-Jost, G. *Juvenile Delinquency in Japan*. Reconsidering the "Crisis". 2003. ISBN 90 04 13253 8
19. Tomida, H. *Hiratsuka Raichō and Early Japanese Feminism*. 2004. ISBN 90 04 13298 8
20. Ueda, M. *Dew on the Grass*. The Life and Poetry of Kobayashi Issa. 2004. ISBN 90 04 13723 8
21. Beckwith, C.I. *Koguryo: The Language of Japan's Continental Relatives*. 2004. ISBN 90 04 13949 4

22. Parker, H.S.E. *Progressive Traditions*. An Illustrated Study of Plot Repetition in Traditional Japanese Theatre. 2005. ISBN 90 04 14534 6

23. Eckersall, P. *Theorizing the Angura Space*. Avant-garde Performance and Politics in Japan, 1960-2000. 2006. ISBN-10: 90 04 15199 0, ISBN-13: 978 90 04 15199 4

24. Gramlich-Oka, B. *Thinking Like a Man*. Tadano Makuzu (1763-1825). 2006. ISBN-10: 90 04 15208 3, ISBN-13: 978 90 04 15208 3

25. Bentley, J.R. *The Authenticity of* Sendai Kuji Hongi. A New Examination of Texts, with a Translation and Commentary. 2006. ISBN-10: 90 04 15225 3, ISBN-13: 978 90 04 15225 0